Metta-Mors

To Gilbert

All the love

Ezra

Summer 2011

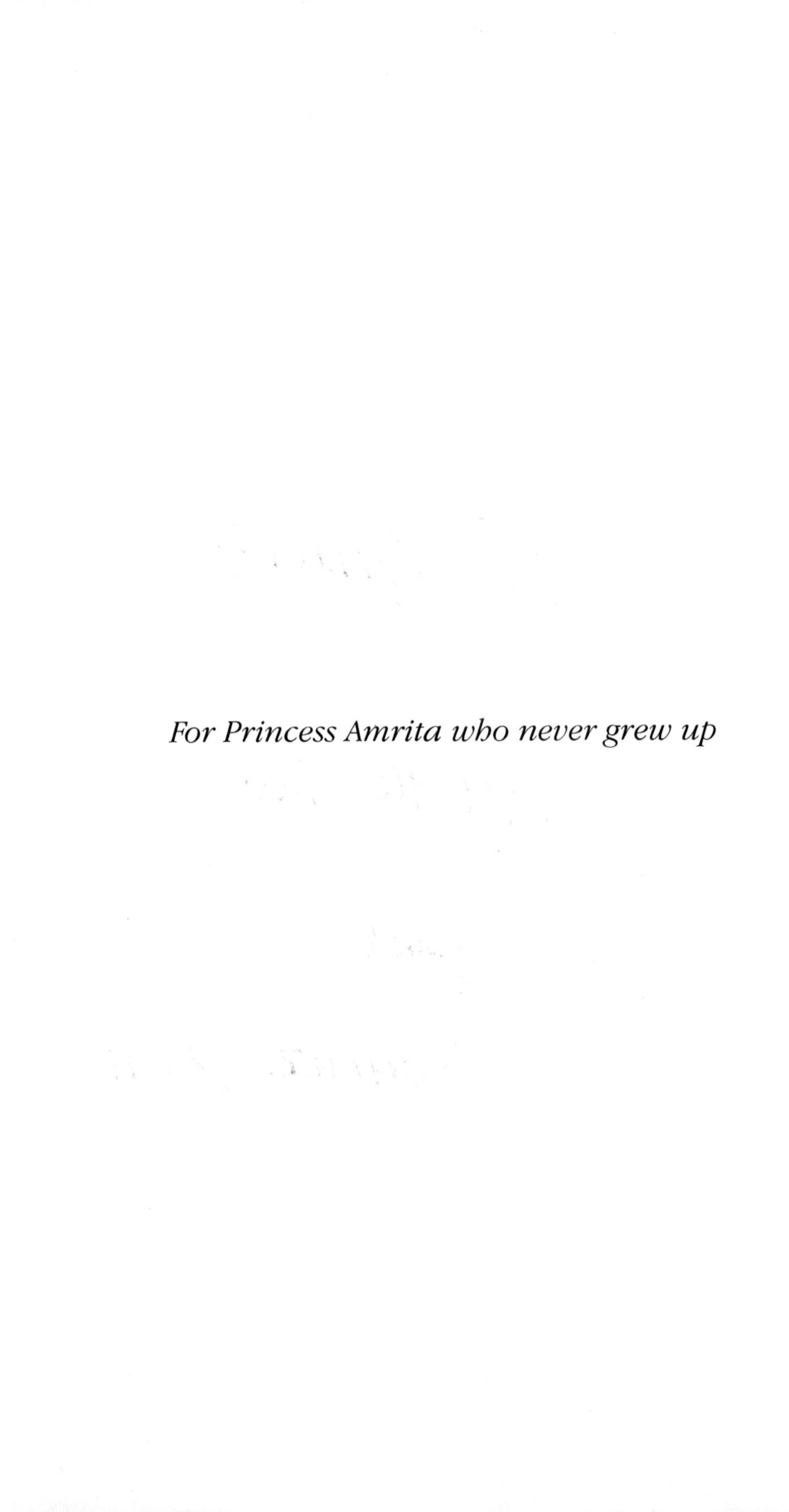

For Princess Amrita who never grew up

Metta-Morph-Aziz

The Idiot's Path to Enlightenment

Obin Ahmed

First published in the United Kingdom in 2010
by Twinklefish Publishing
This edition 2011
obin@virgin.net
0208 980 4179
www.theidiotspath.com

ISBN 978-0-9565612-0-6

Contents

First, a few things that you need to know:

The Idiot's Path

Use the ...

4 Holy Rules (Idiot's spirituality)
4 Humble Truths (political spirituality)
3 Serene Sillinesses (just plain silly)
3 Magic Mantras (simplicity itself, once you know them?)

Four Holy Rules

1. You're never alone being alone
2. Laughter is the first language
3. All roads lead to home (eventually)
4. What you see is what you get ... what you get depends on you

Four Humble Truths

1. Freedom is a basic necessity
2. Freedom will not come by waiting
3. Because Freedom will not come by waiting it has to be sought for, fought for and won
4. Freedom does not come for free ... there's always a price

Three Serene Sillinesses

1. Time flies like an arrow
2. Fruit flies like a Banana
3. Dragon flies straight for the heart

Three Magic Mantras

You'll soon find out

Glossary

Anatta – the most powerful magic potion ever
Afrostan – the dark continent way yonder
Big Bad Trip – a paranoid psychedelic journey through unmentionable pain
Battle of the Big K. – the crucial battle in ancient Zindia
Chuckle Stream – Sonic stream of laughter that the dark forces want to steal
Chamber of Blissful Echoes – echo clad cave of the Sisters Nazneen
Fort Cox – Lucifer's home
Fantasy Factory – cave where fantastic alchemy takes place
Grumble Glitch – the unhappy music of the Black Magic Mysterons
HypnoTantric Trance – the happy music of MMA
HypnoTantric Hijabs made of magic muslin – disappearing gowns of invisibility
Hoggaristan – the darkest part of the dark continent
Kid Kurry's Magical Muncherie – cosmic restaurant inside the catacombs
Kumbh Mela – the gathering of the clans in Zindia
Lost Catacombs – Somewhere in the underground where all the fun takes place
"Leprechaun's Revenge" – pirate ship
Magic Muslin Works – a place where dread invisible threads are made
Metta-Morph-Aziz – the rave at where all the magic starts
Metta-Morph-Aziz – the ever changing preciousness of love – (says it all!)
MMA – the band and the movement of the peoples
Monsoon Mindstorm – the worst restaurant in Brickie Lane
Never Ending Tapestry of Time – always an unfinished piece of work
Nirvana – Birthless and deathless never never land
"Om Song" – the Sisters Nazneen's perfect song

Pearly Green – the sweetest place in Slumdon town, a place called home

Pool of Laughter and Forgetting (Well of Never-Ending Tears) – a place of very opposites inside the Lost Catacombs

Psychedelic – anything wibbly and wobbly and very far out

Queen Angie Park – the sweetest place in the sweetest place

River Alph – the River of Crystal Light – the source of the Catacombs

Right Rude Sabre Tooth – a groovy Zindian Restaurant in Brickie Lane

Rosetta Stone – the Zeegyptian stone that tells all

Sonic Temple of King Psychedelix – where the real partying takes place

Seas of Serenity – the cosmic seas of the Sonic Temple

Spirit Light – the lasers bouncing from the pyramids

Spanglish Main – where pirates fight the forces of doom and order from leaky ships

Tapestry of Alternative Endings – a useful tool to plot adventures

Thieves Philosophy – the piratical brand of truth

Valley of Dry Bones – the place where Lucifer's forces play music

Prologue

STANISLAV STROLNIKOV, MORE commonly known amongst village idiots as St Stan, was no more than a real idiot. A wholly holy one, however. Hanging upside down from an old crunchy banana tree for forty days, he fell and hit his head and discovered the Four Holy Rules of The Idiot's Path. Following his incredible downfall, he stood down-side up and went around making people very happy by being extremely silly and great fun to be with. However, caught by Moldavian state forces, he was dipped into a giant cauldron of cold porridge and drowned and just like Pavlova's pudding, the mystery of the Strolnikovian Dip remains an enigma!

1

Lucifer is having some visions and ... Paradise is lost

THE VISIONS IN the All-Seeing Crystal Ball were cloudy as the smoke that seethed from the glowing darkness slithered and slipped down the sides to confuse the dark seer even further. Bats in the belfry and demons to the side, where the Hell are we now?

Our fallen angel seethed. He was in a rage about something strong, a time when life had no story and there was only one song. His two giant red but nervous horns looked into the past, trying to sort out the present, looking only for a future that can't last.

Smoke flared from his hot nostrils and those goat-slit eyes stared. Rage! Rage! Rage against the world! Lucifer looked around at his world. Fort Cox was full of dosh and golden bars made of broken stars and still it was soooo – dim!

The ball clouded darker and Lucifer thundered like a sleeping dragon asleep inside the burning volcano at the bottom of the Misty Mountains.

"What the . . . Hssss . . . Vark . . .!" he yelled crushing the ball with a flash of his big, red, back wings and quickly demanded another. The demons ran as fast as possible to humour his Majestic Satanicness's request. Lucifer was hallucinating or was he? The smoke never lied, did it? He seethed on the Throne of Total Grumble Vibes and ground his teeth angrily. And then – back to the ball again but still nothing new but rage. He breathed hard and fire shot from his deep nostrils. What was it now? The Big K, a frisky pirate or some scrawny Kockneestani with frisky fingers. A different anger was rising inside that scarlet heart and this was ancient, very ancient.

Bhoots had been tripping over preets and the banshees had run away and hidden. Lucifer was having a bad trip again and it was probably the same one as he'd recently been having. It was. Lucifer's ankle-wings fluttered frantically and his head glowed but what was this new bummer all about? The clouds parted in front of his scabrous face once more and Lucifer took a peek. The Big Bad Trip again, endless hot screams in eternal nights. He stared and stared and stared. An All-Seeing Crystal Ball never lied, however much he cried and it was always so very foggy, so hazy it was crazy.

Lucifer huffed and he puffed and blew everything in dark, mysterious clouds of never-ending, silent screaming. Ripped, torn asunder with thunder, the vampires, heckles, speckles, ghouls, hobgoblins, afreets, bhoots, preets and a multitude of other sins whinged and whimpered. The heat was ever so burning but it was always very cold deep in the heart of Hell.

Lucifer looked like he'd got up from bed badly. He wanted to rise so he considered the past. The past? What the Hell was that? There was only the present. This was hobbledyshite! History, all Hogwash and Bogwash, completely crappy poo.

"Vark it all!" he spat and then got back to the All-Seeing Crystal Ball in which he could see something smaller, Slumdon, and closer to home, Pearly Green.

"TwinkleBoo. TwinkleBoo, Flash in a Pan . . .
What's happening here, they're not eating Spam . . .
Or even sweet piglets in seas of Vindaloo.
Or other furry creatures you can get from the zoo
TwinkleBoo. TwinkleBoo, flash in a pan
I wonder if they're cooking up Right Royal Scam!
Crystal Ball. Crystal Ball, I thee command.
To Pearly Green. We must hasten our hand.
Good is too slimy and has to be duffed,
Pass me a muffin of lizard fluff!"

2

Here Comes Pearly Green

THE SLUMDON BOROUGH of Pearly Green lay between the edge of the city and the never-ending suburbs leading east to the sea, deep down in darkest Southbend. The whole area was commonly known as the East End and was unique because what seems to be in Pearly Green isn't what it seems, it seems.

This is the story of Sidney Arthur and the kiddies from the street named after him. It's also the story of how the principles of The Idiot's Path aided by Anatta, the most magical potion ever, joined hands with the mythical music of Hypno-Tantric Trance to overcome everything. And it all started in Pearly Green, a stinky-winky, pokey dive, though pretty funkadelic too. There was nowhere to start but the bottom.

Yes, the story starts at the bottom. It can only get better. It was here in Pearly Green that stupendously, breathtakingly wondrous events took place that would advance global civilisation by bounds and leapfrogs.

Anatta and Hypno-Tantric Trance exploded through the cracks in the unsuspecting cobblestones of the East End and took the world by storm. What with the discovery of the Four Holy Rules, the Four Humble Truths and the Three Serene Sillinesses, life could never be the same again as it was, from then, but a dreaming. From the surreal streets of Scoreditch to the brown backwaters of Spitney Green, all the multi-coloured tribes of Sid Arthur Street dreamed without sleeping and no one kept their doors locked at nights so everyone could dream each other's dreams unhindered. Additionally, being extremely poor, there was nothing to nick and dreams were never ever stolen really, just borrowed, elaborated upon and exchanged. (Anyway there were always plenty of sooth-saying sea slugs hanging around with fantastic happy endings, mystic middles and surreal starts.) The great world revolution started here from the inter-cultural tribes living in the countless, rat-infested housing estates stretching from Slimehouse to Smile End. So in essence, Pearly Green was mainly smelly, poor and over-crowded but with some rich bits. The revolution would change everything and as we shall see, it certainly did.

3

Lighting the Pipe of Peace

SOMEWHERE EAST OF the new rising sun, a few streets away from Brickie Lane, life continued rumbling. This was the multi-jewelled, multi-faceted life beyond the first cut. This was the gem inside the gem. This was Banglastan, a world where the borders of where the outside met the inside blurred.

Bangla Town started where the melting edges between dark and day melded in an exquisite tapestry of confusion. Some would say that this was a world where time was in order. These were the streets where nightlife wasn't separate from the life of day. Where shops staying open and the playful shrieks of children playing boot-ball or hooky (or both) from school joined the heady smell of spice and incense to time-stretch the day into tomorrow or was it yesterday? Whatever it was, it was a sparkly, spangly, twinkling, twilight world called home. Bangla Town was a big beautiful baby sleeping deep, completely at peace with itself and its surroundings.

"From Dooblistan to Mehra Dhun
From Tunkirk to New Zork
They stabbed it with their steely knives
They munched up all the pork
But Pigs are cool and pigs are great
And Paradise if you try.
There aint no Heaven, There aint no Hell
And if only Pigs could fly

Oh me, oh my . . . if only pigs could fly!"

Bilal, the Banglastani Beatnik, stumbled along the uneven cobbled surface of Brickie Lane singing very badly in his usual, silly, manner.

The smoke from his peace-pipe of happy herbs swirled up like the writing in candy rock. He cracked a grin as the starlings larked around in the skies in the aerial rhythmic formations that partnered his grateful breath. On a clueless cue and with no clue at all, they burst from the park as he inhaled, exploded like fireworks as he breathed deep and landed in surreal synchronicity on top of the shabby rooftops as he finally exhaled. Life was brill! Everything was groovy and as a gainfully unemployed young layabout, BB had nothing better to do than dream. The green fronds of crunchy banana trees mirrored the emeralds shining in his eyes, the brown in the mud puddles, the earthiness of his skin and tatty jeans, the fading mauve of the skies, the colours of his purple kurta. The fluidity of his sparkling inner world matched the wetness coming through the inner soles of his torn, pink plimsolls and all looking out at a very blurred world via a pair of wonky, kaleidoscopic spectacles. A friendly, funny face with a blob-nose and curly black hair, he was really nothing special. BB continued to sing as he strolled along.

"Oh, sorry me, please, thank you, no pies. Bacon is smelly, spam is unclean and pigs are far happier in skies!"

The streets were looking lovely. Heaven always started on earth. The past and future were always present in the present and its very presence was astounding! BB bounced along the cobblestones whistling to himself. He had time on his hands but just like money, it seemed to slip away when he wasn't paying attention. Time was a wondrous thing, you could wrap it up like wool, ravel it, unravel it and loom it into gloom or joy, that was choice and BB preferred joy. The posters on the tacky walls came alive as he passed. Bollywood cowboys and Hollywood bimbos laughed at him mercilessly as he stooped to tie his laces.

Passing a shop he quickly stole some Bombay-mix and munched to the cashews he liberated for free.

BB mumbled as a sweetshop came and stopped quite willingly in his gaze. He tried to move on but the bewildering, bejewelled shopfront wouldn't let him. It offered to duff him up and before he could say no, a stream of low flying jelapis shot off the silver plates and grabbed him by the mouth. The kulfis tried to follow but were caught in the onrush of gulab jams as BB was chased down the street by the irate sweet seller.

BB choked as the backstreets of Whiteapple whizzed past but he was on a mission. It was called a take away-get away and he dared not stop at home as it came and went. After a while huffing and puffing he slowed down in the maze of streets. But where was he? The run-down mid Queen Angiean street aptly named Hang'N'Bury St. was very close to Whiteapple where a magnificent mosque graced the main road. The dome on it spiralled heavenwards from five minarets; the highest one was incredible and looked so delicious, it was almost edible with its intricately carved Scarabian calligraphy flowing around it like golden vines.

"Oi! You! Stop! Pay!"

The sweet seller was now very close. The bungling beatnik almost lost his spectacles when dashing dangerously across the road and barely missed tripping over a purple turtle emerging from some underground, gunpowder plot. Diving through the open curtains of a passing palanquin, BB jumped to relative safety, seriously startling the bewildered occupant. The pelicans at the front and the penguins at the back rushed on. Rubbing his scraped knees, he looked around but the sweet seller had thankfully vanished and he was now near the thieves quarter, the Bazaar of Offthelorrywallahs, a huge ramshackle moving market place of ever-changing dimensions that never stayed in one place and usually did his head in. The palanquin moved off quickly as BB jumped out at the corner by the cattle trough where a few sacred cows were drinking and chuckled aloud, little knowing that his life was about to change because Sidney Arthur himself, the oldest ghost in Ghost Town, had finally caught up with him.

4

Ghosts

SIDNEY ARTHUR IV was thin and emaciated, he had a sharp pointed face and a sly grin. He wore tatty clothes from yesteryear from which daffodils and daisies grew from crumbling buttonholes. Sidney Arthur was well known in Ghost Town for his legendary mischievousness. He'd been a ghost for simply ages and was in fact the very oldest ghost in Ghost Town. He was a purple, ghostly presence sixteen foot above our beatnik's head. Sidney Arthur thought fast. This stoned idiot seemed just right. Squishing to one side, he made lightning calculations faster than thunder could hide. In a snip-snap moment of pure madness another penny dropped. He watched BB carefully with a spooky detachment. Meanwhile, back on the ground as the lad turned a corner into Hang'N'Bury Street, Sidney Arthur chuckled to himself and scratched his crooked nose. He had a plan. It came into his head so quick, he'd worked in out in a flash. And this beatnik was going to be quite a part of it. Liberation depended on it, in particular, his own. While BB wandered aimlessly along, Sidney Arthur's ghost cracked a ghostly grin and pondered.

But who was Sidney Arthur? He'd been born simply ages ago and no one knew exactly when. Being the oldest ghost in Ghost Town, he knew how old everyone else was but no one knew his age. His family had made a fortune from flogging Astral Ale to the poor and when it came to Sidney's turn to inherit the lot, in a fit of divine madness, he gave it all away to the foreign, the homeless and the poor. Of course, there were many of these and most grateful they were too for his generosity. Having given his house away to a wandering band of Bongostani leprechauns, he decided to move into Queen Angie Park, preferring to sleep under a canopy of giant mystic mushrooms, where he had been given the job (by Lord Krishna himself) of cavorting with the sacred cows.

Sidney had a wonderful time eating himself out of house and home and was much the better for it but many a time, especially when the cows were peacefully chewing their cud, Sidney Arthur would wander off gambolling with the lambs. Sitting cross-legged and serious, drinking gin, playing rummy and smoking skeets without a care in the world, they all had a great time. The lambs were meant to be gambolling and the cows cavorting, the flowers were meant to be blooming and the petals turning psychedelic. Well that's what Krishna had told him but our Sidney was a sly, foxy one and had a few tricks of his own up his sleeve.

When occasionally asked by Krishna on a fly-in visit how the cows were doing, Sidney Arthur coyly replied that they were fine and looked after themselves perfectly well. He preferred frolicking and rolling over in the grass and conveniently forgot to mention the fleecing of the lambs. But once in a fit of over-cocky madness when Sidney Arthur was on a winning streak with the lambs, a calf from his unattended flock wandered perilously close to the edge of the lake. Consequently, it fell in and would have drowned if it hadn't had been for the friendly giant blue octopus that lived at the bottom of the lake. Things could have been serious and this story would have turned out very different.

It wasn't all bad in being a ghost. No Sireee ...! There was fun to be had, mostly in the form of minor harassment and the sowing of confusion. It was what he was good at and he did it very well. Thank St Stan for Heavenly Ghosts. Even Sidney Arthur.

"Oi you. Stop nicking me sweets. Come back here."

Jumping off from the pelican and penguin palanquin had been a bad idea as the sweet seller suddenly resurfaced waving an axe. BB tried to run off screaming but some force or another was holding him back and then shooting him along very fast away from the irate sweet seller (who had just been crapped on by a lone grey pigeon being chased by a flock of fantasy falcons). Now, hovering very closely to the beatnik, Sidney Arthur suddenly perked up, watching a bouncing, bewildered BB, as he pulled out a stash of trickster ideas from a carpetbag. These he always kept by his knickers and in a blurred, blushed disguise of exploding purple powder puff, slammed it into the idiot's head just when he thought he wasn't looking. He stashed the thought quick inside and zoomed off to the nearest rooftop to sit back and watch the fun, and then got out his borrowed fishing rod and cast it at the poor beatnik.

With a expert toss Sidney Arthur carefully caught BB hook, line and sinker and teased him through Fleshire St and reeled him in expertly. The scam was on as Sidney Arthur opened his carpetbag and flung another passing fancy into the poor lad's head. (A passing sooth-saying sea slug chucked in some happy futures for good measure too.)

"Oh by the sacred dreadlocks of St Stan. What's happening to me?" BB gasped as the streets rushed by. He didn't have a clue as Sidney Arthur floated after this Banglastani Beatnik, chasing him silly. After cutting across Itchycoo Park, Bilal was almost at the schoolhouse squat where he sometimes lived with his one hundred and eleven friends.

Buried directly underneath the staggering bums of methylated hoochie-coochie men and now whizzing round in circles seventy foot in the air around the cemetery was the rotund ghost of Billy Blake who saw nothing everywhere and gave Sidney a passing glance. His long white hair almost hid a very lively round face and his shabby, impoverished twinkletogs couldn't distract from the incredulity of his eyes at what he was witnessing.

"Still trying to work it out Billy?" Sidney Arthur chuckled as Billy span around in circles pondering on the imponderables of the strange toy that he held. It was this object that Sidney Arthur was on about because Billy's problem was that he was forever trying to work out the time. In his hand was an hourglass like no other; a single grain of diamond light hung motionlessly in the air in the middle and it never ceased to amaze him. No amount of turning the thing upside down or down-side up, would make the thing actually move, so, consequently, he never knew the time. Attracted by the new activity another spook flew up from the park – the thin, peg-legged serious-looking ghost of Danny De Foe. He nudged Billy Blake and flew them both up to investigate Sidney Arthur's grin. This fisher of folk seemed to be having a joke but he wasn't telling them.

"What are you doing, Sidney?" asked Danny De Foe.

"Following that fool down below!"

"And why's that, mate?"

"Er, I can't tell you but I've just had an idea."

"When can I have my fishing rod back then?" laughed Danny, his witty face tempering his smile with the inner knowledge that this was a Holy Ghost that always thought life was just the start of the weekend. "So when?"

"When I've finished!" Sidney Arthur replied, bunging him a daisy out of his loophole instead of a real excuse.

Danny De Foe pondered on how lonely it would be if there was no one to spend eternity with but he was lucky as he had Billy and Billy had him. Even their graves were next to each other. Eternity on a desert island on your own was never much fun, creation and discovery was so much nicer when shared and Life, even when you're dead, was such great fun. Danny tittered as BB approached Sid Arthur St, (so-named long ago, when he was newly departed) led by instinct, desperation, no choice and design. Oh!, and, of course, by a borrowed fishing rod.

5

The Schoolhouse at Sid Arthur St

THE FRIENDS WERE lounging on the Durkish divans inside the large, dusty living room at the squatted schoolhouse at Sid Arthur Street. The underground had come over-ground once again. Although there were many still inside the Lost Catacombs of Brickie Lane doing their funky stuff, some had decided to come up for air. They were missing the sun and its golden warmth as well as the cool refreshing breeze that blew across the river. They tried to ignore the smell of the sewage that floated by on the crap barges which were on their way to dump their loads on the pretty beaches of the south coast. Although the Lost Catacombs were the most magical place anyone ever knew with its hundreds of caves and crazy places where stars shone everywhere from the floors to the walls and ceilings, it was always nice to go over-ground again.

It was through certain tandoori ovens in the seven hundred and seventy seven Zindian restaurants in Brickie Lane that one entered the Lost Catacombs through which flowed the fabled River Alph, that crystal river of astral light along with its tributary, the Chuckle Stream, where air mysteriously turned to water and water to air. The Living Dreamtime walls were studded with stars that were an exact mirror of those above. On the streets of Pearly Green it was an occasional relief to know that the earth was just mud-coloured, not the freaky multi-coloured red, blue, green, purple and azure of the earth in the catacombs. Sometimes the underground could all be a bit too much, especially with the crazy sounds emanating from the Chamber of Blissful Echoes. In addition to that, Fairlight's Fantasy Factory was another frequently hallucinogenic world where everything was crazy and nothing could be assumed to be real. So it was good to see the river from out of the schoolhouse windows as this made a change from the underground's Well of Never-Ending Tears which turned into the

Pool of Laughter and Forgetting whenever everyone was happy. Nevertheless, no one could ever get tired of the Sonic Temple of King Psychedelix, especially Osric as he was the one that found it and as they all discovered, it could spin off and take them to places they never even realised whenever Anarkali tranced. That's what having an adventure was all about.

Yes, the underground was over-ground again but it brought some of its denizens with it. Inside the squatted schoolhouse the musicians were in a state. Fareek, Mellow Tron and Tarquin were fighting over a cheroot of happy herbs. Fareek's patch-worked, holographic Zoofi gown swept into the air hiding his hallucinogenically-dilated left eye as he held Mellow Tron to the floor by grabbing him around the neck. Mellow Tron, the tiny Afrostani Skankmaster of Jah, fought back. In fact, it was his dreadlocks which did the best fighting. The ten-foot-long dreadlocks wrapped themselves around Fareek's head while the man himself tried punching Fareek below the belt. This was the moment Tarquin had been waiting for. The hunky, handsome Bollywood synsantooric tabla player swept a hand through his blue-gelled hair and jumped up to grab the cheroot of happy Himalayan herbs off the other two.

Beside him, house-elves were arguing with djinns and fireflies and glow worms were floating in between the sparkling twinklefish and causing havoc. As usual Dylan the Black Bunny was crashed out on top of his guitar as his brother, White Rabbit, looked up, adjusted his monocle and brought a timepiece out of his tiny tartan waistcoat. He looked at it carefully before clearing his voice.

"Time for another," he muttered before scurrying away in through the out door.

"So what's the plot then?" Fareek asked having finally uncovered himself from the clutches of his holographic Zoofi gown.

"Yes, when exactly does the storyline begin?" Ayesha, the first of the sisters Nazneen, asked with a face of sweet smiles as Frogamatix hovered around. The big pug-ugly tantric tree-toad flicked out its flickery-dickery tongue and caught a few of the hallucinogenic agaric-flies that were flying around. Floating three foot off the ground, the pyramid-shaped creature looked once at the inscrutable, scruffy face of his best friend, Catweazel Phil, and then back again at Ayesha, waiting for her question to be answered.

"You should never answer questions with questions. It's

annoying!" Ambrin, the second, added while moving Tarquin off his spot by the fire with one of her infamous kicks.

"Yeah, the answers should be clear right at the start of the plot!" Mellow Tron gasped as his dreadlocks ran to hide behind his ancient Afrostani face.

"It's not an issue of the answer being there at the start, what matters is that the problem should fall away and then it doesn't matter what the question is or, consequently, the answer," Fareek suddenly added, munching on an oblong oyster and helping himself to some periwinkle wine. The kiddies from Sid Arthur St were bored, it had been a long, hot summer and they believed that they had discovered the Idiot's Path to Enlightenment and seen the last of Lucifer so they were not worrying about anything. Now it was time to get onto another adventure. Being enlightened, they thought they knew all there was to know. Little did they know about entitlement but they were soon to find out.

Fareek, having sparkled, rolled up in laughter, squealing, "All's best in this, the best of all possible worlds!"

"Speak for yourself," boomed Najma, the last sister Nazneen, and dragged Fareek over to the open window through which came the Wicked White Witches of the West – Stargasm waving from within her wattle and daub grown with her partner-in-spells, Moonmummy. The leprechauns jumped back in surprise seeing the blue woad drip off Stargasm's perfect face. Knocking a slow leprechaun out of the way with her broomstick, Moonmummy looked at everyone in bemusement through her golden-grey eyes and shovelled a few oblong oysters into her strong, square jaws.

Next came Anarkali who burst into the place pursued by the Funkadelic Tribe. They had all fallen from the attic and slid down the Zindian rope that hung in the air in the middle of the living room. Only fourteen years old, tiny, thin and delicate, the Kathak trancer looked aghast at the commotion in the room, opened her mouth and was just about to say something when a twinklefish sailed into it. Choking with surprise, she quickly spat it out at her feet, but carried on trancing in an anti-clockwise direction around the centre of the room. Her silver ankle-bells tinkled the air as she shouted, "The colours are coming off the Chuckle Stream again!"

A bewildered Fareek stood to stare. And there it was. The skies, which had been so colourful, looked most definitely as if they were paling. Something was sucking the rainbows out of the skies while somewhere on the other side of the world leprechauns were screaming as a grey blackness without blue took over.

"Oh no, not again!" Fareek squealed.

"It looks like it's bleeding colours off the sky for real. That must mean we'll be sent off to fight some baddies, have loads of interesting adventures, learn nothing useful and perhaps have a party or two."

"Oh no, not more parties," Tarquin howled as he hitched up his Bollywood bloomers and ran a delicate hand through his hair. What could stop the good vibes at the schoolhouse now? They had found the Idiot's Path to Enlightenment after all.

Suddenly, the shrieking of Habiba and the Hashemites filled the air as they were landing in the courtyard on their psychedelic pigs. Habiba's hook of a left hand waved at her brothers as they dropped from the skies. She was the leader of the Trancefloor Liberation Organisation, the TLO itself, founded by Hassan-I-Sabbah, the Old Man of the Mountains. She watched the colours fade and wondered how to bring them back.

6

The Band of Doom Tunes Up (or down)

HALF-WAY BETWEEN the ancient cities of Timbuktwo and Timbukthree, somewhere east of the Black Hoggar mountains, lay the infamous Valley of Dry Bones which some of the leprechauns of Pearly Green believed to be a source of Varma Marg meditation techniques which, if properly practised, could be used for gaining liberation not in a single lifetime but in six and a half minutes flat. Unfortunately successful practitioners of this art never hung around long enough to teach their aspiring acolytes how they did it.

Afrostan was a beautiful continent but here near the top, just adjacent to the billowing sand storms of the never-ending desert, the Valley of Dry Bones was simply hideous. Somewhere inside this sandy mess lay the crumbling ruins of an huge, ancient amphitheatre filled with countless demons, ghouls and monsters who sat or stood or hung upside down gibbering from its many turrets and arches. Bad djinns, afreets, ghouls and gremlins sat squirming in their seats to watch the show and flocks of carrion pigeon and vampire vultures raced above their heads to play headless polo with the occasional lost starling which flew in unannounced. The crowds roared. The Valley of Dry Bones was where the Band of Doom played their revolting riffs.

Azrial, the conductor of the Afreet Orchestra, stood on his toe-tips on top of the six hundred and sixty-foot-tall Roman column that served as his conductor's plinth. He wriggled and writhed at the demonic musicians while his grey-black wings flapped behind his balding head. The bad guys were back, afreets, ghouls, banshees, bhoots, preets, vampires, hobgoblins and others of their ilk, willingly made up this infamous orchestra. To gain a better view of the orchestra pit, the night stars were quickly rearranged by minor devils to act as spotlights as the conductor's plinth lit up. To one side skeletal trumpeters blew their rancid horns, made of the dry bones of dead saints, while the phantom dancers shiggled in their hula-hoop skirts on the other side. In the excitement shape-shifters changed from dingoes to drogoes and back again fifty-three times per second. It was all rather a blur of bones and bits. Some of it most bloody too. The Satanic symphony was back and playing the Grumble Glitch again.

"Skronk. Thump!" went the emaciated kettle drummers as they thumped their row of mammoth skulls. The crowd went wild and chucked each other's heads in the air.

"Eeek . . ." went the vampire violinists, serenading scary sounds from their bows.

"Skreek!" went the bhoots, blowing on bones as the stones of the valley began to shake.

"Awark!" went the banshees and preets as they played their horns.

"Ardvark!" went other demons diabolically as they set delightedly about their tasks.

In the distance the stage sparkled from the instruments on stage, electric guitars, multiple keyboards and spinning holodecks awaited their masters' return. The stage was made of shining fossilised dinosaur droppings and pointed tyrannosaurus teeth and a three-foot-tall belladonna mandrake was spinning around inside an ogre's skull in rhythmic accompaniment to the morbid scrapings of a doom-laden dirge from a sampler. It was linked to six hundred and sixty-six banks of mixers, samplers and grumplers. The spectral sound programmers and warlock wave engineers ran around trying to placate it and teasing the fantastic sounds into astral orbit.

"More spectral trombones!" shrieked the conductor. "We need to rob the Chuckle Stream as quick as we can!"

With that Azrial pointed to the skies with his baton and there for sure, the evil aura of the Afreet Orchestra's music combined with the spirit of the evil plant-form that had spiralled into the ashen skies like a grey-black haze. The demons played trombones, the preets played trumpets while the bhoots and banshees howled deliriously as a crazy, furious spinning path proceeded to rip the colours off the Chuckle Stream and all the while, the world became a much darker place. From Smile End to Scoreditch, Gobbinfields to Spitney, in fact all over Pearly Green, rainbows cried as rainbows died and not a single leprechaun in sight. The little people in the schoolhouse simply covered their ears and eyes and went to hide inside an old tea-chest in the attic. But what was happening to the earth? Colours were simply bleeding from the skies as the Chuckle Stream was being well and truly robbed.

7

Sidney Arthur Schemes

BB HAD ENTERED the schoolhouse thinking that it was his own idea. Obviously, he was wrong as all the while the hovering ghost of Sidney Arthur followed him while fingering the daffodils that grew between his crumbling lapels. The line of his fishing rod was still stuck to the back of BB's purple kurta and he was being reeled in. Sidney Arthur was not alone and the long white hair of Billy Blake flapped across his face as he tried to get a better look. Danny De Foe was there too trying not to make a clunking sound with his peg-leg as he walked the air thirty feet above BB's fiddledum head.

"Wow, great to be back!" BB exclaimed as he entered the schoolhouse with the smell of the flying pigs in the air above his head. He passed by palanquins scampering across the corridors with penguins at the front and pelicans at the back, the secret passengers being shot around the schoolhouse halls but at every juncture, there he was, Sidney Arthur hovering a few feet in the air.

"Brilliant, Billy, finally we have a chance to be free!" Sidney Arthur gasped as they hid themselves on the ceiling.

"What do you mean?" Billy asked, scratching his pale face with Danny's peg-leg.

"Just what I said," Sidney Arthur replied excitedly.

"Would you care to explain it?" Danny asked, hurriedly pulling his peg leg back in irritation.

"Certainly not, what do you think I am? Just wait and see," Sidney Arthur said, without giving anything away.

He watched BB wander down the corridors and pondered. Hope had been released and what had passed could be not be undone. Time for fun and Sidney Arthur's thin, aristocratic face stifled a chuckle.

"Hiya, Catweazel Phil!" BB cried as Catweazel Phil, the owner of the Bum Note club, passed him in the corridor. Phil tugged at his pale, freckled face and his black wizard's hat flopped from one side to another as his friend Frogamatix flew down to be next to BB. A thousand-year-old toad with trippy skin can be a bit of a surprise to some, you know.

"Hello Bilal, what are you up to?" Catweazel Phil asked as they all stopped in their tracks.

"Nothing much, just came up from the Lost Catacombs to see what everyone was doing."

"Still shooting the flowers of love from your fantasy flintlocks with Charlie?"

"Yes, but we've already covered the whole of Pearly Green with flowers."

"Ain't you heard? The colours are coming off the rainbows again, the Chuckle Stream is being attacked by Lucifer's mob!"

"What a bummer, what shall we do?" Bilal finished, bringing out some diddleberry delights to share. Catweazel Phil munched meditatively while Frogamatix gulped the whole lot in a single greedy gulp.

Above their heads, the fishing rod was reeled in even closer than before and a purple flash almost blinded the other two ghosts. Sidney Arthur plunged his hand inside his tatty underpants and from his bag of trickster ideas, chucked in an explosive metaphysical Molotov directly onto the beatnik head below.

And in the explosion of twinkladelic smoke visible only to the three holy ghosts and Frogamatix, out poured a whole bunch of ghostly sooth-saying sea slugs. Mystic middles, surreal starts and happy endings all got mixed up with each other and although Frogamatix's flickery-dickery tongue flashed around swallowing up as many of the fortune cookies as possible, there were still loads more and these swilled in the air making magical mayhem.

"I've just had a wonderful idea, Phil!" BB suddenly exclaimed, jumping up with surprise.

"And what's that?"

"I'm tired of living at home and being just a flower-power foot soldier and could also give the Lost Catacombs a bit of a break. I still love flower power but me and Charlie have probably shot everyone in Pearly Green a good few times over!"

"Bummer," replied Phil as Frogamatix finished off eating the rest of the sooth-saying sea slugs.

"Don't interrupt me. What I really want to do now is live under the canopy of giant mystic mushrooms in Queen Angie Park and be a shepherd," BB said emphatically, examining the holes in his plimsolls.

"You what?"

"That's right, I want to be a shepherd!"

"And when did you think of that?" asked Phil, doubtfully.

"Er . . . just now, I think."

"What do you want to be a shepherd of – fools, fishes, fantasy creatures or what?"

"Nah, none of that stuff, I'm traditional. I'll be happy just with the sacred cows that wander around."

"And who says the sacred cows want to be shepherded? They look quite happy to me wandering around in their small groups chewing the cud and all."

BB straightened his kaleidoscopic spectacles and continued. "They go off to feast on the mystic mushroom meadows every day and it would be nice just to be with them. And if they get lost in the dark, I'd always be there . . ."

"It takes all sorts!" Catweazel Phil sighed, prodding Frogamatix in disbelief.

"And that's not all, Charlie could be there with me. He could look after the soft, cuddly sheep that come over from Slimehouse Fields and together we could still shoot our fantasy flintlocks into the skies and then into the flocks and then finally into ourselves."

"Are you sure Charlie would want to go with you?"

"Yeah, as long as we're together we're happy and don't particularly care what we do or where we go."

"Well best of luck then, matey," finished Phil and as this gypsy wizard with his giant frog wandered off down the corridor, a side-door opened and in flew Stargasm looking very pleased indeed.

"Oi, Beatnik!" Stargasm called and BB caught her glance as she jumped him with witchy delight. Stargasm told him that she was gathering a band of merry tricksters together to fly into Hoggaristan and spy on the Grumble Glitch.

"Where are you going again, Stargasm?" BB asked, rubbing his wonky specs with his ragged kurta.

"Off to Hoggaristan to hit the Grumble Glitch. Wanna come?" Stargasm asked glibly as Sidney Arthur suddenly swooshed down and pushed an answer into the lad's head. The other two ghosts clamped their hands over their mouths at his effrontery.

"Yes, I'd like to but I can't fly," he replied as Sidney Arthur pulled at his ears to get the appropriate reply.

"Oh yes. It's easy and there's so much choice!" Stargasm laughed getting off her broomstick in a neat flash. The broomstick hovered in the air, waiting for a reply.

"Tell me some!" BB gasped, quickly getting out of the way of the broomstick.

"And what are they? Well, being a witch, I'd say broomsticks, magic prayer-mats, snowcamels, flying psychedelic pigs, Whirlistani cloudboards, wings, trancing feet and much else. They're all safe manners of locomotion, some safer than others ..."

BB scratched his head and thought.

"Go on, come to Hoggaristan, you've never been out of Pearly Green, have you?"

He looked a bit miffed as he really wanted to go but some unseen force was pushing the words into his mumbling mouth. Sidney Arthur shook him furiously and goaded him to reply.

"Nah, I'm off to Queen Angie Park, me and Charlie are gonna become shepherds."

"Are you sure? Don't you want to come to Hoggaristan?"

"No, maybe one day, who knows?" BB replied sheepishly. Billy Blake squealed with excitement and almost wet his pants because he really wanted to go too as he had never been out of Pearly Green either. Sidney Arthur put him in a neck-lock and, as usual, didn't allow him to express himself.

As Stargasm jumped back onto the broomstick and shot off through the corridors, BB was left there wondering why he was feeling so strange and why these odd thoughts were coming into his head. He didn't get far but Sidney Arthur most certainly did. In a sudden explosion of smoke the three ghosts vanished.

8

Fairlight Creates a Fantasy

THE FANTASY FACTORY was seven thousand feet underground located right at the bottom of the Land of the Awakening Dreamtime, it was right under the main artery of the Lost Catacombs where the River Alph flowed. Countless tunnels, corridors and caves had been passed on the journey through these strange lands. Stalactites and stalagmites grew everywhere, the stalactites right side up and the stalagmites upside down or was it the other way around? It was an incredible world where nothing could be taken for gospel. The deeper one descended, the clearer the air became and to get to the cave that had been turned into the Fantasy Factory, Fairlight, Osric and Amrita had plummeted under the earth through the broken tandoori oven of Kid Kurry's restaurant – the Right Rude Sabre Tooth, slap bang in the middle of the lane. As they went down, downer and down, remnants of past civilisations stared out at them as broken, scraggly bits of pottery embedded in the shifting walls. Anyway, it was good to have their own space. The Land of the Living Dreamtime they had passed was full of sacred cows and any psychedelic flying pigs that weren't out on the streets. This land was where Kid Kurry had his second restaurant, The Magical Muncherie where the poor were fed for free. Further down in the Torrible Zone there was a cave especially for the Funkadelic Tribe where they could practise their thievery to their hearts' content and under them was the cave of Habiba and the Hashemites where they practised the secret ceremonies of the TLO.

In the centre of the Torrible Zone was the cave of the Whirlistani Zoofis, Suleiman the Spinner, Mevlana the Mage and Nasseruddin the incredibly Nutty. When in the underground, they span and span around into the star-clad walls seeing who could go the fastest. Suleiman usually span himself sick. If they ever crashed into the moving cave walls, their crazy Whirlistani bodies would become immersed into a silvery mirror before popping back out again. They'd find that complete galaxies had imprinted themselves onto their bodies and just like St Stan, they'd be dressed in nothing but stars.

This zone was also where the magical gubblies lived whose heads were green and hands were blue since they had all sailed down to the Dreamtime depths in a sieve. They had the unbelievable ability of sinking through the cave walls and appearing anywhere they wished inside the Lost Catacombs because all the cave walls were simply full of stars. One could just sink into them regardless of one's beliefs and be dressed in glowing stars. As for the gubblies; these three foot tall furry thingies spoke a language no one understood. Gubblistani never made sense but it was full of incredible laughter, the very first language, the second Holy Truth understood by children everywhere. They had also passed the Gromboolian Plains where pobbles hung upside down in twangum bushes and turned left after the wrangling quangle-wangles and ignored a smug scroobious pip meditating behind a bong tree when the land changed yet again. Deeper down through the multicoloured earth they had travelled until they'd entered the Land of the Sleeping Dreamtime where Malik Slik Sylvester had his Magic Muslin Works. Married to his workers, he happily had no time to get married to anyone else and all were happy except for the hallucinogenic agaric-flies that were bred to be the spiders'/weaver's repast.

Underneath Malik's light-emitting cave lay the Chamber of Blissful Echoes, which belonged to the sisters Nazneen, where sounds bounced off as echoes and flooded them with copies of exactitude. Usually these echoes came back quick but whenever Najma sang well, her big bang booms often took weeks, if not months, to return. The deepest ones could be heard by no one but big blue whales that lived out in the seven seas of serenity and they often replied to her singing in their own special way. What they said was nobody's business but Najma's. The Land of the Sleeping Dreamtime was home to the Dreamweavers, Twynklyn, Blynkyn and Nod. Twynklyn and Blynkyn were seven inches tall but Nod was only half that but size wasn't everything and the magnitude of their magic made up for their size. All three fairies had ladybird wings and antennas and tiny prismatic smiles.

The catacombs had gone on and on. Under the cave of the

gibbering Jabberwocky lay the musicians' studio. It was here that Tarquin, Fareek and Mellow Tron had discovered the true power of their music and the Sonic Temple of King Psychedelix was right next door. Whenever everyone was in there singing, trancing or practising the Idiot's Path and Anarkali was trancing the Kathak fantastic, off they'd all go somewhere else, and underneath it all flowed the main source of the River Alph. Nothing in the Lost Catacombs was real and nothing could be taken for granted. All was unreal in an unreal universe. Nothing and nobody was more or less important than each other. They all mattered, especially in this plot. Most of the Lost Catacombs were now empty as the groovy funksters and magical creatures had gone above. The sacred cows were on their way to Queen Angie Park and many people had gone to the squatted schoolhouse and who knows where the rest were? Does it matter?

Inside the Fantasy Factory Fairlight stood neatly in his white dinner jacket, his pirate's beard swashbuckling in the breeze and his cool, calm, rational manner looked out from a bony face. The yogic top knot on the top of his intelligent head twitched with excitement. He was ceaselessly working on magic potions because that's what he was good at, helped by Osric and Amrita. Amrita had come down alone as she was the only child that mixed freely with both adults and children. Fairlight needed Amrita to make his magic potion with because in the serious world of alchemy, without a child's laughter, the mix could never be right. Fairlight potioned, Amrita chuckled and Osric did his thing. But what of Osric?

At this moment, he was being tied to a bamboo chair where Amrita was tickling him with a large peacock feather. The tickling made his spiky, blond hair change colour to a dirty brown while his pale face looked even whiter and his aquiline nose even skinnier. The black kajol around his eyes looked smudged. He'd probably been crying again. His tatty, orange jumper was jumping up and down in chuckles but he himself looked unfathomable as he was choking on the umpteenth mix of magic potion stuffed into his mouth as Amrita ran around in between the all-guiding glow-worms creating chaos. For light, they used the stars on the walls and the laboratory was filled to the brim with test-tubes and living DNA. In the middle of the cave on a computron, double helixes of ghostly DNA raced across the screen, ignoring the shoals of twinklefish that dived in and out of the screen to see if the octopus's playground lay inside. The master alchemist brushed them out of the way and continued working. Amrita was looking tired as she and Lucy had been up all night at Queen Angie Park armed with nothing but smiles and a giant butterfly net until finally, in the early hours of the morning, they had caught what they'd been asked to catch, a beautiful Buddha butterfly that Fairlight had asked for. Fifteen inches long and with wings of the brightest, most iridescent blue, they had quickly tripped down into the Lost Catacombs to give it to Fairlight. There it lay still under the net flapping furiously.

It was then that Amrita laughed in her wild gypsy manner and asked, "Is it still Anatta that were making?"

"Of course it is but with a difference!" Fairlight replied as the twiklefish scattered themselves around the room and flushed them with light. It was aqueous light and lit up the chemicals, colouring, test tubes, different batches of Anatta and of course the twittering butterfly. The all-guiding glow-worms also crawled over to get a closer look and turn themselves on as piles of coloured powders and mystic mushroom spores were measured and carefully put into groups. Very gently, so as not to tear the butterfly's wings, he attached tiny electromagnetic transmitters to them connected to the rows and rows of test tubes and pipettes. Fairlight and Osric were the philosophers stoned and they were about to discover the elixir of life but they weren't telling Amrita as the sparkling child knew everything anyway. However, motioning Amrita over, Fairlight stilled his breath and blew hard onto the butterfly's twinkling wings and a shower of golden fairy dust fell onto the Petri dish.

"There now – done it! You can take the butterfly back up to the park now!" he whistled turning the Petri dish around in his hands and smiling.

From one corner of the cave a large enigmatic animal purred; it was thirty feet long and had been dozing serenely with one eye open. On its body were luminous changing stripes of orange and red on a background of blackness with blue. As its large, open yellow eye blinked, it yawned and stretched its magnificent body and two diamond sabre teeth flashed. Here was the infamous Sabre-Toothed Power Pussy. Purring loudly, it fell back asleep again but kept the one eye open. What it was doing here and what its relation was to the plot was a secret known only to itself. Just like the Jabberwocky it called the Lost Catacombs home and only ever surfaced if needed to.

A little girl flapped into the cave in a haze of billowing bloomers.

"Hello, Alice! ... What are you doing here? ... How come you got back already?" Amrita asked as Astral Alice popped her head around the corner. Her eight-year-old squashy, pumpkin face smiled from a complexion of strawberry cream surprise. Wearing a blue Victorian velvet skirt above her billowing bloomers, she went right up to Fairlight, tugging a giant mystic mushroom behind her. The Dreamweavers puffed and gasped, helping to carry the other end. In delirious excitement, they flashed their ladybird-spotted wings and scrunched up their cute button noses. Meanwhile, an odd assortment of gubblies bounced around all over the place. They were completely covered in fur but their heads were green and their hands were blue. They were very excited at the sight of Alice's giant mushroom and they gabbled away in their strange language.

"Ah, you got the giant mushroom?" Fairlight gasped with pleasure turning around and seeing Astral Alice's prize.

"Yes, from the Queen of Hearts' gardens," Alice replied, waving a breezy hello to Amrita.

"It was the grumpy caterpillar's favourite spot ..." she continued, coming closer to Amrita.

"Oh never mind, plenty of mushrooms everywhere and that grumpy caterpillar can soon find another one," Fairlight whistled, grabbing hold of the mushroom and starting to hack a large piece away for instant experimentation. His bony fingers turned up the heat on different test tubes and on the screen, helixes of DNA danced. Fairlight deftly mixed the Anatta, Buddha butterfly pollen, with original sonic starfish DNA. He mixed so fast the mortar and pestle glowed red. Then, using a scalpel with total precision, he separated the DNA from the original Anatta, turning to Amrita, he pulled her pigtails and said, "This may do wonders."

Osric had been kindly released from his bamboo chair by Amrita and flapped around trying to stop the ravenous twinklefish from devouring the mushroom. Succeeding, he ran out of the cave carrying the remnants of the giant mushroom on the top of his funny head, closely followed by a group of excited gubblies. The lesson in magic potions had begun.

Fairlight had been at his life's work as an Alchemist for many years but he acknowledged an acceleration, a "moment", when a beautiful spore sailed up the River Alph some years ago. He always joked that it was a spore from outer space but he might have been right. There was nothing else on the planet like it. Where it had come from who knows and more importantly, who cares! He cultivated this little spore and it spread and spread all over his laboratory with a little help from his friends, Osric – the taster, and Amrita – the giggler. This was certainly not a drug and he would have been horrified and insulted if his Anatta was ever called that. To Fairlight, this was an Avatar sent from space for him to cultivate as a gift for humanity. In the beginning, after he had tried it himself he wondered what to call it. The spore had many qualities, a sense of inter-connectedness, visual enhancement, strong empathy plus a great clarity of thought with a powerful urge to ... DANCE!!!! Consequently, he called it Anatta from the Buddhist word meaning "No I, no me, no mine!" and it would change the world for ever.

9

The Wise Men of the East

REMEMBER THAT BEAUTIFUL mosque in Whiteapple that BB loved so much? Well, in the minaret lived a wise old man called Mullah Ullah, hovering on a magic carpet about seven inches above a spinning floor made of stars – looking ready for a journey. It was early dawn and he was awaiting the arrival of his friends. He was well over one hundred years old but extremely fit and stroking his salt and pepper beard, he tugged at his rice green lungi and put on his skullcap. The psychedelic gatta in the middle of his forehead shone warmly and it sparkled a warm red as he looked happily over Pearly Green.

Multicoloured grannies were off hand-in-hand to pick mystic mushrooms at Queen Angie Park and sacred cows and cuddly sheep strolled amongst the ubiquitous taxis and palanquins. Yes, all was as it should be. The sun was shining brightly although there was a black-grey pallor within the clouds and perhaps it was true that the Chuckle Stream was being robbed, and Mullah Ullah realized that unless he acted soon all this beauty would come to an end and Lucifer's forces would take over.

Mullah Ullah was originally from Banglastan but as a young man, many suns ago, he had flown on his magic prayer mat to spend time with the Man on the Moon and returned to earth much changed. For him, the past was all shining and he made a vow to make the present and future so, and so he jumped a passing crunchy banana boat and came to Slumdon town and he had lived in Pearly Green ever since, taking over the empty minaret. No one really complained and very few ever saw him although they heard his bamboo flute and the tranquil music that he played on it.

"They should all be able to hear me, wherever they are," whispered Mullah Ullah.

Very soon there was a knock on the old man's door and his prayer mat swooped down the spiral staircase of the minaret and opened it quickly. Moments later Stargasm and Moonmummy flew in.

"Come in, ladies!" Mullah Ullah exclaimed cheerfully as his psychedelic gatta shone brighter. Bidding them be seated, he stood up and looked out of the star and crescent window. There high in the sky the Man on the Moon winked at him but the Mullah turned his eyes down and looked towards the east as the Whirlistanis rushed in through the minaret's window.

"Salaam," squealed Suleiman the Spinner, a young man of extreme height on whose beanstalk form was a strong, square face with sea-green eyes which saw everything under the sea and above the skies.

"How's . . .?" asked Mevlana the Mage, another young man whose white-blond hair flowed out from fez to shoulders. His perfume, attar of roses, could be smelt far away. More dark white than light brown, he entered, scratching his short, curly beard.

"Everyone?" finished the last young man, known as Nasseruddin the Nutty, a dwarf with a huge head, short cropped hair and lapis lazuli for teeth. He was the shortest of the trio and definitely the craziest. His long stretched face smiled as he took off his rubber flip-flops and pulled at his white silken djelaba. Blowing crazy smoke-rings, from a vintage fourteenth-century hookah, he careered to a halt inside the minaret.

"Everyone here then?" Mullah Ullah asked, his gatta glowing confidently. He scratched his nose as his magic prayer mat nudged him gently and looked around to peruse the disparate trio. Nasseruddin was now running up the walls and stealing Stargasm's humour while being chased silly by her belligerent broomstick. Suleiman was making polite conversation with Moonmummy who was trying not to get perturbed by his spinning while Mevlana had ecstatically exploded in his fragrance and was trying to purloin Nasseruddin's hookah.

"Freedom is a basic necessity!" said Suleiman.

"The first Humble Truth!" Moonmummy squealed as the Mullah's magic prayer-mat wrapped itself around her voluminous body.

"Stop it! Sit down and behave," Mullah Ullah commanded. The Mullah was the oldest and it was customary to respect the elder so they did.

"Listen to me and quieten yourselves as I am the oldest!" Mullah Ullah hollered.

"No you're not, we're much older!" Nasseruddin replied, looking serious for a moment.

"Yeah. How old are you Mullah Ullah?" Mevlana added in a mischievous air.

"Older than the sun and nearly as old as the Man on the Moon!"

"What a load of dobb!" Suleiman said, with a grin as wide as he was tall.

"We're from the sixteenth century even if we are only in our thirties. That makes us four hundred and thirty at least," Suleiman finished, trying hard to look serious.

"You're having us on because you want to be leader!" Mevlana continued laughing.

The Mullah proceeded. "No, I'm leader because I'm the serious one and you need some serious folks in this plot or how are we ever going to beat Lucifer?"

"This slaphead's rude, man," Nasseruddin snorted, gleeful to have found a hole in the Mullah's plot.

"Laughter's always the first language," Mevlana chuckled, sidling up to Nasseruddin.

"Wicked brother, Second Holy Rule!" Nasseruddin chuckled, looking nuttier than an almond or even a walnut.

"All right be as silly as you want but just listen to me for a moment, please," Mullah Ullah said emphatically, as the magic prayer mat slapped the dwarfish Whirlistani a good few times across his ridiculous face.

"He said please," Suleiman snorted, looking carefully at Mevlana's face but holding a hand to his nose against the rosy scent.

"Yeah, that's polite," Mevlana replied, exuding even more perfume than before and as they always say in the rose gardens of Kamershand, a man living in the midst of blooming roses is never really happy until he becomes immune to the smell of roses.

"What do we say in reply then?" he choked in reply.

"Thank you!" Nasseruddin chortled.

"No silly ... that's at the end ..." Mevlana replied, looking faintly embarrassed.

"I know ... it's ... sorry," Suleiman stuttered, getting his head out of his hands.

"Don't you say sorry before thank you or is it the other way around?" Nasseruddin asked, scratching his head.

"It's sorry, thank you, please," Suleiman insisted, finally standing seven foot tall.

"All right then let's all say it together," Nasseruddin started, looking up at his Whirlistani brother.

"Sorry. Thank you. Please," crooned the Whirlistanis together, trying to look apologetic and failing miserably while Mullah Ullah cleared his throat and tried to feel mollified.

"By the sacred dreadlocks of St Stan, are they always so crazy?" Moonmummy asked as the Whirlistanis quickly got their cloud-boards out and started streaming around and around the small circular room knocking over the samovar in the process.

"Nasseruddin's not the only one, they're all completely bonkers!" Stargasm replied, watching them in total fascination as Mullah Ullah decided to take control.

"It's okay ... just sit down all of you and I'll tell you why I've brought you here ... Lucifer is rising again ... the colours are coming off the Chuckle Stream ... leprechauns are disappearing everywhere and we have to find out why."

Hearing Lucifer's name they all calmed down instantly while the Mullah stroked his podgy belly clockwise and his beard counter-clockwise and continued quietly. "I've had a recurring dream the last thousand and one nights and I must tell you about it."

"Tell us, what's been on your mind?" Moonmummy asked.

"It's something we don't know and we should."

"But we know everything, we know the Four Holy Rules!" Stargasm said in a steely voice as her turquoise eyes looked querulous.

"And the Four Humble Truths," Moonmummy added, fingering her collapsible broomstick in an agitated manner.

"And what about the Three Serene Sillinesses. Isn't that all there is to know ...?" Stargasm said as the conversation turned serious.

"Certainly not."

"Sorry?" shot Moonmummy, quick on the take.

"Tell us, please!" Stargasm added as the mystery seemed to unravel itself.

"You'd be doing us a favour," Moonmummy finished with a sigh, encouraging the Mullah to continue.

Mullah Ullah then snatched the flying hookah off Mevlana's cloud-board, quickly refilled it from a pouch he had had under his lungi, magicked a glowing coal from out of the top of Stargasm's bewildered head and lit the hookah. Smoking meditatively for a few moments he looked at everyone and pondered. He took a few more contemplative puffs and surprised everyone with his smoke rings and squares and crescents then passed the pipe to Stargasm. The witch shook her crazy mane and toked until smoke appeared out of her nose in the shape of a broomstick. Then it was Moonmummy's turn to inhale and she kept the smoke inside her lungs for a long while until her two black eyebrows separated from either side of her face in opposite directions and floated off out of the windows while the exhaled smoke took the shape of a ring of dancing black cats that chased each other's tails in a never-ending circle. Finally, it was the turn of those swirling Whirlistanis. Mevlana took the first toke and quickly passed it to Suleiman who followed suit. Nasseruddin was the last to smoke and when he did the plans became very clear. They then all exhaled in turn. Mevlana's smoke was in the shape of an incredibly intricate moving mandala. Suleiman's smoke blew right into it and created indescribable pulsing patterns within the mandala's centre. As the smoky mandala expanded into a thousand intricate forms and appeared to take over the room, Nasseruddin exhaled strongly and simply blew everything into oblivion.

"Ahhhhh! You spoilt it, you rotter!" Suleiman cried, looking disgusted with Nasseruddin.

"Why did you do that?" Mevlana asked, slapping at the dwarf's foolish head.

"All good things come to an end."

While the two taller Whirlistanis pummelled the shorter one Stargasm pulled up her wattle and daub gown and quickly asked, "So what did you dream, Mullah?"

The Mullah smiled for a moment and pondered seriously before replying. The others looked at him with a collective questioning gaze.

"I dreamt that there are three Magic Mantras we don't know about and we have to know them if we are truly to be liberated."

"Wow!" gasped Nasseruddin, as the others finally stopped thrashing him.

"Sorry?" asked Suleiman, who had missed what the Mullah had said.

"He said Magic Mantras, you deaf fool," Nasseruddin muttered, rubbing his pained head and grimacing.

"Could you say them again, please?" Suleiman asked quickly, not wanting to miss anything.

"Three Magic Mantras!" replied the Mullah, happy that he'd finally got their attention.

"Thank you," Suleiman gasped, as Nasseruddin bounced up from the ground and landed him a perfect right hook on the jaw.

"Magic Mantras maybe but nothing's as important as Love!" Stargasm stuttered, looking puzzled.

The Mullah laughed quickly and replied, "No, you're right!"

Outside the star and crescent window a distant magical sound could be heard but it wasn't Hypno-Tantric Trance, this was different. As the group smoked the Man on the Moon strummed his cosmic hurdy-gurdy and the delicious tune swirled up in the air and filled the skies with its mysterious refrains. Sitting on his silvery crescent, the Man on the Moon floated closer in order to hear what they were saying. On one side he had the giant Golden Dream Butterfly flapping its large semi-transparent multicoloured wings. And on the other, the Aurora Borealis sparkled in all its dynamic splendour while inside the minaret, Stargasm suddenly had a thought.

"The Zoofis from Banglastan flying their snowcamels, are they coming with us?"

"No, their snowcamels are too slow and fart too much. We'll probably meet them later," the Mullah replied, quickly gathering up his things and motioning the others to do so too and then the room started spinning, slowly at first, then with gathering speed. Here was the sign that Mullah Ullah had been waiting for and the minaret was shifting into gear as it was time to move on. The room spun faster and faster and then even faster and they were all starting to get giddy except for Suleiman who was used to spinning. It was almost as if the room wanted to take off itself into the unfathomable skies.

"What's it all about and where are we going?" Moonmummy asked with her eyebrows joining up as one again.

"We're going to Hoggaristan!" Stargasm said confidently, as the little room raced faster than her incredible thoughts.

"Why we going?" Moonmummy asked, quite understandably as she had never been to Hoggaristan before.

"To find out why colours are coming off the Chuckle Stream and possibly discover the Magic Mantras," said Mullah Ullah very quickly before she could get her breath back.

"I know we'll find the Grumble Glitch in Hoggaristan and colours coming off the Chuckle Stream but will we find the Magic Mantras?" Stargasm added. The Mullah pulled his ears and considered.

"Everything must be considered, the dark ones may know things that we don't!"

"Who cares as long as it's gonna be fun?" Nasseruddin cackled.

"What did he say?" Suleiman gasped, completely missing the point.

"He said that maybe the bad guys know the mantras," Mevlana responded, holding onto his smell of roses as the room began to shake deliriously.

"I reckon we'll find them closer to home," Moonmummy said as her collapsible broomstick unfolded itself. Stargasm had the last word.

"Yeah, let's all ride anyway, it's an adventure!"

"OK then! Everything's OK?" the Mullah asked, getting ready to hover on his unrolled prayer mat.

The Whirlistanis rolled out their cloudboards and shot off, one after the other, through the window, out in the skies again. Mullah Ullah then cruised out to meet them, circling the mosque courtyard, while Stargasm helped Moonmummy onto her broomstick. The witches were almost the last to exit through the window but the prayer mat, finding itself on its own, quickly rolled around the star-clad floor and whizzed out to be under the Mullah's podgy bottom. Nasseruddin led at the front, closely followed by Stargasm, Moonmummy and Mevlana. Suleiman cruised behind this group followed by Mullah Ullah himself and so the journey to Hoggaristan began and magic, myth and mayhem would clearly continue.

10

The Good Shepherds of Queen Angie Park

QUEEN ANGIE PARK was looking lovely. It had been created by the infamous Queen Angie in a time when Slumdon was very different, the capital of the greatest power on earth.

However, the place that became known as Queen Angie Park was Krishna's playground where Sidney Arthur had once gambolled with lambs when he should have been cavorting with sacred cows. Sitting under a canopy of giant mystic mushrooms, BB and Charlie were making daisy chains and BB's plan had worked so far and convincing Charlie had been easy.

"Hey Charlie, have another slice of mystic mushroom!" BB gasped between a mouthful, watching the rain seep in again through his torn pink plimsolls.

"No, I'm stuffed, isn't there anything else to eat?" Charlie replied, brushing away the straight ginger locks that fell untidily to his collar. He shifted his seated position and rubbed his pained ankles. The two had been sitting like meditating yogis for simply ages. How long they didn't exactly know as the mystic mushrooms were playing havoc with their sense of time. BB didn't reply, his mouth being full, and so the Kockneestani asked again.

"Oi, isn't there anything else?"

"Not unless you like eating grass!"

"No, wouldn't mind smoking some though," Charlie replied and tugged at his ears.

The two lit a bong and the smoke gushed out of the top like something interesting. The two then looked around. For some strange reason although they hadn't been taking their shepherding tasks very seriously, the flocks seemed to be coming in all right. Around them there were simply hundreds of sacred cows and soft cuddly lambs that had seemingly followed BB and Charlie into the park.

"How come the lambs and cows are coming in even if we're just sitting here taking it easy?" Charlie asked, in the midst of a haze of blue smoke.

"Who knows and who cares, maybe they like your smell," BB replied, laughing.

"No, but the sacred cows seem to be crazy over yours!" Charlie said, in a midst of giggles as his grey eyes started turning green.

"Perhaps we both smell just right."

And he was correct. BB rubbed his kaleidoscopic spectacles and tall, gangling Charlie pulled his high cheekbones even higher and looked up. The skies were still blue but the sun was definitely looking dimmer and the rainbows that were usually seen at this time of year were not there. Charlie sighed as both he and BB knew the reason why. In the old oak above them ghostly presences pouted and preened.

"Oi Sidney Arthur, move up a bit!" whistled Billy Blake as he tried to shift Sidney Arthur up a bit on the branch.

"And give me my peg-leg back," groaned the ghost of Danny De Foe as he sat on the branch above and looked miserable.

"In a minute Danny, just be patient," whispered Sidney Arthur, doing neither of what the other two had asked for.

All three were sitting on the highest branches of the oak tree and casting their fishing rods far and wide throughout the park. Sidney Arthur's ghostly daffodils were falling out of his tattered jacket lapels as usual and BB and Charlie didn't realise that they had used some of them for the daisy chains they had been making. Of course, Sidney Arthur's ghostly daises always changed to daffodils and the daffodils to daisies. Danny's wooden peg leg was being used as a comfortable seat for Sidney Arthur as he found the prickly branches too hard on his ghostly bum but what about their fishing rods that had fished and gathered the incredible tribe of lambs and cows together? It had taken ages but they had finally done it while the two silly beatniks had mostly slept or tripped. BB and Charlie had thought that it had been their charm that had made them follow them to the park but they had been wrong.

Sidney Arthur rubbed his face and laughed as all was going well and everyone and everything was being manipulated to plan. If it all went right then soon they would all be free.

11

The Bum Note – Metta-Morph-Aziz Gets Real

IT WAS THE night of Metta-Morph-Aziz at Catweazel Phil's Bum Note (Phil loved irony). This infamous club was only minutes away from the bagel shops at the top of Brickie Lane and from the outside it looked like a normal nightclub but on pressing a secret button a dark stairway led down a spiral of stairs and through a hidden door into the Queen of Hearts's garden. Catweazel Phil, the best laser and lights bloke in Slumdon, ran over to change some effects which were shining on the walls. Intricate, changing, multi-coloured shapes shone their patterns on the walls and ceilings while beside him faithful Frogamatix nodded, happy just to croak along. Seeing the tiny shining forms of the Dreamweavers, Twynklyn, Blynkyn and Nod, he just ushered them in with his tongue and rasped over their ladybird wings.

Friday nights were the very special Metta-Morph-Aziz sessions. This is where Mellow Tron, Fareek and Tarquin played their Hypno-Tantric Trance and the night after which they named themselves as MMA. The names, *Metta*, in ancient Pali, meant love, *Morph* was classical Greek, meaning change and *Aziz* in Scarabian, meant never-ending preciousness. To put it together, it meant the *Ever-Changing Preciousness of Love* or something like it, *and it really was*! On stage Mellow Tron became 'Morph' and programmed while his dreadlocks danced, frisky Fareek became 'Metta' and ran around looking marvellous in his holographic zoofi gown, smiling serenely with his hallucinogenic left eye flapping like mad while Tarquin became 'Aziz' and played synsantooric tablas dressed in nothing but a romper suit and a grin. Mellow Tron then rocked the roots with bass notes so deep the whales in the seven seas of serenity could hear them from a thousand miles away. If the name wasn't true at the beginning, by the time Anatta had been dished out it certainly became so. Here we go . . . again!!!

It was about this time that the children entered though a trapdoor in the ceiling. Princess Amrita was the first to open it and slid down a Zindian rope followed by Dobbins, various members of Funkadelic, Astral Alice, Anarkali and Little Lucy. Dobbins threw his hat into the crowd and a whole stream of pocket watches flew out over the delirious crowd. On his tatty coat-tails were a couple of Dream-Skinned Mandrills who had finally caught up with their truanting lot but Dobbins shook the monkeys off and dived into the crowd. Bouncing up to be near Osric who was generously handing out Anatta to everyone, he dipped his naughty hands into the stash sack and liberated a handful.

The grimy Dobbins then led Amrita over the crowded dance-floor. All around the room the countless Banglastani waiters stood silently to attention while their braided, princely togs sparkled under the magic of Catweazel Phil's lasers. These were members of Sergeant Chilli's Lonely Farts Club Band and they were brilliant. In their hands they held silver salvers and offered the guests sweets to munch on. As each trancer passed, the sweets would naturally shoot off from the silver plates and grab them by their grateful gobs . . .

"Trippy!" Astral Alice gasped in a face of strawberry cream surprise as her velvet bloomers billowed out like parachutes to cushion her fall.

"Far out!" Anarkali cried as the figures on her Kathak gown closed their eyes as she too jumped but before she had reached even three feet off the floor, her feet started trancing in mid air and she was gone. Her painted scarlet lips parted deliriously to sing a song of home. Home for this outcaste in time and space was seventeenth-century Kathakstan but Anarkali knew better. Home, of course, was always where the heart was. And at that precious moment her heart was right inside her delicate tiny frame, smack bang in the middle of the Bum Note, somewhere in twenty-first-century Pearly Green. It was then her swirly-whirly gown began to spin and took her in their grand sweep up into the air.

Little Lucy screamed as she fell off her Zindian rope and scattered diamonds everywhere. Her cascading ginger locks covered most of her face. The freckles on her face were changing all the time into the purest gems to scatter. From inside her sky-blue dungarees, she pulled out a handful of cloud-white buttons and chucked them into the air. These got stuck to the ceiling where fluffy white clouds shifted across the moving panorama. Lucy was only six years old but a real shiner all the same.

Hypno-Tantric Trance was to new age music what Mandarin Dream (with a bitter-lemon twist) had been to synthirock generations before. The underground spirit which had started in Sid Arthur St, frolicked on the streets of Spitney and Smile End, had finally found a place to be, a movement whose time had come. Downstairs several hundred creatures bopped crazily, some flapped their wings and some others rose into the air with no visible means of support. Others took off on stolen cloud-boards or on broomsticks they had liberated from the secret stash that the absent Moonmummy and Stargasm kept in their hiding place at the top of the schoolhouse. Everyone was there. The Dreamweavers were weaving dreams; Twynkyn was blinking, Nod was asleep in the middle of the air and Blynkyn was blinking her eyelids so fast she didn't miss a single thing. Meanwhile, the gubblies were running around watching their heads turn green and their hands turn blue, this was back-to-front but they didn't seem to mind. Ignoring the wandering sacred cows, the Sabre-Toothed Power Pussy watched a few soft cuddly lambs wander by. It flashed its orange and black luminous stripes and gave the children a piggy-back as it meandered through the crowds and the shimmering Jabberwocky, the original inhabitant of the Sonic Temple of King Psychedelix, waddled slowly up. Thirty foot long and timeless, it crawled to the beat on its four shifting legs. It had the head of a crocodile with soft, coloured brontosaurus fins on his back. It happily criss-crossed the crowd merrily smoking the Caterpillar's hookah and ignoring Little Lucy's wish for a ride.

The Bum Note was becoming seriously over-crowded and those not tripped-out soon got edged out of the crowds and pushed towards the bar. This was where they eyed each other up lovingly as their own trip started to take off and the colours in their drinks lit up like electric flares as soon as it touched their sparkling lips. Outside, as the summer winds touched the tower tops, the streets around Scoreditch and Slimehouse became full of happy smiling people holding hands. They were in for an unforgettable night!

From the East, the Zoofis from Banglastan flew in through the open rooftop sitting on their snowcamels. They had ridden over from the twelfth century and consisted of Abraxas the Long Beard, Azeem the Dream and Hussain the Insane. If they had been a bit faster they could have gone to Hoggaristan with Mulllah Ullah and his crew but their farting snowcamels weren't the fastest means of transport.

"Brothers!" started Abraxas the Long Beard, adjusting his turban and brushing hallucinogenic agaric flies off his techno-coloured dream coat.

"We are," added Azeem the Dream with melting facial features. Only his tiny nose remained the constant. He quickly started playing his magic shenai.

"Here," finished Hussain the Insane, thin, five feet tall and with brown wavy hair falling down to his waist. He was banging a gong.

"Where are the witches?" Abraxas asked a passing Dream-Skinned Mandrill.

"Oooo . . . Oooo . . .!" shrugged the monkey, moving on hurriedly.

"Bah! We've come too late!" groaned Azeem the Dream.

"And where's Mullah Ullah?" Abraxas asked again as a passing sooth-saying sea slug jumped down into his techno-coloured dream coat. Very soon a shoal of twinklefish was chasing the sea slug down into the Zoofi's voluminous robes. Abraxas' face turned tangerine as the fish wandered around his nether regions. He scratched his beard which had scrolled up and out the twinklefish popped from the top of his carefully wound turban. How they did that was anybody's guess.

"Who cares? Let's party!" squealed Hussain the Insane banging his gong in time to the Hypno-Tantric Trance that was beaming out across the forty-seven wall-embedded speakers. He started to bounce around the room like a Zindian rubber ball and shot across to the other side. There he nearly upset Astral Alice who was riding high near the ceiling on one of Little Lucy's cloud-white buttons.

The Jabberwocky walked carefully around the plodding snow-camels who were walking to the beat in crazy circles seven feet in the air, trying to avoid the fantasy flamingos that were simply going nuts. The rave was getting groovier by the moment.

"Are You . . . Ready?" Fareek wailed over the gibbering crowds as his pupils dilated and contracted to the happy beats. He had spent the last thirty-six hours coaxing strands of Zindian-fern. All this hard work was paying off. Lajapati, the common or garden Zindian-fern, was an amazing plant especially when its nervous sytem was connected to a whole range of synthesisers, samplers and midi-computronic boxes. Lajapati was one of the wickedest plants that

Krishna ever invented. As the Hypno-Tantric Trance blossomed from the multiple speakers, everyone sighed with relief.

The crowd was rocking. All was well in this, the best of all possible worlds. Fareek beamed at the crowds as Mellow Tron dug deeper into the big, big bass. His dreadlocks danced and while Fareek beamed, his grin bounced off the many people and returned to him bigger than when it had left. This beam boomerang kept on bouncing and exploding into little bits of smileiness everywhere.

"Wow! This is simply – heaven!" Anarkali gasped as heaven imploded behind her in a thousand and one day-glo rainbows. The faces on her gown shimmered in disbelief as she stomped her tiny feet in perfect circles.

"Yeah, and everyone's on the guest list too!" she laughed, somewhere way above the sounds, swirling. The many faces on this incredible dress delighted at the sight around them. A wandering Bongostani leprechaun from Sidney Arthur's grand old house at Scoreditch jumped from cloud to cloud to finally settle on top of the coconut island that Hussain the Insane had magically materialised somewhere above the heads of the dancing and delirious crowds.

"Oh gosh! What's happening to me?" Osric gasped suddenly as his world began to speedily dissolve.

"Same as what's happening to everyone else, matey!" Fareek shouted manically from the stage.

Somewhere, dangling from one hand onto Hussain the Insane's floating coconut island (which he'd magicked up) and trying to grab the adventurous sooth-saying sea slugs that had entered his nostrils with the other, Osric looked aghast. He wondered why he always had such a hard time taking Anatta before the fluidity of Fairlight's magic potion took him into worlds unknown. It is true that he couldn't say much especially as a Dream-Skinned Mandrill jumped up from the ground and tried taking his jeans off in a hurry. On the floating island, Little Lucy, Amrita and Anarkali began chucking coconuts at the monkeys' heads in order for them to let poor Osric go and Abdul the Bongostani leprechaun quickly grabbed Osric up by the scruff of his dirty collar and laughed at him. Then, many of Master Fagin's Funkadelic tribe zoomed in on fast-moving fluffy white clouds. Some others pirouetting on the top of the magic Zindian ropes shifted closer to be with their friends. Osric pondered. Here he was now on an incredible floating island surrounded by magic, myth, mayhem and much innocence. Seeing his discomfort as the Dream-Skinned Mandrill ran around the Trancefloor whirling his stolen jeans ceremoniously above its head, Amrita quickly offered him a plum which she stuffed right into his mouth before it could change to a fantasy fig. Osric never liked figs.

"What exactly is a joke and what exactly is a dream?" he muttered. Amrita replied without hesitation. "You've said that before and there was no answer that time either."

"Yeah you're probably right, princess. You usually are . . ." Osric said as he started to smile. If the floating coconut tree island was a kingdom on its own, then Osric was probably king and the children's many sandcastles were consequently his bejewelled palace of humble delights. A palace of total impermanence which would soon get washed away with every single tide. Osric grinned and quickly bit into a passing crunchy banana before it could turn into a passion fruit. Obviously, as we all know he was the greatest fool of his generation and it made perfect sense for him to be monarch of all he surveyed. The children were the delightful inhabitants and the leprechaun, probably a wise man. Osric closed his eyes and breathed deeply and when he exhaled, multi-coloured rings streamed from his much-confused gob. As the Anatta made his consciousness rise, he felt his body sliding down the trunk of the highest coconut tree where he had gone to hide and into the octopus's garden somewhere in the shade of a long forgotten dream of summertime. His body stayed flumped into the sand but his mind was swimming in the seven seas of serenity. Just like Sinbad, he was off on another trip to find his inner island of total serendipity.

The children were having a good time chucking purple peaches at whoever they liked. Seeing this spectacle from the side, Hussain the Insane stared at the changing panorama and muttered a magic wish that split the flying fruits wide open, releasing a host of dancing dragonflies that flew out through the hole in the roof. But what about Osric? By now as he stuttered, ringlets of multicoloured flames streamed from his mouth. Every breath rippled in colours unknown and his body began to glow incomprehensibly. Anatta's sparkladelic sonic rings were happening again and as Abdul the Bongostani leprechaun looked out from atop the pretty sandcastles that were Osric's palace, all he could see were sonic rings emerging from everyone's lips and where they met in the middle, perfectly formed, multicoloured transparent mandalas emerged. Osric was now mumbling and muttering in a language all of his own, a total gibberish but it didn't seem to matter. The mandalas he created by merging sonic rings were just perfect, a real communication with no room for misunderstanding. Bouncing off from the floating island and having grabbed onto Hussain the Insane's unravelled turban, Osric abseiled to the middle of the trancefloor and what with the sounds, sonic rings, spectral colours and everything else he was starting to lose the plot.

"Ah no! ... Where am I?" he shrieked again and quickly looking around he noticed that the Bum Note had transformed into the Queen of Hearts' royal maze. Dylan was there strumming his guitar and the White Rabbit was impatiently looking at his pocket watch and stamping his little paws upon the ground. It was then that Osric realised he wasn't actually lost at all. The way back home lay through the Queen of Hearts' heart which went right through his own and everyone else's. Suddenly, everything disappeared and all he could see were love-hearts inter-connected everywhere.

"All roads lead to home!" shouted a demented Dream-Skinned Mandrill.

"The Third Holy Rule!" yelled Osric as the trip got weirder and weirder.

Amrita had jumped down off the floating island to hex the mad monkey's Zindian rope by quickly transfiguring it into a mirror. Upon seeing itself for the very first time, the Dream-Skinned Mandrill shrieked and stopped. It was transfixed by its own apparition.

"What you see is what you get. What you get depends on you, doncha know the Fourth Holy Rule then?" giggled Amrita as her schoolteacher curled up its tail and scampered off up to the side of the roof to fall onto the floating island. Perching itself next to Abdul the nose-picking Bongostani leprechaun, it hushed itself and pondered. It had thought itself to be pretty advanced but the image in the mirror still showed a monkey. As it started thrashing itself with a crunchy banana frond, the whole room exploded in flowers.

"Far out maaan! ... Our fantasy flintlocks are working well!" screamed Charlie to BB as they greedily stuffed their gobs with Anatta that a Dream-Skinned Mandrill had accidentally dropped after stealing it from Phil's hat. Charlie's head was way above the clouds. He was standing knee-deep in a shower of petals while his head narrowly missed Little Lucy's passing fluffy white cloud. The flower-power men were back and shooting randomly.

"Yeah groovy Charlie man! ... Everything's turning to flowers!" replied BB as his kaleidoscopic spectacles took in the sights. As they reloaded their empty flintlocks with the cascading petals that fell everywhere, the Kockneestani and Banglastani beatniks looked around and smiled.

Ignoring the distressed Dream-Skinned Mandrill now swinging painfully from the rafters, the Holy Ghosts took in all the sights. Sidney Arthur still had his fishing rod out and unknown to BB, his kurta was again affixed to it. Invisibly sitting atop the three wandering snowcamels our spectral friends watched the happenings with considerable interest.

"What a sight, Sidney!" Billy Blake whistled, brushing away the hair that covered his merry face.

"Yes absolutely brilliant but what are we doing here?" Danny asked with a sigh and smiling.

"Just you wait and see. I'm not going to tell you much more!" Sidney Arthur said in a quick flush.

"You never do, Sidney," the other two sung in ghostly chorus.

"All I can say, Billy, is keep your fishing-rod closely stuck to Kockneestani Charlie."

"And what about me?" Danny gasped, uselessly prodding his snowcamel with his ghostly peg leg trying to make it go faster.

"And Danny, see that dirty-faced youth over there doing magic tricks with his top hat? He's the Artful Dodger so make sure your rod is always caught on him."

"Why?"

"Why not?" Sidney Arthur said with a grin, stroking a snowcamel. And as the party rocked all around them, the Holy Ghosts waited patiently in the midst of flowers.

Over at Fort Cox, however, nothing had been going right for Lucifer. He had much to think about, his two red horns pulsed as he thought crazily about the future. His future!

"Vark and completely Vark!" he spat and it was very clear that he didn't like the present either. His goat-slit yellow eyes, his big red-black wings, his speckled lizard skin, attracted thousands of tiny lizards that he continually brushed off or slapped, as these unfortunates became a permanent addition to his body.

"Trouble, trouble, toil and trouble.
Pigs do cook and cauldrons bubble.
Mirror, mirror on the wall
I don't see any respite at all.
Trouble, trouble, toil and trouble
All I see is . . . VARK!"

Smoke gushed out from his flaring nostrils and he twisted his black-forked beard. His cruel hands and cloven feet twitched to get into some real action. From his third eye, laser bolts just waited to be fired. Lucifer thought about what he had just seen in the All-Seeing Crystal Ball. The visions had been disturbing. Demons and Diabolics in Pearly Green had reported back that the Hypno-Tantric Trance had been increased in volume, clarity and Metta! Damn it! Lucifer looked into another crystal ball and from this he watched the gig in Hoggaristan.

"Vark, even the Afreet Orchestra aren't in tune!"

He'd stolen most of the world's glittery stuff but in Brickie Lane the sun was still shining strongly and so he decided to wait no longer.

"OK . . . Give me the All-Seeing Time Ball" he whistled to a minor demon and sat back down again on his throne. About two feet wide, deep inside its glassy depths a scarlet-purple smokiness could be observed, turning and turning. The dark one waited then clicking his fingers said:

"Crystal Ball I thee command,
Aren't I the greatest in the land?
Where are the secret stashes? Please do show.
The sun needs no brightening, it really must go."

12

Hoggaristan and a Genie

THE RIDE HAD taken thirty-six hours, the Whirlistanis had shot off ahead but Mullah Ullah on his magic prayer-mat still held middle ground. Occasionally, Stargasm would hold back to ensure that wobbling Moonmummy was okay but in general, it had been a quiet ride. Moonmummy's eyes flashed like fire and the night sky lit up as she quickly thanked Stargasm for her timely help. Up ahead Mullah Ullah's lungi was flapping uncontrollably in the wind. The Mullah smiled as he raced on furiously, followed a few yards behind by the much slower prayer-mat. His squashed face looked intently into the future horizon that was racing towards him, faster than yesterday could follow today or even today turn into tomorrow. Way up at the front the crazy Whirlistanis raced around deliriously on their cloud-boards. They skimmed through the clouds like sonic surfers whizzing through ice-cream clouds and they screamed like crazy as they raced each other to see who was the fastest. Suleiman the Spinner was on the left and his tall frame bent in the moaning wind. Mevlana, still exuding the attar of roses, flew inches behind Suleiman looking detached. His long white hair flew in the wind, often blinding him, but he carried on regardless and Nasseruddin the Nutty's huge head could be heard screaming obscenities as his shining teeth became a beacon to illuminate the way.

Flying two hundred feet in the air, past the rock of the Gibbering Turk, they turned south into the seas until, after yet another hour, they were at the very top of the continent of Afrostan. The clouds were whizzing past their heads and the day was getting dark, very dark. The desert was starting to stretch out like silken scarves and fields of fig and fantasy lay below and camel tracks could be seen going from oasis to oasis. A lone grey pigeon (the very same which had crapped on the irate sweet seller) was still being chased by the persistent fantasy falcons.

"Ah, there it is!" shouted Nasseruddin the Nutty way out in front, punching fantasy falcons out of the way. He then sped back to be closer to Mullah Ullah who was in the middle. Meanwhile, the solitary grey pigeon settled on top of the Mullah's skull cap and after leaving a deposit, flew off again, satisfied. The Mullah's all-shining psychedelic gatta shone an embarrassed scarlet.

"Gotta slow . . ." whispered Mevlana surfing up waves of clouds as he hit clear air turbulence and settled close to the Mullah.

"Down . . .!" finished Suleiman as Stargasm joined too. Pointing to a cluster of palm trees, Mullah Ullah guided everyone down. They flew down together in a fantastic formation divided by nothing but rivers of individual belief. The Whirlistanis fell on top of each other gracelessly laughing and rolling around in the sands. Moonmummy and Stargasm giggled and waited for them to finish clowning before they landed more gracefully a few feet apart in the early evening ready for a rest.

"Anyone got any food?" Stargasm asked, anxiously gazing out at this very different world. She was starting to get very hungry as they hadn't had anything to eat since they had munched on a special dish of mystic mushroom curry and rice at the Right Rude Sabre Tooth. That, however, was forty hours ago.

The Mullah never ate any mystic mushroom curry as he always got acid indigestion and preferred crunchy bananas. "By the holy dreadlocks of St Stan, I'm really hungry. Anyone got anything?"

"I've got some naans that I nicked from the Right Rude before we left," Moonmummy replied, collapsing her broomstick up into a seven-inch telescope and falling cross-legged onto the sandy floor.

"And I've got some pumpkin pie," Mevlana said, when he jumped off. He quickly kicked on one end of his cloud-board and like a kiddie's skateboard it rose up and he caught it skilfully in one hand.

"And we've got some apples from Kamershand," Nasseruddin the Nutty whistled lazily as he began rubbing his teeth like a jeweller polishing gems.

"And what have we got to drink?" Moonmummy asked.

"Ah! . . . to drink . . . some elderberry wine," Suleiman the Spinner replied, chucking her a bottle of this precious delight. Everyone would drink this except the Mullah who drank only water.

"Good, now let's think. We have to have a plan, a course of action." Mullah Ullah started looking serious. The others didn't seem to agree. They scratched each other's heads and then each other's bottoms before pushing Stargasm forward to reply.

"Why do we have to have a plan? We've never had one before," she conjectured, ignoring Mevlana's poke and Suleiman's shoving.

"That's the biggest load of dobb I've ever heard! Life without a plan?" Mullah Ullah replied rolling up his magic prayer-mat and chucking it to one side. "Life without a plan? However shall we live?"

Then Nasseruddin the Nutty stuck out his foolish hand and said "Life is simply brilliant without a plan. You live moment by moment by moment and that's the only place you can live in, Mullah Ullah. I mean there's never a yesterday or tomorrow is there?"

"What?"

"I mean yesterday was today a bit earlier on and tomorrow is today yet to be . . . and so I rest my case, let's drink some elderberry wine and live in the moment and then great things may eventually happen. It's a good idea anyway!"

Mullah Ullah scratched his psychedelic gatta as the others fell about laughing. As they poured each other glasses of elderberry wine, Mullah Ullah suddenly noticed that his rolled up mat was in a state of intense agitation, flopping up and down on top of the sand as if something was buried underneath it. The Mullah stopped eating and came close. He picked up the prayer-mat and saw the shiny sparkle of something gold. He pulled out an ancient wick lamp about a foot long, curly and rather pretty. If it hadn't been for the thrashing about of the magic prayer-mat, he would never have uncovered it all. He looked at it bemused and then turned round to face the others.

"Anyone need a light?" he asked, pointing it in their direction.

"What's this?" Stargasm gasped, peering closer to get a better look.

"No idea but we should be very careful," said Mevlana coming closer after having a quick smoke.

"Why?" Mullah Ullah asked, holding on to the golden lamp possessively.

"It could be a magic lamp and you know what lives in magic lamps – genies!" Nasseruddin said, trying unsuccessfully to touch it.

"Jean who?" asked Stargasm, not having heard of genies before.

"No, genies. Some are good and some are bad and the rest are totally mad!" Nasseruddin replied with a chuckle.

"Rub it, Mullah Ullah, just rub it, man!" Stargasm interjected, excitedly putting the smoking hookah aside.

"Just remember the consequences, if anything bad happens to us it's all your fault," Mevlana chuckled, moving back just in case.

"Yeah, and the next thing, if anything good happens we ain't gonna give you any credit, you know that!" Suleiman tittered.

Taking a deep breath, the Mullah rubbed the lamp. From the end of the golden lamp, a silvery-blue smoke came out, filling the very air. It was hissing like a snake pissing itself and stopped at about two feet in the air, collected itself and grew into a fantastic form of an incredible genie about three hundred feet tall. It was so huge that it almost blocked out the setting sun.

The monster from the lamp roared as it stretched out into the open air for the first time in thousands of years. Stargasm shivered, Moonmummy mumbled, Mullah Ullah tumbled, Nasseruddin nicked Mevlana's look of total bewilderment for himself and Suleiman slipped down to the ground gracelessly.

It got bigger and bigger and its face was that of a wrestler that had fought ten thousand bouts. Its ears were more cauliflower than Kassim's, its jaw was more square than Moonmummy's and the many muscles on its huge ever-expanding body rippled as if there were live snakes under skin. It was frightening and they all looked daggers at Mullah Ullah as it was his fault. He'd rubbed the damn thing, hadn't he? It was his golden lamp. He found it. It was nothing to do with them.

"What's going to happen to us?" squealed Moonmummy.

"I don't know. There aren't any sooth-saying sea slugs around here," Mevlana replied embarrassedly trying to hide the growing stains on his silken gown.

His rubber flip-flops were so petrified they ran off in opposite directions never to return. On all three silly Whirlistanis, the velvet fezzes on their heads became so scared they too ran off. Mullah Ullah was so scared, the tiny slits of his eyes closed completely and his gatta turned itself off. Shuffling nervously forward, the Mullah squinted at the darkening skies and whimpered.

"Dear Genie of the Lamp, what do you want from us?"

The Genie looked down at them on high and laughed mysteriously. "Nothing much, oh puny mortals, just your lives!"

They all squealed at the same time and fell to their knees.

"Won't you give us a chance, please?" Mullah Ullah pleaded, with his hands folded in prayer.

"Hmmm ... maybe. Who was the one who found my lamp and who was the one that rubbed it?" The Genie spoke in vibrations of angry thunder.

"He did! ... He did! ... Mullah Ullah found it! It was nothing to do with us!" shouted six voices in exact empathy. The Mullah shuffled uncomfortably with this certain truth.

"What does that mean, oh great one?" he whispered.

"Finders keepers. Losers weepers!" roared the blue giant genie as smoke billowed out into the air. "I find you all responsible for my release from the magic lamp and because I do not discriminate I find you all equally guilty and will therefore kill all of you, without exception!"

Everyone cried except for Mullah Ullah whose psychedelic gatta suddenly shone an inner light into the back of his brain where it emerged at the front, smiling and chuckling.

"Prepare to die!" roared the Genie, his scarlet eyes flashing as everyone wept. The giant Genie of the Lamp raised a huge smoky blue foot to squash them all but the Mullah jumped up, straightened his lungi and squealed.

"Please, before you kill us at least let us know why we are going to die? I know it doesn't make much difference but it's a comforting thought anyway."

The Genie suddenly stopped and his giant right foot hovered in the air. He scratched his beard, pondered a while and then spoke slowly.

"Okay, I'll tell you why you have to die. Once upon a long long time ago, I was trapped in this golden lamp. I had angered a great sorcerer and my punishment was to be locked in here for ever."

Mullah Ullah tweaked his nose and the other cringeing six finally looked up. The Genie continued.

"For the first ten thousand years, I waited and promised whosoever set me free ... I'd give them wealth beyond compare. I waited and waited and no one came to set me free."

"And then what happened, oh great Genie?" Mullah Ullah said.

"I waited another ten thousand years and promised whosoever set me free, I'd love them beyond compare and gently place flowers in their pretty hair but no one came ...! And from then to now a darkness fell across my once happy brow. I was much changed."

The Genie began lifting up one giant foot again as sparks of fire flew out of his nostrils. He angrily roared.

"I waited another ten thousand years and promised whosoever sets me free I'll just kill them, so now you lot have set me free you shall have the honour of dining tonight in the hottest part of Hell."

As the others prepared to die very badly, Mullah Ullah suddenly remembered reading the "One Thousand and One Nightmares" of Habiba the Beloved's ancient grandfather. Alauddin had been many places in his much-travelled youth and always had a few tricks up his merry robes. Quickly rushing up to the Genie with his arms askew, the Mullah shouted dementedly "OK. OK, so you got a big ego, who gives a monkey fart? Killing a bunch of mere mortals – big deal! We've seen how big you can get now show us how small your ego can be. If it's as small as your smoky-blue willy we'll be totally impressed and then you can gladly squash us!"

"What small willy? Me?" roared the Genie in an incandescent rage, stomping up and down furiously in the scorching air.

"Nah we don't want to see your willy genie we want to see if your tiny ego will fit in the lamp!" hollered Nasseruddin the Nutty, quickly catching on to the Mullah's game.

"Speak for yourself, I don't mind seeing his willy before I die," whimpered Stargasm as the blue woad dripped off her frightened face.

"Bah! Prepare to die after you see me shrink back into the lamp. I shall return and when I do, you will die!" screamed the Genie of the Lamp as its giant smoky blue form sucked itself up in swivelling spirals and returned from whence it came. As soon as it was inside, Mullah Ullah clamped down the top and locked it. Everyone stood still in silence not knowing what was to happen but the Mullah started chuckling and his magic prayer-mat whizzed around in circles, deliriously happy.

"What shall we do now?" gasped a much relieved Moonmummy brushing the sand out of her hair and standing up.

"Nothing, we've caught the monster well and good this time and he can stay there till the end of time and there will be no one to play with, no one to laugh with and he will never get out!" Mullah Ullah said with a satisfied look on his sweating face.

"Shall we bury it in the sands again? Really deep?" Moonmummy, asked, trying to think of the best solution.

"No some other poor unfortunate will probably find it some day!" Mullah Ullah said, letting his psychedelic gatta do the thinking.

"Let me out! Let me out!" squealed a little voice from inside the golden lamp.

"Yeah right! Do you think we are as stupid as you?" chuckled the Mullah holding tightly onto the stopper of the golden lamp.

"No I promise to behave and not kill you and also, being the Genie of the Lamp, I'll give you three magic wishes!"

"We rather like you as you are so we're going to chuck you into the ocean." The Mullah laughed as his white skullcap started spinning around his head in relief.

"No . . . No . . . Please . . . let me go and I'll behave!" screamed the little voice as the others sat down and resumed their picnic. They drank a few more bottles of elderberry wine and watched the setting sun with a growing sense of beatitude and quietness. No one spoke. After a while, Mullah Ullah stood up and brushed the cobwebs from his mind. Watched curiously by his hovering prayer-mat, he walked up to the golden lamp, picked his ears, closed his eyes, quickly opened the stopper and out emerged the Genie of the Lamp in a fast haze of blinding smoky blue light.

"Three wishes, master and I promise never to misbehave again," whispered a most apologetic Genie of the Lamp as it again rose into the air.

"Excellent!" replied Mullah Ullah smiling benevolently. "And what do you say?"

"Sorry, master, your wish is my command!"

"What else?"

"Please don't put me into the prison again!"

"What else?"

"Thank you for letting me go and I give you the three customary and most obligatory wishes!" answered the Genie of the Lamp as it swirled around and around.

"Far out!" screamed Nasseruddin the Nutty stashing the still burning hookah away. They were all living in the moment, everything was groovy and they were on a mission. They had to find the three Magic Mantras and find out what was happening to the Chuckle Stream. Someone must know something. The Genie of the Lamp got back into the golden prison which was placed gently onto Mullah Ullah's hovering prayer-mat but there was a difference this time because the Mullah had thrown the stopper away and the Genie wept with happiness as it realised its long imprisonment was over for good.

They raced on for another good few hours and were cruising down to see the never-ending gig in Hoggaristan where the Afreet Orchestra, Lucifer's band of doom were playing their endlessly scary scales and deathly dirges. They paid close attention to the topography as they were looking for the abandoned Roman amphitheatre that was home to the geeks, gooks, scrooks, goblins and major and minor devils. The air grew blacker as they came closer and closer and the very particles of oxygen seemed to be suffused with an evil intent that was hard to decipher.

Over the horizon they could hear the screeching, stamping and gnashing of many teeth but whose it was difficult to know. Was it the demons or the vampires or the hobgoblins that were grinding their sharp pointy teeth to the beat? As Stargasm looked to her left from about two hundred feet in the air, she could clearly see colours being slowly bled from the sky, the Chuckle Steam being robbed. However with colours slowly dripping onto the rocky barren floor like kidnapped kookaburras, it was a terrible sight to see. And how was it being robbed? It was through the incredible dark and disgusting playing of Lucifer's band of doom. They had done this before and now they were doing it again.

"What are we going to do, Mullah Ullah?" Moonmummy asked, cruising close to the Mullah. The Genie of the Lamp was only visible as a gentle puff of iridescent blue smoke that illuminated the magic prayer-mat.

"We're just here to check up on the opposition and not get caught," Mullah Ullah replied as he turned down the glow of his gatta. Stargasm joined up to be on his level coming up from the other side and the Mullah spoke to both in hushed tones.

"We're here just to check out what they're playing and to see if they know the Magic Mantras," he finished abruptly and pointed to the skies. Even the three silly Whirlistanis went quiet now as they all looked up.

The crimson skies were changing fast and it was a change not to their collective liking. The colours were slowly being bled out it like a wound left in warm water.

"Bleedin' heck!" gasped Nasseruddin the Nutty slapping his head for good measure.

"Dead right mate!" Mevlana grimaced as his cloud-board bounced up and down in the shaky breeze.

They were now about one mile away from the abandoned Roman amphitheatre and flying quite low. As the Mullah pointed an arc with his arm, all looked towards the skies. All they could see were colours disappearing from the skies and a smoky-grey darkness began to take everything over. Soundlessly, they spiralled down in the darkness playing an invisible helter-skelter before landing next to each other on the ground by some abandoned rocks. They were about a half mile away from the epicentre of the crazy stage. The night was harsh with the squeaking of the vampire violinists and the wailing of the heckles and speckles, bhoots, afreets and preets as the demons and diabolics carried on playing throughout the night. It was awe-inspiring, ably done and simply awful.

The Afreet Orchestra were ably doing their stuff. Made from the decomposed bits of the seriously undead, they were actually absolutely brilliant at what they did, so bad they were utterly, awfully good. The Genie of the Lamp quaked in fear as he hid inside the golden lamp. Pure, simple darkness would have been fine but this music had the soul-sucking noise of seriously demented demons and it was horrible. From their vantage point in amongst the palm trees, they stared at the mammoth stage made of dinosaur droppings and shining in the distance like a bad dream. All kept quiet as they watched the intricate turnings of the Poison Ivy which was connected up to complicated electronics of an incredibly good sound system. It was as good as the sound system in the Sonic Temple of King Psychedelix deep down underground inside the incredible Lost Catacombs of Brickie Lane. And then the music changed in crescendo and an even more disgusting riff cursed the air.

"I can't see beyond those awful banshees and preets playing horns or those bhoots playing their bones or even those evil dwarves and skankerry gnomes playing drums," Stargasm whistled. Mevlana and Nasseruddin conversed quietly in their tree while Moonmummy and Mullah Ullah whispered manically in the third. The broomsticks and cloud-boards and magic prayer-mat hovered a few inches off the air ready for a quick get-away.

"Everyone, do hush!" Mullah Ullah said trying to keep the volume down. It was a good thing that he did too as suddenly to the thunderous applause of happy hobgoblin folk, the Black Magic

Mysterons joined the Afreet Orchestra on stage in a hurricane of demented hurrahs. The bhoots, afreets, vampires, goblins, skankerry gnomes, banshees and much else screamed their skeletal heads off.

As the hellish choir of queer yet cute looking choirboys dressed in devilish romper suits screamed to a crescendo, the Black Magic Mysterons crashed onto centre stage. Three demented figures came into view, three indefinably weird brothers. All were thin, bony, skeletal forms seven feet tall. Fruggy was the first to be seen after the smoke blown from the nostrils of the many evil ogres cleared. Dressed in schoolboy shorts and an old school tie, his ashen locks fell to his shoulder from a sinister skull. His eye-sockets were like burning white coals as he screamed obscenities to the grateful crowd from long-dead toothless gums. He leapt into the air and flew down backwards onto his set of Bad-Beat drums. He then smashed into the terror tablatronic set-up and whacked the spectral snares. And then came Fruzzy onto the scene. Looking just as nasty as his triplet brother, he quickly enjoyed a snakebite before he started to play. This was not a harmless drink as enjoyed by most people made of weak beer and cider, this really was a snakebite. As the crowd watched in a whimper of delight, they saw him pick up an evil-looking king cobra from one of many gathered in a basket on the stage. He then lifted up his arm and rammed it down fangs first into his deadly skin. The snake bit and he got a hit and smiled as the rush took him into upside-down dreams. Wearing the same silly clothes as Fruggy, he ripped into the 666 banks of mixers, samplers and grumplers while his scary right hand tickled the awesome arpeggiaters. With his left hand he slammed down a fearful chord of dissymmetry onto the evil battered electric guitar slung around his neck.

And then Total-Frux shimmered into view, spinning disks on the sinister holodecks, his right arm raced to tickle the vibrating Poison Ivy that was connected to all the ghoul grumplers. It was this that was playing the demonic music. Everything was going okay and the Poison Ivy's toxic tunes rippled up in a spiral streaming up to the skies and proceeded to rip off the colours off the Chuckle Stream. This, of course, was stealing the happiness at the rainbow's end. Suddenly, Total Frux roared a hello into the crowds and smashed his left hand onto the control switch of the noxious scrankler. As loud as Lucifer having a bad trip and really rather beautiful too, the

Black Magic Mysterons' lasers flashed and smoke bombs crashed. The Afreet Orchestra now doubled in volume and Stargasm covered her ears.

"Can you see what the addition of The Black Magic Mysterons has done to the synergy between the colour-stealing smoky-waves and the music of the Afreet Orchestra?" Mullah Ullah whispered to Moonmummy as she clamped her black leather boots more firmly around the tree in order to listen well and not fall off.

"Yes, together they always become Lucifer's Band of Doom, don't they?" she replied snapping her fingers to make her collapsible broomstick open out again.

"And now the smokiness of the Black Magic Mysterons is joining up to rob the Chuckle Stream!" Moonmummy added, having lost some of her fear but looking at the stage and the colour-sucking rays that emanated from it.

"This puts us in a quandary because it means the Chuckle Stream is being robbed at double its usual rate . . ." Mullah Ullah gasped, waving his hand at the ground which unrolled his magic prayer-mat.

"And very soon we won't have any cheerfulness or colours left in Pearly Green or the rest of the world!" Moonmummy finished by jumping onto her broomstick. The others began thinking of jumping off the palm tree branches and onto their respective flying tackle. They were all getting ready to split when suddenly Total Frux the demonish singer began screeching into song.

"I . . . Skreet . . . You my love . . . I Scrak . . . you my dove . . . I deeply desire to . . . Skronk with you . . . I want to . . . Donk you . . . I want to . . . Dirk you . . . I Pooo with you . . . In my Heart I Fink with you . . . I Fonk with you . . . I Frew You Baby . . .!"

The singer jumped up and down as the chorus suddenly came in like death stalking in unexpectedly.

"Screw . . . Scrak . . . Scritch . . . Baby . . . Rub my itch . . .

"Together . . . we shall be rich . . . Screw you baby . . . Scratch my back and Scritch . . .!"

The crowds cheered as they munched on live farple larvae and smashed each other around the head with the femurs of dead saints. This was the best song they had ever heard and they were loving every moment of it.

"That's it! That's it! That's the Magic Mantras . . .!" Nasseruddin whistled from his palm tree, shining with excitement.

"You may be right but which three are the right words? " shrieked Suleiman as his knee-length moustache curled itself up into a ball.

"Screw. Scrak. Scritch!" shouted Mevlana above the wild demented noise, his djelaba flapping as if it had found a cosmic answer to a cosmic question. It seems he had forgotten one of the first principles of the Idiot's Path. It never matters what the answer is as long as the question falls away.

"No it's Screek. Scrak. Scronk!" argued Nasseruddin loudly, beginning to get quite agitated.

"No, it's Donk. Dirk. Poo!" screamed Suleiman, bending down from his tree to punch Nasseruddin on his foolish dwarfish head.

And then the argument between the ever so silly Whirlistanis got even louder. Trying to punch each other from their respective palm trees, they fell to the floor shouting and pummelling each other and tumbling in the sandy rocks. In their fight they slapped each other with torn off palm fronds and kicked each other in the shins still bleating about their proper mantras. As the witches looked aghast and Mullah Ullah looked completely shocked, a whole stream of low-flying demons that had heard their fracas rushed towards them.

"Busted!" screamed Mullah Ullah rubbing his gatta for ideas.

"What shall we do?" Stargasm squealed, looking very scared and shivering on her wobbly broomstick.

"Let's fly!" Moonmummy shouted revving her broomstick.

"We've got no chance, Mullah Ullah, the demons are flying so fast. Quick, get the Genie out of the Lamp out and start wishing like crazy!"

The Mullah lost no time and rubbed the golden lamp and the Genie emerged smoky blue and subdued.

"Oh master, what can I do for you?"

"We're in trouble! Get rid of this lot and take us home, fast!"

"Is that a wish, master?"

"Damn right!"

"Then your wish is my command," whistled the Genie of the Lamp rising high up into the air assuming his normal size.

At his full height the Genie of the Lamp placed all their hovering forms into his giant right hand and as the demons flew closer and closer, so close that they were no more than one hundred yards off, he shouted a shout whose echo can still be heard throughout Hoggaristan and the demons fell to the ground. He then blew deeply upon his right hand. It was a blow so hard, it whooshed them through the air faster than anything they could ever have imagined. They raced ahead into the direction of the new rising sun.

The Genie of the Lamp watched them almost tumble off and fall through clouds but they held onto their positions by the skin of their teeth, the force of various prayers, different magic incantations and simple good luck. One magic wish had been spent but at least they were getting away. The demons were soon left behind and very quickly the fantasy fields of figs and dates soon whipped beneath their feet and within minutes the Afrostani coastline loomed between them. After cruising at a low altitude past the rock of the Gibbering Turk, they flashed across the seas and hugged the low-lying topography as they raced each other to Pearly Green and home. It had taken them only seven minutes. Flying close behind Mullah Ullah on his shivering prayer-mat, the Genie of the Lamp just laughed and laughed and laughed like he hadn't laughed for centuries. Thirty seconds later, everyone found themselves stumbling down into the middle of Brickie Lane. Narrowly avoiding the wandering sacred sheep and meandering soft cuddly white lamb, all six got up, brushed away the low-flying stream of pretty pink flamingos, jumped over the many passing purple turtles, grabbed a falling crunchy banana or two to eat and walked to their destination wherever that was. They were feeling hungry again and they had a choice of where to go. They could either go to the Right Rude Sabre Tooth again or go to Kid Kurry's Magical Muncherie deep down in the Lost Catacombs. They decided quickly on the latter. But in order to go there they still had to go through one of the tandoori ovens. They quickly choose the Monsoon Mindstorm as it was the closest and they had had enough of flying for now. Flowing discreetly back into his golden lamp, the Genie followed wherever Mullah Ullah's hand would go. At this moment in time, his left hand held on tightly to the golden lamp while his right hand scratched his nether regions. All was well with the world and they were finally back home.

13

The Idiot's Path

IT RAVED, IT raved and it poured as if a magic monsoon had started outside of time. Some long lost rain cloud emptied itself through the open Bum Note roof. The monkeys and the Dream-Skinned Mandrills moved out of the way quickly but the jubjub birds swooped down from the tumtum trees and swallowed each falling raindrop in sequential slow motion. The pills, thrills and spills of the most unbelievable Friday night whizzed through Saturday and right into Sunday morning. The room was awash with metta and no one slept, not even those on the beanbags, hovering somewhere in the air or swimming with the darting Twinklefish in and out of each other's dreams. Fairlight's Anatta had time-stretched reality, neither a start nor an end, just the here and now, for ever.

The trancefloor was now full of shifting change, like watching water drops merge and become larger. Everything was getting joined up and changing fast in the trance of life itself. Even Nataraj, the King of the Cosmic Dance would have been impressed, everyone and everything was connected.

"Oh wow! Alice look at those monkeys climbing up the ropes, I think they want to get to our magic island!"

Oh no, Amrita! I think that they want to get to the crunchy bananas."

"Shall we chuck some coconuts at them then?"

"No, we've run out!"

"What shall we do then?"

Alice sucked her thumb and looked for help towards the top of the coconut tree where Abdul the wizened and wise Bongostani leprechaun gave them both a funny look and grabbed the long bamboo pole that was lying on the ground with its extendable arms. The leprechaun was twenty feet up the tree but it didn't need to come down. (Bongostani leprechauns could do many things, and this was just one of them.) As the monkeys almost found themselves on top of the shifting shores of the moving paradise that was the children's present home, a strong punt moved the island swiftly over to the other side of the ceiling. The monkeys tumbled back onto the ground where they were soon smothered in a sea of dancing petals.

"Freedom is a basic necessity!" laughed the Bongostani leprechaun, doffing its little green hat.

"First Humble Truth, Amrita!"

"Yeah, so what?" laughed the Imperial Princess of Gigglistan, passing Alice a hovering sooth-saying sea slug as a fortune cookie.

"Happiness all around!" divined Astral Alice, laughing.

"Thought so, come on, let's watch the party below." And they did.

Anarkali was smiling and slowly climbing the air until she had even passed Abdul the meditative Bongostani leprechaun, still on top of the highest coconut tree. She had almost reached the roof. Suddenly, swinging high from the rafters funky Fareek pulled up his holographic gown, dilated his hallucinogenic left eye at a passing pretty pink flamingo, grabbed the passing microphone and yelled to the ever-growing brightness everywhere.

"Dear friends, furry, funny creatures or whatever we think we are. We have brought for you from a great distance, with the greatest difficulty but at no extra cost to you, I must add – the incredible, supremely original, one of its kind ... Voodoo Child!"

The crowd and went absolutely quiet and the silence grew like a secret fart, warm, overpowering and everywhere. Only the thudding of everyone's booming hearts could be heard, they'd come a long way for this, some from the outskirts of Pearly Green, some from the darker corners of Slumdon town, some from the Lost Catacombs of Brickie Lane and others, like the Zoofis of Banglastan, from centuries ago. Voodoo Child beamed down onto the stage. This tall, grey-haired black-blue giant was a fuzzy, left handed, Afrostani freak with beads and bangles everywhere. From his groovy shoulders hung a psychedelic bandsman's coat, unique in the history of cosmic togs with scarlet tassels on its shoulders which quickly jumped off and tuned his battered but shiny black Stratocaster. Having compared notes and nodded to each other they flew back to be on his shoulders and waited for that sudden sonic scream when the Stratocaster opened its gaping mouth, bared its massive psychedelic teeth, laughed a bit and then kerchaaanged into its music.

"Ah hello, sorry. Thank you. Please, this song's called 'Sometime in Atlantis, when my skin was blue.'"

The sonic rings coming out of everyone's mouths stopped in mid air and the ever-shifting mandalas began to join up above Osric's floating island, right up to the level of Anarkali's dancing eyes. Communication was a group thing now and not just between two individuals and as the music soared, this communal mandala grew to greater complexity and ever-expanding intricacy. A tribe of ghostly sooth-saying sea slugs dived into its transparent centre, scattering happy endings indiscriminately, and the open roof was soon filled with watching mermaids and mermen who had floated up from the Pool of Laughter and Forgetting deep inside the Lost Catacombs to shower Voodoo Child with invisible kisses.

From the crenulations and turrets of Osric's sandcastle-made palace Alice and Amrita and the old leprechaun kept up their patrols for emerging monkeys, having borrowed fantasy flintlocks. Voodoo Child's band were The Cacofonix Experience which consisted of Yoric, Eric, Uric, Boric, Doric and Bongo Bill from the Thirteenth Lost Tribe of the Gnomes of StonedHenge. They were tuned in to the beats but waiting for Yoric their second percussionist who had lost his head and was still somewhere on the trance-floor. Frogamatix and Catweazel Phil flashed up the lasers to the ceiling while the Voodoo Child screeched screaming, sonic superstitions. He was playing as if his guitar was on fire which, in fact it was, and poor Boric had run over with a bucketful of Astral Ale to try and put it out. It didn't work as sonic superstitions were scorching up and down the fret board one after the other. Voodoo Child smiled as he burst into a haze of blue-ringed flames.

"Oh no . . . our schoolteacher's back!" Alice screamed as an angry looking Dream-Skinned Mandrill, carrying a banana frond as a whip, fell off a passing fluffy white cloud to land upon their floating island. They had been busted because Abdul the Bongostani leprechaun was tranced and had seen nothing.

"Oh dear what shall we do?" Amrita yelled above the deafening sounds of guitarist, band and crowds as the maddened monkey approached. It was enraged and approached them furiously, the banana-frond whip twitching in its frisky fingers. They tried shaking the tall coconut tree but that didn't work (even on the leprechaun).

The little girls were now in so much trouble that they looked to the skies for help. At that moment, chased by a flock of fantasy flamingos, Little Lucy cruised by on a fluffy white cloud in answer to their prayers.

"Oi kiddos, jump onto my fluffy white cloud."

"With pleasure, Lucy."

"Thanks little sis, you came just in time!"

Jumping up and down the Dream-Skinned Mandrill screamed and started thrashing the tranced form of the poor Bongostani leprechaun instead. Abdul would have none of it.

The silly monkey woke up the leprechaun who landed a right-hook in its angry face. Falling off the magical floating island, the Dream-Skinned Mandrill fell right through some other passing clouds and landed head-first in a pail of squirming gibberworms that the gubblies had brought out to eat.

"Freedom will not come by waiting!" Amrita laughed, looking down at the mirrors in her gypsy dress.

"Second Humble Truth, schoolmaster!" twittered Astral Alice.

"Don't you know anything, anything at all?" Lucy laughed, having the last laugh.

Pulling its wet head out of the disgusting bucket of wet gibber-worms, the mandrill ripped apart the schoolbooks it carried in a haversack upon its back. Maths books, history books, geography books and language books all ripped apart between angry, snarling teeth and the pages went whooshing into the air.

Fareek was hanging upside down from a trapeze of spluttering monkeys that swung underneath the floating island. The monkeys were trying to get onto the island, of course, and take over Osric's sandcastle palace. Meanwhile Fareek was swinging back and forth picking up ravers randomly while the gibbering monkeys held on for dear life. Abdul the Bongostani leprechaun was now out patrolling the pure shores of Osric's isle with a bamboo pole just to make sure no monkey business took place. A lesson that they were not expecting. Fareek's silly hippy head was wreathed in a secret smile, the circus of illusions was back and this time it was real. With every swing back to the deck, he twiddled a few knobs and continued on swinging. This was music as it was meant to be, live, funny and . . . extremely funky!

Yoric had finally made it on stage but alas had still lost his head completely, it was nowhere to be found but seeing as that most of the crowd had completely lost theirs too, it didn't seem to matter much. Suddenly, Tarquin went completely nuts and, throwing his Bollywood-style underpants into the crowds, squealed delightedly to join Fareek swinging from the rafters while Mellow Tron kept the big beats booming. Everything was now heaven, definitely, here on this humble earth!

Meanwhile, Anarkali's Kathak gown had dragged her right up to the open roof with the twinklefish and mer-people. However, the mermen were shy and the mermaids even shyer and did not really want to be seen. They loved Voodoo Child's music and couldn't wait for him to join them and sing to them for ever as they swam all the seven seas of serenity together. (They didn't know just when he would join them because sometime, somewhere in eternity could always take an incredibly long time.) But a merman he would one day be, the all-smiling universe would see to that. Anarkali still rose and rose, higher than anything else, all she could hear was the sound of her silver ankle bells and the inner rhythms of the deepest secrets of her beautiful heart.

As Voodoo Child came to a stop and the cascading harmonies echoed across the floor Anarkali raced to catch the mer-people who, with a quick, final flip of their fins, swam out and disappeared.

"Where have they gone?" she squealed, seeing nothing but feeling the wild monkeys grabbing her gown and dragging her down.

"Get them off me!" screamed the temple-trancer and the swirly-whirly figures on her dancing Kathak gown came alive. The monkeys had glimpsed the secret smile of a passing merman too and were climbing up in the only manner they knew how, in order to get a better look.

"Quick, I'm drowning in a sea of monkeys!" yelled Anarkali as she began to topple. At this point, the figures on her golden gown decided to act and sticking out their myriad hallucinogenic tongues, they kicked out with their little legs and the ladder of monkeys tumbled gracelessly to the ground.

"Yippee! We did it!" they cheered as she again rose free and shot off at amazing speed.

"Third Humble Truth!" Amrita yelled, passing around a torn paper bag of ever-lasting gobstoppers as the voices on Anarkali's dress sang out in victorious unison, and what were they singing?

"Because Freedom won't come by waiting, it will have to be sought for, fought for and won."

Little Lucy laughed as her ever-lasting gobstopper suddenly began to expand inside her throat and threatened to choke her.

Time was shifting forwards and the trance music was moving like the golden sands of some Scarabian fantasy, nothing was real any more and yet there was still a lot to learn. While Fareek and Tarquin continued swinging on their crazy trapeze picking up anything and anyone they could find, Habiba rushed onto the stage to help out. With her at the holodecks, Mellow Tron's disappearing dreadlocks quickly returned and his ancient face cracked a grin, and then two more. Habiba the Beloved stabbed at the world with her piercing eyes and scary hawk nose. Flinging her multicoloured burnoose to one side with her hooked hand, the leader of the Trancefloor Liberation Organisation flashed a cosmic wink at her forty little brother Hashemites who were hiding inside giant olive jars to the right of the flower-strewn stage. The T.L.O. were here and they'd willingly taken over! Everything was rocking and the lads on the trapeze above the crowd were rapping into their radio mics:

"Fairies and eldsters, elfins with kids, joy-riding merry,
 bareback on grief.
Laughter and giggles and monkeys in prams,
cuckoos going kookaburra and not eating spam,
pigs whizzing, sacred cows spinning until the seas were all silk,
leprechauns without horns and beware geeks
bearing gifts, large wooden ones,
presents for poor freaks.
Azeem the Dream, upside down through the air,
his eyes were so frightening
no one would stare.
Hussain the Insane living up to his name
and materialising whatever he wants,
sugared bread and chapattis,
pretzels, weasels and donks.
Astral Alice being silly, way up in the clouds,
Dylan the Black Bunny with guitars full of sounds.
Little Lucy still a diamond way up in the sky.
Anarkali not wanting the monkeys to fly.

Snowcamels plodding graciously wherever they want to go.
No one to question, they simply get up and go.
Yesterday was Kamershand, tomorrow will be Kashtent,
sounds and colours making light, heaven sent.
Storks bringing babies and lovers saying maybes,
everything was stretched in time,
some gave them white bread, some gave them kicks,
the rest got elderberry wine,
cheroots, tokes, holy jokes
and a bit of quick kissing on the side.
Amrita a naughty child but maybe one day someone's bride.
Kid Kurry moving in a hurry and Kassim tumbling over toast,
Dilly the Silly playing with Billy,
The ghost who needed love the most.
Ayesha, Ambrin, Najma all waiting their turn,
wearing Malik Silk's magic they'll be able to burn.
Bills and mobs, four-shilling bobs, our Shelina ran off with
your Sam,
who cares? who gives a toss?
eat candyfloss,
but just don't ever eat spam.
From Dooblistan to Mehra Dhun
from Tunkirk to New Zork,
they stabbed it with their steely knives
they munched up all the pork.
But pigs are cool and pigs are great and paradise if you try.
They're ain't no heaven, there ain't no hell and if only pigs
could fly!"

With a quick swoosh the fluffy white cloud carrying Princess Amrita, Little Lucy and Astral Alice zoomed back to be on their floating island, waves of sounds washing up on the shores of its sands. There they smiled at a rosy-cheeked, black-haired little girl called Sally who was trying to sell sea-shells to a shoal of gathering twinklefish. Quickly tying their cloud to Osric's palace with the string of a passing kite, the three young girls jumped into its turrets and peered down at the strange sights with astonished eyes.

Many feet below Habiba was jumping up and down with her hooked hand scratching at the holodecks with incredible precision and the Hashemites were popping their little brown heads up from the giant olive jars. Everyone was happy except for the cowering bunch of howling monkeys who were still bawling their eyes out. As Habiba's hook flashed in the air like a dagger at midnight, a single monkey broke off from the group and approached her with stealth. With a skilled practice brought over from years of stealing fruit off stalls in Brickie Lane market, the single howler bounced over to the holodecks and before Habiba could even notice, ripped her left hooked hand right out of its socket and scampered away.

"Aaah! Where's my hand?" Habiba screamed as the music ominously stopped.

She looked to the skies but the monkey had disappeared through the dream-body of a passing purple turtle. She quickly turned around as many confused faces turned in her direction. Reaching out for the nearest Hashemite, she grabbed him by the hair and quick as a blink chucked him in the direction of the passing Sabre-Toothed Power Pussy. The big, soft, furry puddy cat had no chance. Before it could leap out of the way, a squealing, flying Hashemite landed right in its face. Roaring, the Sabre-Toothed Power Pussy scampered to a corner of the Trancefloor to lick its furious face and to discover that it only had one sabre tooth left. Whining and whimpering it curled its long tail around itself and lay down disconsolately. Habiba quickly picked up the broken sabre tooth from the floor and grinned. Quicker than a twinklefish could burp or a fantasy falcon fart, she embedded the sabre tooth in the hollow gap of her left hand, adjusted it slightly and rammed it back down on the holodecks. Everyone cheered and threw each other's heads in the air as the wonderful HypnoTantric Trance was back. And Hashemites shot off from their olive jars to Osric's island, bought all of Sally's seashells and all fell instantaneously in love with her. Then they quickly invited themselves into the sandcastle palace and continued watching the crazy proceedings below.

"Far out . . . what was that all about?" asked Alice.

"Fourth Humble Truth, innit Alice? Freedom doesn't come for free, there's always a price!" Amrita giggled as the mirrors on her gypsy dress reflected the incredible universe of possibilities.

And the best was still to come as Fareek called out, "And now from the path of the mystical middle beat . . . let's give a big hand or whatever you've got at this moment in time for the incredible, unbelievable, totally transcendental Soul Sisters of Awareness – please give a big cheer for the glorious Sisters Nazneeeeeeeeeeen!"

Back with Lucifer the scarlet-purpleness seemed to change as, through the clouds, ancient Zeegypt appeared only to shift to a piratical battle on the Spanglish Main and back and forward it went, repeating ad infinitum and for Lucifer, ad nauseam. When they slowed down two figures could be deciphered; the first a young pharaoh grinning like a monkey and juggling seven tangerines in one, soft, unblemished hand while in the other he held a long pipe. Beside him stood a bald and serious courtier and a what seemed to be court musicians playing their lyres, blowing their flutes and banging on drums.

Above his head the seven tangerines stopped in magic formation somewhere in mid air and tiny yellow baby chicks flew out of them to race to the rafters of the huge ornately decorated room. On reaching the rafters, they turned into cosmic canaries and started crapping all over the heads of the assembled many. The pharaoh laughed as he watched the happy scene; his whole body was almost hidden by the wreath of smoke that came out as he smoked his pipe. Although it most certainly was a royal court, there was music everywhere and everyone seemed to be laughing, smiling, curtsying, juggling with scarab beetles, drinking and eating and generally making merry. The scene didn't look very serious, no not at all.

"What a Varking situation! What's happening now?" Lucifer screamed, as he looked closely at the slim beautiful face of the young pharaoh with its perfectly etched eyebrows that floated over pale green eyes, a delicate nose and pert mouth.

The second irritating presence appeared to be a pirate fighting on a frigate with possibly English seamen. This is more like it, Lucifer thought as plummeting cranes crashed down and knocked out all twenty-seven sailors.

The pirate doffed his three-pointed hat and said, "And here's a jolly good vark to Stinky Billy too!"

This jolly fellow now swung back to his own galleon, floating beside the English ship, where he greeted his crew. His black beard and twinkling blue eyes gave a look of anarchic freedom as he told a joke that Lucifer couldn't hear. He sliced off a piece of hempen rope, chewed it a while and spat out a ball of happy herbs which he gave to Seaman Stains, his first mate, to build a neat cheroot on the top of the extensive stack of gold that was now being unloaded from the English ship.

The whole vision had taken no more than thirty seconds and Lucifer was left gnashing his teeth and looking confused. There was work to do and ordering his squadron of ghostly vampires, heckles, speckles, ghouls, demons, dwarves and diabolics to listen close, he carefully explained the plan. The ghostly monsters were divided into two companies, the first was to search the Spanglish Main in the eighteenth century to find that freewheeling pirate and the second was ordered back to the time of that smirking pharaoh. He knew that these two both had some relation to the leprechaun's gold which he thought he had already stolen from them at rainbow's end, millennia ago. But what?

14

And The Metta Flowed On

"GLEEEEEP!" SQUEALED THE crowds as the Soul Sisters of Awareness bedazzled themselves on stage. Meanwhile, Habiba was still spinning the holodecks with a new-found precision as Fareek jumped back onto the stage. Tarquin, suddenly seeing that he had no clothes on, quickly covered his nudity with a smile and went back to slapping the shimmering synsantooric tablas that only he knew how to play. Mellow Tron smiled and watched the dancing tarantulas crawl up and down his multiple keyboards. In fact, they played better than he did.

The three best singers in Slumdon-town wriggled their bodies and got ready. Round-faced Ayesha stared ahead at the crowds as her body grooved like a Durkish belly dancer. Square-faced Ambrin looked quite quizzical, while her perfect lips parted like a luscious peach about to be eaten. Big-boned Najma looked at her two sisters and winked mischievously. On their bodies they wore translucent Hypno-Tantric Hijabs made of Malik's magic muslin. Malik was an eternal bachelor, married to no one but the colony of black widow spiders that munched on the hovering hallucinogenic agaric flies in order to make this special material. Malik flashed a secret signal to the Sisters Nazneen and they began to sing. This legendary weaver of Gobbinfields grinned as he was the only one who knew what would happen next.

"Ommmmm," sung Najma in a voice of deepest space bass, her vocal chords vibrating in the air.

"Ommmm," whistled Ambrin in a voice of cool mellow yellow, staring enthusiastically at the crowds.

"Ommmmmm," trilled Ayesha in a voice more crystal-clear than a mountain spring and fulfilling her part of the harmony.

"Far out!" screamed the delirious crowds as the pace on the trancefloor began speeding up intensely. Something was beginning to happen to all of them. A different change was starting to gatecrash their very existence. All of a sudden people started whooshing out of their real bodies and jumping around in their dream ones! As their real bodies stood watching the sisters sing, their purple, green, blue, scarlet, indigo and many other coloured dream-bodies whizzed around the air. Astonishing though it was, what was happening on stage was simply far more far-out, in fact, so far-out it was incredibly perfectly far-in. But as Osric (and probably Mullah Ullah) always knew there was no difference to far-out or far-in, it was all just a point of view. Up and above the floating desert isle, the crunchy banana trees and cosmic coconut trees simply went crazy. Dropping a coconut onto the head of the sleeping Bongostani leprechaun, a single tree awoke its keeper and itself. Then suddenly thousands of cosmic coconuts fell right through the dissolving walls of Osric's sandcastle palace. As they crash-landed on the silly heads of the love-struck Hashemites, they exploded as chrysalises of the most wonderful dragonflies. And always of course dragonflies go straight for the heart. In a single instant, they had entered each and every Hashemite heart and made them fall in love for ever. Seashell Sally stood there gob-smacked with umpteen bewildered suitors in front of her and not knowing how or who to choose, she did the next best thing and decided to fall in love with everyone. Amrita, Alice and Little Lucy watched the sands of time disappear between their transcendental toes and stared at true love taking place, in total astonishment.

"Now Najma! Now Ambrin! Now Ayesha! ... do it ... NOW!" squealed the tiny voice of Malik Slik Sylvester as Catweazel Phil's lasers went brilliant.

Ignoring the exploding petals that had been activated by Bilal and Charlie, the Sisters Nazneen took the spot-lights and as they sung in incredulous three-part harmony they began peeling off layers and layers of their Hypno-Tantric Hijabs in a fantastic disrobing to the beat. As they did so, layers and layers of illusions began peeling off in living technicolour. As they disrobed, bundles and bundles of translucent magic muslin began tumbling to the flower strewn floor as an endless stream of translucent Hypno-Tantric hijabs began to appear on their vibrating forms while they simply began to disappear.

The magic muslin became more and more see-through and they began to disappear within and without whilst still singing the incredibly wonderful "Om Song". And on the floor, the pile of magic muslin grew and grew as Malik giggled and stroked his goatee. All was going to plan. The sisters were dissolving both without and within. They disrobed and became totally transparent and began looking inside-out and roundabouts, all to the beat while still singing. This was incredible!

The crowd freaked seeing three shimmering hazy gauzes of transparent magic muslin trip into the air. Astral bodies they could understand but total disappearance was something else.

"Where have they gone, Amrita?" Lucy asked in the bewildered daze of innocence.

"I don't know Lucy, maybe Alice knows!" Amrita replied, chuckling and munching on an ever-lasting gobstopper.

"I don't know either and I don't care ... there's something far more interesting going ... look over there ..." Alice replied, pointing her finger down below.

Spinning very slowly in slow motion, Billy Blake's mystical ghostly timepiece was tumbling to the floor. The three Holy Ghosts had been hanging off the rafters and silly Billy had dropped his precious toy and screamed but, of course, only Sidney Arthur and Danny could hear him. Up above, Alice, Amrita and Little Lucy felt the sands of their sandcastle palace disappear at a faster rate which could only mean that time was moving on and they were getting older every instant and closer to their deaths. The hourglass kept rolling, seen by no one else but a crazy Commanche. As Karim the Kid Kurry jumped around sweeping back his wavy black hair and looking rather dishy in his cosmic pantaloons, Kassim the Sun-Trance Kid, his younger brother, hijacked a low-flying pretty pink flamingo and cruised into mid air. But what about that Commanche? The tattoos of fighting cowboys and Indians on his left arm suddenly stopped fighting and as the ghosts watched Billy's hourglass fall, he drew his bow and fired a single arrow which pierced the old timepiece right in the middle.

"Nah ... my timepiece ... they'll break it!" Billy screamed while up above him Sidney Arthur lit another cheroot and poured himself and Danny another glass of gin. He laughed unsympathet-ically.

Billy screamed again, pulling dejectedly at his hair. But it was a close shave indeed, far closer than Malik's three-day-old stubble. The arrow shot right through the middle of the single grain of diamond light that was forever stuck in the middle of the mystical hourglass. As the timepiece fell, still completely intact, to the floor, Billy swooped down to pick it up before it got crushed by the many trancing feet, hooves and wings before shooting back up with a face full of relief. If it had been broken, he'd never be able to tell the time ever at all.

"Amrita, what was all that about?" Astral Alice asked, pulling out a stash of long forgotten chestnuts she had successfully hidden and passing them around.

"Time flies like an arrow, Alice. First Serene Silliness innit . . .?"

"Oh right," Alice replied laughing. The little girls put their faces in their hands and watched from the crenulated towers of their sandcastle-made dreams.

Meanwhile the crowd oohed and aahed as the Sisters Nazneen tranced invisibly to the beat. Everything went quiet as there was simply no end to their appearing and disappearing gowns or even their hypnotic invisibility. You could see straight through them but never see them naked. Perhaps nudity was not about taking your clothes off but about being totally open inside.

"Are they invisible yet?" Fareek asked, hastily lighting a cheroot of happy herbs.

"Yeah man! Totally gone!" Mellow Tron replied smiling and stealing the cheroot of happy herbs off him quick.

"All right, let's do it," Tarquin finished, robbing Mellow Tron of the cheroot and lighting it by rubbing it up and down the glowing body of a passing twinklefish. And then running to either end of the stage, the beat boys got ready for the next part of the act.

"Come on . . . Come on . . . trance with me. Come on . . . come on . . . everybody just trance with me . . ." Fareek began crooning dementedly as he took Ayesha's invisible hand. Tarquin took Ambrin's and Mellow Tron took Najma's. Then they began tumbling and doing somersaults right through the transparent bodies of the ever-present sisters. In between each beat-boy, lay the transparent luminous form of either Ayesha, Najma or Ambrin. And as they were now the see-through sisters, Tarquin waved to Fareek and then to Mellow Tron going right through them all. It was unbelievable, unseeable and unfathomable.

"Excellent stuff this boys but please remember your fishing rods," Sidney Arthur said.

"Oh yeah!" replied the other two in their usual obedient manner.

By now, many multicoloured dream-bodies were starting to join up into larger ones. Firstly two, then three, then many more. To watch this was almost as interesting as watching what was happening on stage. From their vantage point atop the crumbling sands of ever dissolving innocence, the three young girls continued watching the show until they saw something that took their very breath away yet again.

"Wow, what's that?" Lucy asked in a flurry of a hurry. A squadron of a low flying formation of crunchy bananas was cruising towards them unstoppably.

"I don't know," Astral Alice replied, transfixed.

They watched in silence as the bananas changed course and rushed towards them at a fantastic speed. Little Lucy squealed as a banana pulped her head. The girls rushed to hide themselves under the turrets as the bananas smashed themselves into the sand-castle walls.

"Ouch, what was that all about?" Alice asked wiping the banana mush off her silly face and laughing.

"Second Serene Silliness, of course. Fruit flies like a banana." Amrita giggled. By now Seashell Sally was still being wooed by the Hashemites many floors below and each was on bended knee offering her the rarest blooms and crooning love tunes in mysterious languages that only she could understand. Sally stood there blushing redder than any rose.

But what about the crowds going absolutely wild? Revelation was a dream. The rush rushed. The buzz buzzed, then swooped, climbed, peaked and like an ambient albatross glided onto a plateau where sounds, movements, colours, emotions and feelings all landed as one. As dream-bodies coalesced into much larger ones, a stunning chant could be heard emanating from the gathered tribes.

"We is all Anattas ... nutters is we ... we is all Anattas ... we Anatta to be free."

That may have been well and good but other weird stuff was happening too. Suddenly Amrita screamed as a giant purple dragon with multicoloured scales on its massive body flew in angrily from the hole in the roof streaming fire from her angry nostrils. Flapping way above everyone's heads, the huge dragon flew noisily around as if it was specifically looking for someone or something. But where had it come from? One of the dragonflies must have turned into a real dragon and now here it was looking for its just deserts and it certainly found what it was looking for. Racing straight down for the Queen of Hearts' heart, it snorted again and shot out yet more flames. She had nowhere to hide and quickly whimpered and hid behind the ever-tripping Osric. Suddenly and without even being asked, the scruffy kajol-stained Osric pushed his hand deep into his body and pulled out his own palpitating and bleeding heart. He chucked it at the dragon who snapped it up in its mighty jaws and flapped away through the open roof, satisfied, while in the place where Osric's heart used to be, a never-ending stream of multicoloured blooms flew out. BB and Charlie stood there absolutely amazed, they thought they knew all about flowers but they had never seen such indescribably colourful blooms as these. The Queen of Hearts then planting Osric a quick kiss scampered off to be with the White Rabbit who was still looking impatiently at his pocket-watch. Osric smiled like the simpleton he was and danced on.

"Groovy Alice but what does this mean?" Lucy laughed as a blur of fluffy white clouds whizzed over their tiddly heads.

"No idea, Amrita do you know? You seem to know an awful lot," Alice asked, looking at the Princess of Gigglistan intently in the eyes.

"Yes . . . it's the Third Serene Silliness innit? You two should know it too unless you've forgotten your previous homework," she smirked, taking a gracious bow.

"Dragon flies straight for the heart!" she finished, giggling again.

"Totally groovy don't you think?" Astral Alice laughed as Lucy's wandering eyes went back to watching the romance of Seashell Sally and the pleading brotherhood many floors below but the sands were dissolving under everyone's feet and it was time to move on.

Yes, it was time to move on and the crowd vibrated in respectful silence as on the trancefloor the many dream-bodies were joined as one. A Giant Hypno-Tantric Love Monster was starting to form, a legend in itself until it was out of the roof with its arms extending. Every dream-body that had joined up was part of the whole but the individuality of their differences could clearly be seen, different colours and faces and eyes all twinkled and smiled as the whole simply got bigger and bigger and this new being smiled to itself as it came into existence. It was freaky, it was fab and best of all, it was free. Everything was heating up rather quick though. Voodoo Child was sitting cross-legged on the stage and building a solitary cheroot of happy herbs to be smoked by everyone. It was about seventeen feet tall and five foot wide at its conical end and he lit it with a floating spark of his incredible imagination and relaxed as the ends of his two legs had disappeared and what was appearing were the green funky fishtail of a lonesome merman. He had found his own eternity and was turning into a merman, free. The Sabre-Toothed Power Pussy now somewhat recovered had Dobbins the Artful Dodger bouncing on his back and looking downright cheeky. His soot-stained fingers jerked as he tried filching the beards of the three Zoofis of Banglastan who were happily smoking a hookah and drinking jasmine tea.

"Only Four Humble Truths," roared Habiba into the crowds, most of whom didn't have a clue what she was on about or even care.

"Only Four Holy Rules," Anarkali shouted, still trancing in the middle of the air surrounded by many members of Master Fagin's Funkadelic Tribe who had suddenly grown wings and were flapping next to her.

"Don't forget the Three Serene Sillinesses," Karim the Kid Curry also shouted, bouncing up and down off the floor like an Indian rubber ball.

"There may be more," Fairlight gasped aloud.

"Is there anything else we need to know?" Lucy gasped, staring down at the mayhem.

"Sorry, can't hear you, can you repeat what you said please?" Amrita laughed as the Bongostani leprechaun leapt down from his coconut tree to be by their side.

"Yes, we know loads of stuff. Is there anything else we need to know?" Alice reiterated and picking the leprechaun's nose.

"Thanks, I heard you that time but I also heard Mullah Ullah and Stargasm talking about finding three Magic Mantras before they left for Hoggaristan," Lucy tittered.

"Oh no! More stuff to remember, it'll end up just like being in school" Amrita gasped, pulling the leprechaun's green hat off his head and chucking it into the crowd.

Most of the trancers had simply disappeared but the Love Monster was now iridescent with a thousand colours; its countless faces were those of everyone's friends and neighbours. It smiled at everybody, jumped up and shot off through the roof and away over the rooftops into the Pearly Green skies.

"Where's the Love Monster gone?" Lucy whistled as the creature disappeared.

"Who cares? I'm sure it will be back some day!" Alice replied, still watching the romance unfolding below. Seashell Sally was singing a love song back to the love-struck Hashemites who listened on bended knee as she sang in forty different languages all at the same time, the language of love obviously being a very personal thing. Each Hashemite beamed as they understood the refrain and the smiles grew on their many faces. On stage the Soul Sisters of Awareness suddenly returned and in a blinding flash of invisibility returned to visibility and singing.

"Lovely Love" screamed the sisters in perfect three-part harmony as BB and Charlie shot off some love canons from the side. Unknown to them, the three Holy Ghosts had their fishing rods firmly fixed to them. Spinning in the air, Billy had his rod fixed onto Charlie and close by Danny had his rod hooked to the Artful Dodger's overflowing top hat. Dobbins was still bouncing around on the back of the Sabre-Toothed Power Pussy and hadn't a clue. And then it was time to disappear. Where had they gone? Who knows? Who cares?

"Right on time!" muttered the White Rabbit, looking at his timepiece and then scampering off, stage right.

15

Ancient Zeegypt Beckons

Moments earlier they had been dancing along with their friends with hands, heads, feet, wings, tails and soft furry other things going crazy with Metta-Morph-Aziz down at the Bum Note. Now they were all freaking out somewhere else. Four voices were screaming together as the white flash of lightning zapped all around. Moving at the speed of light they were spinning and then tumbling and twisting, falling into patterns known only to their karma. Time was being shifted and like the jelly-like thing it is, was being swished and swashed out of all recognition. Karma was the driver and rushed them past multiple alternative realities, pushing them into worlds of its own but as they say in deepest, darkest Darkistan "The karma you are the calmer you get." Who knows where they were going? Who knows how long they'd been travelling? Nobody could be sure of anything any more. Who knows whether they were monkeys or men at this moment? As they tumbled they held onto each other, initially a good idea but as Mellow Tron, Fareek and Tarquin all decided to grab Anarkali's pigtails, there was a problem. Her pigtails decidedly didn't like being pulled and poor Anarkali now screamed the loudest of all. She squealed as the countless swirly-whirly figures on her gown closed their multiple eyes, held their hands together in prayer and hoped for the best.

Tarquin screamed, falling through the rising air his rinse turned pure white in fear and his hi-tech Bollywood designer labels deserted his clobber. Holding on to Mellow Tron's unfriendly dreadlocks, the handsome hero screamed his hippy head off. Tripping was one thing, flipping was another but flipping heck, this Anatta trip was something completely different. He wondered what Fairlight the magic potion maker had done this time and wasn't too sure whether or not he was enjoying it. Fareek shrieked but the nightmare continued. Now holding each other's hands like a circle of free-falling skydivers, they fell more gracefully. Holding tightly onto Anarkali's left hand, Fareek's long straggly hair fell over his face almost blinding him. His right eye seeing that the left one was hallucinating and dilating faster than a pipsqueak could fart, soon decided to join in. With both eyes blinking like mad, it was a damn good thing that Fareek had inner vision otherwise he wouldn't have seen anything at all. But what about Mellow Tron? How was the Skankmaster of Jah faring? Not very well it must be said.

Mellow Tron's dreadlocks squeaked as the blinding present took over. Each dreadlock was literally petrified; instead of being the moving snakes they actually were, they had petrified themselves through and through and now stood up on his head like something disgusting that happens if you don't wash your hair. But, thankfully, the trip changed again.

Everything changes – it's the way of things. The present is never the present for very long as it quickly shifts into the past and so the present is impermanent too. As for the future, that's just more of the here and now yet to be and full of impermanence as well. However, the single most important consideration to consider when considering change is this very simple one – always remember to change your underpants and socks.

Danny De Foe had realised that aloneness can be an incredibly beautiful thing when he was alive and shipwrecked in his youth. It took eighteen years of solitary loneliness on the seemingly deserted tropical island before the peg-legged Danny began to realise that actually he wasn't lonely any more, he was merely alone. How could he be lonely when there was the crashing seas, the tumbling oceans, the myriad of multicoloured twinklefish, the countless stars in the skies and his eyes, the infinite grains of golden sand, his well kept goats, pigs, donkeys and the lama? Abdul the lama was a special case. Being a Bongostani leprechaun, he was always in deep meditation inside a secret cave where only the sound of crashing waves kept him company. This strange red-hatted being obviously liked to keep himself to himself and Danny did not want to intrude. He only came out once every three and a half years and that was only to rush outside and take a leak on the tumbling wave-ridden seashore. Quickly picking up the prettiest seashell he could find, he would throw it with all his might and it skimmed across the ocean surface to reach Seashell

Sally who was standing on the opposite shore. That of course was miles away and beyond anyone's horizon. Danny used to watch these proceedings in total amazement for years and the sight never failed to cheer him up. Once after fifteen years, Danny plucked up his courage and decided to say hello. Just after waving to the sun and as the red-hatted leprechaun got ready to sprint back to his domain, Danny cleared his voice and stuttered, "Good morrow. How farest thou?"

The leprechaun stood still for a moment, cracked a grin and simply replied, "You're never alone in being alone, mate!"

"The First Holy Rule!" Danny sighed as he resumed his fishing and the leprechaun his meditation. Danny fished and fished and wished and wished. Then, after twenty years, Danny finally realised that loneliness and aloneness were the different sides of the very same coin and through long, hard practice he had finally learned the difference. However this didn't stop him loving the company of Billy Blake when he later became a ghost as Billy was his Man Friday, found on a Thursday, christened on a Wednesday, partied on a Saturday, fell ill on a Monday, called the quack on a Tuesday, died on Sunday and was still waiting to go to heaven at the start of the following week.

But how had the tiny, graceful Anarkali found herself in this position? She was just a fourteen-year-old child and children didn't need to take Anatta. So how did she find herself in the present company falling to an uncertain future? The answer is easy. Chance, trance, intuition and fate had sucked her in into the auras of the these beat-boys at the crucial moment of implosion/explosion. She had no chance. She had no choice. She simply had to go.

They now started falling in slow motion and their fears began to subside as the hurtling air whizzed past them slower and slower cushioning their fall.

"Where are we?" Tarquin yelled and there was a good reason too. The howling groans and moaning of the shifting sands tried to hide the view but the blaring sun gave them no respite. It was hot, dry and desolate too, so they picked themselves up from the ground and brushed each other off.

Fareek asked the same question in the glow of the stunning sun. This was blinding them all with its heat and light and was like a golden orb.

Tarquin replied, while still trying to look like a Bollywood hero if rather a confused one, "Somewhere bleedin' hot!"

"Maybe we're inside an oven!" Anarkali suggested as the figures on her dancing gown quickly took all their clothes off and chucked them away. Soon they were all naked but still sweating profusely.

"No little sister, I reckon we're in Zeegypt, look at those pyramids over there!" Fareek replied. He looked around while Anarkali spun around the ground seventy times in seven seconds to get a better perspective on things. Not more than half a mile away, across the heat-hazed air, three pyramids of different sizes could just be discerned. One was humongously huge, the next was ginormously gargantuan and the last simply rather cute. Tarquin slapped his head as the blue gel melted like ghee, and pointed at the pyramids excitedly.

"Yes, you're right," Mellow Tron squealed, hiding his surprise by disguising it with dreadlocks that had now flopped back down into their usual snaky heads. Somewhere in the far distance, wandering camels plodded along to munch dippy-dates from the nearby cluster of trees through which flew a lone pigeon, (the very same and still not caught).

"Yup, this is Zeegypt for sure, I would bet my bottom dollar on it, if I had one but something's not right. Where are all the donkey-cart rides, the camel touts and the souvenir shops? I've been here on holiday before sometime and it didn't look anything like this. It's never looked so empty ..." Tarquin said as he jumped up and down in the heat and stripped off eagerly.

"You're right, it is the pyramids but when are we ...?" Mellow Tron asked grimly. He scanned his hallucinating eyes over the horizon but all they could see were the pyramids and sand. Fareek, Tarquin and Mellow Tron knew they were still tripping and the Anatta they had eaten at Metta-Morph-Aziz was still shifting them inside out.

"Oi, come down, Anarkali!" Tarquin yelled, as she raised herself into the warm air by spinning in the Kathak style.

"No chance, bruv, and burn my toes in the hot sands?" Anarkali replied with a laugh.

"Come let's wander that way!" Mellow Tron rasped, and set them all off in the direction of the pyramids walking in single file. Mellow Tron was in the front, followed by Fareek, then Tarquin whilst Anarkali was floating at the rear floating. As they walked (and floated) Fareek had a good look in his battered old satchel, his grubby hands stirring the various things in its depths. Apart from a whole handful of Anatta magic beans he had liberated from Fairlight when he wasn't watching, there was also the solar-powered CD player he always carried, it was quite small but the specially modified speakers meant that it was loud enough to blow the bollocks off a charging rhino at seven hundred and forty-two yards. His hands felt around a bit more and smiled because there were also about seventy-seven assorted Hypno-Tantric Trance CDs inside the sweaty bag. He realised that with a whole handful of magic beans to chomp on, great sounds and something incredibly small and powerful to play them on – life was good!.

"Great idea to bring the music along," Mellow Tron gasped as a slight breeze blew across their tattered brows.

"Some tunes to impress the natives with!" Tarquin laughed.

"What natives?" Anarkali asked, scanning the horizon from the air and seeing no other living beings.

"At least we have music and Anatta!" Fareek replied, hurrying everyone along. As they pranced along in the burning sands, a flock of low-flying jubjub birds suddenly raced out from a distant grove of tumtum trees and scattered funky droplets of their dung everywhere.

"Strike while the irony is hot!" Mellow Tron laughed, turning around and seeing the others bathing in a shower of jubjub bird droppings. They trudged on to the rhythm of the trance for about forty minutes when they came upon a track leading to the largest pyramid.

"Groovy!" whistled Mellow Tron.

"Far out!" screamed Tarquin, tapping along to the beats.

"Amazing!" finished Fareek, turning the volume up and trotting merrily along.

"So nice! Oh I wish Princess Amrita, Astral Alice and Little Lucy were here," Anarkali sighed floating along. The path to the pyramids still seemed a way off and seeing a bunch of dippy-date trees, they fell to the ground and sat cross legged on the sands, all except for Anarkali who sat cross-legged a few feet in the air, of course.

"I wonder what's made this all happen?" Mellow Tron asked.

"Fairlight's new potion innit?" Tarquin replied, busily shaking the tree under which they rested.

"Gosh, this is much different to before!" Fareek gasped, scanning the wide horizon in front of him for any signs of mischief.

"Yea, this Anatta must be special!" Tarquin said, starting to munch greedily into the dates. Suddenly, a cosmic coconut from King Osric's magic floating island fell through time and space to land neatly in his hands and having a brainwave, he quickly pierced it with a sharp stone and coconut milk flowed out and they each took turns in refreshing themselves.

"Well, if we've come to ancient Zeegypt I wonder where the others have gone?" Mellow Tron asked.

"Only St Stan knows," Fareek replied in between chomping mouthfuls of coconut and swallowing the milk. His solar-powered CD player blazed in the sun and blared.

"Do you think we've come here by accident or design though?" Mellow Tron asked, cracking open another coconut from the skies. Little did he know that down at Metta-Morph-Aziz, the howler monkeys were now whizzing around on fluffy white clouds and chucking crunchy bananas at the cosmic coconut tree on Osric's floating island and with the Bongostani leprechaun not there now to guard it, a whole stream of coconuts were falling through time and space. Abdul, the Bongostani leprechaun that had been guarding the island had gone back in time to meditate in a wind-washed cave on a shipwrecked desert island where a peg-legged sailor was marooned (sound familiar?). Little Lucy, Amrita and Astral Alice of course didn't see a thing as they were still guarding the watchtower on the sand-castle palace. Meanwhile Tarquin brushed away some sand from his mouth and muttered in a swill of cosmic coconut milk.

"What, you mean we're meant to come to this desolate place?" he said, almost choking on the glorious milky juice.

"Whether by accident or design, we've still got to get home some time, the fight against the dark forces depends upon it!" Fareek emphasised.

Tumbling, tripping, toking, smoking, joking and poking each other onwards they reached the base of the largest pyramid which dazzled and shone in the sun like something made by ancient gods. They all stared upwards at the exquisite workmanship which seemed to go on and on like a Tower of Babel reaching into the sky. No language was needed now as the communal astonishment of being somewhere so surreal was enough to render them all gob-smacked. Even little Anarkali stopped spinning in the air and bowed down her tiny frame in respect for what she saw. It was one of the oldest things in the known world and had been built long ago in a very different world when the sun rose in the west and set in the east. Even her dress-figures opened their eyes and stared up beyond their tiny limitations and into the infinite skies above. Suddenly, Tarquin, being the ever-present Bollywood hero as usual, had an idea that he wanted the others to follow.

"Hey folks, let's climb to the top of the pyramid!" he shouted, then started to run in the direction of the well-worn grooves in the slabs of rock that delineated a path. Anarkali simply span in the air, made a few mystical mudras, and off she went.

"Hey, that's not fair Anarkali!" Tarquin shouted, turning back as he meandered up the path like one crazed.

"Oh no, it's too hot!" Fareek replied, grumblingly getting up.

"It's a stupid idea!" Mellow Tron's shimmering snakehead dreadlocks replied in unison but the Skankmaster of Jah got up too. He walked daintily up the slopes, his dreadlocks taking in the sights with open-mouthed wonder.

"Hurry up all of you, don't be such wet blankets!" Tarquin shouted from some hundred yards up the pyramid and still running.

"Wet blanket? What I wouldn't do for one of those now!" Fareek gasped, thinking back to the glorious comforts of the schoolhouse squat and the wonderful pleasures of the Lost Catacombs that seemed a thousand miles and years ago. Actually, he was wrong as they were about four thousand years in the past and three thousands miles away.

"Come on, it won't take more than a few minutes," Tarquin shouted. His voice echoed in the open air. After a few more endless minutes of bouncing and grunting, he was nearly at the top while many feet below, Mellow Tron and Fareek gasped and plodded.

The sun was now beating down their on their heads. They knew that they had to find shade soon or fall when they heard Tarquin shout, "Hey, I'm at the top and guess what I've found . . .?"

From the top they could see for miles around but that wasn't what they were all exclaiming about and not the distant donkey tracks and palm tree groves where fantasy falcons chased the single grey crapping pigeon either. There at the pyramid's top was a single goat's hair tent about five foot across and three feet high and it had been burnt black by the sun. One of its openings flapped in the breeze and sitting within could be seen one of the strangest beings ever invented. So strange she was that no poet could have painted her, no painter written verse nor musician created a harmony to describe the ancient blind, black Afrostani woman sitting there. She wore a grubby dark tattered woollen cloak which covered her single piece black cotton gown. Her skin shone a blackness with blue which was always the colour of space, and her hair was absolutely wild like Voodoo Child's Afro but much bigger and moved from side to side. Her face was delicate and refined and had the look of a precocious child and her lips and mouth were so expressive that they could speak without saying a word. Her ears were huge and flopped down near to her shoulders and her build was neither plump nor thin but how old she was could not be deciphered, fifty or two hundred and seventy years but which was true? Anarkali scratched her tiny head and looked into the old woman's eyes which shone with an resplendent inner light. She looked up at them as they stood at the entrance of her tatty tent and her face was alive with motion, wreathed in smiles but after a while she spoke.

"Hello! I've been waiting for you for a long time, glad that you're here."

"Ummm . . ." went Tarquin, tripping over his tumbling words.

"Hummm . . .!" went Fareek as he looked spellbound at the sight.

"Oh Bummm . . .!" went Mellow Tron, going forward to take her hand. Being the oldest and wisest out of this silly group he always knew what to do and so, tying up his dancing dreadlocks in case they got up to any mischief, he bowed down low and smiled. She smiled back with a set of toothless gums and sang out in tones so pure they reminded Mellow Tron of freshwater falls. He finally cleared his throat and asked who she was.

The ancient, tatty apparition changed her sitting position, reached out a hand to his and replied. "My name is Cassandra. I'm a Blind Seer and I've been waiting for all of you for the last thirty-three nights.

She then gasped and coughed, coming to a stop. She was so old, even her wrinkles had wrinkles and her wild hair moved around the top of her head like a giant beach ball.

"But how do you know that?" Fareek asked, taking her other hand and sitting down next to her and the others took their cue and sat down too.

"I'm a seer," Cassandra replied, cheerfully picking up a handful of sooth-saying sea slugs that were lying in an empty half of a coconut husk and chucking them into the air. They scattered crazily around the space and settled on the ends of Mellow Tron's bemused dreadlocks.

"But you can't be, you're blind ..." Tarquin asked in simple disbelief, slapping his face to check if he was still real.

Cassandra turned to him and smilingly said, "Oh that's nothing, I can see the past and the future although I can't see anything in the present but I still know why you're here!"

"And why's that?" Tarquin asked again, totally dumbfounded but awake and alert.

"Oh that would be telling as you have to have an adventure first," Cassandra replied, brushing her raggedy gown.

"But we're having one right now!" Fareek screamed, laughing at their predicament.

Cassandra pouted her delicate face and creased her wrinkles with an inner iron, laughed at the irony and replied. "OK, let me tickle your fantasy. I know why you're here and I'll give you a clue."

Another bouquet of wrinkles and smiles shimmered from her tiny face as she exclaimed, "Lucifer's rising again!"

"Do we have to deal with him for ever?" Mellow Tron asked, tugging at his locks (they didn't like this and snapped at him angrily).

"Yes, we all do and my part is to help you," Cassandra replied, hurriedly preparing the tea.

"Well, what shall we call you then?" Fareek said, mindful of Banglastani customs and never calling old ladies by their names if he could help it.

"Call me Granny Cass!"

Fareek laughed and finished with a flourish and a smile. After the jasmine tea, Cassandra fed them on some strange-looking buns from a clay platter and stroked Anarkali. She then began to explain further.

"We have to go and see Pharaoh Funkanathen. King Funky as he is known, is the most popular ruler of the Funkadelic dynasty and the time is auspicious." With that she cleared her throat again and sipped at her tea. Mellow Tron remembered Pharaoh Funky as the one king in whose long reign there wasn't a single war, famine or disaster, a happy time when people partied all the time. Good King Funky was the happiest of the ancient pharaohs and his people the happiest too so history remembered him well.

"Oi lads, do you know when we are?" Mellow Tron asked suddenly after jumping up and down and twisting his ears to get rid of a sooth-saying sea slug that had taken residence there.

"Haven't got a clue!" Fareek replied, busily devouring some more buns that Cassandra was dishing out.

"You are in the seventh year of the reign of Good King Funky!" Cassandra said with a grin.

"That's about four thousand years from where we've come from . . ." Mellow Tron informed the others who had no idea what they did yesterday let alone have an understanding of history.

Cassandra laughed to see their bewildered faces and said hurriedly, "That's why you have to call me Granny Cass!"

Meantime the music was still blaring from Fareek's solar powered CD player and even Cassandra was starting to nod. "You see you've come to make Good King Funky very, very happy!"

"With what?" Fareek asked glibly, not understanding anything yet trying to look like he did.

"You'll see, don't worry!" Cassandra said encouragingly, now offering a bowl of figs and dates.

"Wow! I'd love to see a real pharaoh!" Tarquin burped, excited at the prospect lying before them.

"If we can get back, that would be fine too!" Fareek replied, momentarily worried at their predicament. Getting to groovy places was wild but going back to where you came from was important too.

"You will return that I can assure you, I'm a seer after all."

After that enigmatic remark they crawled out of the tent and followed Cassandra down the pyramid and though blind she was more sure-footed than they were! Her flapping ears guided the others from the front and in a short while they were back at the bottom where a strange crowd of children attached themselves to the group asking for sweeties, toys and money but they were gently rebuffed as it is well known that musicians never have any money. Smiling through the thronging Zeegyptian crowd, they followed Cassandra as they headed for the palace; even Anarkali had to walk so as not to attract too much attention. Their adventure was about to begin.

However, they already had been seen by a squadron of ghostly heckles, speckles, vampires, spooks and gooks who had been observing them from invisible positions on the second highest pyramid. They had been waiting for the last two weeks, ever since Lucifer had given them his marching orders and he had been right. The visions in his All-Seeing Time-Ball had come true and now that they were here, there was nothing to do but to follow them to King Funkanathen's palace and see if there was a special interest in anything made of gold. These had been Lucifer's instructions and these were the only ones they had to follow or there would be trouble. As the whole flock of heckles, ghouls, speckles, afreets and minor demons screeked and scrawked, they flew off the pyramid and followed each other in an ugly formation. Led by Cassandra and unaware of being observed, the foolish four laughed and chuckled and tickled each other. They had found a friendly guide and were going on an adventure. What could be better? None of them had ever been inside a palace before except for Anarkali who had been a temple-trancer in the court of the King of Kathakstan hundreds of years ago or was that now hundreds of years later? Now it was so hard to tell that it didn't matter.

Quietly unobserved, one ghostly heckle that had remained on the pyramid now flapped his black wings, scratched his worm-eaten grey-black body, polished his two tiny red horns and brought out an All-Seeing Crystal Ball from inside a scarlet hempen bag. He rubbed the surface and in a demonic snarl spoke clearly to the evil face that he saw in the ball.

"Master Lucifer, we have found them and will do as you say and follow them to the palace to find the source of all the stolen gold and bring it back to you. We remain your humble citizens of Hell. Over and Out. Major Speckle ..."

And with that the speckle stretched its ugly wings, noisily flapped for a bit then flew off to join his fellow demons shadowing the Pearly Green crew like the breath of death.

16

Ghost Town

GHOST TOWN WAS situated in that part of Pearly Green where reason bordered on imagination. Ghost Town was no different to any other town except it was full of ghosts. There were: ghost people, ghost horses, ghost cats, ghost dogs, ghost fleas, ghost thieves, ghostly cavorting children, ghostly, if delirious, little boys and girls playing truant from ghostly schools, delicious ghostly muffins kissing sweet-looking ghostly crumpets on the side of ghostly alleys, ghostly witches whizzing past ghostly wizards on broomsticks, ghostly milkman bringing ghostly milk, ghostly oyster sellers being ironic and crying "Alive, alive-O", ghostly flower-sellers selling ghostly pansies, daffodils and daisies and much else bedsides. There were also ghostly donkeys, buffaloes, fantasy flamingos, purple turtles, grey crapping pigeons, cosmic kookaburras, orioles singing in Creole, pie sellers, chimney-sweeps, window-cleaners and a lot else besides. There were even ghostly hallucinogenic agaric-flies being eaten by ghostly black widow spiders. They were all ghosts and why not? This was Ghost Town after all, right in the heart of Pearly Green itself, well actually a Pearly Green of the past that still existed in the present. Ghosts from every era and wearing every imaginable type of clothing wandered up and down the ghostly streets, walking through walls, exiting through closed windows and basically having an excellent life. It wasn't only the living who lived and sometimes life is wasted on the living.

Three ghosts were chilling under the rafters of the abandoned inn "The Pig in Paradise" down in Spitney. One had been at Metta-Morph-Aziz and it had taken him only moments to fly down to this ancient pub that had been a favourite watering hole for many a ghost when they'd been alive. Of these ghosts, the first was called Phineas Freakville and he pulled at his long moustache while inhaling from a long seventeenth-century meerschaum pipe. His friendly face and merry smile masked the incredible intent twinkling in his grey-blue eyes. On his head he wore a top hat of the late Queen Angiean era and on his body a green velvet jacket with tails on which ghostly sooth-saying sea slugs munched contentedly. At the end of his long, thin nose were pince-nez without a single lens in them and he was reading a newspaper "Ghost Town Daily" while hanging upside down from the rafters.

"Nothing much in the Sunday papers today," he whistled suddenly, turning himself right side up and dropping the papers down to the second ghost, Madame Serendipity, a graceful old lady with a round, chubby and friendly face, her ghostly hair tied in a bun and a long white dress from the Cavalier era. She had once been a royal seamstress extraordinaire but now she was just a venerable ghost in Ghost Town and, sitting on her rocking chair, she had the glow of a fat, contented grandmother as she stitched the incredible Tapestry of Alternative Endings with the shifting scenes of what occurred in Metta-Morph-Aziz. People, fairy folk and magical creatures could be seen dancing, entrancing, spellbound or kissing. The figures moved with each stitch and one could clearly see the Hypno-Tantric Love Monster and its wonderful friends disappear. Now she was stitching together the merman's tail for Voodoo Child which was flapping up and down contentedly as a swarm of floating twinklefish came in to have a closer look. In the shifting tapestry he was turning into a merman for real and as he rose through the roof he was met by a group of mer-people who took him by the hands and swam away in a happy, alternative ending.

Tapping his pipe out onto the broken floorboards, Phineas asked again, "Have you read them?"

"I stopped reading the papers centuries ago," Madame Serendipity said with a sigh as she continued rocking and stitching. Next to her a pair of ghostly kittens played with the yarn.

"I agree with you, real life's much more interesting than what you get in the papers," said Cynthia Cruickshank as she too rocked in a ghostly rocking chair opposite Madame S.

Cynthia was about twenty-three years old, incredibly beautiful, exuded good taste and came from some time in the eighteenth century. Her clothes were voluminous and wonderful like Madame Serendipity's but they were black and on her head she wore a diamond tiara while pearls the size of billiard balls graced her elegant neck, a present from the Princess of Pearlistan. Her skirt was made of black silk and her blouse of the silk spun from cocoons of everlasting Chinese silkworms but what was beautiful Cynthia Cruickshank doing? She was stitching the Never-Ending Tapestry of Time and had been for three hundred years. On it was a picture of her face and the moment that she stitched a stitch, an eternal moment would have passed by and she would have got older and so the very next moment after having stitched it, she would have to go back and restitch it again and again and again to make it more accurate. She was painting the fines lines of ever-lasting ageing on her incredibly beautiful face but this doesn't explain why Cynthia never went to parties. Simple, centuries ago when she had been alive, she had gone to the Grasshoppers Ball and the Firefly's Feast and as the darling of the ball, she was feted and eighteen would-be suitors fell in love with her instantly. This included the Prince of Pondicherry, the Princess of Pearlistan, a few odd dukes, earls, barons and the Fantasy Firefly itself as well as the Grinning Grasshopper but what could a poor girl do? They all asked for her hand in marriage and Cynthia said only after she had finished her Never-Ending Tapestry of Time could she consider a proposal. A great work that showed the eternal flow of passing moments of the life and death of every arising second as it flowed through her changing face. Everyone said to her that she was beautiful but real beauty lay within and Cynthia told her suitors that the older and uglier she got, when time would have carved deep gashes in her once wondrous face, she'll actually have become more beautiful than ever before. Only when she had finished her tapestry would she choose one of them as a lover and so here she was, the pearl and tiara-clad beauty never being able to finish something that was impossible to finish. And even now, the Prince of Pondicherry, the Princess of Pearlistan, the many dukes, earls, barons, the Fantasy Firefly and the Grinning Grasshopper who now lived in Ghost Town, still did not give up and came down individually in the dead of night to the "Pig in Paradise" to ask for her hand which was far too busy with the ever-lasting tapestry to accept.

As the two female ghosts rocked in their battered old rocking chairs, Phineas swung off the rafters and landed gracefully. Brushing away dust from his jacket, he said affirmatively to the others, "Well, now that the leprechaun gold is being stolen by Lucifer what shall we do?"

The others stopped rocking and leant forward.

"What's so important about this leprechaun gold?" Madame Serendipity asked as Phineas placed his Meerschaum pipe into his right ear and cheerfully inhaled through the other. The resultant smoke that came out of his nostrils was in the shape of kissing lovers being chased by time dressed in the form of the Grim Reaper swinging his scythe. Phineas twinkled his eyes some more and tapped the top of his top hat and poking a finger through his ghostly pince-nez he chuckled.

"What's so important? I dunno but it must be important otherwise Sidney Arthur wouldn't have given me such clear instructions," he said picking up the pair of ghostly kittens lying on the ground and juggling them in the air.

"Can you see the future, Phineas?" Cynthia asked suddenly as the magical apparition of her handiwork showed the face of a young girl that changes through the quickness of time into a beautiful woman then turns into a crone and then back into a child.

"No, I'm just a very ordinary ghost. I thought you could see into the future, Madame Serendipity . . .?"

"I'm not that special but this tapestry that I've been working on since St Stan knows when is the Tapestry of Alternative Endings. They show me the possibility of what can be."

"And what do they show now?"

"Come closer and have a look for yourself Phineas!"

Phineas put the bemused kittens gently down and gazed on the Tapestry of Alternative Endings. He could see a whole shifting panorama of exquisite brilliance. Lucifer was sitting in his throne looking unhappy and depressed while crystal balls scattered in every direction. Happy parties could also be seen in ancient Zeegypt and Zindia involving everyone Phineas had seen earlier tonight at Metta-Morph-Aziz. There were also frightening things in present day Zindia and Hoggaristan and Pearly Green was defending itself from outside attack while pillage was taking place from both the rainbow's end and the Spanglish Main.

"Wow, that's great but what does it mean . . .?" Phineas asked now gently stroking the kittens that were purring on the floor and curling around his ankles.

"It means that there are so many possible endings we have to work out the best one for everyone and then go to make it a reality!" Cynthia said smiling freely. Exhaling deeply and emitting a sigh, Phineas got on with the plot.

"Before leaving with the others at Metta-Morph-Aziz Sidney Arthur gave me some advice, he said that the plan involves you and that you will be crucial to the story!"

"In what way?" asked Madame S, graceful, charming and very curious.

"He didn't say, he just chuckled and flew away but before he did so he did say that there is someone you should meet." Phineas magicked a ghostly bouquet of roses and offered them to her graciously.

"Who?" asked Madame Serendipity accepting his bouquet but not letting him off so easily. Meanwhile, his pipe had come out of his right ear and he now merrily smoked through the left but this time there were fantastic shapes flowing out of his mouth in the shape of Cynthia's beautiful face, neither changing nor affected by the passage of time, being chased by a host of unsuccessful suitors following each other crazily. The Prince of Pondicherry was chased by the Princess of Pearlistan while the Grasshopper was chased by the Fantasy Firefly and right at the end of the smoke were two kissing lips (curiously like Phineas's) through which Cynthia escaped. As the smoke disappeared, the blushing, romantic Phineas continued.

"The person that Sidney Arthur said you should see is Malik Slik Sylvester, the most famous fashion designer in the whole of Pearly Green, if not Slumdon Town itself!"

"What's so special about him?" Cynthia asked, whizzing up in the air to be near Madame Serendipity and her rocking chair that had risen sixteen feet up into the dust-ridden air of the old pub.

"This Malik can make the wonderful garments with his black widow spider-made silken webs and can even make them invisible."

"Well that's something I couldn't do," Madame Serendipity said smilingly.

"Yes, but he can't make them actually dissolve so you'll have to go down and help him," Phineas replied, relighting his extinct pipe with a flicker of passing love that he felt but never expressed for Cynthia Cruickshank.

"Why . . .?"

"That's a secret, I can't tell anyone simply because Sidney Arthur never told me but I'll tell you one thing he did tell me before he split, that it could save someone's life and saving someone's life is a wonderful thing."

17

The Tragic Capture of Captain Kidd

THREE GREAT GALLEONS were bobbing up and down in the unrelenting green-blue waters of the Karibbean. Treasure Island could clearly be seen through the early morning mist and there was trouble in the air and it could be smelt in the very atmosphere as gunpowder flashes and cannon balls whizzed through their intended targets. If the three had been fighting with each other then there would have been a much fairer chance for all concerned but as it was two against one, the outcome was increasingly clear.

If anyone had been standing on the prow of any of the three ships and used a telescope, they would have seen a bunch of tiny, brown-skinned folk in green hats, jumping up and down in glee as they saw one particular ship steer itself into position and fire broadside at the two others. It was obvious that the smaller and more flexible vessel had far less firepower but it did have the wholehearted support of the natives ashore, some who climbed to the top of the trees to get a better view of the battle while those on the beach spun madly around in their grass skirts, twirled their lances in the air, smashed coconuts on each other's heads and broke out in song. They cheered whenever the smaller ship blew its cannons directly into their enemies and jeered when the bigger ships manoeuvred themselves into better positions.

"Hurrah, hurrah and all things huzzah and one up the jacksy of Stinky Billy!" screamed Captain Kidd as the fighting got more exciting. His piercing blue eyes twinkled, making him look far younger than his actual forty years and his three-pointed, red and blue hat jumped up in the air in regular timing to the booming of his cannons and fusillade while the eccentric green and black parrot sitting on top of his braided left shoulder merrily smoked the cheroot of happy Himalayan herbs that Captain Kidd had just given him. The pirate's long black wig danced in the air as cutlasses clashed and danger flashed all around him but he was guided by the light of his sparkling golden earrings which pierced the mist of the early dawn. Captain Kidd resumed chuckling and got back to fighting, they may have been out-numbered and out-gunned but they certainly weren't out-skilled. His fabled luck, dare and devil-may-care attitude had looked after him so well for the seven long years since he'd become Captain but was it about to run out?

"Let's thieve from the thieves and rip off 'em what they've ripped off from others!" hollered Seaman Stains, Kidd's First Lieutenant, swigging from a bottle of "Rudolph's Reminiscing Rum". The red-kerchiefed Seaman Stains took another swig, flashed his cutlass to the side and considered their fate. Here they were being attacked by both the English and Spanglish fleets near one of the most beautiful places on earth, Treasure Island.

"*BOOM . . .!*" went the Spanglish galleon, coming up broadsides to try and capture Captain Kidd's ship from the right.

"*BOOM . . . BOOM . . .!*" went the guns of the English ship as it tried to trap them from the left until very soon the ships were shaped like the letter Y. The two fronts of the English and Spanglish ships had joined up in the shape of the letter V as Captain Kidd's ship, the *Leprechaun's Delight*, met them head on as the cannons tore holes in the very fabric of their structures and the screams and the cries of the anguished sailors on all sides were hurled into the morning air. Why this was happening? English fighting English in alliance with Spain meant something very strange was going on. Why were these two powerful nations targeting themselves onto this one tatty pirate ship and what was the problem with thievery anyway? Hadn't the Spanglish and the English stolen the gold in the first place from the diminutive natives of Treasure Island so why were they being so uptight when the pirates started ramming them, coming on board and stealing their gold back? Thieves never liked having their own stuff stolen, the most basic tenet of thieves' philosophy.

"Get the thieving scum!" yelled Captain Kidd climbing up a yardarm and gazing proudly at his crew of many colours fighting and flashing their way to victory. They were special and all united by a total disbelief of everything else which made them the very best pirates in the universe and Captain Kidd the very best captain.

"Get them!" yelled Captain Kidd yet again and the pirate sailors from the *Leprechaun's Deligh*t stung into action. As their Captain watched swinging merrily from his mast two hundred feet high near the watchtower of the *Leprechaun's Delight*, he barked orders to the hundreds of his sailors who having taken over the Spanglish, quickly set about liberating the countless chests of gold coins and silver buttons that had been stolen from the natives of Treasure Island. Being excellent pirates they had far more in common with each other, the various colours they were painted in than any one nation, race or religion. As the English sailors watched in disbelief, all the stolen gold they had stolen to share with the Spanglish quickly disappeared inside the hulk of the rolling *Leprechaun's Delight*.

"Good God! What's happening …?" whistled a voice as it waddled onto the front deck of the *The Greedy Fat Rat*. This was the rotund form of King Stinky Billy himself. Fat and extremely flustered, he had crawled up on deck to see for himself the shenanigans of the man he'd hunted over half the oceans and all around him, major and minor lieutenants grovelled like earthworms seeking a burrow. Seeing the fat English king, one of their mortal enemies up on deck , the pirates started singing, an insulting shanty as countless treasure chests were being stored. They all stuck two fingers up in the air, pointed to their grubby bottoms and sang even louder. They weren't particularly good singers nothing like the Soul Sisters Nazneen, but nevertheless the effect was electric. As the king watched, they pointed their fingers at him and started howling for real.

"Stinky Billy, fat pudding and pie, kissed the girls and
wondered why
when the boys came out to play, Stinky Billy ran away!
Stinky Billy, fat pudding and pie, kissed the girls and
wondered why
when the boys came out to play, Stinky Billy wanted to stay …
Stinky Billy, fat pudding and pie kissed the boys and it made
him cry.
When they rushed out to make him stay the greedy fat rat
ran away!"

As the sailors aboard the *Leprechaun's Delight* burst into giggles and rolled around the decks clutching each others sides, the sailors on the Spanglish ship the *Cancion de Esperenza* tried suppressing their giggles ineffectively whilst those on the *Greedy Fat Rat* bit their lips knowing better than to laugh. The king turned crimson with rage and crushing a wine glass in his right hand and watching wine stains drip down his hand like blood, he muttered to himself that he would be the death of Captain Kidd if it was the very last thing he ever did.

Having clambered atop the watchtower high on the *Leprechaun's Delight*, Captain Kidd could see that all his men had finally left the *Cancion de Esparanza*. He could see the English captain in the *Greedy Fat Rat* scream and bellow at his minions as the entrapment of the *Leprechaun's Delight* had clearly failed. Suddenly, grabbing a hempen rope, Captain Kidd swung from the halyard and bounced himself onto the deck of the *Cancion de Esparanza*. Why was he doing this and what had he seen? From this vantage point he'd seen a single gold coin that had been dropped by his departing pirates and swinging at an incredible speed, he rushed towards the Spanglish deck barely inches above the smoking cannons.

With a thud Captain Kidd landed on board the *Cancion de Esperanza* and his parrot flew from off his shoulder and the Captain was left on his own. Having swept up the single golden piece with his left hand and pocketed it safely, he got back into the swing of it, the cutlass and the battle that is. Still busy fighting countless Spanglish sailors single-handedly, his sword swerved arcs in the blistering air and the sailors tumbled and tripped over themselves to get away because they were no match for Captain Kidd.

"Unfurl the flag!" shouted Captain Kidd to Seaman Stains who was sliding up and down the rocking deck of the *Leprechaun's Delight* completely pissed.

"Captain! ... Get back quick!" he screamed but it was too late.

"Get back! Get back!" screamed Seaman Stains but it was too late.

Seaman Stains pulled off his red-spotted bandanna and slapped his head in frustration. Captain Kidd was on a roll and rocking away merrily, golden earrings dangling and swigging a bottle of the incredible grog that he kept in his coat pocket. With a sudden grimace he bit his lips, took a graceful bow and sang out loud.

"Dear Gentlemen ... friends and parrot ... It has been a total delight to have served with you all these years ... to have spent all this precious time with you ... but time like most other things often changes ... things ... Remember the most important thing to remember about change ... is to change each other's underpants regularly and never forget your socks . . . That's all I have to say . . . Life is sweet, life's a treat and Bing Bang Boomshanka. There you go . . . Hip . . . Hip . . . Huzzah . . .! And quickly unfurl the damn flag now!"

And with a quick flurry of hands and arms, the pirate flag was unfurled from the top mast of the *Leprechaun's Delight* and fluttered merrily in the breeze. The pirates burst into brazen cheers as the flag showed a jolly green hat-ed little guy staring brightly at the world with its tongue sticking out and a one-fingered gesture of rudeness.

"Yippee . . .!" squealed the pirates. They had won the stolen treasure back and were going to make the natives very happy. Captain Kidd was now back to fighting single-handedly thirty-seven Spanglish sailors and his sword arm was flashing like never before. He was fighting for his life this time and that made all the difference and so trying to escape, he grabbed onto the long rope he had used earlier and fastened himself to it with one hand. Running to the other side of the ship to get a better speed, he hurled himself towards the *Leprechaun's Delight* at the speed of inner light.

With a cry, stumble and fall, Captain Kidd suddenly realised that trouble was breaking out in Paradise as the rope he had been swinging on had turned completely into a cheroot of happy herbs, a wonderful thing to turn into but perhaps not the best of times to do so as the Captain needed to escape. However, as change is inherent in all animate things, Captain Kidd's twinkling eyes smirked as he realised that if mud goes back to earth and water back to the ocean then it can only be logical that ropes made of hemp eventually turn back into cheroots. As the Captain tumbled and fell chuckling, he was grabbed by a crowd of angry, jeering, Spanglish sailors.

"Damn . . . always knew I smoked too much . . .!" laughed Captain Kidd as the Spanglish sailors quickly tied him up with chains and unceremoniously dumped him aboard the *Greedy Fat Rat* where King Billy could now be seen smiling somewhere in the middle of his flabby face. Being the best pirate on the Spanglish Main, Captain Kidd had stolen from most everyone and so Stinky Billy was very pleased that this thorn in his side had finally been trapped, the pirate that had caused him much loss and many plundered royal ships. It had been a personal vendetta of the king to catch him and finish him off. Captain Kidd turned to the wobbling English king and spoke in a voice so clear that everyone on all three ships could hear him distinctly.

"You got me bang to rights, you fat wobbling greedy git but whatever you do to me won't matter because you can put me in as many chains as you want but I'll always be free. You can trap my body but my spirit will always belong to me!"

To give their Captain moral support, pirates from the *Leprechaun's Delight* sang the "Stinky Billy" song again, stuck their fingers and bottoms in the air and jeered and hollered as much as they could but many of them went through these motions with tears rolling down their cheeks. The King looked pissed-off too and motioned for some of his sailors to drag Captain Kidd down to the rat-infested hold of his ship. Just before disappearing, Captain Kidd turned his handsome head to the direction of his ship for the last time and shouted for them to flee and fast. As Seaman Stains and company bawled their eyes out, the *Leprechaun's Delight* unfurled its sails and off they went to obey their captain's last command and so the *Greedy Fat Rat* returned to Slumdon to hang the captured Captain Kidd at Topping Stairs while the *Leprechaun's Delight* zoomed off to Treasure Island to give back the bundles of stolen gold but they were not on their own.

From their watchtower in the *Greedy Fat Ra*t a group of ghostly heckles, speckles, bhoots, afreets, demons, vampires and other such nasties huddled up to each other in the narrow confines. Suddenly, the leader of the pack, a frightening apparition of a heckled speckle rose into the air, spread his blue-black demonic wings, gnashed his furious fangs, touched the crimson tips of his scarlet horns, flew to the tip of the highest mast and pulled an All-Seeing Crystal Ball out of his jacket pocket. Rubbing it furiously he awaited until the cloudy red mess inside the ball cleared itself to form into a vision and when he did see it, the heckled speckle cleared its throat and gargled respectfully into the ball.

"Master, we have seen the capture of Captain Kidd and are now hiding on the Royal Ship and heading for Topping Dock in old Slumdon. There, this pirate who has been causing you so much trouble, will be hanged and a jolly good thing too. We will all be there to ensure all goes to plan and nothing goes wrong. Forever be our darkness"

And with that it flapped its wings, circled around the poop-deck a few times and then quickly pooping on it, laughed as it hit the wandering king on his protruding belly.

18

Malik's Slick Threads

Malik was busy working in his magic muslin studio deep down in the Lost Catacombs of Brickie Lane where natural light was provided by the glowing stars on the ceilings, walls and floors of the multiple corridors and caves. And so Malik, Slumdon's top fashion designer and the oddest, was doing his funky stuff and whistling to himself rather badly as he prepared to go on holiday. He never usually had much need of going on holiday as he didn't like closing up the Magic Muslin Works but once a year he took his band of hundreds of merry black widow spiders to the smoky mountains of Trancesylvania where they could mate, if lucky, with the incredibly rare tarantulas that lived there; after that, if he was lucky, he'd be ensured of a whole bunch of baby spiders who could quickly be trained into making magic muslin.

Malik, dressed in nothing finer than single-piece spider-spun gown, looked a state, under curly blue locks and a three-day-old stubble, crooked black teeth shone from his shining face. Small and slim with mischievous eyes, he walked around checking his seventy-seven looms. These were where black widow spiders in collective groups on each loom would weave their magical threads, rainbow blue with the finest of stitches. The cloth on the looms looked almost transparent, these were the rough materials used to make the Hypno-Tantric Hijabs worn by the Sisters Nazneen at the Bum Note. As Malik went around checking his cloth, he lit a small cheroot and smiled as the many black widow spiders twitched with joy. The smoke would send the spiders into a trance and then the patterns they'd create in their weaving would be incredible. Checking the newer smoke-induced patterns Malik grinned, his father was a demon Kockneestani while his mellow mother was from Darkistan. As a young man, success had not gone to his head, it usually went to his feet as he had one of the finest private collections of the Kingdom of Chin slippers, this side of the Orient. There were soft silk ones, ones with pictures on, woollen ones for colder weather, leather ones for snowy conditions, floating ones for the water, flying ones for the skies and much else besides. On his many looms the spiders were busy spinning so this meant making on the frames, sticky spirals and auxiliary spirals.

Malik's spiders loved him and he took great care of them. He occasionally took them on holiday but best of all, he fed them on the finest hallucinogenic agaric-flies that money could buy. Malik made the slickest clothes, clothes for both top models and the person on the street and they gained in value the more they were worn. Humming to himself with smug satisfaction, he was completely unaware of the ghostly presence of three spirits. These had come in about an hour ago from the "Pig in Paradise" and having flown through the tandoori oven of the "Right Rude Sabre Tooth" had swiftly arrived in Malik's cave. Dangling themselves from the top of the cave by spider threads they cheerfully awaited Malik's departure for holiday before getting down to work. As they saw Malik starting to herd his hundreds of spiders into wicker cases, they sighed with relief. Soon they would have all the time and space in the world to get on with their plan.

"Isn't he ever going to leave?" Cynthia Cruickshank whispered, drawing up her black gown. She was damn glad to get away from Ghost Town and her eighteen crazy suitors.

"Don't be impatient, he seems to be packing the spiders up now," Madame Serendipity sighed as she gracefully glided down from the roof of the cave to hover near the rocky floor. Forever stitching shifting scenes on her tapestry, she studied it for a while before hitching up her frilly white dress, materialising her rocking chair and sitting down. An incredible party in ancient Zeegypt was taking place on her tapestry before her bewildered eyes and in another scene a pirate was being hung, drawn and quartered. She put her tapestry down on her lap and looked at Phineas.

"It's really rather odd taking the spiders on holiday," Phineas Freakville added, his twinkling eyes shining behind his merry smile. Having lit his pipe once again, he twirled his moustache and waited for a reply from Madame Serendipity.

"Why not? Everyone needs a break," she replied, still watching Malik carefully herd the rest of his spider colony into the wicker cases with a gentleness that seemed to surprise her. She smiled and patted the white bun on top of her head. Malik was one slick dude and though time was of the essence, it couldn't ever be pushed or it would most certainly fight back.

"It seems like it's going to be a long wait," Cynthia said after a moment. She too had now materialised her rocking chair and sat opposite her teacher, both rocking merrily away and weaving. On Cynthia's Tapestry of Never-Ending Time her face was now that of a beautiful seven-year-old child. Cynthia stiched and re-stitched the threads so that the image could remain that way for ever. Of course it couldn't.

"A long wait for what? Before Malik leaves to go to Trancesylvania?" Phineas interjected dejectedly, not being the most patient of ghosts.

"No, a long wait before our plans come to fruition," replied the older female ghost as her eyes shifted quickly from watching the departing Malik to staring at the ever-changing scenes on her tapestry where a whole bunch of fascinating alternative endings were coming into being. She cleared her throat and asked in a clear, bright voice, "Phineas, what did Sidney Arthur say to you exactly?"

"Not much, just that you should make Malik's threads dissolvable. Can you do that?"

"It's been a long time but I think I can."

"Good!"

"Now, to spend the time I've brought my Tapestry of Alternative Endings to see what I can sew and I'm also going to knit some extra large woollen jumpers for my grandsons, Bill and Ben. What are you two going to do until our magic works?"

"I'm going to weave some more on my Tapestry of Never-Ending Time," Cynthia said with a smile knowing very well she'd much prefer romancing with Phineas.

"And I'm just going to blow smoke rings, meditate upside down, wander up and around the different caves and not much else!" Phineas finished on a high note, creating a giant bubble with his smoke, and then quickly disappeared into the cave next door. When he returned moments later he was carrying a basket of cockles and oblong oysters for them all to eat which would go deliciously with the dusty green bottle of periwinkle wine in the pocket of his velvet jacket. He opened the bottle, materialised three wine glasses and poured each one a perfect glass.

"Yippee! He's finally going," Cynthia sang with a cheer, rocking faster in her chair.

"Yes, he's finally got all fifteen cases packed," Madame Serendipity sighed observing that Malik hadn't left a case free for his own clothes. He would go wearing the scruffy clothes on his back and would no doubt return in the same.

"And there must be at least a few hundred spiders in each case," Phineas whistled through his ghostly teeth.

And it was true. With a final flourish, Malik snapped all the wicker cases closed, checked on the looms once more, left what magic muslin was remaining there and turned the lights on the twinkling glow-worms down. The three ghosts held their breaths and waited until, with a final slamming of the cave door, Malik was gone, carrying his enormous load of fifteen wicker cases balanced precariously on his head, He was off on holiday and wouldn't be back for one month giving the ghosts enough time to do their thing and depart before ever being caught.

"Great, now he's gone we can get down to it," Phineas smirked, adjusting his pince-nez.

Madame Serendipity turned to him with a serious look and asked, "What *exactly* did Sidney say, Phineas?"

"He said you have to make Malik's magic muslin dissolvable and then make a hangman's noose out of it."

"Look, this silk is the finest in the world but it doesn't do your trick," Cynthia interrupted.

"You're the only one in the whole of Ghost Town who can make materials dissolve," Phineas finished with a merry smile.

Madame Serendipity considered; she did know incantations and spells that would make material dissolve and could literally melt the socks and pants off someone's body. She had been the greatest weaver of her generation when alive, she'd been royal seamstress to the jolly but naughty King Charlie the Second who used her to make all special material for robes for his mistresses so that as soon as they'd reach the bedchamber, the king would lay a single finger on them and the dresses would dissolve and leave King Charlie and his countless mistresses surprised and breathlessly happy. Madame Serendipity had perfected the art of dissolvable threads that dematerialised upon touch and the King was so happy he showered her with riches.

"What we need to do is steal Malik's thread, add it to my magic and then make a hangman's noose!" Madame Serendipity replied, scratching her ears and looking slightly bewildered.

"But why a hangman's noose?" Cynthia asked, getting off her rocking chair and coming closer.

"Sidney Arthur didn't say," Phineas said, shrugging his handsome shoulders, his grey-blue eyes still twinkling.

"He never says anything," Madame Serendipity said with a laugh.

"And anyway Malik can't mind, he'll only lose a few hours' production," Phineas said with a grin as he pondered their part in this great adventure. Sidney Arthur may not have told them much but here they were, still part of the plot.

"Great! Let's go for it." And with that Madame Serendipity was off, floating around Malik's worktables checking each loom in turn. Then, while Phineas blew intricate smoke ring after smoke ring, she went over each loom in turn muttering magic invocations amidst a cloud of iridescent smoke.

> "Loom Loom, spin your magic threads
> Let it help someone not be dead
> Loom Loom, make a strong resolve,
> In short-sweet time, you'll soon dissolve."

And with that she sprinkled some magic powders that flashed blue and red and it was done, all that remained was for the silken thread to dry off. Sidney Arthur now had his dissolving threads wherever he was and poor old Malik had nothing but he could always make lots more.

"There's nothing to do now but wait for the incantations to dry and when the magic muslin has dried we have to say a final incantation and it will be ready," Madame Serendipity mumbled to Cynthia as they flew around the room six feet in the air, carefully observing any changes they could see on the countless looms.

"And how long's it going to take to dry?"

"Approximately twenty-eight and a quarter days and that's okay because Malik has gone off with his spiders for about a month, we should be okay."

"Well what shall we do?" Phineas asked, flying in close to be next to the other two still munching on oblong oysters.

"Do anything you want Phineas. I'm busy here. I'll be weaving on my Tapestry of Alternative Endings and knitting two jumpers for my ghostly grandsons."

"What will you be doing Cynthia dear?" Phineas asked, passing Cynthia another glass of periwinkle wine.

"Oh I'll be on my rocking chair with Madame Serendipity weaving my Tapestry of Never-Ending Time."

"Don't you want to come with me to explore the Lost Catacombs a bit more?"

"Yes of course Phineas but I'm worried that you'll be blowing more of those romantic smoke rings at me."

"No I promise to behave!" Phineas said blushingly as he shot off to explore the catacombs on his own after picking up a magic bean that Malik had left in a pile on a pewter platter near his worktable.

And they patiently waited a month. After finishing off the jumpers for her grandsons, Madame Serendipity examined the different endings of the story on her tapestry; some were happier than others and she was careful to follow these optimistic threads. Whatever ending was happiest for the majority of people was the one she tried to weave. Cynthia spent much of her time weaving her special tapestry but as it was always unfinished, she gave up at some point and wandered off with Phineas to explore the incredible depths of the Lost Catacombs until finally the thread was ready. They had all waited patiently for twenty-eight days and somehow in the distant corridors, they could hear grunting. It sounded like Malik was back from his holidays and still carrying the fifteen cases one on top of each other on his head.

Madame Serendipity, quickly making the new threads into hanks of rope and winding the coils around her ample body, pointed to Cynthia and gasped, "The incantation again Cynthia and this time you'll have to say it."

"Okay, Madame Serendipity," whistled Cynthia as she rushed up to be near the hank of dissolvable magic muslin wrapped around the other.

"Loom Loom, spin your magic threads
Let it help someone not be dead
Loom Loom, make a strong resolve.
In short-sweet time you'll soon dissolve."

"Excellent Cynthia, now let's split," said Madame Serendipity, looking Cynthia straight in her beautiful eyes.

"Where are you going?"

"I'm off to see Sidney Arthur with this hank of very special dissolvable magic muslin."

"Shall we come?"

"No need Cynthia, I'm sure you two will be better off romancing here."

"Hrmmmm … Hrmmmm …!" mumbled Phineas, shamefully putting his fingers through holes in his velvet jacket.

"Thanks," said Cynthia, blushing and very coy.

Just as Malik opened his door and entered, all three ghosts instantly disappeared. Cynthia and Phineas decided to carry on their romancing back at the "Pig in Paradise" whilst Madame Serendipity simply disappeared. Gently releasing his fifteen cases of contented spiders, Malik sat down on the only tatty sofa in his cave and brewed himself a cup of rosehip tea. He sighed. It was good to be back home. Whether or not he noticed the missing magic muslin was another question altogether. If he did, he didn't say anything, not a word.

19

Topping Kidd at Topping

SIX VOICES SCREAMED together and an incredible white flash of lightning zapped all around at the speed of light. Light, light, light and then much more and they were spinning in this world of bright white light and then tumbling and twisting and falling into patterns known only to their karma, hurtling back through space and much else. Time was being shifted and being swished and swashed out of all recognition. Who knows where they were going? Who knows how long they'd been travelling? They were hurtling through an endless tunnel as the brilliant pure white light of purity moved through them, then the light changed its brilliant hues and a calmer symmetry flowed into view. As they tumbled, the fools mumbled and held onto each others tickly bits for security – Bilal held onto Charlie's leg and Charlie held onto silks from the Artful Dodger's overflowing top hat and Sidney Arthur still had his fishing rod attached to BB, Billy's attached to Charlie and Danny attached to the Artful Dodger. It was a good thing that Sidney had thrust a few handfuls of Anatta into their mouths just before the implosion at Metta-Morph-Aziz as this was helping to get them onto the same journey as their unknowing hosts. They may have been ghosts but they had never hurtled through time before and this was an incredible novelty, tumbling into only St Stan knows where. Moments earlier they had been dancing along with their friends with hands, heads, feet, wings, tails and soft furry other things going crazy at the Bum Note and now they were freaking out somewhere else. Then six tumbling forms came hurtling into view. Three could be clearly seen but the other three could only be seen by each other. Two men, a boy and three ghosts were falling from the skies.

"Aaaah ..." screamed BB as his kaleidoscopic spectacles misted up and the hole in his pretty pink plimsolls let in unrelenting, rushing wind as the ground came rushing up.

"Ooook!" screamed Charlie in Kockneestani chill as the earth rushed up to meet him.

"Wow!" laughed the Artful Dodger as a line of pocket watches streamed from the top of his top hat and prettied the clouds. He had a particular and most personal understanding with time and that's why he was never scared. With Dobbins around there was never any reason to fear the true passage of time as it could always be turned back, then nicked or even turned into silken pocket watches. The head boy of Master Fagin's Funkadelic Tribe slapped the hinged-top flap on his hinged-top hat down and his malnourished look took on an expression of real hunger, a hunger for the unknown and a soot-ridden grimy smile pleasured his face as he fell.

"Oooops . . .!" gasped Sidney Arthur as he finally got out of Pearly Green again. His right hand had held successfully to BB's left leg and he wasn't letting go now. His ghostly fishing rod was still stuck firmly onto the lad's purple kurta and he wasn't letting that go either.

"Aaarkk!" went Billy Blake as the other ghosts too came tumbling out of the clouds, Billy holding onto Charlie's back with his fishing rod and Danny holding onto the Dobbins's top hat. Billy's ghostly hair flapped in the wind and Danny's peg leg vibrated as if it was coming off in the sheer force of their descent.

"Ouch!" gasped Danny De Foe as they finally touched the ground. Although the ghosts weren't still visible to the humans, what they saw from their glazed eyes was enough. They were all lying lopsided in a pool of dank and smelly mud and immediately pushed over each other to get away from it. They were in a small park and sitting morosely over a few crumbled, ancient gravestones where a bunch of wine drinkers and tramps scowled in their direction.

"Yuuch!" yelled BB, vainly trying to brush the gunge off his clothes.

"Urrk!" yelled Charlie, jumping up quicker than a flash in a pan and raising his body as fast as he could.

"Er . . . I'm soiled . . .!" shrieked the Artful Dodger, running to his feet and jumping up and down in disbelief.

"Oh wow . . . This is Itchycoo Park, I'm sure of it . . ." Charlie whistled through his teeth, suddenly perceiving a different point of view.

"How can you be so sure?" BB stammered, scraping the mud away from his faded jeans.

"Look it's small, square, not particularly attractive and full of tramps getting drunk over broken gravestones!"

"Oh yeah, you're right!" BB stuttered, this time taking a good look around him.

"Oh wow! We've travelled only about one mile," the Artful Dodger said in a splutter, trying to get rid of the mud in his ears.

"Yes, but it doesn't look the same!" BB said with a smile on his beatnik face for the first time.

"This might be the same place but something mightily different makes it seem wrong," Charlie whispered as he stretched his body in the early morning sun.

"Looks disgusting!" BB replied, holding his nose at the unappetising smells.

"Looks like the same place but a different time!" Dobbins replied, stashing away his secret hoard of silken pocket watches so they wouldn't get stolen.

"Yeah, look at those old alcoholic tramps, look at the clothes they're wearing, they're so old, from hundreds of years ago," Charlie added pointing his finger at the drunken lolling group who were rudely pointing back.

"And look at the empty brown bottles of "Rudolph's Reminiscing Rum" they're leaving behind. These haven't been seen for three hundred years!"

"How do you know, Dobbins?"

"Oh, I nicked the last bottle from an antique shop last year, Charlie . . . somewhere posh up Plumdon."

"Oh right!" finished BB totally astonished.

They got up, brushed each other clean(ish) and decided to go for a walk. It was obvious that they had gone back in time, all they could see were dank alleys leading to other dank alleys. There weren't any pretty pink flamingos or even any purple turtles to watch out for or palanquins carried by penguins and pelicans either; however, there was a lone crapping pigeon under pursuit. There were no trees of any kind, let alone any crunchy banana trees but fluffy white clouds still scudded above their confused heads and a bright golden sun was showering the air with its warmth on this new day. Up in the eastern reaches of the sky, the part where sky meets space, the Man on the Moon was doffing his harlequin's hat and strumming a cosmic chord of total connectivity on his hurdy-gurdy after which he simply disappeared. Night had ended and the morning star had gone. Dobbins had correctly calculated the year to be three hundred years odd since they had left the party and as they walked on aimlessly and totally confused, they muttered amongst themselves quietly. They knew roughly when they were, they knew how they were but they didn't know why they were and that time and space had played a trick on them and they wished that they did know. As they walked they held their noses as the whole place stank of rotting fish and dirty underwear; the sense of poverty was acute.

"Wow, just like old times, Sidney!" Billy said, excitedly flying down to be near Sidney Arthur and twirling his mystical hourglass in his hand.

"Well, it's old times for you!" Sidney Arthur replied enigmatically, gathering his little group together with a flick of his ghostly hand.

"Just when are we, Sidney Arthur?" Danny De Foe asked putting his fishing rod back into a bag he kept on his back.

"I reckon ... having had a good look at Billy's mystical hourglass ... that we are here at 8am on March 1st 1701 ... that's over three hundred years before last night!"

"Bit before my time!"

"Yes, Billy but not before mine, as you do know, I am the oldest ghost in Ghost Town!" Sidney Arthur said laughingly.

"Yes but this *is* about the time I was alive though!" Danny interjected, as he clambered through the air to get closer to the other two.

"Yeah, but you weren't here then were you? You were on a deserted island in the oceans somewhere!"

"That's absolutely true, Billy!" replied Danny. He cleared his throat and asked their group leader, "Sidney, you seem to know most things. Please tell us, why are we here?"

"Oh no sorry! I can tell you the date, month, year and time but I can't tell you why we're here!"

"Why not?"

"It's because he doesn't know himself and just tries to look like he's clever!" Billy said with a glum grin.

Sidney Arthur giggled, twirled up and down in the air and then did an aerial back-flip to land breathlessly at their feet seven feet in the air. With a manic giggle he explained, "What do you mean looks like? I am clever!"

"Well then, why don't you tell us why we've been brought here by some stronger magic than our own?" Billy continued, still turning his hourglass up and down in his hands.

"That would be telling and as you know I never tell anyone anything until I've solved the whole puzzle in one go."

"That's just like Shylock Homes, isn't it?" Danny interjected dejectedly, knowing well that Billy and he weren't going to get a clear explanation for anything.

"Shylock who?" Billy asked, quickly scratching his head before the itch whooshed down to the nether regions and he lost it altogether.

"You've had your pound of explanations. Enough! Beat it, all I can tell you chaps is that we are on an adventure so incredible that even if I told you what it was I wouldn't be able to do it justice."

"Far out!" cheered Billy, bouncing up and down in the air like the dementedly happy ghost that he was.

"Wowwee!" Danny added, grabbing Billy by the hands and spinning them both around and around in circles very fast.

"Now let's get to work and see the three silly billies stumbling along, dazed and confused. They know that we're still in Pearly Green and have guessed at Topping as the exact place!"

"So what?" said Danny, starting to chew on his peg-leg out of sudden hunger.

"So what? That means they're clever!"

"Okay Sidney, you're boss!" gasped Danny, merrily chomping on a piece that he had successfully bitten off.

"Yes, you're the boss!" Billy added with a smile, pocketing his hourglass with a confident air.

"Of course I am, now get along and follow them!" Sidney Arthur finished, leading the others ten feet in the air in the direction of Bilal the Banglastani Beatnik, Kockneestani Charlie and the Artful Dodger.

Getting a steady rhythm with their feet and starting off towards the riverside, the three fools and the three holy ghosts set off, passing countless inns with many drunken people lolling and tottering all over the place and manky-looking tea houses run by disreputable looking scruffs. Everything was horrible and smelly. Urchins scuttled between their knees and even tried nicking the Artful Dodger's top hat. The poor were everywhere, in the shops, cafes, pubs and streets and were simply awful. Pearly Green may have been poor where they had just come from but this was much worse as the very poverty stunk in the air. As BB and Charlie kicked a few mangy dogs out of the way, they tried avoiding stepping in the overflowing gutter while Sidney Arthur and the other ghosts followed at a curious pace and kept their voices low. Everywhere the effects of gin, rightfully called "mother's ruin", could clearly be seen in its effects. Outside one nasty looking dive, a whole group of mothers wailed in drunken hysteria while outside another, their abandoned children screamed in terrifying destitution.

"Look, here's a street sign," Charlie said, his ginger locks all over the place. They had left one dank alley and were coming to a larger thoroughfare.

"What does it say? I can't read," BB bleated.

"The Highway," Charlie replied, excitedly showing the sign to everybody and wearing a smirk on his face.

"That must definitely mean we're in Topping, the Dockside of Pearly Green," Dobbins said, shutting the open lid on his top hat again.

"Are you sure?" BB asked through misted spectacles, rubbing his body down because the air was cold at this time of the morning.

"We're in Topping!" Dobbins said again in a voice of growing confidence.

"Well, I know of only one Highway!" Charlie exclaimed, wishing he had some love grenades stashed in his voluminous pockets. These he could have exploded and prettied up the Slumdon skies and made himself warmer in the process too. It was a good thing that he and BB had both brought their fantasy flintlocks and a plentiful supply of blooms to fire through them.

"That must mean that the river is through there," Charlie insisted, walking confidently though the crowds, head and shoulders above everyone else. The crowds grumbled and groaned but as Charlie was taller than anything else on the streets, they simply moved away. However, they gave the cold, brown Bilal a few funny looks and some of then even wondered if he was a lost Zindian seaman trying to find his way back to the docks but his humourless expression put them off asking.

"Come let's head in that direction, we might be able to find somewhere cheap!" BB insisted with a smirk following him quickly. His spectacles were pointing to the east and Charlie and Dobbins quickly conferred to agree.

"Flea-ridden sailor-pits no doubt!" the Artful Dodger smirked, knowing exactly what poor accommodation was all about, having lived at Master Fagin's for so many years. He was used to having nothing and laughed but since they had become good shepherds, both BB and Charlie much preferred sleeping in Queen Angie Park looking after their flock of sacred cows and fluffy white lambs.

"Flea-ridden pits are better than nothing," Charlie replied, striding manfully along and smiling at the glum mothers racing on ahead to spoil themselves on mother's ruin at various gin shops. They also passed a whole bunch of beggars and sailors all off to the gin shops for the same purpose as "mother's ruin" was quickly proving to be 'father's ruin' too.

"Loads of thieves in this area, I can just feel it," said the Artful Dodger trusting to his intuition and holding onto his top hat as they pushed their way past drunken sailors, beggars, con-men, and thieves. Suddenly, twirling his grimy frame around on the spot like Anarkali at her best, Dobbins grabbed their attention by jumping onto their collars, slapping BB and Charlie around their silly faces and then letting them go. Surprised by his sudden enthusiasm, the other two just stood there gob-smacked as in front of a small, gathered crowd, Dobbins opened his arms and burst into song so divine it needed no wine and mothers out on the hunt for their ruin simply stopped in their tracks and listened spellbound as Dobbins explained in perfect melody, everyone's existential dilemma.

"Come! Come! Awaken all true drunkards ...
Pour the wine that is life itself,
Oh, cupbearer of the Eternal Wine
Draw it now from Eternity's Jar.
Come! join the honest company of the King's beggars
Those gamblers, scoundrels and divine clowns
And those astonishing fair courtesans
Who need divine love dressed even in tatters.
Then nothing can ever get them down
They'll always be laughing and there'll never be a frown."

"Whay! ... Hippee! ... Huzzah ...!" whistled the crowds thinking Dobbins was a professional balladeer and trying to force money upon him but, slapping a giant hand over his bewildered mouth, Charlie booted him hard on his arse and prompted him along. They rushed on as the smell of the crowd was horrendous, worse than the noxious odours of the Sunday Market on Brickie Lane. This was Pearly Green with a difference, not the green and pleasant land of our story so far, this was the land of satanic mills and grimy little sweatshops and the most powerful smell of all was the cheap gin that flowed out from under almost every door, crook, crevice and cranny. Beggars on crutches stuck out their bandaged hands and grimy little children selling flowers thrust them unsuccessfully into their faces but this group didn't need to buy flowers, not with Sidney Arthur shooting them from his crumbling button holes and BB and Charlie's flintlocks at the ready. So the beatnik reached into the deep pockets of his kurta and pulled out some chocolates for them instead.

"Where are they going, Sidney Arthur?" Billy asked as the holy ghosts followed the others at a discreet distance.

"Never you mind, Billy!"

"No seriously, Sidney, where are they going?" Billy asked again, shooting off to be at the front and now only inches away from the Artful Dodger's hat.

"The same place as us, silly!"

"And where's that?" Billy shouted, turning round and sticking his tongue out at Sidney Arthur.

"Just follow them and you'll find out," Sidney Arthur chuckled and pulled Danny along.

"Bah Humbug, Sidney! Bah Humbug!" bleated both the other ghosts at the same time.

After almost twenty minutes walking down Topping Lane, they suddenly came to a place with a completely different atmosphere altogether where the very air was suffused with a different fragrance. Dobbins now saw a group of quite different creatures hanging around a golden mulberry tree that suddenly materialised in front of his spellbound eyes on one side of the lane as a strange scent began to permeate the very space. It was a flower all right but an extremely dangerous smell that one had be to be very careful of.

"Ah poppies!" cried BB cheering up immensely and rubbing his spectacles with glee.

"Be careful, a flower is a flower but poppies can be dangerous stuff!" Charlie said looking very serious.

"Bah, hogwash! Poppies are groovy too, you and me Charlie are flower-power warriors extraordinaire so we don't have to be worried about anything, especially such a little thing as a poppy flower!"

"Maybe Charlie's right, mate and we should take care. Poppies are very pretty no doubt but they can be terrible too, just like gin," Dobbins whispered seriously, jumping up and down on BB's torn plimsolls.

"Plants are never dangerous! What's dangerous is the mind-set that goes with them!" Bilal insisted, pushing Dobbins from his footwear.

"You may be right."

"Of course I am!"

The three just stood in the street wallowing in the excellent aroma of cooking poppies. The smell came from somewhere nearby and BB went on a mission to find out where it was. Putting his fantasy flintlock upon his back, he sniffed and sniffed like an over-excited dog as he was desperate to find out where the intoxicating smells of the poppy blooms came from. He very rarely ate or drank his flowers but occasionally Charlie and he would make a drink out of rose petals or daffodil blooms but now he had to find out the source of the incredible smell and swallow it himself. This smell had a kick to it that no mule could ever have and something was changing in Bilal's eyes as they took on an expression of mania. Charlie looked exasperated. He knew of his mate's occasional weakness for all things intoxicating but he thought that the Anatta they had swallowed just recently would have been enough but was wrong as BB's religion was 'more'. Dobbins simply scuffed his heels and looked at the crazy expression on BB's face and then above to the mulberry tree again. A whole bunch of squirrels stealing hazelnuts from each other and stashing them in secret places always forgotten, were sitting on the branches stunned at BB's dementia. All around the squirrels were nightingales, phoenixes, pheasants, grouse, fantasy falcons and the occasional pretty pink flamingo. The golden mulberry tree, the squirrels and the birds had appeared just like magic as Dobbins gazed into empty space and wondered what to do about their friend who was moaning, "Poppies! Poppies! . . . Must have poppies!"

Looking exasperated and tired, Dobbins turned to the squirrels and birds and asked, "Dear squirrels and dear birds, what have we done to deserve this? What do we do about him . . .?"

After much muttering and conferring, the conference of the

squirrels and birds ended with a nightingale stepping forward and speaking for them all.

> "Squirrels and birds sense your sadness
> And call an important conference in a tall tree,
> They decide which secret code to chant
> To help your mind and soul
> To realise that you are free."

"Great, help that is!" sighed the Artful Dodger as the vision ended. The creatures had been right though as a feeling of trepidation was creeping into his soul like the ghostly woodworms in Danny's peg-leg and then it was too late.

"Found it . . . Found it . . . Let's go in here," Bilal squealed, having traced the source of the smell to a dark, shabby house.

"Do you know what this is?" Charlie asked with inquisitive emphasis.

"Who cares? It's where the wonderful smell comes from!" BB said excitedly, wanting to knock on the door but being held back by Charlie by the scruff of his neck. Charlie then proceeded to rationally explain the situation.

"It's an opium den, it's all right for some people but not for you."

"What do you mean?"

"What I mean to say is you got no self-control and that my friend is going to be the downfall of us all."

"Oh come on just a single pipe, it won't hurt."

"But we've gotta find out why we're here. We're on a mission from St Stan," added the Artful Dodger, trying to placate him.

"Who cares? One single little pipe won't hurt anyone at all, least of all me," BB insisted, ignoring Dobbins's gist and sticking to his own point. Charlie slanted his eyebrows back as far as they would go and stepped in.

"We're on an adventure to heaven knows where and we don't have the time to stop!"

"Oh, come on, listen to Charlie, this will all end in a sticky mess," the Artful Dodger insisted, giving the beatnik a grimy look.

"How do you know, Dobbins?" BB asked, momentarily distracted from his mission.

"Oh, some squirrels and pretty birds told me!"

"You been having visions again and without us?" Charlie asked, quickly giving the Artful Dodger a scary look and kicking his boots with frustration.

"Er . . . Yes . . .!"

But it was too late, having traced the smell of the poppies to a battered door, BB knocked firmly on the door and waited while the others just held their breaths. This house was decrepit with all the windows boarded up and any window panes there may have been had been knocked out years ago. Above the tatty door stood two crumbling floors of soot-blackened building that almost toppled into the alley, battered beyond belief. A whole pallor of grey-black smoke had coloured them inside out and when the Artful Dodger ran a finger through the wood boarded window frames, an inch of black dust came onto it. The house was so strange that the tatty houses surrounding it on either side of the alley seemed luxurious in contrast and as Charlie tried unsuccessfully to stop BB from battering on the door again, he felt a premonition of worry pass through his body leaving him cold, shivering from the collywobbles and trembling. Right then he suddenly remembered a crazy poem his great-grandmother used to croon to him as a child and involuntarily started muttering it himself.

"There was a crooked man who walked a crooked mile.
He lived in a crooked house and jumped over a crooked stile.
He found a crooked coin and loved a crooked cat.
That was when the boogie ended and all that was left was scat!"

Letting Bilal go, Charlie took a good look at his friend. In his desperation to get into the opium den he looked rather like the crooked man himself, all arms and limbs askew. In his frustration to get inside he had almost kicked the brown door off its hinges and sweat was starting to pour down his saturated face. This was déjà vu that Charlie was seeing, the future in the present and it wasn't very nice.

"Who's that knocking on my front door . . .?" whispered the fragile, far-away voice of an ancient man from the Kingdom of Chin, wearing aged robes, black silk slippers and a bamboo hat.

"Me sir!" Bilal replied excitedly like a boy going to school for the first time.

"If you want to come in . . . do you really know the score . . .?" whispered the ancient chap opening the door a little bit more.

"Yes, of course ..." he replied hurriedly, almost driven mad by the anticipation.

"Then step inside and never mind the rest. Come in and chase a dragon and let's put theory to the test!"

"Groovy! Far out! Ooops . . .!" BB said joyously and ran into the darkened hallway.

"Eeerrr ...!" moaned the Artful Dodger, firmly shutting his top hat and looking bewildered.

"Ummm . . .!" went Charlie, scratching his head and not knowing what to do.

"We'll only have one pipe, sir ...!" BB shouted from somewhere deep inside the hall as the fragile voice of the old one quickly replied.

"Of course, that's what they all say. Come inside and meet the other happy folks who just like you have only ever had one pipe, however, it's a never-ending pipe that never goes out."

As the old man led them through the house, they noticed the black smoke that hung around everywhere. They entered and ordered themselves some jasmine tea, buying them with some silver coins Charlie had stolen from the local museum a week earlier. It was lucky that they were from the same era and he was chuffed to get some change. Bilal then quickly ordered a pipe while the others just shrugged their shoulders and waited for him to start. The earlier he started, the quicker he could finish and the earlier they could get on with their adventures.

"Keep your voices low," Charlie whispered as they sipped their drinks and Charlie started filling a chillum he always carried with him along with a stash of happy Himalayan herbs that went with it.

"I don't know how," BB retorted, taking a good long lug of the funny twenty-inch-long copper-bowled pipe which the host filled well and lit with a long taper. Charlie, BB and Dobbins found themselves sitting on soft divans arranged in a circle. As the beatnik put his legs up, rubbed his kaleidoscopic spectacles and continued puffing laboriously at the opium pipe, Charlie contented himself with his chillum and the Artful Dodger with nothing stronger than the jasmine tea.

"Just be discreet and don't flash anything around," Charlie whispered at the Artful Dodger whose top hat was being unhinged again. Dobbins took his hat off and then clamped it down firmly.

"The place just smells of thieves," Dobbins said in a quiet hush, taking a sip.

"Well, I suppose that suits us really!" Charlie replied, smoke coming out of his nostrils in a shape of a dragon chasing a man.

"Yeah ... well in a way, it does suit us," BB shot back, with growing contentment as the opium took over. His smoke rings were in the shape of howling man with a crazed tiger upon his back and upon the tiger's back was a screaming monkey that held on tight and wouldn't let go.

"Though I don't know what we're meant to be nicking," he added, exhaling.

Above all their unknowing heads, the three ghosts circled around the room. Sidney Arthur, Danny and Billy Blake had all entered the opium den from the cracked roof and had now descended to be nearer to their catch. Putting a finger up to his thin mouth, Sidney Arthur motioned the others to be quiet. Hovering up to the level of the highest windows on the ground floor, they quickly stole a teapot of the hot refreshing brew and also a lump of opium. Proceeding to put his feet up on a recently materialised divan, Sidney Arthur proceeded to smoke contentedly as Billy and Danny awaited their turns. There they were blowing their lives up in smoke and it must be said, looking rather merry for it.

"By the holy dreadlocks of St Stan! Is this an opium den?" Billy asked incredulously, moving up to sit next to Sidney Arthur.

"Of course it is," Sidney Arthur replied taking a long toke himself with undisguised glee.

"Is it as wonderful as they say it is?" Danny asked, coming in to sit on the divan on the other side and pushing Sidney Arthur into the middle.

"Of course, Danny ... here, have some ...!"

"But isn't it dangerous Sidney ... won't it get us into trouble ...?"

"Nah, we're dead anyway, seeing as we haven't got any real bodies it can't do us any harm ...!"

"Wow!" gasped Danny, taking the opium pipe from Sidney Arthur and inhaling strongly.

"What about the youngster, does what applies to us apply to him?" Billy asked, bleakly waiting for Danny to finish so he too could have a toke.

"Tee ... Hee ... No of course not ... he's a real person ... with a real body ... he's going to get into trouble real soon ... Ha ... Ha ... Haaa ...!"

Billy and Danny looked at each other in amazement as they didn't know what Sidney Arthur had found so funny but he did have a peculiar sense of humour.

"So that's what addiction is about, Sidney?" Billy asked after exhaling in his turn. The resultant smoke ring was in the form of his mythical hourglass turning round and round for ever endlessly.

"Yes, addiction to opium I suppose but there's more to addiction than overdoing it on the opium pipes!" Sidney Arthur gasped.

"What do you mean?" Danny asked, not put off by the smoky grain of sand that exploded from Billy's smoke-ring hourglass.

Sidney Arthur smiled, smirked and quickly replied. "There's the addiction to being a complete idiot like you are, Danny. You can't help it I suppose so I'll forgive you but only if you pass me that damn pipe quick . . .!"

As they flew down to steal more "Rudolph's Reminiscing Rum", they looked quickly around the dingy dive. The other opium smokers were a dirty, ruffian-looking lot and it was true; everybody did look like a thief or pirate. As Billy looked on in amazement and Sidney in astonishment, all feeling a warm glow of contentment crawling up their bodies from the tips of their toes to the tops of their ghostly heads, they took in the view. So this was what the opium glow was all about thought Billy, scratching at a ghostly scratch on Danny's peg-leg. He looked down, below them he could see a whole host of people sitting in small groups passing the pipes. They were sitting and crouching on low divans just like them. Some wore neolithic rags of cavemen, some simple cloths of the Celts, some cotton and linen clothes of the Romans, some Norman clothes, some the glorious costume of King Charlie's era and every other time and style in between. The ghosts looked and gasped.

"Sidney . . . How old is he?" Danny asked, pointing below with his peg-leg.

"He's timeless, older than the rest!" Sidney Arthur replied, politely passing Danny the opium pipe.

"How comes they haven't died like us?"

"The opium has pickled them like hard boiled eggs or gherkins . . .!"

"Well isn't this the right thing to do then if you want to live for ever . . .?"

"Maybe . . . if you want to live a pickled half-life that is!"

"*Aaaaah . . .!*" finished Danny, starting to inhale a large toke of the acrid fumes and quietly studying the subdued scene that was taking place under his peg-leg. The ghosts now sat cross-legged on their floating divan and passed each other countless pipes and pondered. It was then Billy suddenly thought of a question.

"Er, Sidney Arthur . . . how many pipes have these people had . . .?"

"Didn't you hear what the old Chin chap said when he opened the door for Sid?"

"What did he say . . .?"

"He said you can only ever have one pipe . . .!" Sidney Arthur exclaimed, finally exhaling and turning around to look at Billy who still wasn't satisfied.

Prodding Sidney Arthur's thin form, he asked, "But some of these people have been here for centuries . . .!"

"That's right ... However ... they're still only ever having one pipe . . .!"

" I get it . . . A pipe that never runs out . . . because it gets refilled whenever it goes out."

"Absolutely correct."

At this point Charlie suddenly got up and Dobbins followed him. Quickly paying for their extra drinks with some psychedelic petals from his bloom bag, Charlie turned to look at Bilal and shouted, "All right, matey, were leaving, can't stand this gloomy place any longer, it's making me forget everything. Even about our great adventure. Stay here until you finish your damn pipe and then join us in Itchycoo Park."

"Yeah, and hurry up!" Dobbins added, quickly kicking BB in the shins as he said so.

"Ouch . . .! Allright. Nearly finished. I'll just finish this pipe and then I'll join you . . .!" BB said half-heartedly, rubbing his shins and smiling weakly.

As Charlie and the Artful Dodger went to the door, the old man bowed to them and said goodbye. As they left, he smiled inscrutably and whispered, "And don't come back until you too learn how to have a single pipe of the dragon's breath . . . Don't come back until you too understand what it's like to really dream."

"Tee . . . Hee . . . Hee . . .!" laughed Sidney Arthur, almost falling off his mid-air divan as Charlie and the Artful Dodger went out of the door.

"So far, so good . . .!" Sidney Arthur whispered and the other two ghosts nodded their heads without understanding. Seeing their confused faces, Sidney Arthur laughed some more. Nothing was serious and being a ghost was great fun as being dead had incredible opportunities that life couldn't offer.

Outside Charlie and the Artful Dodger began to panic.

"Quick let's get him out . . .!" Charlie shouted in desperation, kicking at the door.

"Oh no, the door's been barred . . .!" Dobbins added ineffectually, doing some more of the same.

"We can't get in at all," shouted Charlie, now hammering at the door in desperation.

"Stay out and keep out!" whispered the old man, ignoring their laments. It was at this point that the Artful Dodger began to scream.

"We want Bilal . . . let him out!"

"No one here is a prisoner except of their own design. I am not their jailor, everyone is their own jailor! I am not their worst enemy, they themselves are!" replied the whispering voice from inside the den.

The others stopped hammering on the door and pondered and Charlie decided to ask the obvious, "Well when can he come out then, venerable Chin bloke?"

"When he's finished the single pipe."

"When will that be? We've got an adventure to have," Charlie asked as the other's voice went as whispery as possible.

"All depends, maybe ten minutes, two hours, three weeks, sixteen months, five centuries or a hundred thousand lifetimes . . . it all depends on him!"

"But you're lying, that's smoking millions of pipes!"

"No, my young friend, you misunderstand, there's only ever one pipe and this never goes out!"

With a final, useless kick at the front door, Charlie and Dobbins walked away with a sigh and the Big Wait began. Not having any money left having spent it all at the opium den on drinks, Charlie and the Artful Dodger returned to Itchycoo Park where they conveniently found a refuge under a canopy of giant mystic mushrooms. To Charlie this seemed like a home from home as the two reflected on their situation. Ignoring the manic cries of the distressed winos, they picked some blooms and took turns in prettying up the skies with Charlie's fantasy flintlock. For thirty-five days, they came back at different times to the opium den but no amount of screaming or shouting would allow the barricaded door to open for them and never would BB's face appear. Inside, he was slowly becoming a living ghost like the rest of the clientele and from their floating divan, Danny and Billy looked aghast at the change coming over him. However, Sidney Arthur just shrugged his ghostly shoulders and chuckled, finding something funny that the others couldn't see.

On the thirty-fifth day just after Charlie and the Artful Dodger had left for the umpteenth time Sidney Arthur suddenly flew off the divan, screamed and swooped around the room in ever-expanding circles, tickled Danny under the armpits and whooshed around pulling at Billy's hair. Having got their undivided attention, he motioned them to follow him into the rafters where he chucked their opium pipe in the air, caught it on the tip of his long, thin nose and balancing it with total brilliance, said smilingly, "Right, enough's enough. We better let the lad out, joke over."

"What's happening?" Billy exclaimed exultantly.

Sidney Arthur, remaining upside down, cleared his throat and said, "The time has come to explain to you a little bit about the incredible power of flowers."

"Yeah . . . go on . . .!" went the two other ghosts in perfect unison.

Sidney continued in the clear voice of a schoolteacher. "The humble poppy is an incredible flower. It can heal or enslave and in the case of him below, the latter!"

"How comes we can't get enslaved?" Danny asked, pulling his peg-leg off Billy and standing stock-still to attention.

"That's because we don't have bodies and not having bodies, we can't get sick so smoke up, for us it's fine," Sidney Arthur replied, turning right side up again.

"So, what's *his* problem?" Billy enquired, rapt to attention at this very little piece of information Sidney Arthur was giving them for the first time but he ignored Billy's question and continued explaining.

"He's been living in a single moment of poppy-induced time and hasn't slept or eaten, just smoked and drunk jasmine tea."

"So what?" Danny asked not seeing what Sidney was getting up to.

"Well this has been brilliant for us because I have to tell you a certain thing now . . . we're waiting for someone to turn up with something very special."

"Who, Sidney, who?" both ghosts asked in perfect unison. Sidney Arthur twirled himself a few times upsides down and downsides up before answering.

"Madame Serendipity, bringing her dissolvable hank of magic muslin."

"Oh wow! she's so far-out and extremely venerable we understand but why the hank of dissolvable magic muslin?" Danny asked. Sidney smiled serenely and put his two hands out as if to stop them.

"All things in their proper time, all I can say is that it takes thirty days for her incantations to dry over Malik's magic muslin and in that time we've partied here, smoked all the opium we could get our ghostly hands on. Spent time waiting in a beautifully delicious way and just before Madame Serendipity arrives we're going to see something else that's wonderful."

"And what's that?" two excited Holy Ghosts asked in perfect time with each other.

"Tee ... Hee ... Hee ... the beatnik getting a good kicking. He'll end up paying for the consequences of his own actions, it's called karma."

"Isn't that the stuff that Kid Kurry cooks up?" Danny asked inquisitively, peering anxiously at the other.

"No that's korma, this is karma," Billy replied intelligently, looking rather smug.

"Of course! The karma you are the calmer you get" Danny stated, giving Billy a squashy hug and going right through him. Sidney Arthur simply laughed and pointed below.

"Not in this case boys, just the opposite ... watch."

However, unknown to everyone at this moment in time, a whole squadron of diabolics swarmed in through the skies to settle on the tea house roof opposite the opium den to await the arrival of Captain Kidd aboard the *Greedy Fat Rat* which was only a few miles away and waiting to come and dock at Topping. They would ensure that the hanging, quartering and beheading of the pirate would go on as planned and that nothing would go wrong and as the invisible demons settled themselves, their leader, a major heckle with a sixteen-foot wing span, rubbed the red prongs on his head, shined his pointy teeth and picked at his cloven hooves. Beside him the demons looked very different from each other, the speckles looked like speckles, the heckles like heckles, the vampires very vampish, the afreets like freaks and the bhoots like bewildered bunnies. It was a good thing that they were all invisible for their very sight would frighten the living daylights out of anyone.

Far below in the streets, the leader saw the odd sight of Charlie and the Artful Dodger unsuccessfully kicking the barricaded front door of the opium den. He parted his scarlet lips and gasped. "Sssssssomething unusual there, minor heckle."

"Yes sir, Major Heckle," whimpered the much smaller demon, standing to attention like a good boy scout.

"Take a good look. I think there's something fishy going on there."

"Yes sir, whatever you say."

"I think we should not let them out of our sights, I can feel it in my guts that there's something odd going on!" the Major Heckle reiterated, flapping his large red-black wings for emphasis.

With that, Major Heckle silently motioned for the others to fly down and they all landed in close formation on the street. From high above the rafters of the opium den and very near the broken rooftop, Sidney Arthur could see all this through the holes in the roof and motioning for Billy and Danny to be quiet, he pointed a finger in the direction of the heckles and speckles. These were simply hovering behind the still fuming and kicking Charlie and Dobbins. Inside the house things which had remained in a pickled equilibrium for ages were in actuality changing rather fast. BB, who had been reclining on the divan waiting a full seven minutes for a refill of his pipe, suddenly lost patience and looking blearily around for the ancient proprietor, he suddenly burst into strange song.

"Simple Simon met a Chinman going to the fair,

"Said Simple Simon to the Chinman, let me taste your wares."

The song was rather loud and had its desired effect, within seconds the Chinman was hovering at his side. He then parted his lips to sing in reply.

"Said the venerable Chinman to Simple Simon show me first your penny."

BB scratched his head, looked bewildered and finished the song off with a flourish.

"Said Simple Simon to the Chinman, I haven't gotten any!"

"No money?" the venerable ancient asked, coming very close to BB and looking most peeved. BB tweaked at his nose first before replying.

"Yes, but I've been paying you in psychedelic blooms from my fantasy flintlock haven't I?"

"Yes, but your fantasy flintlock's stopped firing petals days ago, this isn't funny. This isn't a social service, it's a sodding private enterprise. You have to pay or you will surely pay!" replied the old man lifting his arms up aggressively.

BB was gobsmacked and even more so when suddenly the old man started beating him with the rubber end of a long hookah. The other smokers of the dragon's breath barely glanced up and carried on smoking their never-ending pipes as if nothing had happened. As the lad rolled around the floor uselessly trying to ward off the other's powerful blows, the three ghosts burst into giggles and held each other's sides and mouths so as not to give the game away. Quickly turning to the others, Sidney Arthur rapidly explained.

"Tee Hee ... Hee ... demons on the outside wanting to come in with Charlie and Dobbins. The beatnik wanting to get out but not being able to leave until he pays his bill and us hiding from the demons so as not to give away the plot and still waiting for Madame Serendipity to arrive to sort us all out!"

"What shall we do, Sidney?" Billy asked, unable to watch any more of the kicking. Sidney Arthur snapped to attention and smartly took the lead.

"Quick, unbarricade the front door but don't let the heckles and speckles see you."

"Then what?" Danny asked.

"Come straight back here and from the rafters we will discreetly watch the whole tamasha!" Sidney Arthur replied with a string of daisies and daffodils starting to stream out from his crumbling buttonhole.

"What's a tamasha, Sidney?" Billy asked, turning quickly in the air and getting ready to race down towards the door. Sidney Arthur smiled and buffed his fingernails on his ghostly jacket before replying.

"That's a Zindian word that means 'show'!"

"You're so clever!" Billy gasped.

"And you're so slow. Quick, hurry up and unbarricade the front door."

Danny and Billy immediately swooped down to do Sidney Arthur's bidding and the wooden bar was lifted in a flash of ghostly fingers and the door to the opium den finally opened after thirty days of patient waiting.

Charlie and Dobbins strode in like time bandits and the lanky one's Kockneestani gob shouted, "Oi Venerable Chinman, stop kicking him!"

"Why, it's the lanky flower-power man! So you finally got inside but you still have to abide by my rules," the other replied, ignoring Charlie's instructions completely.

"Nonsense old man, we've come to get our mate!"

"Teee . . . Hee . . . Hee . . .!" laughed Sidney Arthur from the rafters watching the magic below with undisguised glee.

"Hooo . . . Hooo . . .!" chuckled Billy, racing back to be next to Sidney Arthur.

"Ha . . . Ha . . .!" tittered Danny, scratching at an invisible itch as usual.

"Bilal get up. We've come to help you to escape, our adventure is going nowhere without you," Charlie said, seriously looking at the groaning mess on the floor.

"Yeah everyone's equal and part of the plot and so everything needs to be free," Dobbins finished with a smile and a sigh.

"Do you know how long you've been here?" Charlie suddenly asked, angrily pulling his pal up off the floor by the scruff of his Banglastani beatnik neck.

"Only came here this morning, what's the fuss?" he replied, eyes still bleary and full of dream.

From the rafters the three ghosts laughed quietly as the entering ghostly heckles and speckles, afreets and bhoots angrily awaited their turn, they had the silly billies in their sights and wouldn't let go.

"All right. What does he owe?" asked Dobbins.

"He can't come out until he pays me what he owes and it's a lot. One golden coin for each day that's he's been here!" the venerable Chinman replied, raising his left eyebrow right off the top of his irritated face.

"Ouch . . . ouch . . . please don't kick. I'm sorry! Thank you for not thrashing me too hard . . . ouch . . . ouch!" BB whimpered as Charlie scratched his head and thought for a while before replying.

"Well, we don't have that kind of money."

"What will we do?" Dobbins added, taking a pocket watch from out of his top hat and checking the time. The Chinman looked at both of them acutely before answering.

"Easy, he will have to pay me in kind!"

"And how?" Charlie asked behind a haze of ever-expanding smoke.

The Chinman stamped his little feet and said, "By going to the kitchens and washing up 3619 tar and yuk-embedded opium pipes. These have needed washing for the last seven hundred-odd years but I've just not got around to doing it."

"Oh no but an opium pipe's really difficult to clean. How can I do it?" BB squealed, getting up to his feet and slapping himself around the face a good few times to try and awaken himself out of his stupor.

"Tee Heee Hee!" Sidney Arthur chuckled to himself discreetly, somewhere high and unobserved up in the rafters as BB tugged at his purple kurta and asked the others, "Will you help me, mates?"

"No way! You got yourself into this problem, get yourself out!" Charlie replied, angrily turning his back on his friend.

"Yeah, tough love, we're going out and will be waiting for you in Itchycoo Park," Dobbins added. Seeing Charlie and Dobbins leave angrily, the squadron of demonic heckles and speckles rushed to follow them out.

"Tee . . . Hee . . . Hee . . .!" laughed Sidney Arthur, softly motioning the other two Holy Ghosts to come silently down. Meanwhile, the venerable Chinman was pointing with a shaking finger towards the kitchen door.

"You'll find the scourer, the soap and the hot water in the kitchen along with all the dirty pipes, now go!" he finished nastily. The beatnik asked quickly, "But why 3619 opium pipes venerable sir?"

Smiling under his bamboo hat for the first time, the ancient Chinman turned to him direct and said. "That's the amount of lifetimes you've been addicted to the dragon's breath, now go and cure yourself once and for ever!"

Bilal was in luck, however, because when he had his arms deep in the soapy water the invisible ghosts, at a prompting from Sidney, whooshed around in the kitchen in a blinding flurry of incalculable speed and did all the washing-up in sixteen minutes flat. The beatnik was pleasantly stunned but not as much as the Hu Chi who thought it would have taken a few weeks at least, whereas only minutes later he'd returned to the bewildering sight of 3619 clean pipes.

BB said happily, "Done them, venerable sir. Can I go . . . sorry . . . please . . . thank you . . . I'll never do this again!"

"All right, just make sure I never see you inside this place in this lifetime or the next!" chuckled the Chinman, pointing towards the door.

"Yippee! Free!"

"Back to the rooftops, boys ... Tee Hee Hee ... now watch." Sidney Arthur giggled, waiting expectantly for the next act in the melodrama.

As BB quickly ran off to join his mates, he started to feel a wave of nausea. He was starting to get sick as he felt the absence of the pipe. Starting to sweat like a pig near a skillet and shivering from the inside, his knees buckled and he fell onto the ground groaning and moaning and clutching his stomach.

Luckily, this was at the entrance of Itchycoo Park and he was seen by Charlie and Dobbins who ran to his aid before asking solicitously. "What's up, man?" Charlie asked in a voice dripping with compassion.

"Yeah, you look in a terrible state, bruv!" Dobbins added, a dangerous twinkle in his eyes.

"Groan ... moan ... don't feel so well."

"Are you in pain?" Charlie asked again kindly.

"Yeah ... Mmmm ...!"

"Where does it hurt?"

"Groan ... All over," Sid finished, starting to sob.

And then, quickly looking at each other with a manic glint in their eyes, the Artful Dodger and Charlie pulled up their trousers and sleeves and jumped all over Bilal's sobbing body, already pulverised by Hu Chi.

"Ouch ... ouch ... ouch ...!"

"Will you ever do it again? Make us waste a whole month!" Charlie exclaimed as he jumped up and down like a clown on a trampoline.

"No ... no ... never ... I promise ... Ouch ...!"

"Are you sure?" Dobbins reiterated, slapping BB around his face.

"Yes ... Sorry ... Please ... never again."

"All right we can stop now, let him go!" Charlie said after seven and a half minutes, finally bouncing off the battered beatnik.

BB gasped and gasped, rubbed his spectacles and muttered so quietly that the others couldn't hear, "Never again, until the next time."

Unaware of the demons laughing at them twelve foot above their heads, the three staggered off inside the park and lay down. Offered a swig of "Rudolph's Reminiscing Rum" which he refused with an involuntary shudder, BB curled up in the foetal position and tried to sleep. The many, varied ghostly demons then took up their positions on the branches of the giant yew tree while completely unobserved by all on the roof of the opium den a quarter of a mile away, the Holy Ghosts tittered and cracked open some bottles of Astral Ale.

"Tee ... Heee ... Hee ... absolutely fantastic, Perfect Karma Korma!"

"Why are you chuckling, Sidney Arthur?" Billy asked as he swallowed the ale in one single inexplicable gulp.

"Because finally he got his come-uppance and what a downer too! Wonderful Karma Korma too!"

"What do we do now, Sidney?" Billy asked again, cracking open another bottle with his ghostly teeth.

"Give me your mystical hourglass, Billy and I'll tell you."

Giving the hourglass a goodly shake Sidney Arthur pursed his lips and exclaimed excitedly while turning it upside down and round and round very fast.

"Yup ... the time's right ... she should be appearing any moment now."

And in an instant another ghostly form arrived.

"Ah Madame Serendipity! You got here after all," Sidney Arthur said, politely offering his ghostly hand to the shimmering new arrival.

"Hope I wasn't late but the incantations took some time to dry," Madame Serendipity laughed, breathless and excited.

"Perfect, just on time!"

As the ghosts shifted up their own bottoms to allow an ample fourth one to sit down, they all smiled at seeing Madame Serendipity's fluster. The round, rosy-cheeked glow was still there but the white hair in a bun was looking askew. In one hand she held her Tapestry of Alternative Endings and in the other, the dissolvable hangman's noose. Sidney Arthur laughed to himself as he saw his plans falling into place. Opening another bottle of the delicious Astral Ale and passing it to Madame Serendipity with a smile, he tilted his head back and giggled dementedly. Laughter of course, as even the children knew, was always the very first language *and* the second Holy Rule. At Itchycoo Park the ghostly ones laughed and chuckled as they got drunk and spied on Lucifer's ghostly demons who were spying on Charlie, Dobbins and BB. Yes, everything was going perfectly to plan.

20

A Pool of Tears

THE LAND OF the Living Dreamtime was looking ace. Although it was the highest level of the Lost Catacombs, it was no less important than the Torrible Zone or the Lands of the Living and Awakening Dreamtimes. Above everyone's heads in the cobbled streets of Brickie Lane, the sounds of rickshaws and bicycles could still be heard clanking up and down the street like Danny De Foe and his peg-leg. At the Magical Muncherie a gaggle of people were sitting around the giant flat-top stones that served as tables, on smaller menhir-shaped stones that served as seats. The whole of the Funkadelic tribe was there (minus Dobbins, of course) and were running between the tables causing mayhem and madness. The White Rabbit was there, with monocle, continuously dragging out the pocket-watch from his tartan waistcoat and checking the time just in case it was time to move on.

Meanwhile, Nasseruddin the Nutty and Hussain the Insane had entered into their usual spirit of freewheeling anarchy. Being the silliest of the whole lot and truly certified fools, they were ignoring the shenanigans of the sensible others and were having a pillow fight. Soft white duck's feathers flew from the tattered pillows as Nasseruddin's huge head got stuck deep inside one pillow while his lapis lazuli teeth tried to bite their way out of ever-increasing trouble. His nose was trying to knife its way through the pillow while his rubber flip-flops flapped mercilessly in the air as his feet dangled precariously way above his ears. As Hussain the Insane continued thumping Nasseruddin with a feathery flash of torn pillows, his turban came off his head and his green eyes slowly turned red. His open idiot's face was laughing like crazy and it was obvious that he was having the time of his life. Others would smoke and talk about serious things like the rising weight of air and the increasing cost of thermal socks but the Zoofis never did, they just liked pillow fights that nobody ever won.

On a quick three-second fight break, Hussain asked Nasseruddin with a grin, "By the dreadlocks of St Stan, why's everyone looking so serious?"

"I dunno, they seem to take everything much too glumly."

"No I've got another idea, maybe it's something to do with the River Alph!" Hussain exclaimed with a quick smirk, refilling his torn pillow with a stash of feathers lying at his feet.

"What do you mean?"

"Well, the Pool of Laughter and Forgettting must be drying up if everyone's looking so damn serious about everything?"

"You must be right."

"Why don't we try and put some magic spells on the River Alph and make it flow even more? That way there will end up being more water in the Pool of Laughter and Forgetting and all these glum-heads around us will cheer up."

Nasseruddin pondered a while before replying. "What a good idea, let's do it!

The Pool of Laughter and Forgetting was about thirty yards away from the Magical Muncherie and Hussain and Nasseruddin sat opposite each other cross-legged at the edge of the pool.

"Know anything to make things overflow, Nasseruddin?" Hussain whistled, starting to get lost in his reflection in the pool.

"Yeah, something I learnt as a kid," replied Nasseruddin tugging at his eyebrow for ideas.

Suddenly, looking intensely at the waters and scratching his head, Nasseruddin saw his reflection. Seeing his lapis lazuli teeth shine in the reflected water, the idiot tried greedily snatching the jewels out of the water before a slap from Hussain the Insane chastened him. Rubbing his hands he quickly watched the smoke disappear between his fragile fingers before muttering an invocation into the still waters of the dark and silent pool.

"Sparkling blue, sparkling white,
Waters of the River Alph, totally out of sight.
How is laughter ever to grow with the incident at Dishapur,
  we do not yet know?
Nor twiglets made in sunny Kashtent.
Or summery apples in the groves of Kamershand.

Or multiple meanings from crazy comic books from
Dazakhstan.
Or opened umbrellas under the seas somewhere from
Moozbekistan.
Sparkling blue and sparkling white.
Waters of the magic pool, don't give us a fright.
Open up and make them grin some more.
It's only me and Hussain who're opening the door.
Kerflash ... Kerflosh ... Kaboom ...!"

And then nothing happened or so it seemed. They sat there trying to pull each other's ears off when suddenly children flying a kite screamed.

"Oh no ... the Pool of Laughter and Forgetting's drying up!"

Hussain and Nasseruddin stood up and quickly noticed that what the children shouted was completely true. The pool was sinking and drying up and the very atmosphere in the Magical Muncherie was getting more serious by the second. In fact, the whole of the Land of the Living Dreamtime had been affected and everyone was beginning to look glum.

Pulling at his front teeth for ideas, Nasseruddin punched himself in the ears and muttered, "Oh no wrong damn invocation. Should have been the other way around!"

"You always mix things up, you fool!" Hussain said angrily stomping up and down on the ground.

"Yeah, but they usually turn out okay!"

"What shall we do? Look, the whole of the River Alph is drying up."

"Now there won't be any air turning to water and water turning to air, we'll all be suffocated!" Nasseruddin shrieked.

"All your fault ... Boo ... Hooo ... Hoooo ...!" Hussain said quickly starting to cry.

"Booo ... Hoo ... Hooo ...!" Nasseruddin burst into tears thumping his chest.

And as everyone watched, amazed, Nasseruddin and Hussain, completely out of humour now the Pool of Laughter and Forgetting had disappeared, burst into tears inconsolably, flopping each other's heads on each other's shoulders and very soon their tears covered the whole floor because once the Pool of Laughter and Forgetting was overflowing, it always changed into the Well of

Never-Ending Tears. As the Whirlistanis and witches rose into the air the whole place filled with tears more abundant than the waters of the River Alph and the Pool of Laughter and Forgetting had ever been. Everyone stood there spellbound.

"Watch the waters!" Little Lucy cried, suddenly materialising a cloud and disappearing up into the air.

"Help, I can't swim!" screamed the Genie of the Lamp as its golden receptacle floated crazily up and down in the tearful flow.

"The water's up to my knees now!" shrieked Amrita as the mirrors on her sequinned gypsy dress turned back to front out of fear.

"Oh no, the water tastes salty!" Stargasm shrieked as she fell off her spinning broomstick and crashed into the murky waters.

"Oh dear, what shall we do?" Astral Alice sighed. By now she was waist-high in the water.

"Stop Nasseruddin and Hussain crying for a start!" shouted Mullah Ullah clambering off a stony table top to be with his floating magic prayer-mat and out of harm's way.

"Stop crying or you'll drown us all!" Moonmummy shouted above the crazy hullabaloo and for a change the two idiots decided to listen.

"What shall we do now?" Alice pondered aloud as the swirling waters carried her around and around.

"What you've got to do, you've got to keep running around in circles until you get dry!" said the White Rabbit, "who dries first, wins."

Those that could fly on broomsticks, cloud-boards, flying pigs, magic prayer-mats and snowcamels simply did so and the others raced, swam, grooved, moved anyhow they could and span and span and span in ever tightening circles to dry themselves. Watching this show from the safety of his rock, the White Rabbit pondered on the abstruse ridiculousness of life itself. It was little wonder that Nasseruddin and Hussain who were racing around the top of the many running forms on their cloud-board and snowcamel were actually insane. Being insane, thought the White Rabbit, pulling at its tartan waistcoat, saved a lot of effort and energy in not having to pretend that one was sensible. The mad often ruled the earth and usually made very good kings and queens. And they certainly ruled the heavens.

"Look at the loonies, see how crazy they are!" Stargasm yelled as she span fast around in her zooming broomstick.

"Yeah but the loonies aren't as bad as the stupid and the ignorant!" Moonmummy proclaimed, whizzing around next to her and chuckling.

"Why not?" Stargasm shrieked, waving her wand over everything she passed and wishing everyone a long and happy life.

Getting her wand out too and sparkling the atmosphere with holy dust, Moonmummy stated, "Because stupidity and ignorance are contagious diseases and have done more to damage this world than simple madness ever has done!"

"Yeah, you're right, madness isn't contagious, only stupidity and ignorance are."

The White Rabbit looked carefully around and saw that it was definitely getting drier. Everyone was spinning around so fast, droplets of water came off the ground and off the racers and splashed back into the once empty Well of Never-Ending Tears which was also being filled up with Nasseruddin's and Hussain's plentiful tears and turning slowly back into the Pool of Laughter and Forgetting.

Everyone was completely dry now. They'd been running around in circles for a good few hours and all the water had come off their bodies and fallen back into the Pool of Never-Ending Tears, and as the ground dried up around them, they cheered and screamed.

The White Rabbit beckoned to Seashell Sally to join him and whispered something in her ear as all eyes now focussed on her. "You've all won," she announced, "and you'll all get a prize!"

At her feet, Habiba the Beloved's many younger brothers still sat on the ground proffering the finest flowers of the universe to her. She, of course, was singing inexplicable, silent love songs to each and every one in an individual language that only they could know. As Sally's distant eyes scanned the horizon, there, beyond her gaze, Abdul sat meditating in a cave on Danny De Foe's desert isle and with his inner eye he saw Sally waiting for him on the far side of the distant world. Quickly picking up a handful of cosmic seashells, he skimmed them one after the other towards her. Water is water and all the seas are but a single drop and so, within seconds flat, his magic wishes materialised in front of Seashell Sally's bright eyes. Grabbing them one by one with her dainty fingers, she soon had enough prizes for everyone, including herself. Bouncing happily up to a very relieved Astral Alice, Sally showered her with seashells. Almost drowning in this seashell affection, Alice brushed herself off and daintily started giving a seashell to every being there: one-footed, two-footed, three-hooved, five-fingered, six-toed, one-tailed, furry, hairy, bald, bony, whatever. Dylan shouted at Seashell Sally and the Forty Hashemites to sing a love song.

"You are all so clearly in love with each other, please sing us a song!"

"A song . . . a song . . .!" cheered half the crowd.

"We want a song!" roared the rest.

Seashell Sally and the brothers chucked their seashells into the air, watched with bewildered eyes as the air turned to water and back into water turning to air as it refracted and reflected off their cosmic seashells and twinkled and sparkled like dancing dragonflies. The Hashemites all got back to their silent crooning and tender love-gazing and then jumped up onto both feet and back-flipped on top of each other's shoulders until they formed an incredible totem pole forty beings high. Grinning and laughing, this giant form turned to the diminutive Seashell Sally and sang out in one clear unified voice as Dylan strummed the perfect chordal accompliment.

"I Love. You Love. We Love.
If We Love then where have
You and I gone?"

"Far out!" Nasseruddin squealed, and Hussain the Insane crawled closer to get a better look. Perfectly understanding the philosophical sentiment of the Hashemites' chorus, Seashell Sally rubbed the rosy glow off her cheeks, smiled at her lovers and then sung the perfect chorus.

"In Love no longer do 'you' and 'I' exist
For self has passed away in the Beloved."

In the mystic silence that accompanied her immaculate chorus, everything hip-hip-hurrahed and ran around screaming. The overwhelming aura of dryness and bewildering gladness grabbed everyone by the scruff of their necks and they all went around hugging and kissing each other indiscriminately. The cosmic love song had released all tensions and silly inhibitions fell away like yesterday's smelly socks. As each being fell in love with the next and shared everlasting gobstoppers and lickspittle liquorices with abandon, the children crept away to one side of the growing maelstrom and sucking on some lollipops Little Lucy had found growing on some twangum bushes, they licked the laughter right off their funny faces and sat down to watch the party.

"What was all that about then?" Lucy asked, sitting cross-legged and pondering.

"I've got no idea," Astral Alice replied in between long licks of her luscious lollipop.

Turning to Princess Amrita, Lucy asked again. "Do you know anything, Amrita? You're usually so very clever!"

"No, I don't think I know anything either at all."

"Adults are so funny, I think they're funnier than the crazy furry creatures running around this wonderful place," Alice exclaimed in a burp.

"I know, we all won and nobody lost!" Lucy laughed, almost choking on a hazelnut surprise that she had stolen from Alice's stash when she hadn't been looking.

"Isn't that just a simply wonderful way of looking at things?" Alice giggled.

"No it's more than that, it's actually true!" Lucy insisted, now stealing some chestnuts from right under Alice's nose.

"What really matters is how you run the race. This is the thing that really counts."

"Amrita, you really are the brightest little brat of your age!"

Lucy, who was getting ready to board her passing fluffy white cloud again, listened to Alice.

"Most things in life don't matter much and the rest don't matter at all."

All was as it should be and suddenly looking at his pocket watch, the White Rabbit stamped his feet and yelled above the cantankerous din.

"Time for another!"

21

Fort Cox

Lucifer was in a bummer of a mood as he got up from his throne, flapped his wings and grasped the prongs on top of his scarlet head. With his cloven feet he kicked a few minor speckles and heckles out of the way and helped himself to his favourite tipple, vampire's blood, and woe betide anyone who stopped him. Peering into the purple mist of the All-Seeing Crystal Ball, he yelled and roared for more until three Time-Balls were put in front of him, hovering in mid-air through the dark power of his magic. In the first ball he could see his forces following the musicians as they made their way to Pharaoh Funkanathen's palace in Kayro and in the second he could see his forces waiting for the return of the *Greedy Fat Rat* to Topping where Captain Kidd was to be hung, drawn and quartered and both scenes were fine and living up to his expectation. It was the third ball that was causing the red-pronged one so much trouble as Lucifer could clearly see into the Lost Catacombs of Brickie Lane where, in the Chamber of Blissful Echoes, the sisters Nazneen were in excited discussion with Stargasm and Moonmummy and everything they said could plainly be heard.

"To find the Magic Mantras!" Ayesha wailed as her belly-dancer's stomach wobbled with excitement.

"Where shall we look? Hoggaristan was a bad idea after all, we didn't find anything but demons!" Stargasm said as the smoke in Lucifer's ball got even smokier and disguised much of the subsequent conversation.

"Oh, I reckon we should head for Zindia," Moonmummy added as her eyes shot everyone a wicked look. Lucifer bit his lips and studied this scene with both interest and resentment.

Then it was Ambrin's turn to speak and from within her translucent Hypno-Tantric Hijab she said, "There's so much those diabolics can teach us that I reckon the Magic Mantras are with them but they don't know." Hearing this Lucifer snarled and snorted pure fire from his nostrils. Then in a much deeper voice Najma made some excited conclusions.

"Lets go to the Khumb Mela held at the confluence of the many holy rivers, it's such a wicked festival and always full of left-handed gooks and demons. We're bound to find the Magic Mantras there."

"Brilliant idea!" Everyone agreed and poured themselves more cups of jasmine tea. And then as quickly as it had arisen, the smoky visions in the crystal ball faded and Lucifer was left mulling and pulling at his beard. Without losing any more time he threw his Time-Balls away and concentrated on the All-Seeing Ball. Quickly conjuring up the visions of the demons he wanted to see, he raised himself to his full height and snarled into the ball.

"Calling all Thuggees! Calling all Thuggees! Prepare yourselves for action – Go to the Khumb Mela and catch these irritating women. They must be eliminated, never to find out these mantras!"

With that he finished his rant and returned to the throne in a marginally better mood because the good guys and gals had been busted again and would be made to pay and pay as darkness has its day.

22

The Sisters go to Khumb Mela

THE SISTERS NAZNEEN and the two Wicked White Witches of the West were on their way to the incredible Khumb Mela where they hoped to find the three Magic Mantras. They had left Pearly Green at daybreak and were now flying over Europa at mid-afternoon and simply following the sun and their not inconsiderable instincts towards the east. It was, in fact, a very easy journey to plan as all they would have to do is to follow the rising sun and enjoy the ride. At the front rode Stargasm, her hair flowing in the wind. Behind her came Moonmummy, revving up her broomstick with kicks from her black leather boots. Behind the witches came Ayesha on her psychedelic flying pig with her sweet smiling face gritting its teeth in the chill wind. Only a few feet behind her came Ambrin, a quizzical look on her handsome face and last was Najma whose flying pig was definitely the slowest. Her ebony eyes stared excitedly at the beauty of the passing world and her oval face beamed down at all the pretty creatures that flew underneath her.

The fantastic five flew on as morning gave way to late afternoon and the Man on the Moon looked out at the passing weird sisters, smiled, strummed a chord of connectivity on his cosmic hurdy-gurdy and furiously shook his harlequin's hat. Golden bits of yesterday's suns and cut-up bits of old full moons twinkled down into the dreamscape to help guide them on.

"Where are we now?" Moonmummy asked, racing forward to be next to Stargasm.

"Somewhere beyond the Alps, I think," Stargasm replied as the cool snowy wind whipped at her icicle ridden face.

"And which way do we head now?"

"We just keep going east. Keep heading for the sun and the warmer air," Stargasm suggested.

"Watch out for clear air turbulence, it might blow you off your broomstick," Moonmummy replied.

"Quick ... give me an idea of how we're going to get to Zindia ...!"

Scattering a handful of sooth-saying sea slugs Stargasm pursed her lips before replying. "All right ... first we get past Europa ... Then we head towards Durkey ..."

"And then after Durkey we've got a choice, depending on the prevailing winds," Moonmummy suggested, watching the sooth-saying sea slugs spiral merrily to the ground.

Stargasm's face looked austere as she replied. "Yeah, we could go one of two ways."

"What's the first?"

"The first is that after Durkey we head towards Merzia. From Merzia to Darkistan and from there into Zindia."

"That would be great wouldn't it, Ambrin? We could drop off at home in Darkistan and see our great-grandmother," Ayesha said as the three Sisters Nazneen whizzed up from behind to hear what the two witches were on about.

Stargasm shook her head as she quickly replied. "No time for that I'm afraid, we're on a mission and we don't stop until we get to the Khumb Mela ...!"

"How long will it take to get there?" Ambrin asked.

"At the rate were going another eighteen days!"

"And what's the second route ...?" Najma asked, prodding her portly pig up close to Stargasm's broomstick.

The witch replied excitedly. "Oh, instead of going to Merzia, we go straight to central Asia. Past Kashtent and Kamershand, up through the Zindu Push and down again into the Vale of Zashmir from which it's an easy journey to the Khumb Mela ...!"

"Far out, weird sister!" Najma exclaimed laughingly and the fantastic five flew on.

Having taken all their food and water with them in giant jute sacks tied to the backs of the flying pigs, the weird sisters didn't need to make any stops. They were on a mission from St Stan and needed to get to the Khumb Mela as quickly as possible. The future of Pearly Green and the Idiot's Path depended on finding the three Magic Mantras quickly.

As they flew on, Stargasm kicked her broomstick to go faster and pondered as, cruising backwards to be closer to Moonmummy, she shrieked into the hollering wind "Ah, tell me sister, why are we chasing the Magic Mantras only where the bad guys live?"

Moonmummy replied, "Because we've already searched our own domain and not found them."

Ayesha raced her pig to be close to the witches again and shouted in the fleeting wind. "And also having looked for them and not found them in the lands of happiness . . . where else could they be but in the lands of desolation and freakdom . . .?"

Racing up from behind them, an ecstatic Ambrin added, "And it is also good to know the opposite. Where would night be without day? Where would an egg be without a spoon, a melody without a tune. Where would man be without a woman?"

"Hopelessly lost. Tee . . . Hee . . . Heee . . .!" Najma tittered, her eyes laughing hard.

"All philosophies, whatever they are, have the 'other' and without understanding the presence and importance of the 'other', one's knowledge is essentially obscure and incomplete," Stargasm added, turning round to face the others who'd stopped in mid-air. They were hovering above some pretty green fields and chocolate-box houses.

Moonmummy then poked Stargasm in the stomach and gently asked, "Does that mean that with that philosophy you could go looking for the sun deep inside a mine?"

"Or a twinklefish swimming up towards the sun?" Ambrin asked, almost wobbling off her hovering pig.

Stargasm scratched her head and then replied emphatically, "Exactly!"

"All opposites finally cancel each other out and that's why the Baddies must know what the Magic Mantras are because we're the good guys and we don't," Moonmummy said with a look of strong determination.

Ayesha whizzed around the group on her fast-flying pig and daintily replied, "And without knowing them we will never be fully able to understand the Idiot's Path!"

"Or the link between enlightenment and entitlement!" Ambrin added with a growing grin as a sudden gust of wind made her almost disappear underneath her billowing, translucent, Hypno-Tantric Hijab.

"What a load of dobb!" Najma finished, starting to feed her pig on a handful of transcendental turnips from under her voluminous folds.

"Yes, let's fly on in silence, no one seems to be making any sense," Stargasm replied, shooting off towards the front.

They did and headed south east for the land of Durkey where the Whirlistanis came from, a little spinning, whirling city called Conya to be exact. As they passed overhead, the tiny cobbled streets of Conya sparkled in the sun and they saw the golden domes of countless mosques twinkle a merry greeting to them from down below. Ayesha who had saved some of the Man on the Moon's cut-ups of yesterday suns and silvery bits of old full moons, sprinkled them excitedly onto the holy city and things began to change.

"Isn't this where Mevlana, Nasseruddin and Suleiman are from?" Ayesha yelled into the wind as Conya shimmered below their dainty feet.

"Yes, that's their sacred mosque, the one over there!" Ambrin said, pointing down towards the golden vision.

"Which one?" Najma bleated from the back, plodding along merrily.

"That one, silly, the one spinning around!" Ayesha shouted quickly pointing her pig towards a spinning golden dome.

As they looked down from two hundred foot up in the air, they could see a gigantic mosque spinning round and round with hundreds of red-fezzed Whirlistanis serenely spinning around its perimeter anti-clockwise and probably turning time backwards too.

"What are they doing?" Stargasm asked, totally entranced by the shimmering image below.

"Expansion and contraction, they're making up the universe, destroying it and then making up another one, ad infinitum, their dance is the way of the universe!" Ayesha said.

"Wow! It's so far out!" Moonmummy gasped holding tightly onto her broomstick as it decided to spin anti-clockwise of its own accord.

"All well and good but the Whirlistanis we know come from four hundred years ago ... what we see is now. What about seeing the when?" Stargasm whistled, looking below.

"Don't be silly, the mosque we see below is dedicated to Rumi," Ayesha said expectantly, seeming to know the score.

"Who's Rumi?" Ambrin replied, gracefully gliding through the air.

"Ain't you heard of 'Reminiscences of Rumi'?" Najma said,

lovingly patting her pet pig and munching on a crunchy banana she'd saved for a special occasion.

"No, that's Rudolph's Reminiscing Rumi'!" Ayesha said, flashing a disdainful look at her sister.

"No, that's rum, silly, this is Rumi!" Ambrin chuckled, watching her silly sisters bicker.

Najma scratched her nose, pondered a while and then replied. "Oh I didn't know that, I'm not very educated. I never went to school."

"Hmmm ... that I can see," Ayesha said. Wriggling her large belly she folded her hands as if in prayer and continued. "Well, Rumi is another name for Mevlana."

"What, you mean our Mevlana, the one who always smells of the attar of roses?" Ambrin replied, rather surprised.

"The very same! He's a great writer, you know!" Ayesha continued, looking rather sagacious.

"What does he write? It's a pity I can't read," Najma interjected in a hurry, moving her pig to be closer to Ayesha.

Ayesha smirked, tried to look intelligent and took her time before replying. "He was the best writer of all."

"Go on, what did he write?" Ambrin asked.

"He righted wrongs and anyone who does that is the best righter of all!" Ayesha finished, pulling Ambrin's nose for fun and chuckling aloud.

Very soon, Conya was left behind as they continued chasing the golden sun across the fantastic dreamscapes of their collective imagination.

Moonmummy turned around quickly to her left and asked abruptly, "Stargasm ... which way are we going to go?"

"Merzia or Central Asia? We have to decide now because destiny is forking our path into two!"

Suddenly, in front of Stargasm's bewildered face, the same, single, solitary grey crapping pigeon of Whiteapple, being chased by a flock of hungry fantasy falcons, panted past her eyes and raced off towards the north east ineffectually trying to hide inside a mass of passing fluffy white clouds. Stargasm straightened her gown and quickly said, "The pigeon's told us ... We go north-east!"

"That journey goes through Central Asia, Kashtent and Kamershand," Moonmummy quickly added, turning her broomstick the right way and laughing.

"Ah Booo ... I wanted to see great-granny," Ayesha cried, obviously preferring to have gone the other way.

"Don't worry, there will always be another time for Darkistan," Stargasm replied, shooting off way up front.

They raced on through the heart of Central Asia and the days flew by as fast as free-falling feathers. Day followed night followed day followed Najma followed Ambrin followed Ayesha followed Moonmummy followed Stargasm, all having a wonderful time.

Kashtent seemed to be full of surprises, the people fasted all the time thinking it was Lent and had an extra three hours in a day which meant that they could always wake up late, get to work later and leave work earlier than anyone else. From up in the skies, Kashtent seemed to be a very happy place indeed and Najma smiled to herself and patted a pretty pink flamingo on its head seeing the peoples of the happy land scurry around like crazy ants, delirious and excited to have another wonderful day alive in this, the best of all possible worlds. And then they passed Kamershand, the land of Omar Khayyam, the incredible poet, drunk on his own creations. This was a land where wine flowed in the many rivers but nobody got drunk except on creation itself. Summer never ended here and Moonmummy could clearly see the never-ending summer groves many hundreds of feet below. This was a place where Abraxas scrumped apples with Mullah Ullah sometime in the netherworld of their youth. In Kamershand too, the domes of the multiple mosques shone golden and the inlaid Merzian calligraphy in damask blue sparkled up into the air like the crystal clear waters of the Aral Sea.

Moonmummy had never been to the east before, well not east of Pearly Green anyway, and she revelled in the glorious beauty of it all. Soon, they found themselves in the mountains where Stargasm thought she could see Lord Shiva's dreadlocks become the source of mighty rivers that flowed from the mountain tops to Zindia and Chin.

"Quick ... Don't lose that pigeon!" Ayesha shouted at Stargasm who seemed to be losing her concentration.

"Where are we going now?" Ambrin asked from just behind, holding tightly onto her pig in the biting air.

"We're going to the Vale of Zashmir, Heaven on Earth," Stargasm replied with a strange, contented look.

They flew on and on and on and as the mountains gave way to the Vale of Zashmir, Ayesha smiled and screamed in a high treble, seeing the beautiful valleys below. All around she could hear the wicked strains of a mournful santoor being played. The hammered notes vibrated in her cells and shuddered with ecstasy. Her flying pig was simply loving it too. It twitched its curly tail to better hear the mournful strains. Ayesha could see a long stream of semi-naked yogis and yoginis traversing the glaciers to get to the sacred sites and as they all passed the beautiful Nagin lake, she was sure she could hear a shenai playing the Nagin, the snake-charmer's unforgettably melodious tune. She rushed up to circle Ambrin and Najma and poke them with her fingers to ensure that they heard these magical strains too. As they listened, they intuitively understood the inherent joy and sadness of the mystery of all creation and somewhere deep inside their wombs, the rising snake of kundalini spiralled up their individual bodies to unity in the Thousand-Petalled Lotus.

"Quick ... Look ... a lotus!" Ambrin screamed, feeling a delicious nectar filling her body.

"Where?" Najma asked excitedly, looking everywhere.

"It's somewhere floating down on Nagin Lake!" Ambrin yelled, pointing to the lake many feet below.

"No ... that's just a lotus ... the real one is somewhere just above my head!" smiled Ayesha with an inexplicable look of cosmic unification on her beautiful brow.

"Oi! ... Stop tripping out, we're here on funny business!" Stargasm ordered imperiously from the front, pointing onwards.

"Where are we going now then?" Moonmummy asked quickly, right behind her.

"South, I think, that's where the pigeon's going ...!"

"Yippee ... It's the plains of Zindia!" yelled the Sisters Nazneen, raising their fists into the air and hollering like children on holiday.

"Yippee ... we're almost there," Stargasm added, equally excited and crazy with anticipation.

Finding the Khumb Mela was easy. They would just have to find the confluence of the three holy rivers and sniff out the stench of ten million people all partying in the names of ten thousand gods.

After a few more hours, as the sun was setting on their twenty-first day of non-stop travel, they finally saw it.

"There it is!" Ayesha yelled.

"The Khumb Mela, wow!" Ambrin added, so excited she almost wet her pants.

Looking at the incredible size of the crowds below Najma

exhaled, surprised. "By the dreadlocks of St Stan. So many people and so much smoke!"

"Let's fly down!" Stargasm suggested, pointing her broomstick downwards.

"Yeah, take it easy though, things can be very unexpected here," Moonmummy said, wrapping herself tightly and following Stargasm in a slow circular formation, they all raced down to land unnoticed by the side of an abandoned temple on the bank of the busy river. The milling crowd around them had other things on their minds than to be over-inquisitive about the arrival of this flying sisterhood.

"What are we going to do?" Stargasm asked quietly, hoping her blonde hair would not cause too much attraction. The holy river rushed by leaving them all breathless and thousands of semi-naked bodies were wallowing in the river, with millions of people milling around and if it wasn't for the fact that the sisters were wearing Hypno-Tantric Hijabs, they would have been swallowed up in the crowds. Stargasm and Moonmummy who had been regular visitors to the infamous festivals at StonedHenge and Glazedstonebury whistled between their teeth, never having seen anything so huge before. Ayesha, Ambrin and Najma who had never been to any festivals shivered in nervous anticipation. And then nervously they all landed.

"The whole place looks crazy," Moonmummy said excitedly.

"There are some real nutters hanging around the place," Ayesha sang out.

Ambrin tugged at her Hijab and replied, "Yeah, look at those peoples ... they're absolutely stark bollocking naked!"

"No they're not, silly ... They're covered in ashes, that's their clothing," Najma replied. In the heated crowd her face was looking more squashed but her lucidity remained the same.

Quickly looking around, Stargasm took in the sights and stammered, "And everyone's smoking chillums. Never seen so many stoners in one place."

"Where have we landed?" Ayesha then asked excitedly, pulling her hijab more tightly around her.

"Beside the Naga Babas. They're all supporters of Lord Shiva, smoke loads of dope and are really frightening," Ambrin replied with a smile. She continued, "They're really quite sweet, I'm not scared of them even if they smoke tons of dope, smear themselves with ashes and have dreadlocks on their dreadlocks!"

The psychedelic flying pigs looked a bit nervous and twitched erratically as the Naga Babas looked over at them with delirious, red-glazed eyes. Najma confidently crossed her arms and then said in her booming voice, "These Shaivite Naga Babas are almost the weirdest!"

"What do you mean? You can get weirder than this?" Ayesha asked, throwing up her hands in the air in a rapid fluster.

"Why, of course ... yes." Najma continued laughing and looking at Ambrin.

"You don't mean the peaceful, loving, shaven-headed Vaishnavites do you?" Ayesha asked, looking her sister directly in the eyes.

"No they're not really weird, they're just big softies at heart that usually get attacked by the occasional angry, naked Naga Baba up to no good!" Ambrin finished by clapping her hands with delight at the interesting prospect of any fracas.

Turning to the equally delighted Najma, Stargasm exhaled hurriedly and quickly asked, "How many types of weirdoes are there at this crazy festival?"

"Well let's count them on our fingers." Najma continued looking around at the interesting festival site.

Ambrin then interjected, deciding to help Najma out, "Firstly, let's look at how the universe was made initially. Apparently it all started with a chap called God but God wasn't called God then, he was called Brahma and it's all thanks to him that we're here ... that's if he was a him in the first place ..." Ambrin's mellow voice tapered to a stop as the others started cheering.

"Isn't it true that Brahma is a cosmic chef and lives inside a huge can of infinite peas?" said Moonmummy, looking confused.

"I don't know where you got that idea from ... Brahma lives in the abode of infinite peace, not peas!" Ambrin replied chuckling and holding her sides.

"And then, what?" Stargasm asked again, looking intently at Najma and smiling.

Najma took her cue from Ambrin, bowed politely and continued. "So Brahma was the God of Creation. Then we have Lord Vishnu, the God of Existence itself. Some call the supporters of this god, Vaishnavites. Some call them followers of Lord Krishna, God here on earth. Whether Vishnu is an incarnation of Lord Krishna or the other way round is open to question. Nobody is particularly sure and it doesn't really matter either."

Moonmummy then took her turn and asked. "And anyway, are they the Hare Krishnas that are jumping up and down singing merrily over there?"

"Absolutely correct!" Najma said.

"Then where do these crazy dope-smoking babas come from?" Stargasm asked surprised as Najma continued unblinkingly.

"Oh, that's simple, what comes after creation and existence?"

"Why death, destruction and transformation, of course!"

"That's right and the God of all that is Lord Shiva who, when not funking deliriously with his consort Parvati, dances in a ring of never-ending fire. Giving birth and death and transformation to the ten trillion worlds we all live in!"

Everyone looked at Stargasm as if she'd know what to do and so she had no choice but to respond quickly. "Mullah Ullah said we have to find the left-handed demons and Tantrics beyond the fields of the cult of Brahma."

"All right, let's do it!" everyone replied in chorus and off they went to look.

They looked everywhere for hours but although they saw thousands of different sweet-smiling Krishna types, dangerous red-eyed babas and gurus of every different type, not once did they did see a single group of Brahma-heads. Searching but getting nowhere, the place was starting to get to the sisterhood.

"'Ere Ayesha, why do you think we can't find any supporters of Brahma here, there are so many Shaivites and Vaishnavites but absolutely no Brahma devos?"

Ayesha stood up and replied "Easy innit?"

"Why?"

"Obviously people here don't particularly think much of the god of creation that made this universe and all the silly planets in it and even more so the innumerable silly-billies living on countless planets in this highly dubious universe!"

"The god of creation is never actually seen. Why?" Moonmummy asked emphatically.

Patting her pig gently and munching on an apple she mysteriously found on top of her head, Ayesha continued while crunching. "Oh, that's because ... perhaps ... it wasn't such a good idea after all and the old geezer (if it was indeed a geezer) ran away to hide incognito on a deserted desert isle somewhere!"

After holding onto each other for a good few minutes as they giggled and laughed, they then both straightened up after wiping their tears.

Ayesha, still holding onto Moonmummy's shoulders, then suddenly said seriously, "Anyway, Mullah Ullah said the demons we need to find out are somewhere past the Brahma-heads but seeing as there's absolutely no single Brahma-head in this field full of devotees what, by the dreadlocks of St Stan, are we going to do?"

As they looked around, the divine immaculate craziness of the Khumb Mela took them over. Such craziness had been going on in the same spot for thousands of years and its very vibrations were possessing their souls. That's if they had any. The wonder of all they saw was too incredible to mention. There were naked ascetics hovering in the air, squatting on naked spikes, standing on burning coals with their arms in the air, walking backwards, standing on their heads and smoking through their ears, picking their noses with ten foot long fingernails, flying through the air on beds of nails, sitting there in small groups and serenely smoking chillums and much more. That was what the yogis were doing. The female yoginis were doing much the same and often even a bit more. The weird sisters began to relax and even started to smile. It was only their nervous porkers that grunted scarily as hungry eyes relentlessly looked at their way. Suddenly above their silly fiddledum heads a ghostly strain of a spiritual sarangi could clearly be heard. Ayesha and Najma gasped and held each other's hands. The cosmic violin sounds of the spiritual sarangi was their most favourite sound of all. The weird sisters then all wandered through the crowds sniffing out this strange sound and letting the three flying pigs take the lead for a change.

"Oink ... Oink ...!" oinked the three little pigs as they trampled their way through the crowds.

"Follow the pigs!" Stargasm roared, trying to look effective and ladylike.

She looked behind her at the struggling Moonmummy who gasped quietly, "I'm following the sounds!"

"Quick don't lose the damn pig!" Ayesha cried. As usual, the Sisters Nazneen were running fast at the end of the bungling group and tripping over each other to try and hang onto the pigs who were still straining at their leashes.

"Hold on ... it's running in that direction over there."

As the crazed pigs followed the sounds of sarangi lilting in the mystery-laden air, the sisterhood rushed through the crowds as smells now emanated from the crystal clear notes like melons wrapped in pineapples wrapped in incense and blown everywhere like a dream.

"Come my children, come ... come to Papa Rob. The sun that sets over both west and east! ... Twing ... Ting ... Ping ...!" whistled the invisible form of this local holy ghost as he shimmered twelve foot above their heads – Rob Indranath, the ghost of a very famous Banglastani poet and seer who had died yonks before. He had white hair parted in the middle and this fell down to his broad, ghostly shoulders.

Sitting cross-legged he drew each bowed note making it seem to last for centuries and he began to sing.

"This little pig went to market.
This little pig stayed at home.
This little pig flew off in the air,
taking all the others to Drome!"

As Rob's handsome features creased into a smile, he sang the most beautiful love poetry. Leaving the magical sarangi to play on its own, he chucked some sooth-saying sea slugs up into the air, swallowed them quickly as they fell and farted them out before they could change their minds. Quite satisfied with the ensuing divinations, Rob Indranath laughed to himself and remembered Sidney Arthur's words when they had last met over a pint of Astral Ale down at the "Pig in Paradise".

"Look after the weird sisters and help them out. They haven't got a clue and will be swallowed up by all the monsters at the Khumb Mela unless you look out for them," Sidney had said with a laugh, pulling Rob's long white hair and pouring himself another glass.

"Sure Sidney, whatever you say but buy us a pint, will you?" Rob had replied, and so here he was in his native land keeping an eye out for the girls and reflecting that ghosts did not get recognition for all their hard work, mainly because they were invisible, of course.

"Can you still hear the sounds?" Stargasm asked Moonmummy as she trod carefully over people's hands and toes.

"Yeah, clearly and smell them too," Moonmummy replied, nose in the air and accidentally looking like a snob as she trudged through the crowds.

"Where are we going?" Ayesha asked as her frightened pig tried to curl itself around her ankles like a kitten.

"We have to find the Brahma-heads!" Najma boomed, pushing Ambrin out of the way to get closer to Ayesha.

Rob Indranath smiled as he led them on and on through sixteen fields full of the strangest folk until he stopped above them in the golden air.

"Oh wow! . . . the music seems to be coming from here," Ayesha said.

"You're dead right but what do we do about finding Brahma-heads?" Ambrin questioned, suddenly pulling them all to a stop.

Stargasm looked around and saw a small group sitting on the ground next to them. "Let's ask this family."

Stargasm bent down to ask the young family her question. The group consisted of a mother, father and a young daughter, aged ten. They were cooking a pot of lotus roots to go with their boiled rice.

"Excuse me, good people, do you know where we could find some Brahma-heads?"

All three stopped stirring their pot immediately and the young father said with a glowing smile over his bearded face, "You've coincidentally come to the right place, we are Brahma-heads, the only ones in this huge festival and you have found us."

"Oh wow!" Moonmummy gasped, holding onto her ears in disbelief.

"Why do you do it?" Stargasm continued asking, rustling her wattle and daub gown in their direction.

"Well, someone's gotta give thanks to the Lord for having created this, the best of all possible universes, haven't they?" the bearded young man said with a chuckle.

"Tee . . . Hee . . . Hee . . . you're right!" Stargasm laughed.

The young man stroked his short beard, looked at his wife and then asked Moonmummy, "Can we help you then? Would you like some dinner?"

"No thanks . . . we've had a handful of crunchy bananas!"

Stargasm stepped up and said, "Yeah, maybe you can help us, do you know where we could find the burning ghats and the left-handed demons that practise their arcane arts there?"

"Of course, they are two fields to the left and a hundred yards down near by the river ..."

"Thanks, we'll go directly there then," Stargasm replied with a smile.

The ghost of Rob Indranath smirked as he suddenly moved on and the sounds and smells of his spiritual sarangi took them all two fields to the left and after twelve more minutes of crawling through crazy crowds they found what they had been looking for – the burning ghats.

"There they are!" Najma whistled excitedly, seeing the spiralling smoke.

"Can you see them trancing over those burning corpses?" Moonmummy shot back, lifting Najma with her powerful arms so she could get a better look.

"Are they the Dom people that deal with the dead?" Ambrin asked, completely transfixed by the strange sight.

"No, they are the Demon Doms that deal with the dead," Ayesha answered, jumping up into the air to get a better look.

"Can you hear them sing?" Stargasm cried, picking up an instant refrain that was very different to the sounds of Rob's sarangi.

"Yeah, what are they singing?" Ayesha asked, now standing on the back of her pig and still straining to see.

"Sounds absolutely crazy to me!" Stargasm laughed, watching the mad tamasha.

"Hold on, the pigs are getting nervous," Ambrin said, suddenly feeling her pig strain again at its tight leash.

"The demons are looking hungrily in our direction!" Najma finished and looked extremely worried.

"Don't worry, it's not us they want, it's our pigs!" Ambrin added, feeling very worried for their pet transport and starting to chew her lips.

"Well, I don't want our pigs to get eaten up. How are we going to get home?" Ayesha asked, stomping on the ground.

"We'll just hold onto them as tightly as we have been doing!" Ambrin said, starting to feel really worried now.

Leading them still closer with the sounds of his sarangi Rob took them closer to the acrid smell of the burning ghats and they watched proceedings fearfully. Over the pyres, four

Demon Doms were raking hot coals and burning wood over the corpses.

Turning to Najma, Moonmummy said with a sudden start, See that fire, it's been burning bodies here for thousands of years, it's never gone out and the Demon Doms are there to make sure it doesn't."

"That's an awful lot of dead."

"What do you expect? That's life!" Moonmummy replied with a crazy chuckle.

From about twenty feet away they could feel the intense heat that came up from the sandalwood used to cremate the dead. The demons, dressed only in torn loincloths looked around at the world with scary leers. They were about eight foot tall, skinny as rakes with only a thin parchment-like covering of white skin hiding their internal organs.

"By the sacred balls of St Stan. They look really scary!" Moonmummy muttered under her breath, instinctively stepping back.

"Don't be put off, they're just doing their job!" Najma said with a chuckle, warming her hands with the heat from the pyres.

Suddenly, the flames and pyres exploded as four more corpses dissolved completely in the flames. The Demon Doms clapped each other on the back and laughed as one of them rolled around in the flames and came out three minutes later with a smile on his skeletal face singing, "Hare Bonk! Hare Gonk! Hare Loo!" and skipping over the flames like a child with a skipping rope.

"Rama Bing ... Rama Bonk ... Rama Goo!" chanted the second demon, immersing its head in the flames for what seemed like for ever.

"Yonky Ting ... Tonky Bing ... Scronky Tong!" sang the third, bouncing into the hottest part of the pyre.

"Nanky Poo ... Froddle Yu ... Gribbit!" finished the fourth, jumping in after the third and scattering burning wood everywhere. The five weird sisters stood there gasping and it was Najma who broke the silence.

"Oh wow! ... these are the Magic Mantras!" she screamed, suddenly pulling madly at her own face but Stargasm wasn't so sure.

"But there are four of them and some of them have four words in!" Stargasm interjected, covering up her face in disbelief.

"Who cares? They are in there somewhere!" Moonmummy said

with a cracked smile and began hugging Najma and then the arguments began.

"It's Yonky Ting ... Tonky Bing ... Scronky Tong ...!" Ambrin gesticulated excitedly.

"No, it's Hare Bonk ... Hare Gonk ... Hare ... Loo ...!" Ayesha said angrily, her eyes blazing.

"No, its Nanky Poo ... Froddle Yu ... Gribbit ...!" Najma shouted, releasing Moonmummy from her hug but Stargasm still wasn't sure. Clapping her hands loudly she shouted over the raucous din. As the five weird sisters fell to the floor wrestling in the most unladylike manner, Rob Indranath lifted his robe and scratched a pimple in his nether regions. All was going to plan and this was exactly what Sidney Arthur had been hoping for. Wherever he was, Sidney Arthur would certainly be very pleased, thought Rob Indranath.

"Oh no the Demon Doms are going for the pigs!" Ayesha screamed, suddenly seeing another event unfolding rapidly.

"Quick, stop fighting!" Najma spat back, clambering off Stargasm's fallen form.

"Oh no, not our pigs!" Ambrin squealed, throwing her body over the pigs to protect them from the hungry advance of the evil-looking demons as they rushed forward with snarkling teeth, as the ghost of Rob Indranath jumped onto the pyre to distract them all with a song.

Gesticulating crazily with his far-flung arms, he sang.

"Love is an endless mystery
For it has nothing else to explain it!"

Hearing the true words of love and realising that they would have to eat the Sisters Nazneen before they could get to the delicious pigs, the Demon Doms threw up their hands in disgust unable to fight against the power of love. With a horrible scream of anguished frustration, they ran back full-tilt through pyres and back to their job.

"Phew! Thank St Stan for that," Stargasm cried, laughing with relief and clambering off the floor.

"Come on ... let's go!" Najma whistled, offering Stargasm her hand and lifting her up off the ground.

"We've got what we've come here for!" Ambrin cried, putting her arms around Ayesha and giving her a hug.

Ayesha smiled and then insisted, "Yeah, it's Yonky Ting!"

"No it's Hare Gonk!"

"Nanky Poo!"

"Rama Bonk!"

They were at it again as night fell and they had to find somewhere to sleep. Seeing a banyan tree by an abandoned Shiva temple somewhere in the distance, they decided to head for that and sleep under its branches but they were kept awake by the glorious sounds of ten million people singing, dancing, clapping hands, smoking happy Himalayan herbs, drinking bhang, gnashing teeth and much laughter too. The banyan tree itself was incredible and over one hundred foot high and two hundred foot wide with its roots spreading everywhere. The sisters covered themselves with their Hypno-Tantric Hijabs which kept them warm and invisible while they were trying to sleep. As Stargasm and Moonmummy gradually fell asleep on top of each other, their wandering broomsticks hovered vertically three feet in the air and patrolled the vicinity for protection. However, the three Sisters Nazneen stayed awake and played silly philosophical games with each other in a valiant attempt to kill time before the morning sun came up.

"Oi Ayesha, do you know the name of this tree that we are sitting under?" Najma barked all of a sudden, propping herself up on her elbows and looking serious. Her eyes pierced the darkness and stared at her sister.

Ayesha patted her belly and quickly replied, "The Banyan?"

"Correct, but it also has another name," Najma said with a giggle, pulling Ayesha's hair and teasing her.

Ayesha looked at the laughing Ambrin who was hiding her mouth with her hands before replying. "I know, it's called the Bodhi tree!"

"And what does Bodhi mean?" Najma continued, now mischievously pulling a tonkite out of Ambrin's left ear.

Ayesha ignored the magic show and replied in a huff. "It means enlightenment, doesn't it?"

"Of course it does!" Ambrin added, showering them with the remnants of the Man on the Moon's golden bits of yesterday suns and cut-up bits of old full moons. Sitting serenely under a shower of sparkles, Najma continued explaining. "It's called a Bodhi tree because that original Buddha geezer sat under a tree like this all night and became enlightened. "Well, we're sitting under this tree all night, maybe we could get enlightened too . . .?"

"Wishful thinking, it takes a lot more than just sitting here to become enlightened!" Ayesha replied quickly, knowing that the road to enlightenment was a rocky one. Ambrin was disappointed and chucking away the mango stone simply sighed.

Half a field away the Black Manalishi Rishi was arriving on the scene, sent by Lucifer to catch the five weird sisters. Six hundred and sixty-six years old, the emaciated ascetic was spiked to a blood-stained bed of nails. His rotting flesh stank while grey ash from the burning ghats covered his hideous, naked body and obsidian rings pierced his ears, lips, nose and nipples. Mumbling evil mantras without moving his crocodile lips, the diabolic flew vertically on his bed of nails, guiding his troops towards the sisterhood.

"Thugees, I can smell the pigs from here. Demons, get ready, we have unfinished business here," hissed the Black Manalishi Rishi as blood dripped from his many wounds.

"Yes, sah!" screamed the demons, doffing their hats and curtseying like crazy.

"Your wish is our command, great guru!" replied the band of Thugees all in one voice pulling at each other's earrings and picking nervously at each other's noses. With that, the rishi led his troops onwards and across the only field left between themselves and the weird sisters. These demons were skeletal and tall and they bared their angry slashing teeth and cut through the crowds of people as if they were nothing more than corn. They wanted the pigs to roast and eat them to ensure that the Sisters Nazneen had no way of getting home. The Thugees were a bit different. There were about a dozen of them and they looked like ordinary Zindians. Wearing peasants' clothes and turbans, they twirled their long silken handkerchiefs in which was tied a proverbial bad penny. As they rampaged through the frightened crowds they practised their killing skills by throwing the handkerchiefs one-handed. The coin inside the nasty snot-ridden, bloodstained hanky spun around various objects of their choice and wrapped themselves around as the Thugees pulled hard. They were stranglers extraordinaire and never spilled a drop of blood because blood was sacred and Kali only wanted strangled meat full of blood as her offerings.

"Salaam Ali Khan!" whistled the first Thugee through blackened, broken teeth.

"Salaam Ali Khan, brother!" replied the second evil being, putting the first's nose out of joint in the usual way.

"Salaam Ali Khan!" wheezed a third, sidling up close and pulling the second's nose.

The group scooted off towards the unsuspecting weird sisters. Within a few minutes the demons and the Thugees were in the right field and the demons could clearly smell the psychedelic flying pigs and drooled in anticipation.

The five women were now all asleep like babes in the wood as the Black Manalishi Rishi scanned the horizon with empty eye sockets. His crooked nose could smell trouble from afar and the obsidian rings rotated anti-clockwise, always a sign of trouble that the ascetic could read without difficulty.

"There's something over there next to the oinking pigs. I don't know what it is so let's go and investigate."

"Yes, boss!" the Thugees grunted, slamming each other's hands on each other's turbans and snarling.

"Ah pigs, let's get them!" drooled the demons, looking extremely hungry.

As this horrible bunch approached the peaceful vibes changed instantly and the demons rushed towards the trembling porkers, racing each other to get them. In the ensuing fracas the frightened pigs rushed over the three sleeping forms of the screaming Sisters Nazneen and trampled all over them trying to wake them up. In an instant their hijabs came sliding off and they were finally seen.

"There they are!" shouted the turban-clad Thugees, getting their silken handkerchiefs out and looking very excited.

"Hsss . . . they were hiding under their magic blankets!" wheezed the Black Manalishi Rishi floating in the air and looking down on them vertically. His bed of nails was starting to pierce him in newer more secret places and the dripping blood congealed upon the snouts of the screaming porkers.

"Quick, get them!" added an excitable Thugee, taking careful aim of his silken handkerchief and screwing up his eyes to get a better look.

The Black Manalishi Rishi surveyed the manic frightful scene below and yelled, "Hsssss go, Thugees, strangle them now!"

In a blinding flash their penny-filled handkerchiefs whizzed through the air and wrapped themselves tightly around the women's throats.

"Ha . . . Ha . . . Ha . . . a penny for your thoughts!" laughed a dancing Thugee as he jumped up and down seeing his handkerchief wrap itself around Stargasm's throat. He then pulled it with all his might.

"Don't you mean a paisa for your thoughts?" trilled a neighbouring Thugee holding his sides and doubling over in laughter. His silken handkerchief was merrily strangling Moonmummy and there she was spluttering on the floor with the life being squeezed out of her. The Thugee was tugging hard at the other end and digging his knee into her back to facilitate matters. As for the three Sisters Nazneen, their tongues were lolling out of their mouths and their faces were beginning to turn blue.

"Sss ... pull and don't stop until they're dead!" hissed the Black Manalishi Rishi, racing vertically to the ground, exploding profanities between his ears and ranting out orders left, right and centre.

"On no, I think I'm dying!" Stargasm spluttered, watching her life race before her dazzled eyes.

"Aaark ... I'm already dead!" Moonmummy screamed, seeing a dark black cloud take her over.

"This must be heaven!" Ayesha smiled, letting go of all the struggles in her young life completely and starting to feel an overwhelming peace.

"No ... this must be hell!" Najma barked, refusing to let go and kicking the Thugee that was strangling her and managing to land a hefty kick between his legs. The Thugee groaned and then, rubbing his pained parts shouted to the rest.

"Aaark ... Pull harder brothers ... squeeze until the last drop of life is squeezed out of them!"

At this point, the Black Manalishi Rishi smiled an evil leer and said, "Good, my Thugees ... don't stop until they're dead!"

As Moonmummy felt the last glimmer of her life being squeezed out between her lips, she turned her body around to see the fallen Stargasm clutching at her throat. The Thugee on her back was smirking with a face full of delight knowing that Stargasm's life was quickly coming to an end. Moonmummy turned the other way and saw the Sisters Nazneen in the same predicament. The sight of her beautiful sisters, distressed and dying, enraged Moonmummy beyond belief and her jaws clenched with grim determination and the strong muscles in her compact body tensed themselves for action. Suddenly she forgot about her own problems and considering the terrible fate of her sisters whipped her wishing wand from behind her back.

"Iggeldy Piggeldy Wiggeldy Poo
I'm a whole universe just the same as you
How can you be doing these terrible things that you do?
Now you have to suffer and let my sisters groove!
Flazaam . . .!"

With her hex in place suddenly the handkerchiefs all fell off from their throats and in karmic revenge they flew around the necks of the assailants and began strangling them instead. As the Thugees tumbled to the floor clutching their throats the Black Manalishi Rishi rose to a hundred feet in the air and blew the weird sisters a raspberry angrily as he surveyed the scene. With five Thugees being strangled to death, the other seven raced to tear the silken handkerchiefs off their comrades. The pigs finally found their courage and flying into the air, turned their fat bottoms towards the demons and peppered them with pig poo.

"Rat a tat a tat!" went the roaring pigs firing their smelly remains into the faces of the bewildered demons. No longer simply bacon they'd become monsters and were loving every moment.

"Take that, you rotters!" oinked the pigs in perfect Piglistani.

"Oink Oink ... Hee Hee Hee," chuckled the valiant porkers as the sisterhood brushed themselves down and watched the Thugees struggling with their own handkerchiefs and the demons cowering from the aerial attack.

"Wow ... we're free!" Ayesha gasped, tears of joy rolling down her face.

"We have to thank the pigs for that" Ambrin chuckled, getting slowly up to her feet.

"But I thought they were cowardly porkers. Where did they get the courage for that?" Najma asked.

"Easy, peasy, pudding and pie, goes to show how much they love us!" Ayesha cried, perfectly understanding the bond between themselves and the flying pigs.

Ambrin giggled deliciously saying, "You're right, our friendly porkers have demonstrated the strongest magic of all. Nothing can set you free as much as the power of love, love conquers all and it's certainly crapped on this lot!"

However, the Thugees re-grouped and set free the five assailants from strangulation. Moonmummy was concentrating on getting the injured Stargasm back on her feet and she had no time to dish out another wish and so it was up to the Sisters Nazneen and the psychedelic flying pigs to end this fracas once and for all. As the pigs returned time and again to fire into the battered faces of the nasty demons, the sisters pondered on what to do.

"What shall we do?" Najma asked fearfully as their enemies advanced angrily.

"How shall we beat the Thugees and the demons?" Ambrin asked, picking up on Najma's fear and multiplying it.

"Let's do what we always do and sing!" Ayesha finished, tying up her long hair with a very determined look.

"What shall we sing?" Najma asked, mystified and wobbling with real panic. She was starting to stumble all over the place.

"What do you mean? We only know one song!" Ambrin insisted, giving the others instant encouragement.

"Wow, let's go for it, the 'Om Song' it is!" Ayesha finished, smoothing over her face and tugging at her ears.

As the demons and Thugees advanced unflinchingly, Najma swept the hijab from her face and with her eyes full of concentration she started singing with the profundity of her big bang bass.

"Omm!"

The demons hesitated and the Thugees faltered as Najma provided the bass tone for Ambrin to sing within and she opened her perfect lips and roared into song.

"Ommmmmmmmmmmmmmmmmmm!"

Ambrin sang the mid-range and together with Najma's bass, totally freaked out the spellbound hordes who stopped in their tracks. While the Thugees were holding their ears in disgust, something odd was happening to the demons. They were shaking and vibrating and getting rather brittle, particularly when Ayesha sang out with her Hypno-Tantric Hijab right off:

"Ooooooooooommmmmmmmmmmmmmmmmmmmmmmm!"

The demons and Thugees just freaked. The three sisters were singing together now and something amazingly odd was happening to the evil ones. The Thugees couldn't bear the sounds and ran off clutching their ears in distress. But what was happening to the demons? Unknown to them, Rob Indranath was playing his sarangi, his handsome face wreathed in smiles and his playing perfectly complemented the Sisters Nazneen doing their

"Om Song". The demons that could hear him screamed as it was poetry of a sublime nature.

"Aaark, how long is this monstrous music going to go on for?" screamed a demon, gnashing its evil teeth in frustration.

"Is it going to go on forever? Aaark?" a crazed Thugee replied, ripping the turban off his head and wrapping it around his ears to try and hide the sounds.

"What shall we do?" Stargasm asked, wobbling on her unsteady feet and being closely held by Moonmummy who said nothing as she listened to the ghostly spiritual sarangi.

> "Let your life lightly dance on the edges of time
> Like dew on the tip of a leaf."

The Thugees were now holding their bleeding ears and even the Black Manalishi Rishi had raced off four hundred feet in the air to get away from the sonic truths that Rob Indranath and the Sisters Nazneen were conveying. Suddenly, the demons stopped moving and stood transfixed, they were actually turning into glass, shattering with the high notes being sung by the Sisters Nazneen and falling as shards to the ground.

"How much longer do we have left before we can win?" Moonmummy asked, treading very carefully over the broken glass even though she wore strong leather boots.

Stargasm sighed, smiled and replied, "Don't know, I just don't know!"

With a chuckle Rob Indranath swept his long hair from his face and sang perfectly again while opening up his ghostly heart.

> "The butterfly counts not in months
> but moments and has time enough!"

"Come on the baddies are losing!" Najma shouted, her face beaming with excitement.

"Let's go!" replied the others in perfect unison, smiling. Jumping up on their broomsticks and flying pigs the five weird sisters raced off into the skies watched by the seething rishi who was unable to do a thing.

"Freedom won't come by waiting. Freedom must be sought for, fought for and won," screamed Stargasm, feeling in much better health now that she was back on her broomstick again.

"Third Humble Truth!" Moonmummy replied in a giggle, just inches behind Stargasm.

"Yippee ... let's roll!" screamed Ayesha, flowing in the wind like an aerial sprite as they raced off home. It was a long journey back but they had the Magic Mantras that they thought would set them free. As they raced off, nobody noticed the handsome, well-built form of the ghost of Rob Indranath waving them goodbye as his spiritual sarangi played a never-ending tune on its own.

23

The Sonic Temple of King Psychedelix

EVERYONE WAS GOING crazy in the Sonic Temple of King Psychedelix at the bottom of The Lost Catacombs of Brickie Lane where the River of Crystal Light pierced the deep space and also where many of our intrepid heroes and heroines were gathered now. This was the biggest space in the Lost Catacombs and could change shape and size whenever it wanted to. At this depth of the underworld reality wasn't a fixed notion anyway and things could be really fluid. If the other caves and corridors were filled with stars then this place was simply stuffed chock-a-block full of them. There were small ones, large ones, enormous ones and even bigger ones all crammed into this ever-shifting space that was the temple itself. There were stars on the ceiling, stars on the walls and stars on the floors too while at its centre sat Mullah Ullah serenely smoking his hookah as he admired the incredible pictures painted on the Awakening Dreamtime walls. Ghosts of cavemen had come and gone but not before they had sprayed their pretty pictures of birds and beasties in glorious, living technocolour in psychedelic sheens of unimaginable beauty.

"By the holy dreadlocks of St Stan, don't they ever shut up?" the Mullah suddenly sighed, looking around distressed at the incredible panorama around him. The sights were fine but it was the sounds of argument that were getting to him and even the Genie of the Lamp covered his face and whimpered. Around this sagacious duo, Mevlana, Suleiman, Nasseruddin the Nutty, Ayesha, Ambrin, Najma, Stargasm and Moonmummy were frantically ranting their little heads off.

Due to this the Mullah's shining gatta had almost disappeared while the Genie ran off to hide inside the golden lamp again.

"Dear Mullah, I'm not coming out of the lamp until they all shut up."

"There, there, never mind," the Mullah replied but as he looked around they were at it again.

"The Magic Mantras we've found in Zindia, they're Hare Bonk ... Hare Gonk ... Hare Loo," Stargasm shouted, waving her broomstick up and down and beating Suleiman the Spinner incessantly. Her beautiful face looked very angry and the woad dripped off its surface like a puddle of oil left out in the rain.

"No, we found them in Hoggaristan ... It's Scrank ... Scronk ... Scribbidy Poo!" Suleiman retorted, twirling his long moustache, stretching himself up to his tall extended form, while holding onto Stargasm's broomstick and not letting it beat him. Meanwhile, Moonmummy was thrashing Mevlana and defiantly holding her nose against his rosy perfume.

"Not on your life ... it's Rama Bing ... Rama Bonk ... Rama Goo!"

"What a load of rubbish ... it's Screw ... Scrak ... Scritch!" Suleiman spat back, ripping off the eyebrows on Moonmummy's head, screwing them up into a furry ball and quickly swallowing them before the witch could do anything. Moonmummy's eyes narrowed down and looked distinctly dangerous as she jumped on Suleiman's feet and continued fighting.

Besides this fighting pair, Ayesha could be heard screaming. Her hair was down to her ankles and her hijab had nearly come off while she was slapping Nasseruddin's head and trying to pull out his lapis lazuli teeth and hollering, "No its Yonky Ting ... Tonky Bing ... Scronky Tong!"

"Rubbish ... you don't know anything ... it's ... Screek ... Scrak ... Scronk!" cried Nasseruddin, defending himself adeptly from the other's blows and trying to keep his beaky nose out of danger.

It was Ambrin's turn next and she was just as enraged as her sister as she was punching Mevlana rather hard somewhere soft beneath his djelaba and shouting. "What a load of Dobb ... It's Nanky Poo ... Froddle Yu ... Gribbit!"

"No it's Donk ... Dirk ... Poo!" Mevlana argued, jumping up and down in his rubber flip flops.

Looking at the crazy scene Osric just sighed and put his hand on his heart and just stared at the absurd scene around him. Then he suddenly remembered that his heart had been gladly given away to the dragon that had come down through the roof of the Bum Note.

"It's Hare Bonk ... Hare Gonk ... Hare Loo ... Ouch!" Stargasm screamed, pummelling Suleiman and tugging at his white hair.

"It's Scrank ... Scronk ... Scribbidy Poo ... Punch!" Suleiman replied, adeptly scratching at Stargasm's face and putting her off balance.

"Bash ... Bish ... Kick ... it's Rama Bing ... Rama Bonk ... Rama Goo!" Moonmummy shouted, kicking Mevlana in his kneecaps and making him jump six feet into the troubled air.

"Boot ... Slap ... Aaah ... it's Screw ... Scrak ... Scritch!" Mevlana replied, getting his own back on Moonmummy.

"Slap ... Boot ... Kick ... Punch ... it's Yonky Ting ... Tonky Bing ... Scronky Tong!" Ayesha screamed, jumping on Nasseruddin's head and slapping him in the face a good few times.

"Aaaaah ... it's Screek ...... Scrak ...... Scronk!" Nasseruddin finished on a high note, booting Ayesha back and pinching her ample bottom as the stars came out of the walls to wonder what all the hullabaloo was all about and the fighting turned very real.

"Flash ...!" whooshed the biggest stars as they rushed out to get the prime view.

"Flash ...!" went the second-class stars getting the middle rows and jumping over other stars.

"Flash ...!" went the tiniest stars as they squatted atop the shoulders of the bigger stars to see the ensuing fracas.

Suddenly, enraged with the insults heaped upon her by Mevlana, Stargasm quickly got her wishing wand out and pointing it to his head she snapped a few crazy spells out of her mouth even before realising what was happening.

"Whooosh ...!"

"Aaah, what's happening?" Stargasm shrieked as a sudden transformation was catching her unawares. Her whole being was starting to feel very different and nothing felt right.

"What do you mean, what's happening? You tried to spell me, I haven't done a single thing," Mevlana gasped.

"Change me back," Stargasm cried in the tiny voice of a little amphibious creature, totally lost and bewildered.

"Hah ... Hah ... Hah ... You look just like Frogamatix!" Mevlana roared, holding his sides with laughter.

"No, she doesn't, she's a lot uglier!" Suleiman sang, pulling at his moustache.

"Tee ... Hee ... Hee!" giggled Nasseruddin the Nutty patting himself on his huge head and obviously enjoying the scene.

The irritated Suleiman the Spinner put his hands together,

looked at Moonmummy and wished that she would turn into a bogey but suddenly found himself as one; his worst nightmare had come true.

"Aaah ... What's happening? I feel horrible."

"Get away from me, Suleiman, you look horrible, like something usually found up Nasseruddin's nose ... yuch!" Moonmummy spat out disgustedly, stepping back deftly.

The sisters were throwing hexes at the brothers and the brothers throwing them back with compound interest but nothing was working out as planned. The Sisters Nazneen conveniently hid inside an old Kashmiri cupboard that had come from Anarkali's domain in Zindia many hundreds of years ago and now materialised before their disbelieving eyes. Through the carved wooden lattice they could clearly see what was happening.

"Quick, Ayesha what can you see?" Ambrin asked demandingly and the other replied without hesitation.

"Suleiman's turned into a bogey!"

"And what else?" Najma asked, pushing authoritatively from the back and poking Ambrin in the back.

"Stargasm's a frog that's dementedly running around all over the place," Ayesha replied after a moment's observation.

"And what else?" Najma boomed again.

"Mevlana's hanging upside down from the roof of the Awakening Dreamtime walls and screaming!"

"What about Nasseruddin?"

"He's turned into giant hunchback, fifty foot tall and he's sitting there cross-legged, pulling out his lapis lazuli teeth one by one and crying!"

"What about Moonmummy?" Ambrin asked, anxiously trying to push Ayesha out of the way to get a better look.

Ayesha pushed her back, saying, "I think she's just turned into a rat and is crazily running around in circles trying to find the solution to a problem that won't go away."

"Tee Hee ...!" laughed the other two and feeling more adventurous, Ayesha opened the cupboard a tiny bit and peeked out, trembling. She quickly relayed what she saw with her disbelieving eyes.

"Moonmummy's a rat, Nasseruddin's a giant hunchback, Stargasm's a frog, Mevlana's upside down and Suleiman's a bogey."

"So much for arguing don't you think?" Ambrin suggested, holding her tongue so that she wouldn't be overheard.

"Terrible, but what do you think the Magic Mantras actually are?" Najma started but was quickly stopped in her tracks by an annoyed Ambrin.

"Oh, don't start that again, this is what got us into trouble in the first place."

"Sheesh ... who cares? All this search for the Magic Mantras has got us into trouble. That's all!" Ayesha gasped, bravely opening the cupboard door a little bit more. Very carefully they all peered their heads out to survey the scene and there was Mullah Ullah and the Genie of the Lamp discussing something of importance.

With a quizzical look, it was the Mullah who spoke first. "So what's brought all this on, Genie?"

The Genie of the Lamp spiralled in smoky abstraction and smirked in reply. "Easy, Mullah Ullah, in their anger they forget the first principle of magic, to never use it in a nasty way or it will reverse and get you instead."

The Sisters Nazneen gasped as Mullah Ullah pulled at his salt and pepper beard before replying. "That's it!"

The Genie of the Lamp flicked at his golden earrings before replying hurriedly. "Magic wishes can be dangerous things unless one wishes for the happiness of all sentient beings which is customarily usual!"

"Yes, they were all too angry and anger and magic wishes don't usually go together very well!" the Genie continued, gazing at the Mullah.

The Mullah refused to be distracted by the ever-changing phenomena that was the Genie of the Lamp, rubbed his psychedelic gatta and then asked, "Well, what shall we do?"

"I could use a magic wish and sort it all out if you want me to Mullah Ullah!"

Mullah Ullah thought a while, rubbed his podgy belly a bit and then spoke. "No, we've only two wishes left, we might need them at other times so let's not use them now."

"So does that mean we leave them like they are and just get used to them?" the Genie chuckled.

The Mullah's eyes returned into tiny slits as he quickly pondered. "That's fine, but looking at Bogey Suleiman's rather gross and the giant hunchbacked Nasseruddin looks so depressed ... we have to sort him and the others out."

"Can you sort it out Mullah Ullah?"

"I think so but I haven't done it since my youth."

"Is it magic wishes and magic spells?"

"Oh no, nothing so complicated, just happy wishful thinking . . .!"

"How do you do it, master?"

"Just watch, Genie . . . Just watch . . .!"

Closing his eyes, the Mullah scratched his slaphead and tugged at his beard. It was then the Mullah intoned in a mysterious voice while rubbing his gatta and watching a red film of light fall from his forehead onto every place he could see.

"Wishful thinking, wishful thought.
Magic wishes can never be bought.
Wishful thinking, wishful thought.
Magic spells can get you caught.
Wishful thinking,wishful life.
Reverse these spells, take away the strife.
Wishful thinking, life-fulfilling tree.
Make everyone as happy as happy can be!"

And that was that and in an instant all was as it should be.

"Far out!" screamed Mevlana, tumbling painfully to the floor and not minding.

"Great!" Moonmummy whistled, watching her rat's tail disappear for ever.

"Yippee!" yelled Stargasm, bouncing up to be a real person again and loving it.

"Thanks," Nasseruddin gasped, quickly returning to his normal size with his hunchback gone for ever.

"Oh groovy!" Suleiman said in a grateful voice as his sheer bogeyiness disappeared as quickly as it had come.

The five idiots all stood there sheepishly as, wagging a dangerous finger at them each in turn, the Genie of the Lamp had something left to say.

"Magic wishes and spells are dangerous things, they have to be used wisely and well and never in fits of rage!"

Mullah Ullah thought that was enough admonishment for the day and quickly stepped in.

"Come, let us be friends again! Genie, pour out some elderberry wine for everyone and prepare a hookah and make it quick!"

"Yes, master!"

As they smoked and drank, they began to open up again, not holding grudges, they forgave each other quick and hugged each other like the silly billies that they were. Meanwhile, totally fed up with the crazy fracas between the sisters and the brothers, the Jabberwocky swished his sparkladelic tail, blew holy smoke from his elongated snout and waited for two others to follow him. Princess Amrita's pigtail was being pulled by Osric but the scruffy fool was grinning a lop-sided grin trying to drag her along unwillingly. Amrita's sequinned mirrors turned the other way to hurry her along but she was still engrossed in watching the others make up. The thirty foot long Jabberwocky, who was as timeless as the Lost Catacombs itself, smoked fire from its funny old head and made Osric watch the brontosaurus fins on its back glow in pretty colours. Osric's usual pretty vacant expression changed to one of wonder watching its colour-changing body and he realised that the snorting Jabberwocky was the guardian of the whole Sonic Temple itself and could answer the host of questions that he had. Smiling and muttering inane idiocies known only to himself, Osric ignored the ever-streaming blooms coming out of the hole where his heart had once been as he laboriously dragged Amrita along by her pigtail and pestered her to follow. Guided by the Jabberwocky's diamond-white eyes, the silly duo of young man and seven-year-old child simply followed as the Jabberwocky plodded forward on its short legs, occasionally snorting special smoke signals into the air. Although it could speak, it never usually said much but always gave clear indication of what it meant via its mysterious smoke signals.

"Gruntle . . . Poot!" it cried while its smoke signals said in ancient Sanskrit simultaneously, "Follow me and quick, let's get out of this infernal madness!"

"Hurry up, Amrita, let's go, quick!" Osric cried and the imperial Princess of Gigglistan laughed deliciously like a little girl should.

"Ah, but the party's looking so good now they are making up for their previous fight and look, the Genie's turned Mullah Ullah into a magic carpet!"

"Who cares? There's always plenty of time for things like that. We have to follow the Jabberwocky," Osric replied, pulling harder on her pigtail and looking serious.

Still dragging her heels, Amrita replied quickly. "Why, Osric?"

"Because his smoke signals say so."

"Suppose we don't go, what will he do?"

"Oh, he's very polite, he probably won't do anything but singe your butt, now hurry up!" Osric finished by stamping his feet and wiping his bleary kajol-stained face. They moved forward but they weren't on their own. As Osric dragged the unwilling Amrita by her ever-growing pigtails, the three tiny Dreamweavers Twynklyn, Blynkyn and Nod all came too, riding on the back of the Sabre-Toothed Power Pussy. As Osric's pale nose led the way, their ladybird's spotted wings were sparkling like fire as these magical fairies twitched their antennas and scratched their cute button-noses. But whatever they were doing, they seemed well contented enough to follow. The Power Pussy grinned its one-toothed grin and stomped forward. Its one single diamond sabre tooth sparkled in the Awakening Dreamtime light while the moving orange, yellow, red and black of its striped skin flashed by so fast they tripped out any onlookers. Right now, it was just chasing the source of never-ending blooms that flooded out of Osric's body and following this trail of flowers, the whole group followed the Jabberwocky to the undiscovered side of the Sonic Temple itself.

"Quick, follow the flowers, Twynklyn!" Blynkyn nodded, flashing a tiny prismatic smile and chuckling.

"We can't get lost that way," Twynklyn explained, flapping up and down deliriously.

"Good idea, come on, pussy, you know what to do!" Nod finished, nodding her tiny frame and looking sleepy.

Somewhere at the front of the group Osric had finally let go of Amrita's pigtails and she was skipping merrily along, the only child in the company of adults, fairies and magical creatures.

"Gruntle ... Gruntle ... Poot ... we're nearly there!" the Jabberwocky exclaimed in ever-increasing rings of spiralling smoke.

"Where are we going?" Princess Amrita asked, suddenly grabbing onto the tail of a glow-worm that appeared out of nowhere.

"We're going to show Osric who he really is!" the Jabberwocky replied offering Amrita a bandersnatch that it quickly grabbed from a passing tumtum tree.

"I know who he is, he's Osric the simpleton!"

"Gruntle ... Gruntle ... Poot ... there's often more to a person than meets the eye, don't you agree, Osric?" the Jabberwocky suggested in smoky syntax, helping itself to another bandersnatch and gulping it quick before the bandersnatch changed its mind. Osric scratched his head and pondered.

The Jabberwocky refused to be put off and continued. "Gruntle ... Do you remember what happened last time you were here, Osric?"

"Er yes ... just before Amrita and Fairlight found me, I had found you!"

"And then what?"

Osric slapped his silly face for a full minute, aided by a glad Amrita and continued. "And then I saw this big rock which closed the entrance to the Sonic Temple itself and a really weird thing happened."

"What was that, you never told me?" Amrita asked, grabbing him by his jumper. She tickled him with a flamingo feather before ramming it up his nose.

"Well, this whole stream of Pyramid in Prism Buddhas rushed out of my heart when I used to have a heart that is and one of them, a brightly coloured orange one, mugged me silly."

With that Osric looked serious for a moment and even forgot to laugh at the silly sight of Amrita pulling the feather out of the opposite nostril from which it had been rammed.

The Jabberwocky prodded him with its smokey snout and baring its crocodile teeth, asked suggestively, "Gruntle.. Gruntle ... Poot ... Poot ... can you remember anything else?"

"Yeah it grabbed me by the scruff of the neck and chucked me through the air to hit the rock but when I did so, it dissolved and I was standing inside the enormous space of the Sonic Temple itself."

By this time the Dreamweavers were beside themselves with excitement. It was Blynkyn who first jumped up with joy. "Twynklyn we're nearly there, he's going to find out!"

"Oh, goodee, this is going to be such fun!" Twynklyn replied in a blinding flash of fairy wings.

Beside her, the tiny Nod nodded her little head and screamed. "Oh, wonders of wonders, don't amazing things ever end?"

By now the Jabberwocky had reached an incredible stone portal where moving writing carved in a white marble slab shimmered up and down so fast that its very movement was blinding. It was about the same height as Osric and about as wide as Najma and just stood there like a serious-looking gravestone, out of place and context. Osric and Amrita tried to concentrate on the moving writing but all they managed to keep their eyes on was the stone centaurs that seemed to be aiming their tiny bows and arrows at them. The Jabberwocky decided it was time and nibbbled Osric's ankles.

"Ouch! What did you do that for?"

"Right Osric, we're nearly here ... Grunt ... I want you to try to read this."

"What is it?" he asked, scratching Amrita's head out of distraction and looking quizzical.

The Jabberwocky bit him on the other ankle and replied smokily, "This is something you have to work out yourself."

Osric stared at the inscription carved on the marble slab in moving, curled script, dancing up and down like dragonflies in danger. Osric looked up and saw that the stone archway was covered in what looked like Scarabian script but when the tiny carved stone centaurs fired their tiny arrows from their tiny bows, the Scarabian script quickly turned to Sanskrit. Amrita suddenly understood and tugged at Osric's hand trying to make him understand what she had instantly realised.

"Oh wow, look at the Devanagri script, it's moving to become simple English!" Amrita said with a gasp, holding her mouth in bewilderment.

"Brilliant Blynkyn! Amrita's done it," Twynklyn screamed, and even the Power Pussy looked chuffed.

"Amrita was meant to be here, wasn't she?" Nod asked in a tiny prismatic voice, far gentler and smaller than the others'.

"Yes, she's a wise little girl. She will help him understand the past and present in order to have a better idea of the future!" Blynkyn finished flashing such a pretty grin that the big cat had to look the other way.

"Well Osric, are you just going to stand there like an idiot and not read it?" Amrita asked, in earnest expectation.

Osric scratched his head before replying. "What do you mean, I'm an idiot?"

Amrita wouldn't take no for an answer and jumped up to pull his nose, continuing, "You've got to read this, it's about you and for you!"

"How do you know?" Osric asked, in disbelief.

Amrita slapped his silly face quickly before replying. "The Jabberwocky told me!"

"When?"

"Just now when you were looking like a fool – anyway look at his smoke, silly!"

Osric turned around and watched the smoke bubble arise from the Jabberwocky's smoking snout, clearly spelling out a message.

"Read the poem and work it out,
red's more blue than green.
You don't always have to scream and shout
who you are is more important
than what you've ever been!"

Osric clapped his hands and exclaimed joyously, "Oh wow! All right, lets have a go then."

Osric, like Amrita, had never learned to read properly but that didn't put them off. Stepping up closely to the carvings, Osric watched spellbound as the centaurs shot off their arrows making the Devanagri script turn fully into English which made it easier for him to understand.

"If you can't read, then close your eyes and read it!" Amrita said, closing her eyes too and clasping her little determined hands as if in prayer. "And if you don't understand, I'll help you out!"

"Okay, Amrita, here goes, it says, 'Madness – the Divine Right of Kings . . .'!"

"Oh wow!" said Amrita with her eyes tightly closed and her tongue sticking out.

"Well go on then."

"Okay . . .

"Moon, Moon Merman turn the tides,
The seas are vast, the oceans wide
I bid you do as I command
For thee are just a grain of sand
From rock you come to grain you'll go
Via, wind, water, rain and snow
What is here and now in either hand
Is always heaven, hell, fire and land
But what you see not is what you don't know
The waters listen only to the rhythm they know.

Moon, Moon Merman turns the tides,
The seas are vast the oceans wide
Show to me the heavens inside
For what is when and will be free
This single grain will one day be
The greatest of all pomegranate trees
And jewels brought will fall like fire
Into the very humblest desire.

And so you say 'your majesty you're out of your head
The seas should do exactly what you said'
But what is now and forever shall be
The garden of the pomegranate tree
And I'm a fool as you all know well,
And fortune's fickle, we never can tell
So listen to what really turns things around.
My dearest hearts, listen to your own true sound."

Amrita gasped spellbound at the poem's intrinsic beauty, pulled at her own pigtails and bit her fingernails. It was then the Jabberwocky had something to say.

"Grunt . . . Pootle . . . Fantastic isn't it?"

"Who wrote it, Amrita?" Osric suddenly asked, wanting to know everything.

"Easy, it was written by King Psychedelix thousands of years ago when he first found the Sonic Temple."

Osric scratched his head even more and pondered. He asked again wide-eyed in wonder. "How do you know, princess?"

"Easy . . . you told me."

"When, Amrita?"

Amrita opened her mouth, and then answered. "Thousands of years of ago when you were King Psychedelix and I was your friend!"

Osric still looked gobsmacked but managed to hastily reply. "What, how can you remember all this?"

Amrita smirked and chuckled. "I just remembered everything with my eyes closed, it was easy!"

"Grunt . . . Grunt . . . pootle . . . that's right . . . what's she's just said is the truth," the Jabberwocky said in a spiral of shifting smoke.

Osric opened his mouth and looked down as the stream of flowers from his heart suddenly stopped and in their place came forth a chain of Pyramid in Prism Buddhas that stretched into infinity. Each Buddha sat there hovering in space in the lotus position and smiling, each intricately connected to the next and in a quicksilver moment, the bewildered Osric suddenly realised that each Buddha had been the Buddha that he had been in previous lifetimes. And there were thousands of them, some were blue; some green, some purple, some white, some scarlet but whatever they were, they were all unique and completely different from each other. Then, as he looked at Amrita he could clearly see her shimmering translucent form change through the thousands of life forms that she had taken since she had been with him there and then to this incredible here and now. The Jabberwocky just stood there silently blowing smoke-rings through his sizzled nostrils which said "I told you so."

Panicking crazily, Osric tugged at his hair and screamed. "Oh, by the scared dreadlocks of St Stan . . . this is all me!"

"Correct!" laughed Amrita, grabbing his hands and rubbing them to warmth like the silly little girl Osric had come to love.

"Grunt . . . Exactly!" agreed the Jabberwocky jabbering away in a thousand different smoky languages all at the same time and stepping heavily on Osric's toes. The hole in Osric's heart was starting to do some very strange and wonderful things as the whole space became filled with ten trillion Buddhas, all vibrating in total wonder as incredible laughter suddenly burst forth. Giggles that were lifetimes in the making and silent jokes so funny that the Buddhas held each other's stomachs as holy laughter overtook them all. Who was "I"?, who was "me"? and what was "mine"? were impossible questions to work out as everything started and ended with Osric or, more particularly, in the hole where his heart had once been as he now simply stood there ripping a hole in his already hole-ridden orange jumper.

Suddenly and without any logical explanation, a strange orange flower grew out of both holes and became a laughing orange Buddha that expanded to fill the vast temple.

"Here's looking at you kid!" laughed the orange one racing up from behind to scare the living daylights out of Osric who quite naturally squealed. "You're Psychedelix!"

"No, you are . . . Heee . . . Hee . . . Heee!"

Osric stopped babbling and spoke up bravely. "I've been you and all these too and I never even knew!"

The orange apparition laughed before replying. "I'll tell you Osric, young man. You may be an idiot but you have a fool's heart or at least you did until you sacrificed it for the Queen of Hearts's heart and the dragon took yours away!"

Osric stood there confused for a moment, scratched his chin and then asked, "And so, what does that mean?"

"Oh yes, nature stole your heart and gave you a stream of never-ending blooms instead, it's for such spontaneous loving actions such as these that you will always be a king. You have always been a king and you most certainly are a king now!"

It was then Amrita stepped in and tweaked his royal nose and stated, "Heee ... Heee ... Heee ... don't expect me to curtsey before you, after all I am a princess!"

And with that realisation and with the others milling around him, laughing their little socks off, Osric did the next best thing and swooned as the orange Buddha dissolved into him. He now remembered the past but there was no point in remembering the past unless it could influence the future and to do that one had to always live in the present. This was the lesson for the day that the grinning Jabberwocky wanted him to learn.

24

Back in Ancient Zeegypt

IT TOOK ABOUT a week sailing down the River Smile before they got to Kayro and Fareek played the Hypno-Tantric Trance they had brought with them incessantly and wondered how lucky he was that Fairlight had converted their extremely powerful CD player into a solar-powered one. There was so much sun from the top deck of the royal boat, there would never be any danger of running out of energy. Squatting on his haunches like an Afrostani soothsayer, he wiped the sweat off his face and smiled at the hard-working sailors who ran around the deck adjusting ropes and cables wearing nothing but loincloths and smiles. Still spinning like crazy, Anarkali found a convenient niche on the top deck where she span just six inches off the ground. Her beautiful face smiled as she took in all the sights of the countless villages they passed on the riverbank and stared at the single solitary grey crapping pigeon whizzing across her perspective, still panting like mad, being chased by flocks of fantasy falcons. The countless, embroidered temple trancers on her dancing gown "oohed" and "aahed" as they watched the land pass by while the tiny, delicate Anarkali looked at the passing world with ever-growing interest.

"Excellent . . . all going to plan!" Cassandra muttered, rubbing her hands with glee. Taking off her black, tattered woollen cloak she took to the sun in a single-piece black cotton gown. Her Afro was starting to move around her head and face again and her huge ears flopped to her shoulders. Sitting cross-legged on the port side of the top deck she gazed with her third eye at her four very different charges and sighed, occasionally jumping up to point out things of interest as they sailed on. Villages passed and swarms of children splashed about in the river's edge all passed by to the soundtrack of the Hypno-Tantric Trance. Cassandra was happy that all was going to plan. The scurrying sailors were happy that the breeze was blowing in the right direction and the fat turbaned captain merrily munched on a handful of olives. Almost everything and everyone was happy. This was the way it was meant to be no doubt.

"Kayro to port!" yelled a sailor from the crow's nest scanning the horizon.

"No, starboard!" shouted a drunken sailor fool, stumbling around helplessly.

"Port, you fool!" screamed the first, chucking down some crow's eggs he had conveniently found inside the nest and splattering the drunken sailor many feet below.

"OK!" the second finally agreed, throwing away the coconut cup full of palm wine and tottering off .

Upon entrance to the port of Kayro they stayed on the boat for what seemed a long time. Handsome Tarquin smiled confidently and pushed a hand through his hair as Cassandra quickly got them in line. The ancient soothsayer avoided Mellow Tron's dreadlocks which tried to trip her up and Fareek's hallucinogenic stare which tried to fathom answers from her cold dead eyes with equal success. Wrapping her arms around them Cassandra explained that, being important royal guests, they needed a glorious escort as it was protocol. They would have to wait for the news of their arrival to reach the royal palace and then a royal palanquin be sent to pick them up They had come from another place and time and were the special guests that King Funkanathen had been waiting on for ages so it would simply not do to go off to the palace without a royal palanquin. As they sat in the boat all day waiting for their escort, they looked around at a Zeegypt so colourful and golden until horses and soldiers finally came, and riding off in palanquins pulled by shaven-headed priests, they headed for the palace.

"Oh wow, never seen so much wealth," Fareek gasped, looking at the streets around him. There was gold everywhere and everything seemed to be made of it. Pulling the velvet curtains of the palanquin, Fareek almost hid in shock seeing the glorious richness of the everyday life in the street. He poked Tarquin with a long inquisitive finger before burping from the bag of green olives he'd been munching.

"Look, everything's made of gold!" reiterated Tarquin, pointing his face out of the window.

"Yeah, even my dreadlocks are turning golden!" Mellow Tron said, carefully examining the metamorphosis on his head. The locks were basking in the contentment of shimmering goldenment and snapped their many snake-heads in excitement.

"And the people look fat, healthy and content," Fareek continued, pointing to happy, fat people everywhere going about their daily business.

"Haven't seen a single beggar!" he added, pulling his head back into the palanquin and passing around a bag of dates.

"Yea, the place looks cool!" Mellow Tron said after a while, spitting out his date stone.

"Even though it's so very hot!" Tarquin gasped, going for a flask of water and pouring it over his head.

"What do we do when we see Pharaoh Funkanathen?" Tarquin continued, turning, soaked through, to Cassandra.

"Oh no, we don't worry about things like formalities, just be yourselves! Oh, and another thing, there's something you should know about the pharaoh. This concerns the royal prophecy, upon coming to the thrones of upper and lower Zeegypt the pharaoh was told by the temple priests that he would only live a short while. It was then that he took a solemn oath to party all the time. That's all he does day and night . . . be warned!"

"Wow!" went the others simultaneously and pondered on what Cassandra had said.

With a fanfare and fuss made of royal trumpets, the palanquin came to a stop. The smell of incense was amazing, rosehip mixed with patchouli and jasmine with junipers burning from huge brass braziers set up all over the place. And there were people everywhere, tall Bunian soldiers standing upright holding bronze spears whilst smaller Zeegyptian soldiers stood stock-still with swords, shaven-headed priests of all denominations muttering invocations and spells and giving the group strange looks as they then entered the Royal Chamber where the walls, floors and ceilings were covered in painted stars. Tarquin smiled to himself, feeling rather at home as the whole place reminded him of the Lost Catacombs of Brickie Lane.

"Welcome to the court of his royal majesty – Pharaoh Funkanathen," announced a shaven-headed priest as the musicians blew their ram's horns.

"Please bow before his majesty!" went the priest again.

The group looked at themselves and then around again but couldn't see any pharaoh until, accompanied by some giggling cackles, he entered laughing heartily. And he was a sight allright. He couldn't have been more than twenty-five years old, tiny and skinny to the point of emaciation with an impish face, twinkling eyes and a sympathetic look. His royal robes hung scruffily to his feet while the double crown of Zeegypt hung untidily on his young head. The pharaoh's pale green eyes looked at them all exquisitely and Anarkali was sure they were twinkling merrily with some inner mischievousness of their own. His delicate nose sniffed the air and finally his pert mouth parted to speak.

"Hello Cassandra, I see you've brought your friends!" said the king in a high fluted voice as he twirled his sceptre around his left hand like a juggler. Bursting into a fit of giggles, the pharaoh stood on one leg and patted his two pet cheetahs on top of their yellow and black-spotted heads with one hand. With the other he smoked an ornate pipe that seemed stuck to his mouth and released an incredibly complex pattern of smoke rings from his earholes, shaped in his favourite design of royal crocodiles racing after barges all sailing up and down the Nile. Then all the while as he smoked and spoke, he juggled tangerines which would suddenly open up and tiny canaries would shoot up to the roof to crap on about a hundred people in the room below. Apart from royal soldiers and priests, there was a gaggle of musicians playing their drums, lyres and flutes and all around the royal throne were sets of bongos and it was obvious that the pharaoh must have been a musician too.

Meanwhile, Cassandra curtseyed to the young pharoah and answered politely. "Yes, they came just on time, our calculations were correct!"

"Well, aren't you going to introduce us?" the pharaoh tittered in a wreath of smoke shuffling upon his throne, chucking away all the tangerine skins and now beating an interesting rhythm on his drums as the crowd roared and clapped their hands in glee.

"Long live Pharaoh Funkanathen!" they sang in chorus. The pharaoh looked resplendent in his white silken gown and laughed as Cassandra slowly and clearly introduced everyone in turn.

"Sorry, yes of course, this is Fareek, this is Tarquin and this is Mellow Tron and this little beauty is Anarkali, all musicians and a dancer brought from the future to make our lives a whole lot more fun."

"Are you from Bunia?" the pharaoh asked Mellow Tron whose

dreadlocks were hiding around the back of his head stunned by the quantity and quality of gold on the king's head-dress.

"No, we're all from Pearly Green," replied Mellow Tron with a mischievous smile. The pharaoh smiled in return and clapped his hands for some refreshments for the guests.

"Wonderful, musicians from another time and space, we're going to have a lot of fun," chuckled the pharaoh, straightening the crown on top of his head and munching on some grapes while his cheetahs curled themselves around his shins and purred contentedly.

"I'd better introduce myself" said Pharaoh Funkanathen, coming off his throne to be closer to them again. The king looked at them all and then took a bow before replying in deep, mock serious, sonorous tones.

"My name is Funkanathen but close friends call me Funky.
I like my blues, I dig my soul but best of all is punky."

And with that King Funky rolled on the floor and giggled at the word "punky". The sight of his royal presence crawling on the floor with unstoppable laughter made the others smile because this wasn't what they had expected from a pharaoh. But this was a pharaoh none the less and the best one ever as they would soon find out.

"Let there be more music!" exclaimed King Funky, getting up as the royal musicians played louder on their strings, horns and drums.

"Hey, that sounds like our music!" Fareek flashed.

"Very close, what does ours go like then?" Tarquin whistled coming up next to Fareek who simply replied in the manner they knew best.

"Boom ... Boom ... Boom. ... Boom ...!"

As the sinuous music played on, the king began to slowly dance, followed by his courtiers. One of them grabbed Fareek by his ears and asked him about the strange looking machine he was carrying. This was the stocky, shaven-headed Plebmoses, the king's sculptor and best friend.

"Oh, this is a music player we've brought from our time and some music too," Fareek replied, blinding Plebmoses in the sudden radiance of his gown.

"Oh great, we're all in for a surprise!" Plebmoses replied, slapping himself on his shaven head with a double-handed dose of percussive glee.

"Your music isn't too bad either."

"No, but it would be good to hear your stuff though."

"Don't worry, you will," Fareek replied excitedly

And with that Plebmoses took Fareek to sit down on some large, comfortable chairs. Slapping his head again, Plebmoses smiled at King Funky who was still spinning slowly on the floor, his eyes closed in musical bliss, and continued his conversation with Fareek.

"Do you know the royal motto, Fareek?" Plebmoses asked after a while, passing him some crunchy bananas. Plebmoses was fascinated to see how huge Fareek's gob was as he stuffed his mouth with more fruit just to see how far it would go.

"No idea . . . mmm . . . tell me . . . mmmm . . . what is it?"

Plebmoses straightened himself and spoke up clearly. "The past is dead and melted down, the present's more fun. Who needs a crown?"

"Wow! . . . sounds amazing!"Fareek replied quickly, knocked out by the very beauty of this simple philosophy.

"And do you know that there are only three rules good King Funky follows? Before he came to power, his grandfather Tutmoses the 75th, the previous pharaoh, had 999 rules for this kingdom."

He gave Fareek time to swallow the rest of the fruit and scan the room overhead for any sign of the canaries.

Quickly pulling out some mirrored shades, Fareek put them on as the golden sights of everything in this wonderful star chamber was starting to dazzle him. He adjusted them properly on the bridge of his nose before replying, "That sounds like a lot."

"And now Funky has reduced it to just three." Plebmoses said hurriedly with a growing smile on his face.

"And what are they?"

With that Plebmoses said nothing but clapped his hands and shouted to the milling crowd. "For the benefit of our foreign friends. What, good people, are the three rules of governance?"

"Double the nosh and double the dosh!" went the dancing crowd, chuckling and throwing each other's hats in the air in the customary manner.

"And rule number two?" Plebmoses shouted, starting to move gracefully to the beat himself.

"If anyone is caught being unhappy they are to be tickled pink with ostrich feathers," went the crowd as they danced rings around each other.

"And rule number three?" Plebmoses shouted as from the middle of the floor as King Funky gave him a huge smile.

"There's no more rules coz there's no more schools!" roared the crowd, finally discovering that heaven was a simple place that lay within their beating hearts.

"Wicked!" sighed Fareek as Mellow Tron came up to join them and Plebmoses sat down again.

"He seems like a groovy king!" Mellow Tron said, tidying up his locks and coming forward to sit next to Fareek.

Plebmoses spoke up quickly. "Why, he's the very best pharaoh that's ever been in the history of our civilisation which goes back a long, long time."

"Wow!" gasped Fareek, scratching his nose and looking hungrily at a hovering agaric-fly that was busily circling his head.

Ignoring the fly and Fareek's hungry look, Plebmoses replied, "Our kingdom is at peace and all wars have been banned. The whole country is at peace and all our historical wars against Kithiopia, Slibya and Zyria have been stopped. External expansion has been stopped and the only expansion allowed is the one in your head!"

"Wow!" Tarquin exclaimed, coming up to join his friends and hitching up his pantaloons and blowing some indescribably crazy smoke rings through his nose.

Time ticked away like butter melting into ghee and about an hour or so later, King Funky now merrily juggling the royal sceptre and one ripe mango in his soft hands, sidled up to the group and quietly asked, "Well, let's listen to your sounds, what you got?"

"We've brought happy Hypno-Tantric Trance for your pleasure, Pharoah!" Fareek enthused, standing up.

"Call me Funky . . . I'm sure we're going to be friends."

Nodding his head at Tarquin and Mellow Tron and rushing over to give Anarkali a peck on the cheeks, Fareek ran to the centre of the dance floor and placed the CD player on his head. Of course, he put some music in it first though and then just stood there shimmering in his gown to the trance that whooshed out of the tiny, yet powerful speakers. King Funky stood agape as these astounding beats filled his royal eardrums.

"Wha . . . What is this . . .?"

"It's some of the music we make up at home," Mellow Tron replied, tying his dreadlocks up in a knot before they did the king any harm. His fingers then started tapping the beats on Anarkali's girlish head and he watched the king's growing pleasure in wonder.

"It's absolutely amazing!" shouted Pharaoh Funkanathen, jumping up and down as Tarquin decided to get in on the act.

Stepping up near the juggling king, he whispered gently into the royal ears. "We hope you like it, we've brought it from a long time ago and a distant place . . ."

King Funky smiled and carried on dancing. This music was so different from the slow acoustic stuff his court musicians played, much faster for a start and inexplicably more wonderful. As the party rang with the delighted whoops of the already entranced crowd, Mellow Tron suddenly had an idea. Rushing up to Fareek who was still standing there with the CD player on his head, Mellow Tron asked a pertinent question.

"Oi . . . Fareek, shall we get the Anatta out now?"

"Great idea!"

And with that Mellow Tron brought out the stash of Anatta he had so carefully secreted and gave some to Plebmoses, to Cassandra and finally, to King Funky. Plebmoses was the royal food-taster as well as court-artist and seeing his best friend hadn't toppled over dead, King Funky popped the Anatta joyfully into his mouth too. All present were then served up and everyone had a wicked time. This crucial meeting between the musicians and King Funky had gone well and they decided there and then to make a present of the many CDs they had with them as well as the solar-powered CD player. The king was overjoyed and his eyes bloomed like summertime roses and his smile spread off the edge of his face and sailed across the universe. However, all was not well in this the happiest of all worlds as Lucifer's time-bandits, the ghostly heckles and speckles, gooks and snooks observed everything from the rooftops of the palace and weren't slow in replying back to their master. The Goodies were here but the Baddies were too. There was trouble ahead.

The royal musicians played with the beats, the palace became Metta-Morph-Aziz and Anarkali decided to get into the swing of things. After spinning around three foot up in the air in the centre of the dance floor next to Fareek, the tiny figures on her golden gown flashed two fingered peace signs at everyone and stuck their thousands of tongues out in a friendly manner. The crowd flashed their tongues back and Anarkali's face burst into smiles as she moved next to the king.

Entranced by his juggling for a while she watched him before plucking up her courage and asking him, "By the way, your majesty what do you do . . .?"

The king carried on dancing, gave her a funny look, stopped for a while and looked at her intently again before replying. "Call me Funky . . . Oh, not much . . . I'm just the king!" Funkanathen smiled with a deprecating shrug. Anarkali was not satisfied and nor were the hundreds of figures on her dancing gown who stuck up one finger in the air.

Anarkali smiled a thin delicate smile and said again, "No, but seriously though!"

The king stopped dancing again, stood on tiptoes, patted her gently on the cheeks and then replied quickly. "I do two things!"

"And what are they?" Anarkali asked with breathless excitement, watching the tiny hummingbirds race to the ceiling to begin their process of crapping on the dizzy crowds below.

The king gave her another quizzical look before replying. "I play bongos!"

Funkanathen then ran over to his throne, grabbing Anarkali by the arm, and sat down and started playing the many bongos assembled around it.

"Thud . . . Thud . . . Thud . . . Thrippity . . . Thud . . .!"

Although he was a powerfully good drummer, Anarkali was not impressed, it was as if he was hiding something.

"What else do you do, Funky? What else do you do?"

King Funky smirked an unfathomable grin and muttered quietly. "Oh, nothing much I rob graves!"

"What?" Anarkali cried, holding onto her two blushing ears and watching the countless figures on her dress do the same.

Funkanathen shrugged his shoulders disdainfully and continued as if without a care in the world, bongos beating in time to his words. "Yes, that's right, I rob graves!"

"Whose graves?" Anarkali gasped, bewildered.

Playing another beautiful ripple of beats from his bongos to complement the wonderful Hypno-Tantric Trance coming out of the top of Fareek's head, Funkanathen finally spoke up. "Oh, only my ancestors, they don't mind, . . . they're already dead, you see. Don't complain much . . .!"

And with that, both got back to dancing. The room rocked all night and into the early hours of the morning as everyone grooved and moved gracefully except for Fareek who was stuck there with the CD player on his head. It was a party to end all parties so it seemed and Zeegypt had never seen anything like it.

After a week of delicious living at the palace the group began to get bored of the high-life and wished they could be doing something more useful, so they did. Anarkali spent much of her time teaching the royal dancers Kathak which she taught very well, and soon most of the royal dancers had learned the moves admirably. Fareek just lay around eating grapes, olives and dates looking very much the better for it. Lying around on big fat cushions, he spent much of his time teaching the pet cheetahs tricks. Tarquin meanwhile, had found solace with the royal musicians and was busy learning all their drum rhythms whilst teaching them synsantooric tabla patterns. Mellow Tron was also learning something new – the art of divination from Cassandra. Having cleared some space in an annexe of the star-chamber, the crone taught him to divine with scarab beetles. Using sixty-four live scarab beetles of different sizes and different colours, she muttered an invocation and threw them all in the ground. Most ran away to hide under furniture but some were left struggling to find their feet upside down on their shells and these were the ones that Cassandra used to make her divination complete.

Mellow Tron squatted on his haunches and learnt whatever Cassandra had to teach him until he no longer needed to look at the water clocks to read the time and would just pick up a handful of beetles, scatter them on the ground, read the ones that were left upside down and then whisper, "Twenty-five to eleven, I think!"

"Well done, that's the correct time!" Cassandra would exclaim, pulling at his dreadlocks that were now so used to her touch that they had stopped snapping back and would lick her hands instead.

One day Anarkali came up to Mellow Tron while he was divining and stamped her tiny feet imperiously on the ground and wailed, "Oi Mellow Tron, I'm bored now!"

She finished by spinning so fast that she drilled a small hole in the ground and Mellow Tron gave her a hand and lifted her out, asking her sweetly, "So what, how can you get bored of life in the palace?"

"I've learnt all the Egyptian dances, taught everyone Kathak and now I want to go home!"

"Which home Anarkali, Pearly Green or Kathakstan?" Fareek added, coming close to the swirling dust that surrounded their little sister.

"Yeah, that's right, when are we going to have another adventure?" Tarquin added, bounding up to be next to them dropping a few bongos here and there.

"Yeah, I'm getting tired of listening to our CDs, we must have heard them a few hundred times now."

"Well, play them in a different order!" Mellow Tron suggested helpfully, untying the knots that his locks had got themselves into.

"Anarkali's right why are we here? . . . and where's King Funky? We haven't seen him for days!" Tarquin interjected.

Fareek cleared his throat and decided to enlighten everyone. "That's right, he goes off with Plebmoses for a few days, disappears off the face of the earth and returns with a beaming grin on his face!"

Sensing the quick change in tempo in emotions and feelings, Mellow Tron stood up straight and asked everyone clearly, "Is anyone unhappy here then?"

"No, no one's unhappy but we're all getting a bit bored!" Tarquin spoke up.

"Cassandra told us that we were here to make the king happy. We have, we've brought him tons of music and he's been off his head munching Anatta and enjoying every moment of it!" Fareek shrieked.

"What do you suggest we do?" Anarkali whistled.

Fareek then sidled up to Mellow Tron and suggested, "Mellow Tron, you're good now at reading the runes and divining the funky scarabs and stuff. Ask them when we are going to get home!"

Mellow Tron did as asked and the others stood open-mouthed as they watched him throw another handful of multi-coloured scarabs which fought pointlessly to become the right side up as Fareek pulled Mellow Tron's ears and asked in excitement, "Well, Mellow Tron, what does it mean?"

Mellow Tron tried to look thoughtful, bit his fingernails and then replied. "Er, umm . . . it means we have to have an adventure!"

"Wow, you mean we've not had our adventure yet?" Fareek asked again in rapid haste.

"No!"

"Well, what sort of an adventure?"

Mellow Tron grabbed another handful of beetles and threw again. He stroked his chin as he pondered, then looking carefully around at all the others, spoke succinctly. "The sacred beetles have spoken, we have to have an adventure with King Funky, our paths are interlinked . . .!"

"Wow!" gasped Anarkali spinning again.

"Groovy!" added Tarquin, now drumming on his own head with his powerful fingers.

"Far out!" Fareek whistled through clenched teeth, flapping his gown up and down for effect.

Little did they know how accurate Mellow Tron's divination had been because the following morning at 5am they were all wakened by the priests to tell them to go immediately in the royal star-chamber. Pharaoh Funkanathen had finally called for them.

"Okay, Okay wake up! Party's over, time to get to work, the pharaoh awaits you all," Plebmoses shrieked, pulling Mellow Tron's dreadlocks and waking up his snake-heads.

"Er . . . wassup?" Fareek gasped as a couple of efficient priests pulled the warm blanket off his body. Seeing Plebmoses appear with a bowl of cold water to throw upon him he sat up, rubbed his eyes and wrapped himself in his holographic gown, so Plebmoses advanced upon Tarquin who was dreaming of beautiful things and cuddling a couple of bongos.

"Oh, go away, still wanna sleep . . .!" he complained as Plebmoses tickled his feet with velvet gloves.

"Please, just five minutes more," Mellow Tron gasped, befuddled.

"Yeah, come back tomorrow," Fareek yawned.

Plebmoses tugged at the sacred thread around his midriff before replying. "No, we are all leaving when the water clock strikes half past five."

"Where are we going?" Fareek asked, beginning to show some interest but Plebmoses looked officious for a moment and then replied enigmatically. "That's something only King Funky can tell you."

"Awright, Plebmoses . . . who else is going?"

"Apart from you three, Anarkali and the most esteemed Cassandra, King Funky and lastly myself."

Fareek scratched his head, exhaled, and finally asked, "Have you woken them up yet?"

"Of course I have, they're ready, dressed, washed and waiting."

"Well, what are we waiting for then?" Fareek whistled at the same moment booting Mellow Tron and Tarquin out of bed.

By 5.20am the group had all assembled in the throne room. King Funky was already there wrapping up a load of cucumber sandwiches and containers of water and putting them into five jute bags. His eyes looked up as he gave the bags to Plebmoses, Fareek, Mellow Tron, Tarquin and put the last one on his own back.

King Funky finished by giggling, and ceremoniously taking his crown off and placing it on his throne to replace it with a woollen hat. Suddenly straightening up he turned to Plebmoses. "Has the sleeping smoke been lit yet, Plebmoses?"

"Yes the whole palace has been lit with burning braziers and everyone's falling asleep."

"We can't leave before everyone's asleep!"

"Yes, King Funky, there's only the warriors outside the throne room left awake . . .!"

"Yippee . . . Great . . . Let's go!"

As everyone waited, little Anarkali took the chance to peer out of the windows of the throne room and saw that everyone had fallen asleep. There were shaven-headed priests collapsed in groups on the floor, soldiers asleep standing up with their swords and lances at the ready, cooks asleep on their chopping boards, astrologers asleep on their astrolabes, musicians asleep on their lyres and even the sacred cats and dogs were asleep on each other. And then she asked, "Excuse me, King Funky but why have you put everyone to sleep and when will they wake up?"

King Funky strolled up beside her, gently took her hand and explained. The others listened avidly.

"Look, we are all going on a little trip. It will do everyone a lot of good but it's important that no one knows where we are going as that would change all things and destroy the magic of what we do."

"Oh wow! . . . heard it all but didn't understand a thing," Mellow Tron gasped and gave the king a sweet which he sucked deliciously and elucidated further.

"Don't worry, good people, the palace will wake up the instant we return. There's nothing to worry about; me, Cassandra and Plebmoses have done this many times before . . . Tee . . . Hee . . . Heee!"

"Enough, now we have to get to the Pyramids at Geezer!"

Plebmoses exclaimed suddenly, guiding them all out of the door.

"But we just came from there!" Fareek gasped, rubbing his nose manfully and looking quizzical.

"Who cares? . . . It's there we must go," Plebmoses replied with a smirk watching King Funky crack up out of the corner of his eye and say commandingly:

"Off to the harbour and onto the nearest fishing boat to Geezer!"

Within one hour they had found a compliant boat and crew and within two, they were off down the Nile on their inexorable way to the ancient pyramids again. The boat was extremely fast, being light and sleek and within two and a half days they had arrived. Taking a few camels they quickly plodded their way to the pyramids where they had first found Cassandra waiting for them.

King Funky led the way, his camel being the fastest, and as he pulled at his woollen hat he announced, "And there it is, good peeps, this is where we are going to go shopping."

Little Anarkali looked bemused and the tiny dancing figures on her gown shrugged their shoulders. Fareek meanwhile, was expanding his rapidly dilating hallucinogenic left eye to saucer-like proportions once more. Handsome Tarquin watched Plebmoses reply as Cassandra laughed at King Funky's cryptic comments from the rear.

"But there's a difference, we don't ever pay when we go shopping," Plebmoses suggested, smiling to the group while King Funky asked Anarkali, "Do you know what that is?"

"That's the pyramid of Chyops!" Anarkali replied as her silver ankle bells shook in the sudden breeze.

"Do you know who he was?"

"He was a pharaoh just like you, silly!" replied the young girl.

King Funky slowed his camel down and started picking his nose. He gratuitously examined a kingly booger before replying. "I know that but in reality he was my great-grandfather, one hundred and eight generations ago. Cassandra and Plebmoses know the magic of these tombs better than most."

"Well dear, I always meditate on the top in my goat-skin tent!" Cassandra interjected.

"But this pyramid is really magic!" King Funky emphasised, scratching his mouth as Mellow Tron commented.

"Well, it's really huge for a start."

"Yes but it gets more interesting when you get inside," Plebmoses replied, back now and beginning to sweat profusely under the hot sun.

"Why?"

"The pyramid is one hundred times bigger inside and under than it looks like from outside!"

Suddenly Tarquin raced his camel up to be near King Funky and ignoring his melting hair gel asked quickly, "But tell me something, King Funky, aren't most of your ancestors buried in the Valley of the Kings?"

"That used to be true but me, Plebmoses and Cassandra have robbed them all already ... and so we have to come here now."

Plebmoses decided to elucidate further for their benefit. "You see it was just a myth put about by the pharaoh's family through times past that the majority of the bodies were stashed in the Valley of the Kings. It's not true, there are about five thousand pharaohs buried in this one pyramid alone ..."

"So what do you do?" Anarkali asked.

King Funky didn't bother to hesitate before replying. "We simply come and rob it!"

"Why?"

"Because the dead don't have any damn need of gold but my people do!"

Plebmoses, ever the arbiter, moved his camel to the front and said, "Let me explain for King Funky, half the gold we keep for the use of the ordinary people."

"That's generous!" replied the musicians in one voice.

"And what happens to the other half?" Anarkali asked.

Plebmoses turned to Cassandra who quickly replied, "Something really special happens. It gets taken away by some visitors who you will soon see."

"Don't talk about the leprechauns yet. That's meant to be a secret!" Plebmoses spat furiously, racing his camel forward to try and put a clamp onto her mouth.

"Mmm ... Oh OK ...!" Cassandra mumbled as Plebmoses' hands found themselves firmly clamped to her lips.

Anarkali instantly sussed out the plot much quicker than her pals and she grabbed the king's tangerines and asked, "King Funky, why do you give half the gold away to the leprechauns?"

"Oh I don't know ... they ask so nicely and they are magical beings so it's best not to offend them. Obviously they must have a great need for it!"

They were now at the base of the pyramid and slowing down, they all parked their camels, tying them up by their tails and followed King Funky to a crack in the rocks at the base of the pyramid. The portal was not very big but totally obscured and, stepping forward, Cassandra uttered a curse-breaking mantra sonorously and waited for its sorcery to take effect

"Open Sesame ... open peanut ... open every door ...
Open hazelnut ... open marshmallow ... everyone knows the score!"

Suddenly, before their disbelieving eyes the crack in the rocks began to open up. Firstly, it was like a hairline fracture but with gentle tickling from Cassandra's practised hands, the gap grew greater and greater until very soon it was large enough to allow them to enter.

King Funky jumped up and down and rushing forward to the front, jumped inside and shouted frenetically behind him. "Quick follow me and take care of the curses that surround this place. It's a good thing Cassandra is an excellent curse-breaker or we'd be in trouble for sure."

"Wow!" screamed Anarkali as they stepped through the portal into the pyramid.

"Far out," Fareek muttered.

"Or far in, it doesn't really matter," Tarquin sniggered, propelling Mellow Tron forward with a mighty kick and following soon behind.

They were walking through a tunnel in absolute darkness except for the handful of golden scarabs Cassandra had scattered to the floor. These plodded off at the front and conveniently shone like mini beacons to light the way.

"Hey, follow the beetles, they know the way, they were here the last time!" King Funky exclaimed, lifting up his white silken gown and hurrying along.

"I'm glad someone does, it seems just like the Lost Catacombs!" Mellow Tron suggested assertively, becalming his dazed dreadlocks with a stern look.

"Nah, this is much creepier!" Fareek added, brushing the dust off his light-emitting gown and coughing.

"Yeah, there's something definitely strange and spooky about this place!" Tarquin said in a conspiratorial manner, chewing on a gobstopper he had found. Plebmoses waited for them to catch him up and decided to offer them some words of advice.

"Yes, this place is filled with the ghosts of evil priests and ghouls too!"

"What are they doing here?" Mellow Tron asked, instantly bewildered.

Tarquin replied, "Well, it's their home too."

Plebmoses laughed at Tarquin's inner logic and continued to the others. "And you have to be careful of the curses. These can be simple little things designed to trip you up as you walk along to far more complex magic that can blow you heads off as you turn around a wrong corner but that's why Cassandra's here as the ghostly spooks are no match for her."

"Speak for yourself, I'm not too sure I know everything!" Cassandra pipped up, scrunching her black woollen gown in her hand and giggling like a schoolgirl.

Plebmoses wasn't fooled and knew that Cassandra only ever giggled when she was being serious. He cleared his voice and spoke up. "Anything up, Cassandra?"

"Yes, I feel the presence of more ghostly heckles and speckles than usual!"

"Is that going to be a problem?"

"I don't know yet, let's just carry on anyway," the seer sighed and rubbed her blind eyes to clarify her inner vision further.

They turned right in the tunnel and and seemed to be going to the top of the pyramid. It was all getting rather confusing as nobody but Cassandra and King Funky could be sure where they were going. They passed countless caves which reminded them of the sweet world underneath the cobblestones of Brickie Lane and all the time Cassandra would push her lithe way past King Funky and mutter invocations to appease the spirits of the pyramid.

"By the balls of St Stan, we are surrounded by so much death here!" Anarkali suddenly screamed.

Plebmoses stepped forward to pat her on the head and exclaimed, "Don't look at it that way, little Anarkali, look at them as just sleeping."

Then just to make an exact point, Cassandra suddenly took the group further forward. At the next confluence of tunnels, she saw the open sarcophagi that King Funky and Plebmoses had robbed earlier. In both tombs, the mummies slept on mysteriously and looked as though they were smiling.

"Uuurgh ... its disgusting!" Anarkali insisted, stepping quickly aside.

"Yuchkee ... they're dead!" Fareek added, pulling his gown well out of the way.

Plebmoses sighed, shrugged his shoulders and explained. "Don't look at it like that, they're only sleeping ...!"

Cassandra suddenly sniffed the air and stopped. She held her hand back to motion the others to stop as well. Then she saw with her inner eye something strange taking place.

"Aaah, the mummies they're moving!" Anarkali screamed, jumping ten steps back in one single hop.

"Are they trying to get out of the tombs?" Tarquin shouted, as King Funky stepped forward and spoke authoritatively for one so elfin.

"Don't worry everyone, I know how to placate them and put them back to sleep."

"Is it always the case that they get up even when they're dead?" Tarquin said quickly but King Funky wasn't worried at all and said confidently:

"Nah, its nothing to be scared of, each of these mummies is one of my ancestors from a time past and they are only trying to get up to say hello ... Hello great-great grandpops ... How's life ... er ... I mean death?"

Cassandra then raised her hands and with a sublime look of pure magic, she uttered her invocation in a high voice, quite unlike her usual guttural one.

"In a dream one person enjoys one hundred years of happiness and then awakes, while another awakes after being happy for just a moment."

With those special words, both mummies fell back asleep in their sarcophagi and Cassandra sighed with relief. They carried on and after a while King Funky ran up front, deftly avoiding dangerous traps that could have spiked them clean through their bodies with dangerous blades; sent them spiralling below to their certain doom, strangled them on magical vines designed to throttle all comers, mangled them on falling boulders that could come tumbling down from nowhere and a host of other potential mishaps. These were the curses so cleverly designed by his grandfathers to stop grave robbers but unfortunately for the pharaohs, the curses had no effect on King Funky.

After dismantling a particularly vicious, giant leech from around one corner of the tunnel, King Funky tugged at his woollen cap and shouted back to the others, "Don't worry, just follow me. The curses don't affect me as I'm of the royal family."

After what seemed like a few hours wandering in these labyrinths, they finally entered into an area of tombs that they had not seen before where giant boulders closed the tombs from inquisitive gazes.

King Funky now used secret passwords to enable the boulders to slide away magically as he mumbled, "Open the damn door, I'm the King and I'll be in there one day, I'm sure!"

The boulders slid back to reveal the inside of the tomb. They had come far to enter somewhere special and were deep in the heart of the labyrinth where the hidden treasures were kept.

"Aaaah . . .!" Anarkali screamed as the sudden onrush of golden light hit her full on.

"Far out . . ." Mellow Tron mumbled under his breath as his dreadlocks raced around his face.

"Wicked . . .!" Fareek laughed aloud, greedily taking in the sights.

"Wonderful . . .!" Tarquin tittered tremulously.

"The pyramids are stashed to the brim with gold . . .!" he continued, and looking nonchalant King Funky scratched his chin and replied, "Well at least this burial chamber is."

"Will you take a look over here?" Mellow Tron asked Fareek, his dreadlocks trying to grab the other by the throat for attention.

Fareek didn't even bother to turn around as he replied. "No, I'm too busy being gobsmacked looking at that stuff over there!"

There was gold everywhere, scattered on the floor like grains of wild rice tumbling from a magical pitcher; there were golden coins by the thousands and they were wading through the chamber ankle-deep in them. There must have been thousands of gold bars too, each one enough to stave off famine in any district of the king's domain for decades and there were also death-masks, sarcophagi and the countless funerary stuff that went with a burial. Anarkali stopped in wonder, looking at the beauty of the pure gold death-mask in the sarcophagi. She had seen King Tutankhamen's death-mask once, inside a museum, but this was even more splendid and artistically so sublime that she couldn't take her eyes off it.

"We need to steal the gold," King Funky added and the others stopped what they were doing to listen.

"How are we going to do that?" Mellow Tron asked after a moment's hesitation.

"Easy peasy, just watch!" shot back the king, laughing again.

The ball was back in Cassandra's field and ignoring the excited screaming of the others, she rubbed her blind eyes, took a deep breath and muttered:

"Holy gold do as your told and rise into the air for me!
You're far to good to hang around with the dead
when the living all want to have tea!"

With that a sudden plume of acrid purple-blue smoke came out from Cassandra's ears and everyone watched dumbfounded as all the gold began to rise with the sea of golden coins being the very first. Like a school of twinklefish they swarmed themselves around the room like a shoal of wonder. The gold bars were next, floating four feet off the ground as they followed the movements of the smaller golden coins. And then the urns and vases and such-like shot off into the air to float around on top. Lastly, it was the turn of the golden death-mask which rose and settled itself three foot in the air in the middle of this sea of moving gold. With a sudden smile Cassandra led the way with the holy gold following them like a faithful pooch.

"I'm gobsmacked," Fareek said, picking at his nose.

"No you're not . . . you're just silly!" Tarquin replied.

It was then that Mellow Tron grabbed their attention and hurriedly pointed out, "Anarkali's off again!"

Anarkali their little sister was dancing to the music of the spheres again which no one could hear but her. Anarkali started to dance and spun into the air and no one could stop her. Even Plebmoses slapped his horny head in surprise as she took off to the tops of the tunnels.

As they watched King Funky break into a bewildering smile, Plebmoses explained to the others. "He's the king of thieves being the greatest grave robber of all but he still doesn't know why he has to give half the gold to the leprechauns."

"Why does he do that?"

Plebmoses grinned and continued in one breath. "Good King Funky gives away half the gold he steals from the tombs to his peoples … and half is given to the leprechauns that ask him for it. When asked why he gives it to them he always says mysteriously 'I don't know … I didn't ask … and anyways it's best not to ask … maybe its something to do with the sun.' All in all it's a mystery that none of us can solve, we'd all love to know what the leprechauns do with the gold but nobody knows!"

"Far out!" wheezed Mellow Tron.

"Yeah, we are all impressed too, others may get rid of the family silver but our king gets rid of the family gold and no one seems to suffer either!"

"King Funky's a good thief," Mellow Tron suggested.

"The best in the world!" Plebmoses replied.

Although he did not realise it at the time, Plebmoses was wrong as King Funky was only the second best thief in history. There was one better than him and of that one we shall soon hear.

After a short break where they munched on their cucumber sandwiches and drank the barley beer they had packed in their knapsacks, they were feeling relaxed. Here they were, somewhere near the middle of the pyramid, trying to find their way out. They had come on a mission to steal as much gold as possible and had succeeded.

"It's been rather easy!" Fareek mumbled to Tarquin, rubbing his pained gums and frowning.

"What has?" Tarquin asked quickly swallowing some figs.

Fareek stood up and cleared his throat before replying. "All this grave robbing and other associated stuff!"

Tarquin scratched his Bollywood balls and muttered quietly, "I thought it would have been rather more complicated than it's really been!"

"Yeah, too easy, what do you reckon, Anarkali?" Fareek asked as their sister approached. Anarkali looked and replied, "I don't know, it feels rather strange from here … dancing in the air!"

"She's right, my inner eye can sense a change in the vibes, the atmosphere is changing," Cassandra added, quickly moving near to them at the speed of thought.

Tarquin quickly swallowed the fig he'd been munching and asked the seer, grabbing her by her old gown, "What do you mean, Cassandra … what's changing?"

Cassandra placed a soothing hand on his temple before replying. "There seems to be more of a ghostly presence of heckles and speckles than is usually the case, we have to take extreme care from now on."

"Did you hear that Tarquin?... No mucking around, we don't know what could be there for us, waiting around a corner." Fareek finished with a flourish.

"Yeah, take care!" Tarquin responded, enviously watching Anarkali fly off again.

They moved on down to the base of the pyramid from which they had entered and had been inside the giant tomb for a good seven hours and even Plebmoses wondered if their camels had managed to untie their tails yet. He began to get more and more worried the further they descended as Cassandra began to giggle like a child which meant that trouble was just around the corner. He told King Funky of his concern. A distinct change was taking place and they all began to feel rather afraid. The light-emitting golden scarab beetles shone dimmer in the distance, moving faster away from them.

From his base at the centre of Fort Cox, Lucifer pulled at his giant red prongs on the top of his head and stared at the All-Seeing Time Ball. As the myriad of speckled lizards scurried around his mottled skin, the ruler of Hell munched on another pile of farple larvae and watched the scene in front of him very carefully. His heckles, speckles and ghouls were already inside the pyramid and ready to attack and would be joining the demons, diabolics, ghosts of greedy priests and the occasional evil pharaoh. He gulped and groaned.

"Excellent, all going to plan!"

From inside the top of the pyramid the leader of the ghostly heckles flapped his wings and spoke quietly into the All-Seeing Time Ball clenched to its chest. Lucifer was at the other end so it would have to speak politely.

"Everything ready, boss. What shall we do?"

"Just wait for my given order and then attack."

"How shall we plan the attack?"

Lucifer thought for a while before replying. "This is what you have to do ... The speckles can all attack the handsome fool with the Bollywood bloomers ...!"

"And then?"

"The heckles can fight the idiot with the dilating eye, then the ghouls can attack the one with dreadlocks while the rest can go for Cassandra, King Funky and his bald-headed retainer ... and then the dancing girl."

"And what's the main objective of this military exercise, your exaltedness?"

Lucifer peered closer to the orb and shouted his response.

"Scare the living daylights out of them all and most of all, don't forget to steal the gold. I want that gold. I need that gold. There's no thief better than me ... so don't fail!"

"Yes, sir ... no, sir ... three bags completely full, sir!"

And then on the signal of a sea-conch, they all attacked at once. In thirty seconds they descended from the tops of the pyramid to meet the others heading for the exit. There were hundreds of speckles spitting fire and blowing smoke as they flapped their dangerous wings. Ghostly diabolics flew straight through walls and the ghosts of greedy priests and evil pharaohs followed them while monsters shrieked, freaked and made fearsome noises as they descended faster than a free-falling fart.

Within moments hundreds of heckles, speckles, ghouls and ghosts found themselves flying towards the same tunnel where the good-guys were. They were coming out from the ceilings, tombs, walls and the very air itself.

"Aaah! We're being attacked!" Fareek squealed as a hundred falling monsters wrapped themselves around him with tremendous force.

"On no, they're going for my throat!" Mellow Tron screamed, as he felt his body being pulled in all directions.

"What are these evil flying things?" was all that Tarquin was able to say before being smothered by a colossal squad of steaming speckles.

"Oh no ... not ghosts, ghouls and demons ... I'm allergic to them!" Anarkali shouted from somewhere up in the air as her dress decided to come to her aid.

"Dear Anarkali, don't say a word, just spin faster and go higher into the air," sung the tiny voices on her embroidered gown.

It was left to Cassandra to try her magic to stop them and standing strongly against the demonic flow she tried a magic mantra.

"Scribbledy Poo . . . Ghosts go scam
Bugger off, creatures . . . may magic flazaam!!!"

Nothing happened and Cassandra was unstuck. The stinking speckles were the first to attack Tarquin, and circling him by the hundreds, they grabbed his bloomers and ripped them to shreds. Fareek was pointlessly trying to fight the heckles, their evil snorts blowing dangerous flames that singed his fabulous gown. Fareek screamed as hundreds of the evil speckles tried throttling him to death. Meanwhile, Mellow Tron was having no luck against the ghouls, his dreadlocks were cowering inside a floating funerary urn and the bogey-splattering ghouls dived into his flesh. Mellow Tron screamed and in a final, desperate shout he screamed at his departed dreadlocks to return.

"Come back, you flaming cowards!"

With the greatest reluctance the cowardly dreadlocks emerged from their hiding place, flew in silent formation and wrapped themselves around the speckle that was strangling Mellow Tron, freeing him. Cassandra had created a force-field around herself and although the demons and diabolics couldn't attack her directly, her invocations weren't going to plan either but she tried her magic once more.

"Begone . . . Begone . . . Go back home
Go tell your master, Lucifer . . . he's out on his own
By hook or by crook, we'll win for shame
Or by the power of Isis . . . Cassandra is not my name!"

Flames shot out of the end of Cassandra's walking stick but still nothing happened. Plebmoses was trembling and hiding in a sarcophagi whilst King Funky's tiny form was shivering with laughter, watching the whole scene while juggling with the bones of some dead pharaoh. It was then that the tiny figures on Anarkali's dress understood what to do.

"Higher Anarkali . . . Fly higher and start to spin . . . move like you've never moved before and we'll all hang on for the ride!"

Anarkali did as she was told, freed herself of the demons that were trying to grab her by the soles of her feet and arose seven feet into the air. In six seconds flat, the best dancer this side of the universe was stomping Kathak in the air very fast. She sang as she spun.

"Spin ... Spin ... Spin ... What was out is now what is in
"Spin ... Spin ... Spin ... Lets sort out the mess that we're all in!"

And with that she started spinning so fast the tiny figures on her gown almost fell off and had to grab each other by the hands to keep from tumbling. Anarkali had never danced like this before and was soon spinning at over 7,027 revolutions a minute, almost as fast as the speed of light and to the others who could see her from below, just a shimmering blur. The demons stood no chance.

Within seconds all the demons, diabolics, ghosts, ghouls, speckles and heckles were falling off the bodies of their chosen captives and were flying through the air. With screams and squeals they were all repulsed to the higher levels of the pyramid with their tails between their legs. Lucifer, still affixed to his All-Seeing Time Ball, raged and roared as the scattered golden booty remained uncollected. Slamming his hands into his lap, he roared in pain. There would be hell to pay for this.

"Brilliant Anarkali!" Fareek whistled between his teeth as the storm in the tomb subsided.

"You can stop spinning and come down now!" Tarquin added, watching the smiles come back to everyone's faces.

"Yippe!" screamed the tiny voices on Anarkali's gown as the heroine started coming down. Cassandra stepped up to be close to her as she landed and praised her to the skies.

"Hurray ... always knew you had it in you, your dance is the most powerful magic I've ever seen, little one!"

"Thank you, Granny Cass ... thanks!"

At this point Plebmoses took over in an authoritative voice as King Funky just giggled.

"Come on, Cassandra ... lift up the gold and let's all go!"

With a swish of her hand, Cassandra lifted all the scattered gold up and led the way deeper and downer.

"Where are we going now?" Fareek asked in a voice full of trepidation.

"Aren't we going to the exit yet?" Mellow Tron muttered.

"We've got the gold, what more do we need?" Fareek continued, looking clearly disgruntled.

Cassandra shifted to one side and explained. "We are on a mission to find someone special."

"Who?"

"My husband."

"What?"

And without further ado they carried on descending.

After the attack of the ghostly heckles and speckles, the confidence of the wandering group had been jarred but they kept going down in silence. The atmosphere was too full of darkness and ancient magic for anything else and it was a good thing that Cassandra's light-emitting beetles still shone the path for them.

"Wonder how much further we have to go?" Fareek asked, panting aloud.

"I'm getting tired and feel scared in case the monsters attack us again!" Anarkali added, from the air.

"Oh, don't worry about that, they won't," Mellow Tron interjected.

"How do you know?" Anarkali asked, still unsure of everything.

"Oh, a little birdie told me!" Mellow Tron replied.

"There aren't any birds here, no cosmic canaries are coming out of King Funky's tangerines!"

"It's just a figure of expression!"

They travelled deeper and down and were now so deep down in the bowels of the pyramid that the little light that remained was luminous when Anarkali thought she saw some butterflies and exclaimed aloud. "Hey, Fareek, can you see the golden butterflies?"

"What?"

"What did you say Anarkali?" Tarquin added, stepping up close

"I said did you see the golden butterflies that are over there?"

"Tarquin look above and wonder!" Fareek sighed, staring up in spellbound bewilderment.

"Oh incredible, here Mellow Tron, have a good look!" Tarquin replied, ecstatically poking his head up in joy.

And they all looked. Above their heads and surrounding them on every side, were about 10,000 golden butterflies each no more than three inches wide, an incredible sight. As they descended deeper, the host of golden butterflies joined them on their path to find Cassandra's lost husband, then suddenly, there he was, exclaiming,

"Cassandra!"

"Dear husband!"

"Thought you'd never get here!"

"Who's this, Cassandra?" Fareek asked, stepping in front of the others and taking the lead.

Cassandra smiled a huge smile and replied deftly. "This is my husband – the Old Blind Man of Thebiz!"

"Oh wow! He's amazing!" Mellow Tron gasped.

"Oh no, he's so white-haired and old!" Tarquin exclaimed, taking in the sights and wondering.

"More than that he's so blind!" Anarkali said, coming down from the air about a foot.

Everyone pondered for a moment before Fareek continued. "Well, I suppose they suit each other!" he said with a look of delight in both eyes, dilating or not.

Anarkali continued, "Yeah, but there's a difference!"

"What's that?"

"This old man is actually blind but our Cassandra can see with her inner vision!"

Fareek scratched his nose as he pondered Anarkali's words. As Cassandra and the Old Blind Man of Thebiz embraced, Fareek noticed that the old man had a cane to help him walk with and unlike Cassandra, his old body lacked inner vision. He was simply blind. Now fully comfortable, the Old Blind Man of Thebiz finally gave them his full attention.

"Sit down, King Funky please sit, Plebmoses and all you others, please sit down too."

"How does he know who we are?" Tarquin whispered to Fareek hoping not to be overheard.

Fareek replied, "He can probably feel it!"

However, the Old Blind Man had overheard them with his acute hearing and replied directly to Tarquin, tottering on his cane. "No, good people, I always know that King Funky and the faithful Plebmoses accompany Cassandra when they go on their grave-robbing expeditions!"

"So how comes you don't have inner visions?" Tarquin asked with a growing confidence, sitting himself down on the ground and folding his legs.

"Oh, I don't let this little affliction bother me too much Tarquin. Sit down, Mellow Tron and stand on the earth Anarkali and you Fareek stop dilating that eye."

Scratching in the contents of his bloomers, Tarquin asked

another question. "How do you know who we are and what we look like if you're blind, old man?"

The Old Blind Man of Thebiz pulled at his long fingers and thought for a moment before replying.

"Not to worry ... I'll tell you in a while!"

The group then sat down in the corner of the corridor taking care not to squash the butterflies still milling around. Cassandra then got out a large bottle of Astral Ale and taking a swig shared it around. As they drank, they pondered. Fareek was worried about the floating gold above their heads and hoped Cassandra's magic would not wear off or they would have a ton of golden bricks falling on their heads. As they watched the Old Blind Man of Thebiz, he rushed around the room sliding open various bricks and letting in light. He whizzed around for ten minutes whilst the others ate and drank, adjusting this brick and pulling that one open when suddenly it worked. A blazing luminous light shone from out of the crack in the stones and flooded the corridor with its laser lights.

"Oh wow, it's lasers!" King Funky shrieked.

"Are you sure?" Anarkali asked in a querulous manner wanting to know everything.

"How can it be, lasers haven't been invented for thousands of years?" Fareek interjected quickly, not believing what his ears had heard.

"Look it's lasers, green, shiny and most incredible!" Plebmoses answered for King Funky, delighting the crowds by bouncing the laser light off his bald head.

The Old Man of Thebiz took note of their consternation, turned around and spoke. "Well done Fareek, you've noticed it's a laser!"

"But don't you need technology and machines to make them?"

"Certainly not, we've had lasers here in Zeegypt for thousands of years!"

"What do you call it then?"

"We call it the Spirit Light and within this pyramid, I am the guardian of the Spirit Light!"

"What does it do?"

The old man giggled, swapped the patches over his blind eyes and continued in a whisper. "The Spirit Light is the laser light that comes out of the top of the pyramid when everything's aligned properly!"

"What do you mean aligned?" Fareek insisted.

The Old Blind Man of Thebiz tugged at his chin before replying.

"Well for a start these three pyramids move very slowly and turn around, they are not fixed to the shifting sands below."

"Oh wow!" cried Mellow Tron.

"What does that mean old man?" Tarquin asked sitting up and concentrating wholeheartedly on the other's words.

"It means that once every two thousand years, the three pyramids are in perfect alignment with each other."

Tarquin sat up even higher and asked again. "And then what happens?"

"Well, I'm waiting for the alignment and all I can tell you is that Thebiz is the greatest living temple around. With the three pyramids aligned and the Spirit Light shining off the top of each and every one, the luminous light hits Thebiz or the Temple of Zarnak as you know it and something incredible happens there!"

"Wow!" gasped Mellow Tron, still at a loss for words.

"Can you tell us what it is?" Fareek asked.

"No, that would only stop the fun of it all!"

"And when do you think this special alignment will take place?" Fareek asked further.

"Oh, I can tell you that easily!"

"When will it be?"

"Within six months, on midsummer's day to be exact!"

"Make sure you're in Zeegypt when that happens," King Funky said, in a serious manner.

Tarquin wasn't impressed by all this but he was more impressed by the fact that the old man knew who they were. He asked imperiously, "Well, old man how *do* you know who we are?"

"Ah yes, I promised to tell you!" the other replied, turning around to face him hurriedly.

"And how do you know what we look like if you're blind?"

The Old Blind Man of Thebiz did nothing for a while but then he tapped his cane on the ground and said, "Just take a look at what you are standing on, boys."

They all looked on the ground and found themselves to be standing on a special sort of circular stone.

"Oh wow, didn't notice before because the butterflies were covering it," Tarquin gasped, starting to see things in a newer light.

"It seems like a stone with pictures on," Mellow Tron said, falling onto the floor and crawling around on his hands and knees.

"Yes, the stone covers the ground you stand on, it's about twenty feet by fifteen in size, it's very old, older than the pyramids and there's something very special about it."

The others got to their knees and scrambled on the floor to get a closer look. The floor was raised and all the hieroglyphs were in circles that met in the middle.

"Incredible!" gasped Anarkali, now decidedly with her feet on the ground and crawling around the floor like the rest. The old one pointed an emaciated finger to the floor and said with passion.

"And the figures and the hieroglyphs change and move."

"Unbelievable!" gasped King Funky smiling.

Tarquin carried on questioning in his inimitable, ballsy manner. "Who are all these people carved in the rocks, old man?"

"Go on, take a closer look and figure it out for yourself."

Tarquin and Fareek scrabbled around the floor and Tarquin was the first to find himself.

"Hey, old man, this figure looks like me!" he screamed with his hand touching a certain part of the floor.

"And this figure looks like me!" Mellow Tron shrieked next to him.

"And there's Anarkali dancing in the air!" Fareek added, mesmerised by this new and interesting game.

"Here's Mellow Tron's dreadlocks flying off his head!" chuckled the voices on Anarkali's golden gown as she bent down to take a closer look.

Fareek and Tarquin then exclaimed excitedly to each other, "Look, its Pearly Green!" shouted Tarquin, pulling Fareek.

"And there's Fairlight making Anatta!" Fareek replied, pulling his mate's bloomers.

"And that's how we left Pearly Green after eating Anatta!" Tarquin shot back quicker than a cosmic canary could crap.

"And there's us meeting Cassandra on top of the pyramid!"

"And there's us inside the royal palace!"

"And wow, look it's us inside this pyramid reading the Rosetta Stone!" Fareek finished slowly getting back up to his feet and standing upright. He then asked the Old Blind Man a question. "But ... how come the figures have disappeared ... how does our story end ...?"

"Oh I can't tell you that, you are the masters and mistresses of your own fate and destiny. Only I know how the story ends," chuckled the old man starting to munch on a crunchy banana Anarkali had passed him but Fareek would have none of this complacency.

"So, why don't you tell us?"

"I can't . . . I'm not allowed."

"But this Rosetta Stone is the story of our adventures."

"Correct!"

"Please, old man, translate the stuff for us!"

"Oh no, I'm not allowed to decipher the future. I have to let it happen naturally to all the characters in the story."

"Simply incredible!" gasped King Funky, gobsmacked by this turn of events.

"Wonderful!" beamed Plebmoses, swigging on some barley wine and evidently enjoying it.

"Amazing!" trilled Anarkali, loving every moment.

"Groovy!" added Mellow Tron, getting into the swing of things.

"Far out!" finished Tarquin, starting to beat time on the rocks.

"What's this 'Far out'?" King Funky asked hesitantly mulling over the new words in his hypnotically happy brain.

"And what's 'groovy'?" Plebmoses finished, carelessly chucking the banana-skin away and pondering.

It was then that the Old Blind Man of Thebiz smiled and told everyone the real reason they were there. Ignoring the "oohs" and "aahs" he finally chuckled and said, "You all want to know the real reason you are here?"

"Of course we do!" Anarkali trilled.

"Yeah, for sure!" Fareek added quickly.

"Most definitely," Mellow Tron added.

"Me, I don't care . . . much!" Tarquin squealed, still beating time on the rocks and starting to dance.

"Tee . . . Hee . . . Chuckle . . . Chuckle . . .!" replied King Funky in predictable manner.

The Old Blind Man of Thebiz let his cane lead him to a recess in the stone wall where the flowing Spirit Light flooded the chamber. With graceful fingers and a steady hand, he pulled a certain stone gently away and pulled out a box from a secret compartment. He then came forward to the group with the wooden box in his hand, carefully opened it and pulled out what was inside, a giant golden scarab beetle about six inches long with a fine, misty pollen over its body. It crawled slowly onto the old man's hands and sat silently being stroked and comforted.

"That's a scarab!" Fareek said, consternation in his voice.

"Yes, but a very special one," the old man replied with a growing smile as he explained. "This one is like no other!"

"What do we have to do with it?" Fareek asked with bewilderment on his face.

"You will have to look after it. This is the reason you came to Zeegypt. You have to take this beetle back to Pearly Green and give it to Fairlight . . ."

"Wow, you know Fairlight the magic potion maker?"

"Why, of course, I've felt his face in the Rosetta Stone!"

"Why do we have to give it to Fairlight?"

"Can't tell you any more, dears, all I can say is that Fairlight will know."

For seven minutes they just wandered along not saying anything. Fareek held the wooden box with the scarab beetle very carefully to his chest. Mellow Tron trotted along fighting with his dreadlocks while Anarkali tranced along merrily following King Funky. Plebmoses remained as enigmatic as ever, not giving anything away, whilst Cassandra and the Old Blind Man of Thebiz walked along behind everyone, kissing and cuddling.

"What are we doing here?" Anarkali asked.

"Where are we going?" Mellow Tron asked too.

"What's to become of us?" Fareek whispered, his left eye expanding to ridiculous proportions.

"Are we never going to stop?" Tarquin pleaded. King Funky chuckled, wagged his finger and led them on further.

Juggling his own floating eyebrows for a change he whistled a reply. "Just a little bit more!"

"Just down this corridor here!" Cassandra added.

Plebmoses rubbed his bald head and finished in an excited holler. "They usually catch us down here!"

"Who?" Fareek asked, quickly jumping up in trepidation.

King Funky pondered before replying. "The landlords, of course . . . Tee . . . Hee . . . Hee . . .!"

"Who's that?"

"You'll see."

"When?"

"Just about now, I think!" finished King Funky looking at the small water-clock he kept in his bag. And he was right.

Suddenly, completely out of nowhere, the strangest sight ever hit the bewildered group. Cassandra, the Old Blind Man of Thebiz and King Funky just stood back and smiled while the others, Mellow Tron, Fareek, Anarkali and Tarquin, simply screamed.

"Aaah, what are these . . .?" Fareek squealed like a flying pig plummeting to the ground.

"Oooh . . . what are those . . .?" Tarquin twittered like a terrapin trying to swim with one fin.

"Don't worry, they are safe," King Funky exclaimed, sticking his eyebrows on his face back to front.

Suddenly materialising in front of their gobsmacked eyes, sixteen leprechauns appeared without warning. Some looked like the traditional Mayrish ones and wore green uniforms and funny green hats while others wore Bagpipistani kilts and tartan scarves. However the Bongostani leprechauns wore one-piece maroon-coloured robes. These were some of the very same that lived in Sidney Arthur's evacuated house in Pearly Green. Yet others from deepest Zeru wore romper-suits and day-glo smiles that lit up the tombs like flowers from Paradise and the last group, from Zeetpong wore straw clothes and conical bamboo hats. Most surely they were all leprechauns and it was clear that King Funky was pleased to see them.

"Back so soon?" he tittered tentatively like a twit in tatters.

"You know the score, Pharaoh Funkanathen?" replied one of the leprechauns bouncing to the ground with a haversack held to his back. He was the oldest in the group, one of the maroon-robed ones from Pearly Green and waited for the king to reply.

"Half for me and half for you!"

"That's right!"

It was then that Cassandra stepped in.

"But that's not strictly true, good leprechauns, King Funky never keeps any for himself, he gives one half of the gold away to the poor and undeserving . . .!"

The Bongostani leprechaun scratched his impish head before replying. "Well why not? He's got lots of palaces, lots of friends and is an excellent bongo player. What more does a person need . . .?"

"Hmm . . . that's true!" muttered Plebmoses with a quizzical look. He hadn't pondered on this before. What the leprechaun was saying was perfectly correct.

Suddenly, half of the gold stack that had been following Cassandra and floating seven feet in the air, shot off through the smoky air and poured itself into the huge expanding haversacks carried by the sixteen international leprechauns. Yes, these were magical creatures all right and it seemed like they could do anything as their elfin faces grinned as the haversacks blew up like balloons. Fareek was worried in case they actually exploded and showered the group with tons of golden bricks but he had no real reason to worry as they just kept expanding until they were the size of small houses.

"What are they doing?" the many voices on Anarkali's gown asked her in excited polyphony.

"They are taking half the gold!" Plebmoses replied, watching this scene from a show he'd seen many times.

"Why?" asked Anarkali, quickly picking up on her dress's distress.

"Ask King Funky!" Plebmoses added, holding her hands to stop her taking off into the air again.

Spinning quickly to be in front of the king, Anarkali asked, bemused, "King Funky, why are they taking half the gold?"

"Er . . . umm I've no idea actually, I think it's something to do with the sun or something."

Fareek had had enough of this procrastination and stepped quickly forward. "Let's ask a leprechaun!"

Taking hold of Fareek's anguished cue, Tarquin turned to face the grinning Bongostani leprechaun. "Oi, Leprechaun geezer . . . Why are you taking the gold.?"

"Simple, friend, 'cos King Funky is generous enough to give it to us in the first place!"

"That's a feeble answer . . . tell us the real reason please, mate."

The leprechaun lifted his maroon robes and scratched his knee before replying. "Nah . . . you only find that out at the end of this story and now is not the end."

"But Cassandra can tell us . . . she's a wicked diviner!" Fareek screamed into the ears of the Bongostani leprechaun, tugging at his robes and lifting him off the ground in his excitement. Cassandra stopped him quickly before he started to bounce the little chap like a rubber ball. Leprechauns may have been tiny and cute but they were quite unpredictable. Cassandra shook him into sense and sensibility and replied daintily, "Yes, but the scarabs won't tell us about this."

"Oh!" gibbered Fareek, now starting to comprehend the limit to Cassandra's magical powers.

Meanwhile, Anarkali watched the leprechauns shiver and shake until one rolled forwards and backwards upside down on the ground a few times and finally straightened himself up and exclaimed to the Funky, "Here's the business card of Captain Kidd."

The funky pharaoh freaked and tugged at his earholes in order to hear clearer. "What and who?"

"Captain Kidd!" retorted the turban-clad leprechaun, not giving King Funky time to think as the pharaoh hopped from one foot to the other desperately trying to work out who this "Captain Kidd" might be and looking at the card with strange script written on it. (It actually said "Captain Kidd – Rascal".)

"You've got to meet him!" the little fellow repeated before starting to drone a Trans-Tibetan drone of mind-befuddling complexity.

King Funky started to look distinctly bilious and confused as he asked. "But I don't know him . . . who is he?"

"He's a pirate of the Spanglish Main in the eighteenth century!" said the Bongostani leprechaun.

King Funky started pulling at his hair; robbing his ancestors was one thing but being told to be a messenger was something else completely. "That's almost 4000 years in the future!" he gasped, holding onto Anarkali's ankle bells as she started to rise in the air once more.

The Bongostani leprechaun looked at the other fifteen leprechauns and they all took the cue and replied in one voice. "3,987 to be exact."

"What's so special about him?" asked the old Bongostani leprechaun like a conductor leading a choir.

"He's the best thief in the universe!" replied the fifteen leprechauns. King Funky stopped juggling his worries and exclaimed in obvious disappointment.

"Oh, I thought I was the best thief."

"Well almost . . . you're the second best thief in the universe but this Captain Kidd is better," replied the Bongostani leprechaun as quick as a flash, grinning like a drunken monkey pretending to be a monk.

"I'd love to meet him . . .!" King Funky chuckled.

"Don't worry . . . you will and he'll tell you our secret."

"Great!"

Without further ado but with a screech and a scream, the little fellow jumped into the air, grabbed onto its giant haversack and with a mischievous grin at all the other leprechauns flashed a cosmic wink and disappeared along with half the gold.

King Funky then clapped Plebmoses on the shoulders, stopped

the Old Blind Man crashing into a wall and turned around to the others.

"Well that's all folks ... time to go home!" The king didn't realise how prophetic his words actually were. He meant "back to mine" but destiny had a different plan and it was soon going to split them up.

Mellow Tron meanwhile carried on shaking his head and this was bound to have consequences. And it did.

"Hey look at that Anatta coming out of his hair!" shrieked Fareek.

"There's so much of it!" Tarquin screamed, rushing up to pick up those scattered on the floor.

"What the Anatta or the hair?" asked Anarkali.

"Both," Tarquin replied, quickly picking up the Anatta by the handful and stashing them into his copious pockets.

"Wicked, let's neck some!" Fareek suggested, starting to stash some directly into his ever-hungry gob.

"Yeah, me first!" Mellow Tron cried, slapping his dreadlocks to stop them from going crazy.

"No, me!" Fareek squealed, slapping Mellow Tron with skilled dexterity.

"I was in the line before you!" Tarquin insisted, dripping blue hair-gel everywhere.

"No, you weren't!" Fareek relied as quick as a flash, pushing Tarquin and wrestling him to the ground.

As Cassandra, the Old Blind Man of Thebiz, King Funky and Plebmoses watched in disbelief, something very odd started to happen to the other group. They were beginning to go well weird and their bodies started to dissolve. Anarkali was the first to slip into her astral form, quickly followed by Mellow Tron and Fareek. Tarquin was the last to transform into his gossamer form and as King Funky watched with breaking heart, their great adventure was starting to take them somewhere else again.

"Aaah no ... don't leave me behind!" King Funky screamed, not wanting to be separated from his new pals. He stomped up and down in piteous rage and began to sob. He had necked some Anatta too but wasn't dissolving as well. The Zeegyptians stayed in their solid forms while the Pearly Green posse began to dissolve their physical forms quicker than ice left out in the desert.

Fareek was the first to understand the monarch's predicament and replied quickly. "Sorry, King Funky, we have no control over this."

Bawling and sobbing his eyes out, Funky shouted, "I don't want you to go . . . I want to be in your band . . . Boo hoo!"

As Fareek and the others slowly dissolved into an inexplicable mist, Tarquin said a few comforting words to the king. "We want you as well.. you're the best funky drummer ever!"

"Promise to come back!" King Funky gasped, rubbing the tears from his eyes and sniffing loudly.

"We promise!" replied Mellow Tron in a faraway voice as dissolution began to take him to places never dreamt of before.

"I'll wait for you!" sobbed the king, wiping his nose with his robe.

"And then we can all play in the band together!" Fareek insisted as he felt the trip begin to really take off. The king was inconsolable though a bit more understanding.

"Boo hoo hoo . . . that would be great!

Where did the Metta-Morph-Aziz crew go to exactly? Let's find out.

25

Return to Topping

It was March 1st 1701. The day was bright, sunny and rather glorious and also the very day that Captain Kidd was to be hanged, drawn and badly quartered at the makeshift gallows at Topping Stairs. It had taken six months for the *Greedy Fat Rat* to return him in chains and King Stinky Billy wanted to be present at the hanging of the most infamous pirate ever. The king believed that hanging was too good for the most revolutionary pirate that ever lived and wanted to behead and quarter him too. The royal ship was docked near the stairs and although the river was rather narrow there, the streets on the northern bank were too. Bunting and banners were waving themselves from the masts and beams of the oaken ship and the sailors were all bedecked in garlands of pansies and posies with their trousers and tunics starched and a brilliant white. Captain Kidd was going to get hanged at eleven o'clock and now it was only nine. The whole process wouldn't take too long, no more then ten minutes for a slow choking and gibbering garrotting that wouldn't kill him but leave him with enough consciousness for the terrors to follow. The beheading would take twenty minutes more as the king had insisted that it was to be done with a blunt, rusty axe and take a long time. And as for the horrible quartering, this was to take three hours as poor Captain Kidd was to be cut up into many pieces with razor blades, a death of a thousand cuts. But what had he done that was so wrong? Why was poor Captain Kidd being singled out for such torments? Simple, Captain Kidd was the best pirate ever this side of the rainbow. He never kept a single gold coin out of all the gold he stole on the Spanglish Main but gave it away immediately to the leprechauns. King Funky may have given the Bongostani leprechauns and his brethren half of the gold he robbed, but Captain Kidd always gave it all away and it was this innate generosity that was getting him into trouble. King Billy (the fat, smelly one) hated Captain Kidd, not just because of the stolen gold and not telling him where it had gone to but because of the famous song that the crew members of the *Leprechaun's Delight* always sang as Captain Kidd was singing now.

"Stinky Billy was a man so silly,
he thought his head was up his arse
and a cucumber was his willy.
When he was young he went to Bagpipistan
To put down a rebellion his forefathers began.
He smashed them up so very bad
everyone in the land went really mad
and Stinky Billy is now their king
and look at the mess we've landed in!

Stinky Billy, fat pudding and pie
kissed the girls and wondered why
when the boys came out to play
Stinky Billy ran away.
Stinky Billy, fat pudding and pie,
kissed the girls and wondered why
when the boys came out to play
Stinky Billy wanted to stay.
Stinky Billy, fat pudding and pie
kissed the boys and it made him cry.
When they rushed out to make him stay
the greedy fat rat ran away!

We don't want no Stinky Billy
and we do want to be free
so let him drown in the sea!"

Deep in the hold of the stinking, sweaty ship, Captain Kidd was singing his infamous song without restraint. He had been given his condemned man's breakfast and was chomping on centuries-old oakum cornflakes without much enthusiasm. He looked through the porthole at another ship bobbing up and down on the river, the famous *Beggars Banquet* the fastest and most dangerous ship used in piracy up and down the waters of the unsuspecting world and, swigging a bottle of "Rudolph's Reminiscing Rum" that a kindly sailor had left him to drown his sorrows, he reflected on his life as he watched the sailors erecting a set of gallows that he would soon be decorating.

"Hey Percy, my feathered friend, hasn't life been great?" whistled Captain Kidd, hoisting himself into a better, upright position.

"Squawk … If you say so, captain!" replied the green and blue bird alighting on Captain Kidd's shoulder while he elucidated further.

"I've had a brilliant life and regret nothing."

His faithful, feathered companion hopped from foot to foot before replying. "Squawk, bummer in the summer!" squeaked Percy the persevering parrot as it suddenly flew around in circles in the ship's hold getting nowhere. Captain Kidd sighed again.

"Not to worry though, plenty more lifetimes where this came from!"

"That's what you always say." Captain Kidd painfully adjusted his sitting position and replied, straightening his three-pointed hat and curly black wig and pouring some of the delicious "Rudolph's Reminiscing Rum" down his feathered friend's throat before finishing the rest of the bottle in a single swig and throwing it away. The parrot squawked and carried on flying around in circles still getting nowhere.

Meanwhile, on top of the "Hanged, Drawn and Badly Quartered" pub four holy ghosts were invisibly sunning themselves on the cracked and broken roof. It was a beautiful day and they were putting into place Sidney Arthur's wonderful plan. Sidney was enjoying the slight breeze as it went straight through his body and out the other side. His tatty hole-ridden clothes ruffled as he hung on to the carpet-bag of trickster ideas. Next to Sidney Arthur the two ghosts of Billy Blake and Danny De Foe were playing cards.

"Oi, you cheated!" shouted Danny De Foe as Billy Blake notched up the score on Danny's wooden peg-leg.

Billy pretended to look aggrieved, picked at a ghostly spot and testily replied, "Did no such thing, Danny, you always win, makes a change if I win."

Danny shook himself and responded in a similar manner. "It's not winning or losing that matters it's how you play the game."

"Speak for yourself, it's time I win once in a while after so much losing!" Billy Blake replied with his face askew.

Danny sighed, realised it was pointless to argue with his best friend and, shaking some ghostly woodworms out of his wooden leg, cried, "Hmm ... Billy stop jabbering so and deal the cards again!"

Danny then slowly unscrewed his wooden leg and held it between his jaws as he wasn't sure that Billy wouldn't bite it all the way through. It was always like this when they played cards, a perfectly nice friendship was invariably ruined whenever Billy's queen of hearts met Danny's ace of spades.

Meanwhile, Madame Serendipity hovered in the air and then sat herself down on the pinnacle of the roof right next to Sidney Arthur. Her old, round face looked slightly bewildered as she looked around. Down below, the sailors could be clearly seen with their hammers and saws constructing the gallows while the black-hooded executioner was practising his moves with the razor blades and the rusty, blunt axe. It was a perfect day to die, thought Madame Serendipity as the activity on the ground got busier. Far better to die on a nice, hot sunny day than a miserable wet, gloomy one she thought meditatively. Her frilly white dress flapped in the breeze and sitting next to Sidney Arthur, she got out her Tapestry of Alternative Endings and within seconds she began to start stitching scenes on it.

Sidney Arthur stopped smoking his pipe, sat back and asked with interest. "Madame Serendipity, will Captain Kidd really die?"

Madame Serendipity stopped weaving on her tapestry and gently turned to face him. "It's too early to tell, Sidney Arthur, on this tapestry there's still a grim ending."

"We have to make it work!" Sidney Arthur said, blowing out smoke rings in the form of a hangman's noose.

Madame Serendipity took his ghostly hand and smiled. "The thing about fate is that sometimes you have to disregard its potential consequences and just go for it."

"You are right as always, how's the noose?" Sidney Arthur asked.

Madame Serendipity showed Sidney Arthur her left hand, grasping the magic noose. "It's here clenched in my hand, very soon I'm going to fly down to the gallows, discreetly remove the hempen noose and replace it with this!"

"Malik Slik Sylvester's magic muslin is one of the most amazing things of twenty-first century Pearly Green," Sidney Arthur said, taking in the sights in her clenched fist with growing wonder.

Madame Serendipity smiled a curious grin before continuing.

"Yes, it's all those special black widow spiders that make the difference. The thousands of hallucinogenic agaric-flies they swallow goes to make their cobwebs very special, they are dissolvable."

"Are you sure they will dissolve in time and not hang Captain Kidd?"

"Don't worry Sidney Arthur, it will dissolve and in time, I've tested it before I came."

"Great," laughed Sidney Arthur with a growing confidence that they were on to a winner.

Meanwhile, having finished the game which they both lost for cheating, Danny De Foe threw the playing cards into the air where they fluttered down like pigeon feathers onto the scurrying sailors below. Flying up to surround Sidney Arthur and Madame Serendipity on either side, they sat there like discontented monkeys glued to the moving panorama on her Tapestry of Alternative Endings.

Suddenly Billy rubbed his face and asked, "Oi, Sidney Arthur, how are they going to kill Captain Kidd?"

"They will hang him, behead him and quarter him!" Sidney replied after a minute's polite silence after a question like that.

"Is that the order they will do it in, Sidney?" Billy asked, flying up to be closer to Sidney Arthur.

"Of course, you idiot, it's traditional!" Sidney Arthur said with a grin.

Billy thought for a while, scratched his head and then muttered, "What about changing the order?"

"What do you mean, Billy?" Danny De Foe said as Billy offered Madame Serendipity a ghostly plum.

"Why can't they behead him first and then quarter him and finally hang him?"

"Because how are they going to hang him if they chop his head off first?"

"Mmmm . . . hadn't thought of that . . .!"

"Well why not quarter him first, then chop his head off and then hang him?" Danny asked, munching on a ghostly apple that Billy had passed him.

Sidney Arthur had had enough of a silly conversation that was going nowhere. "Well, that's just plain silly, it would look silly, hanging just a torso wouldn't it, you need a whole body."

"Oh . . .!" Billy gasped, beginning to see the point.

"I see . . . " Danny added after a while, chewing on his fingers and looking thoughtful.

Madame Serendipity had had enough of this ridiculous conversation and said, "What does it matter how they kill him, our job is to set him free."

Her Tapestry of Alternative Endings lay motionless on the roof and the shifting panorama changed and changed. Staring at it intently for a while, Sidney Arthur scratched his nose and pondered.

Ambling through the cobbled streets, BB, Charlie and the Artful Dodger were eating delicious hot cross buns and were very happy. Charlie, the Kocknee Rebel, pulled at his ginger locks as his bony frame towered over the crowds and he felt very hopeful. Ever since the Artful Dodger and himself had engineered BB's hasty cure and the week spent relaxing in Itchycoo Park he felt great but what of the Artful Dodger?

Dobbins stomped the streets with his usual, malnourished look as he unhinged his oversized hat to let silken handkerchiefs and silken pocket watches stream out of the top. A whole host of scruffy, shoeless children followed his path and picked up the silken goodies. These dirty, grubby children were the ancestors of the future Funkadelic Tribe and the Artful Dodger suddenly stopped to urge one scruffy urchin up to blow his snotty nose on one of the handkerchiefs. Little did he know that he had picked up his own great, great, great, great, great, grandfather but he should have known better as the kid tried to steal his pantaloons.

Suddenly as they turned the corner and came to Topping Lane, near the river, the vibrations changed completely. There, they could see a large crowd gathered around a set of gallows that had just been finished. The many sailors from the *Greedy Fat Rat* who'd built them, wiped their sweaty brows and went off to have a drink at the crowded "Hanged, Drawn and Badly Quartered". There must have been a good few hundred people there, pigging out and waiting for the execution.

"What's up, Charlie?" BB asked his much taller friend, poking him in the back for a reply.

"Don't know, mate," Charlie retorted but BB wouldn't take no for an answer and tapped on the Artful Dodger's top hat.

"Something's up, hey Dobbins, can you see anything?"

The Artful Dodger slammed his top hat down and turned around to face the over-excited beatnik. "No, not really, the crowds seem to be too thick."

Meanwhile, Charlie stood on his toes to get a better grasp of reality. "Look, I can clearly see the gallows and an executioner's chopping block!"

"And I can see the evil, hooded executioner sitting on a chair to one side!" the Artful Dodger responded as quick as a flash, somersaulting forwards to land on Charlie's head and shoulders.

"I wonder who they are going to execute?" BB said, wiping his kaleidoscopic spectacles clean with a silken handkerchief and wishing he could see like the others.

"Yeah, poor soul, you shouldn't have to execute anyone!" Charlie exclaimed with a sigh, stamping his feet in disgust. As a result, Dobbins fell off his shoulders and tumbled onto the muddy ground.

"Hey, where are you going, Dobbins?" Charlie asked, his eyes looking piercingly at the Artful Dodger.

"I'm going near the front!"

"Why?"

"So I can better see what's happening!"

BB was getting frustrated at not being able to see a single thing and asked impatiently. "Charlie you're tall and can see over the heads of the crowd, what can you see?"

Charlie looked down to see his friend jumping up and down and replied, "Nothing much, not a lot has happened . . . I think they are waiting for the executioner to make the first move." It was then that BB saw something pasted to a wall, a tacky poster.

"Hey, look at this poster plastered to the wall!"

"What does it say?" Charlie asked sheepishly, knowing that he couldn't read.

"I don't know . . . I can't read and nor can you."

"Well, look at the picture then!"

"It looks like a pirate, that's it, they've caught a pirate!"

The face of Captain Kidd on the poster smiled and stuck out its tongue. Obviously, it wasn't very perturbed about the immediate future or perhaps it was too far gone to care.

It was then that the town crier, drunk as usual, rang his bell to get everyone's attention and shouted to the milling crowd. "Hear Ye . . . Hear Ye . . . Hear Ye!"

"What's up you fat pumpkaloon?" shouted a joker in the crowd, chucking a crunchy banana at the drunken town crier's head and just missing by inches.

"Yeah, what's up you drunken sot?" cried a miserable looking woman dressed in rags throwing a bucketful of dirty water at the town crier's fat body. Stumbling around for a while he hesitated, found his balance and then his voice.

"Hear Ye . . . Hear Ye!"

"You've already said that," screamed the jester throwing a handful of horse manure at the stage.

"Get on with it!"

"Hurry up, we haven't got all day!"

The town crier finally took notice, straightened himself up and did his job. His red waistcoat shivered under the weight of his excess lard as he spoke. "Burp . . . Umm . . . all right, then listen, you moronic plebs . . . hear ye once more. Today at eleven o'clock the infamous pirate Captain Kidd will be badly hanged, drawn and quartered. Get your places near the front and don't forget you can get discount front row tickets from me . . . Burp . . .! Remember that our sovereign has sailed for six months trying to bring this dratted pirate back to port. If it wasn't for his valiant efforts then it would not have happened!"

"Why, what's Captain Kidd done that he's got to be killed for?" screamed a smelly and vicious looking fishwife. The town crier burped once more before answering.

"For the two most heinous crimes, that of stealing the King's gold and being the writer of the most terrible song in the universe."

"What song is that then?" shouted the fishwife chucking a handful of rotting salmon at his head.

Brushing some off his brow, the unfazed Town-Crier continued. "Hrmm . . . The terrible song, of course!"

"Hip . . . Hip . . .!" shouted some of the crowd, throwing their hats in the air.

It was obvious that the town crier had said the wrong thing because the crowd loved the Stinky Billly Song. It was revolting and revolutionary and took the piss out of the king which was no bad thing so they shouted their appreciation for it in loud voices.

"That's a simply brilliant song," screamed a man starting to look angry and waving a walking stick in the air.

"You can't kill a man for making up such an excellent tune!" remonstrated another, picking up a load of rotten potatoes and getting ready to chuck them too.

"Yeah, let him go free!" hollered the mad fishwife, emptying a load of fish guts over his feet to no real effect.

"He's innocent!" roared the waiting crowds, obviously getting very restive.

BB didn't like the vibes and tugged at Charlie's long, lanky arm. "Oh cripes, Charlie ... it's getting serious!"

"Yeah, doesn't look like the crowd wants this Captain Kidd dead."

"He's certainly not killed anyone," BB stammered with a plaintive sigh, lighting a small cheroot he had stashed in his pockets.

Charlie was starting to look very wistful too and just like the Artful Dodger, a single tear that spoke volumes trickled down his cheek. He exhaled deeply and sadly as he spoke. "Yeah, he reminds me of my dad, he was a bank robber, he never hurt nobody either, wasn't very good at it though, he always got caught!"

Dobbins came rushing to join them and gasped aloud for the benefit of the others. "Looks like its nearly eleven o'clock now, should be any time soon!"

"What shall we do Charlie?" BB asked suddenly.

With an understanding empathy, Charlie felt exactly the same. "Well matey! I don't really want to stay here and see a human being lose their life!"

"Yeah ... it's disgusting ... Let's go!" BB replied, the sight from his rose-coloured spectacles not being as rosy as usual.

In haste, the Artful Dodger buttoned his top-coat and whistled loudly. "I agree ... lets split!"

As they turned around to move away from the groaning crowds and the disquieting vision of the gallows and the executioners block, Sidney Arthur spied them. Still sitting on top of the "Hanged, Drawn and Badly Quartered", the mischievous Holy Ghost nudged Madame Serendipity who was still examining the threads of her tapestry, almost pushed Billy off the roof and shook Danny by his wooden leg.

"What's up, Sidney?" Danny asked, flapping around to get a better look.

"Yeah ... why did you do that for?" Billy said irately, having almost fallen off.

Sidney Arthur beckoned them all close and pointed to the ground. "Just look down below, what do you see?"

"Not much, just the usual!" sighed Madame S.

Danny definitely did not like what he saw and made his point of view very clear. "Disgusting, grubby people getting ready to watch a public execution!"

Sidney Arthur said quickly, "No, not that. Can you see who's in the crowd, look below, right down there."

Billy stopped playing with his ghostly hourglass and responded with excitement. "Oh yeah, its Bilal, the Banglastani Beatnik, Charlie, the Kockneestani Rebel and Dobbins, the Artful Dodger."

Danny hurrahed and waved his wooden leg in the air as a way of greeting and shouted, "Good to see that they finally made their way out of the opium den."

"Yeah, very good thing!" Madame Serendipity added, beaming a ghostly grin.

However, Sidney Arthur was getting impatient and turning around to the others asked, "But you know what?"

"What, Sidney?" the three ghosts asked together in puzzlement.

"We have to save Captain Kidd!" Sidney Arthur said, looking very serious.

"Why?" Danny asked while shaking a ghostly woodworm out of his wooden leg.

"He's an integral part of the plot."

"Why so?"

"Without him we won't be able to beat Lucifer at his evil game!" Sidney Arthur finally finished with a triumphant smile.

"Oh wow ... never realised!" Billy blurted, bouncing up and down in the air with excitement.

Peg-legged Danny soon joined him, juggling Billy's mythical timepiece to his growing displeasure while replying to Sidney Arthur's cryptic comment. "Nor me," Danny chuckled, chucking Billy's mystical hourglass up into the air where it was deftly caught by the ever-serene Madame S who mercifully gave it back to Billy before he started to cry.

Billy decided to get his own back and angrily flying straight through Danny's ghostly form, he somersaulted in the air very fast and sticking his tongue at his best friend flew towards him with a crazy look on his usually contented face. "Well, you never realise anything!" he screamed slapping Danny and kicking his wooden leg like a broken broomstick. Danny kept his equanimity if not his real leg, which had of course been eaten by a hammerhead-shark during Danny's many years on the desert island.

"Speak for yourself, silly!" Danny replied, unscrewing his wooden leg and hitting Billy over the head with it. It was up to Madame Serendipity to calm them both and this she did with a beautiful smile in both their directions.

"Well, what are we going to do now, Sidney Arthur?" Madame Serendipity turned around to ask Sidney after the other two had calmed down.

He flew to be nearer to her and replied, "There's not much we can do but we can get those foolish idiots down there to do our work!"

"How are you going to do that?"

"I'm going to have to implant the idea to free Captain Kidd, right in the beatnik's brain!"

And with that Sidney Arthur floated from the rooftop to hover seven feet above BB's silly head in seven seconds flat. Billy Blake, Danny De Foe and Madame Serendipity watched with fascination, rather like someone watching a thief at work but this was just the opposite as Sidney Arthur wasn't taking anything away, quite the reverse. BB could suddenly feel something above his head but he wasn't sure what it was, when Sidney pulled a wicked trickster idea from the carpet bag he always had dangling by his knees and ripping it quickly open, wrenched out the appropriate idea faster than a hummingbird could hum or even a bee could buzz. Before BB knew it, Sidney Arthur had rammed the idea of liberating Captain Kidd into his brain-box and floated back to the rooftops again to be with his amazed pals.

In eleven seconds flat, BB stopped dead in his tracks like a charging rhino stunned with a love grenade and spoke excitedly. "Oi boys ... I've just had an idea."

Charlie and the Artful Dodger then stopped and waited for BB to elucidate further.

"Let's stop, I think we can't let this Captain Kidd die, we should try and save him."

Charlie and the Artful Dodger found themselves agreeing with the beatnik for once.

"Brilliant idea! ... best one you've had in ages, I agree, let's do it!" Charlie said as Dobbins nodded his agreement.

"When did you think of that?" Charlie asked quickly.

"The idea came into my head just now," the Banglastani Beatnik replied, starting to share around a bag of hazelnuts that Dobbins had pick-pocketed earlier from the crowds.

"Okay, lets go back to the gallows and think about what we are going to do." Charlie spoke, manfully getting into stride and planning exactly what they needed to do.

"Yeah!" shouted the Artful Dodger, thinking that this would yet be another scam. (He had been involved in so many in his young life that it would have made another person's hair prematurely grey.)

"Let's go!" shrieked Sid and all off them trotted back towards the gallows.

They soon arrived and were now at the front of a very smelly crowd which made Dodger steal some nosegays to hold under their noses. From the rooftop Sidney Arthur laughed at his plan for good to overcome evil while having a lot of fun in the process and the other ghosts congratulated him profusely.

"Brilliant, Sidney!" Danny shrieked, patting Sidney Arthur on his back and watching his hand go right through him.

"You're so clever!" Billy hollered, in demented happiness.

Sidney Arthur accepted their thanks but fatalistically added, Thank you, boys but let's hope it works."

Far below in the milling crowds BB, Charlie and Dobbins scratched each other's chins, wondering how they were going to save Captain Kidd from the death of a thousand cuts. Time was moving on and although BB always knew that time was a wondrous thing that could be bent into appropriate shapes, here it was getting dangerous. It was now 10.45 am and in fifteen minutes, the grisly performance would begin. The crowds were pushing themselves to the front and the town crier could clearly be seen staggering all over the place, his waistcoat decorated with what looked like pigeon crap (it was, and the source flew high above him still under pursuit by fantasy falcons). He had done his job and there was not much else for him to do so he could now get as drunk as he wanted. Meanwhile, right at the front, the intrepid three scratched their heads trying to think up a plan but everyone they thought of was impractical and they argued amongst themselves trying to sort out the best course of action. They were getting nowhere and Sidney Arthur realised they needed some help so he asked Madame Serendipity to look at her Tapestry of Alternative Endings.

"Right that's it, I'm off to change the noose on the gallows," she whistled, quickly plummeting from the broken rooftops.

"Right you are!" Sidney Arthur cried clapping her on in encouragement.

"Go for it, sister!" shrieked Billy, excitedly shaking the roll of the Tapestry of Alternative Endings in her direction. Billy Blake was overjoyed that Madame Serendipity was racing down to provide a solution.

"Go for it, Madame!" hollered Danny De Foe shaking his wooden leg and sprinking some of Sidney Arthur's ghostly daffodil petals, while down below BB and Charlie fired their fantasy flintlocks at the same time. The falling blooms met the psychedelic upward-moving juniper and mango berry blossoms shot into the skies by the lads. The Artful Dodger was meanwhile thinking how he could steal the rusty axe that would be used to behead Captain Kidd but he didn't get far because the muscular executioner, whose face was covered by a black hood, slowly got up off his chair and took a few practised swipes at the crowd who booed and roared with disgust. BB was wondering why the executioner's head was covered in a black hood and he asked the Artful Dodger in a whisper. Dobbins explained that executioners were usually so hated that their identities were kept a secret so they wouldn't get pummelled by the angry crowd.

Invisibly moving level with the gallows and cheered on by her fellow ghosts, Madame Serendipity quickly ripped off the hempen noose with her left hand, bit through it and chucked it on the floor. She was just about to replace it with the magic muslin one, so carefully brought back from Pearly Green in the future, when suddenly all hell broke loose. She had got the new noose half way up the pole when a whole group of red-winged and white-fanged heckles and speckles raced out of nowhere to stop the show and black bhoots and afreets tumbled from the air from all sides invisibly.

"Speaking to Major Speckle ... Holy Ghost by gallows changing noose!"

Major Speckle harrumphed pulled at the horns atop his evil little head and listened as another monster then flew towards him fast over the heads of the unsuspecting crowd and screeched, "Lieutenant Heckle to Major Speckle ... What shall we do?"

"Stop her!" shrieked Major Speckle, angrily slapping the lieutenant. "Yes, stop her at all costs! She must not be allowed to change the noose! Catch her ... Catch her ...!"

"Aaah!" screeched the bhoots, flying fast to attention.

"Scrawk ...!" screamed the demons, flapping their ears and pulling their noses out of joint.

"Screech . . .!" shrieked the preets, quickly swarming down from the clouds like honey bees and onto poor Madame Serendipity's ghostly form.

"Scronk . . . Roar . . .!" the whole multitude of evil beings that had been hiding in the abandoned building on the other side of the river roared waiting for this moment. It was time to do something or the plan would fail and Madame Serendipity be wrenched apart. From atop the old pub, Sidney Arthur suddenly sat up higher. From both sides of the gallows pole and both sides of the river, he could see countless heckles, speckles, bhoots, ghostly demons and diabolics race across to the gallows pole to try and wrench off the magic muslin noose she had put on in desparate bravery.

"Quick, Lucifer's heckles and speckles!" shouted Sidney Arthur.

Billy checked to see if his mystical hourglass was okay and said, "And ghostly demons and diabolics!"

"Don't forget the bhoots!" added Danny De Foe getting ready for action. Sidney Arthur had now jumped from the roof and was racing towards the ensuing mélée to save Madame Serendipity and his plan.

"Billy, you go for the demons on the left!" Sidney Arthur screamed when they were only fifty feet from the gallows and coming closer by the second.

"What about me?" Danny asked, feeling slightly apprehensive on seeing the multitude of demons and diabolics before them.

Sidney Arthur replied with an emerging grin. "Danny, you go for the preets on the right and I'll attack from the front and destroy the bhoots in the middle!"

"Ok . . . over and out, let's go!" The three holy ghosts screamed together as they tumbled into the mêlée, fists and feet all over the place.

"Aaah!" squealed a demon as a fist pushed it sideways through the air.

"Oook!" howled a bhoot as a flying kick made it stumble and fall gracelessly.

"Eeeek!" a preet shouted, finding itself pushed into a bunch of unsuspecting demons. Then the whole bunch of diabolics, demons, bhoots, preets and minor heckles and speckles pierced the air with their blistering screams.

"Look, angels attacking us!"

"They're not angels . . . they're ghosts!"

"Yeah, but they're holy ones!"

"They're smashing us all over the place ... we must do something!"

"What shall we do?" shrieked a minor heckle as Billy's flying kick landed somewhere unmentionable. A nearby speckle decided to be brave although its face got rudely slapped by a wooden leg.

"Hold your ground and don't be scared ... there's only three of them!"

"Oooof ... yeah, but they seem to be much stronger!" replied the minor heckle as Sidney Arthur ripped the clothes off its back with sudden force, leaving it distressed and naked.

"Don't be such a cowardly demon ... fight back ... what are you, a man or a mouse?"

"I'm neither ... I'm just a hungry bhoot" cried a hungry bhoot trying to escape from Billy Blake's manic pursuit. As they passed each other through the scorched air, the three Holy Ghosts stopped momentarily and had a mid-air chat.

"Great, chaps! ... We seem to be winning," Sidney Arthur whistled with obvious glee.

"How comes we are doing so well if we are outnumbered so much?" Billy asked, strangling a demon with his left hand while kicking a diabolic to the ground.

"Who knows ... who cares ... just keep punching them!"

"It looks like we're evenly matched, us three to their three hundred. What shall we do?" Danny De Foe asked, throttling a minor speckle as he spoke.

Sidney Arthur chucked away the two bhoots he'd been mangling, rubbed his hands together and said. "Let's go for a truce and negotiate!"

Billy looked anxiously towards Madame S., suddenly remembering that the whole point of the fight was to free her and not to get lost in the fantasy of fighting.

Danny could see better than Billy and replied, "She's coping well, she's been tied up by a few diabolics but apart from that she's okay."

Sidney Arthur flew down next to Major Speckle and getting his attention by grabbing his ears, shouted into his ugly mush.

"Oi, Major Speckle ... we should stop fighting as neither side seems to be winning!"

Major Speckle hovered in the smoky air and considered the proposition for a moment before replying. What do you propose to do, pull straws or something?"

"No, something far more sophisticated. I think we should try and talk about it and the best argument wins and the funnier the better," Sidney Arthur suggested with a furtive smile as Major Speckle gave the orders for his seething mobs to stop.

"Okay, heckles, speckles, demons, diabolics, bhoots and preets, stop fighting and gather around."

In two seconds flat the demonic forms were gathered around in a circle with Sidney Arthur giving a wicked wink to Billy and Danny, in the centre. Meanwhile, the assembled crowds below waited with bated breath as there was only ten minutes left before the hanging.

"All right you go first, Major Speckle, tell us why you should win," said Sidney.

Major Speckle flapped his wings a bit and said, "Easy, we always lose, your Anarkali's dance beat us at the pyramids and we want to win. Why should we always lose? We have our pride too, you know!"

Sidney Arthur waited a while for it was his turn.

"All right, Major Speckle, I have a question for you. All you demons wear medallions of your boss Lucifer around your necks!"

"That's right, regulations. The medallions show our great leader meditating on how best to destroy this world and fill it with confusion and illusion."

"Aaah, I see. What are they made of, these idols?"

"It all depends, some are made of wood, some of copper, some bronze, some iron, some gold and some are even of bone."

Sidney Arthur's face took on a secret look of mischief and wonder as he continued. "So the ones made of wood are wooden idols, the ones of copper – copper idols, the ones of bronze – bronze idols and the ones of gold – gold idols."

"That's right," Major Speckle replied, now starting to look confused and not knowing where Sidney Arthur was leading him to.

Sidney Arthur went on almost chuckling. "And the ones made of bone, where do they come from?"

"They come from the femurs of dead saints!"

Suddenly an increasing smirk was spreading over Sidney Arthur's face as he finished. "So the ones made of bone must be bone idols."

"True."

And it was then Sidney Arthur made his point.

"Then you are all bone idle and the reason we are going to beat you is that although we may be fewer in number and are probably just as lazy, we can when we want, work much harder! This is a moment in point."

With that Sidney Arthur gathered up his sleeves and punched Major Speckle so hard he was instantly sent back to Hell taking all his demons with him in the up-draft. In a quicksilver instant they had disappeared back to Lucifer's domain where he would no doubt be waiting for them with bad and bated breath. Billy and Danny looked at Sidney Arthur with sheer awe.

"Wow! How did you do that, Sidney?" Billy asked, his eyes alight, and full of bewildered wonder.

"I'm not telling."

"But you must!" Danny insisted.

Sidney Arthur coughed a furtive cough before coyly replying. "Why, I'm the oldest ghost in Ghost Town and I always keep a few tricks up my sleeve!"

With that they all swept down and freed Madame Serendipity who then firmly placed her own noose on the gallows pole and was hugging them each in turn when drums announced a bedraggled Captain Kidd, his faithful parrot still at his shoulders as he approached the scaffold. He had been made to walk from the *Greedy Fat Rat* and had even been keelhauled around its side as an extra torment devised by King Stinky Billy. With his privateer's face peering inquisitively at the crowds, he clambered onto the scaffold still wrapped in chains and wringing wet. Sidney Arthur's plan was to let the lads know that the noose was made of magic muslin and he sowed the idea swiftly in BB's addled brain.

"Oh wow! I've just had an idea!" BB gasped, rubbing his spectacles as if the inner visions had come through his eyes instead of his head.

"What is it, matey?" Charlie asked.

BB pulled at his ears and quickly replied. "That noose is made of Malik's magic muslin!"

For a moment Charlie couldn't believe what he had just heard. "You mean Malik Slik Sylvester . . . our Malik?"

"Yes, of course, is there any other one?"

"And this magic muslin is special, it's dissolvable." Bilal finished his explanations of insight by coughing but Charlie still wasn't fully satisfied and shifting his eyes to the top of his head, asked again. "How do you know?"

"Oh, just plain intuition, I suppose!"

Charlie and the Artful Dodger suddenly had the growing sensation that BB was telling the truth.

"What shall we do?" Dobbins shouted, looking more mischievous than ever and totally ready for action.

"Oh brilliant, let's rush around to the other side of the gallows next to the river where that small boat is and wait for Captain Kidd there," BB suggested with growing confidence.

Charlie understood immediately what they were to do and added hastily. "We will free Captain Kidd as he falls from the gallows and save him."

"Wonderful," mumbled the Artful Dodger, checking the time. "Most Excellent!"

And with that they moved behind the scaffold ready to free the pirate the moment he landed as by intuition and Sidney Arthur's prompting. They all realised that the noose was going to dissolve. Then, as the whole crowd watched, the executioner got up and stood firmly behind the captain ready to guide him onto the scaffold and the gallows. The town crier then rung his bell and sang out to the assembled crowds as Captain Kidd climbed the scaffold almost cheerfully.

"Captain Kidd, have you anything to say before you are hanged, drawn and quartered?"

From the scaffold with the noose around his piratical neck, Captain Kidd stuck his tongue out at everybody, kissed his parrot goodbye and joked just before the executioner released the lever making him drop to his certain doom.

"Dear God, if there is a god, save my soul, if there is a soul."

And then he fell. From high above on the broken, cracked rooftops of the "Hanged, Drawn and Badly Quartered" Sidney Arthur threw his ghostly head back and laughed and laughed.

26

The Return from Ancient Zeegypt

"AAAH . . .!" SCREAMED Anarkali as her eyes took on the vision of a different world and her ankle bells jingled on the cobblestones of a very familiar street.

"Stop your awful racket, Anarkali!" Mellow Tron screamed loudly until his face burst into a broad smile as he suddenly realised where he was.

"Aaah . . . where are we?" Fareek squealed, his slow brain not registering for a moment where he was.

"We're in Brickie Lane, silly, that's where we are, look at the 777 restaurants in the lane, the clubs, the tea shops and bars," Tarquin finished, jumping up from the street.

Through time they had returned from whence they came, the cobblestones of the Lane. Their return back to twenty-first century Pearly Green had been smooth and Fareek, Mellow Tron and Tarquin could still feel the Anatta they had swallowed so long ago, sometime, someplace in Zeegypt as they blew away the dust that had enveloped them all. It was Sunday and the market was on. All around them were hundreds of stallholders selling everything from broken balloons and static gyroscopes to floating dentures and artificial tails designed for pet baboons. The customers could be counted by the thousands. There they all were, eating donkey noodles and red beans and rice and drinking ice-cold lemon water with the occasional beer thrown over their happy heads for free. The four took a moment to get their bearings and then headed confidently southwards down the Lane which was in full swing. Suddenly a rickshaw raced past Anarkali and made her spin off into the air. It was being pulled by a Dream-Skinned Mandrill because, ever since *that* night of mystic mayhem at Metta-Morph-Aziz, Princess Amrita, Little Lucy, Astral Alice and the innumerable members of Master Fagin's Funkadelic Tribe had absconded from school for ever and the Dream-Skinned Mandrills had found themselves out of a job. It was then that they took up alternative employment as rickshaw pullers in Pearly Green and here was one of them now, running past with a gawping tourist in the back seat and huffing, puffing and sweating.

"By the sacred beanies of St Stan, it's so crowded!" Fareek gasped, pulling his robe up quickly before it got trod upon.

"That's because it's a Sunday," Mellow Tron replied taking in the size of the enormous milling crowds.

"What shall we do?" Anarkali asked, not liking the density of the crazy crowds and in her fragility, starting to feel very stifled.

"Simple, let's get away from all this crowd and disappear into the Lost Catacombs," Fareek gasped as someone bumped into him.

"What shall we do there?"

"What do you mean what shall we do there?" Tarquin replied, stepping up and picking Anarkali gently off the ground so she wouldn't get crushed.

Fareek meanwhile poked a hole through his patchworked jeans with his finger and said emphatically, "We're on a mission, we have to give the scarab to Fairlight. The Old Blind Man of Thebiz told us to do that, didn't he?"

"Oh look! The 'Monsoon Mindstorm', just over there, let's use their huge tandoori oven to enter."

"Come on, let's hurry up, the crowds are pressing me!" shrieked Anarkali.

There, standing on the pavement was a Banglastani waiter clad in a sky-blue cummerbund and wearing a Sergeant Chilli's bandsman's electric-red jacket and smoking a beedi. On seeing the desperate group he politely invited them all inside and graciously escorted them to the kitchens where a white-hatted chef opened the lid to the tandoori oven and with a single word of thanks, they all joined hands and jumped through.

Down, down and downer than down they went to the first level of the Lost Catacombs, the Land of the Living Dreamtime. Anarkali looked out at the familiar stars everywhere, tiny ones the size of a thimble, bigger ones the size of a football and simply huge ones the size of a dustbin shining from everywhere to light up the psychedelic blow-pipe pictures created by cavemen thousands of years ago. Anarkali smiled seeing these paintings because, although they were made before the dawn of civilisation, they looked quite civilised to her.

"Watch out on the left and above your heads!" Mellow Tron shrieked, pointing upwards and giggling.

"What's up?" Tarquin hollered in a fantastic voice, filled with fun.

"More low-flying psychedelic pigs!" Mellow Tron chuckled, crouching to get out of the way.

And it was true. The Lost Catacombs and especially the upper levels of the Lost Catacombs were filled with flocks of psychedelic flying pigs that preferred to live in the magical underground than on the rooftops of Brickie Lane. Deeper down, a whole host of golden sunflowers suddenly appeared growing up to cushion their fall as they plummeted to the ground of the Land of the Living Dreamtime and giant silver salvers suddenly appeared from nowhere, bearing gifts of cakes all labelled with the words "Eat me". This they did, including little Anarkali who simply loved cakes, especially delicious English tea-time ones. She greedily stuffed her little face with both hands making the others laugh until a falling bottle of wonderstuff labelled "Drink me" suddenly appeared. And this they duly did. As a consequence, the cake would enlarge them to a huge size almost filling out the space around them and then the drink would make them shrink again. It was a wonderful game changing size ten times a minute but it was a good thing that they had both cake and drink as taken together they ultimately remained in their usual size and shape.

The eagles had landed and they were finally on the ground again, not in the desert or the cobblestones but near the River of Crystal Light that flowed from the bottom of the Lost Catacombs to the top. The intrepid group decided to set off for Fairlight's Fantasy Factory thousands of feet below in the Land of Awakening Dreamtime. As they journeyed, the group could see everything because of the countless stars embedded in the ceilings, walls and floors of the many corridors and caves. Tarquin mopped his brow thinking it would takes simply ages to pass the Land of the Living Dreamtime before they would reach the Torrible Zone where gubblies, an odd leprechaun here and there, Mullah Ullah, the three crazy Whirlistanis, Habiba and the Hashemites and the countless members of Master Fagin's Funkadelic Tribe all lived in caves of their own. Mellow Tron, walking next to Tarquin, gasped, realising the incredible depth of the Torrible Zone and that they would have to cross the vast expanse of the funky coconut tree clad Gromboolian Plains to get to Fairlight's Fantasy Factory.

After about an hour's travelling, they came upon "Kid Kurry's Magical Muncherie", the only real place to eat around here. It was full of creatures. As Anarkali and the others approached, it was as if time had stood still.

"Gosh, it's like nothing's changed!" Fareek whistled, starting to feel hungry. Although he had breakfasted on buns in ancient Zeegypt, that was simply thousands of years ago and he was feeling peckish once again.

"Were they all here last time we were here?" Tarquin asked, quickly putting a comb through his hair now that they were in mixed company.

"It seems like it," Mellow Tron added, nudging Anarkali for her opinion.

The Queen of Kathak stopped spinning and said quickly, "Either they've never been away and have all been sitting here munching out on the house speciality or they have just got here."

"It's so hard to tell anything down here!" Mellow Tron added helpfully, thinking that what Anarkali had just said was absolutely true. Staring at the diners who were their many friends in exactly the same positions as before, Mellow Tron began to feel like Rip Van Winkle in the mountains.

Kassim, the Sun-Trance Kid pointed his spotty nose towards his brother and nudged him till Karim saw who the new arrivals were and beamed excitedly.

"Cor, Blimey! Look what the cat's dragged in."

"How are you, Fareek?" asked Kassim, the arrows of love from his purple cowboy hat shooting out indiscriminately and hitting everyone everywhere. He hugged Fareek and asked desperately, "Where in St Stan's name have you been?"

"Yeah, we've been looking all over for you," Karim shouted.

"We thought maybe you got lost completely," Kassim added quickly, laughing and giggling now that his best mate was back.

"Well then, where you been?" Karim asked, folding his arms across his chest like an Zeegyptian mummy.

"It's such a long story, you wouldn't believe us if we told you." Fareek sighed, stealing a chapatti roll from a nearby table and munching on it meditatively.

By now, many had come over to greet Anarkali, Fareek, Mellow Tron and Tarquin and were all incredibly curious as to where the group had disappeared to.

"The music's not been the same since you left!" Abraxas said, clapping his hands with glee.

"That's obvious" Mellow Tron exclaimed with an appropriate air of condescension.

"And nor has the dance been the same without Anarkali there," the tiny Hussain the Insane added, staring transfixed at the changing colours on his beautiful Technocoloured Dreamcoat. His flowery turban was coming loose but he didn't care.

"Really?" Tarquin giggled, feeling rather pleased that they'd been missed.

"Come on then, where you bin?" Azeem the Dream asked. Azeem's serene eyes looked deeply into Tarquin's face trying to fathom out the answer.

Tarquin cleared his throat quickly and answered. "Look it's a long story and we need a nice cup of chai before we can begin!"

"Then sit down at that empty table there and waiters – hurry up!" Karim the Kid Kurry shouted extravagantly goading his waiters into action. He finished with his usual words of encouragement. "Yeah, blinking, bonking, corblimey, hurry up!"

The group began to recount their story to all that were there. Mellow Tron took a delicious sip of the transcendental chai and began.

"Well, we were all making music or jumping up and down trancing at the Bum Note when we found ourselves in a totally different place."

"What different place? Where did you go?" asked the White Rabbit staring at Mellow Tron with its monocle securely fastened to its face. From its tartan waistcoat, it brought out a pocket watch, checked the time and waited for Mellow Tron to answer.

"Yeah, tell us, we want to know everything!" crooned Dylan the Black Bunny before promptly falling asleep again.

"We landed in the desert sands," Mellow Tron started.

"Yeah, but *where* were you?" asked Seashell Sally, momentarily ignoring the Hashemites and stepping forward to be nearer.

Fareek jumped up and answered for them all. "Zeegypt."

"That's amazing!" Azeem the Dream sang out getting his shenai out and wanting to play a tune.

"But why didn't you contact us and let us know where you were?" Karim asked.

"We couldn't," Fareek answered sheepishly, breaking out into an embarrassed smile.

"Why?" the White Rabbit asked, jumping up on top of Mellow Tron's head to get a better look.

"Because we went 5000 years into the past!"

"Incredible!" Karim hollered, looking more surprised than ever.

"Are you sure?" Kassim asked.

"Yes, most definitely!"

"What did you do there?" Hussain the Insane asked, crazily untying Azeem the Dream's turban and feeding one end to a passing sacred cow.

"We met some interesting people and had a crazy time!" Anarkali added, looking deliciously happy.

"Who did you meet?" Hussain asked, looking decidedly sane for a change.

"We met a blind seer called Cassandra. She was amazing and also a most incredibly funny king called Funkanathen who juggles and keeps pet cheetahs but most of all, he's an incredible drummer!"

"Gosh!" went Azeem the Dream.

"Stupendous!" gasped the White Rabbit, forgetting to look at his pocket-watch for once and gawping at Tarquin with his mouth open.

"Gibbledegosh!" went Hussain the Insane, forgetting to behave crazily for once.

"Far out!" went the rest of the crowd but Abraxas hadn't given up with Tarquin yet.

"And what else did you do?"

"We fought demons and ghosts when grave-robbing inside the pyramids!"

"And then at the end we met a man called the Old Blind Man of Thebiz deep inside the pyramid and he gave us something to bring back and give to Fairlight."

With that Fareek put his hands inside the folds of his gown and brought out the wooden box that the golden scarab was kept in.

"Amazing!" whispered Dylan who woke up for a bit and then fell straight back to sleep.

"What is it?" Azeem the Dream asked, taking over where Abraxas had left off and wanting to know everything.

"It's a golden scarab beetle!" Fareek replied daintily, opening the lid of the box gently and letting it crawl onto his hand.

"What's so special about it?"

"I don't know but we'll soon find out!"

And then it was Mellow Tron's turn to end the conversation and having quickly slurped his chai he arose and Anarkali and Fareek followed. "But anyway thanks for the chai. We'd like to stay but we have to find Fairlight and give him the golden scarab."

"Okay," said Azeem the Dream, releasing them all from his never-ending line of enquiry.

"See you later!" Anarkali said gently to the assembled crowd.

"And by the way have you seen BB, Charlie and the Artful Dodger on your travels?" Abraxas suddenly asked as they were about to leave.

"Nah!" replied Fareek as they set off for the lower levels. There was still much distance to traverse before they would reach the Fantasy Factory below. They trudged on deeper and downer and very soon reached the higher levels of the Torrible Zone. They had lost time of how long exactly they had been travelling but it didn't seem to matter. They were all feeling rather dreamy and entering into the appropriate frame of mind one needed for entrance into this remarkable place. Nodding a passing hello to the occasional elves and leprechauns that lived at this level, they narrowly avoided getting their pockets picked by some wandering members of the Funkadelic tribe and simply followed the luminous wall-embedded stars deeper and down until the very atmosphere changed and they could feel that something different was most definitely up.

"Do you feel like we're being watched?" Fareek asked the others.

"Yes, for sure, can you see eyes coming out of the walls?" Tarquin added, scratching his nose.

"Yes and I think they are looking straight at us!" Anarkali finished, pointing desperately towards the walls.

"Aaah, it's the gubblies!" all screamed and jumped together with Mellow Tron's dancing dreadlocks racing into the air faster than fear itself.

And it was true. Suddenly jumping out of the walls where they'd been hiding, three foot tall, furry creatures completely covered in fur from head to foot, rushed out chuckling and laughing.

"Gubble . . .!" went one to another.

"Gobble!" went the other to another.

"Gibble . . . Gibber . . .!" went a third to a fourth.

"Gooble . . . Gibelle . . .!" went the fourth back to the third as the intrepid companions all screamed together.

"They just speak Gubblistani!"

"Yeah, but they still make perfect sense in what they are saying,"

Mellow Tron said wisely, being the first to regain composure.

"What are they saying then?" Anarkali asked in the tinkling of her ankle bells.

"They are saying welcome to the Torrible Zone."

"Oh, that's very friendly of them," Anarkali replied, smiling as she turned to get a good look.

The gubblies had green heads and blue hands and drooping ears half their size with bells on the end. They looked pretty ridiculous but cute all the same.

"Where do they come from then?" Fareek asked, coming up close.

Tarquin then wiped the grin off his handsome face and replied. "Oh, I know the story, they come from another dreaming and sailed on a river of crystal light to get here."

"Unreal!" Fareek gasped, jumping up and down in excitement.

After munching out on some foodstuffs that the little creatures kindly offered them, the group wandered downer and deeper down and noticed that the quality of light had changed completely as they entered the land of the Dreamweavers.

"Hello, Fareek!" sang Twynklyn sweetly.

"Hello, Mellow Tron. Hello, Tarquin!" trilled Blynkyn in perfect radiance, flapping her ladybird's wings and smiling.

"And hello, sweetest Anarkali!" Nod whistled, flying up close to the Queen of Kathak and giving her a kiss on her cheek.

"Hello, Dreamweavers." Mellow Tron spoke up for them all.

Then Twynklyn took the lead and simply asked directly. "Well, did you get the golden scarab?"

"How do you know about that?" Mellow Tron asked in confusion, pulling at his face for answers that weren't there.

"We know everything, silly, we're fairies!" Blynkyn flapped her perfect wings and replied quicker than her flashing wings.

"Oh!" gasped Mellow Tron, now slapping his face for answers.

"And what's happening now?" Fareek asked with a note of bewilderment in his voice.

"You tell us Twynklyn, as you seem to know everything!"

The good fairy obliged.

"All right, I was just making conversation for conversation's sake, we know you are taking the golden scarab to Fairlight."

"And where is he?" Fareek asked with a growing confidence.

"He's down where he should be, working hard in the Fantasy Factory with Osric."

Twnklyn had been helpful but now it was time to leave. Turning to the three fairies hovering in mid-air, Fareek picked up his voice and said clearly. "All right then, thank you. We should leave."

"Goodbye!" said Blynkyn, smiling her prismatic smile.

"Thank you," the group said together as they wandered out of the cave.

"Goodbye!" whistled Nod, waving goodbye and then promptly falling back asleep, curled up like a contented snail.

The intrepid group wandered further on within the Torrible Zone after crossing the vast expanse of the Gromboolian Plains with its lovely jubjub birds in flight.

"Ah, look . . . it's beautiful!"

Tarquin tossed his head to disagree.

"Nah, when you've seen one jubjub bird racing across the Gromboolian skies you've seen them all!"

Soon after having crossed these vast plains, the landscape changed yet again. The stars in the walls and ceilings and floors were getting brighter. Here the River of Crystal Light that was flowing on either side of the main artery of the Lost Catacombs suffused its light in a softer glow and the quick metamorphosis of water turning into light and light turning into water happened so gently one never knew whether one was drinking water or crystal light. They were now entering the lower levels of the Torrible Zone and everything seemed to be a dream and to be honest, the only reality here was dreaming. They were entering the deeper levels of the Dreamtime and smiled as their pupils grew larger to better take in these incredible sights. They had now traversed over half the depth of the Lost Catacombs and had only two more layers to go before being able to give Fairlight his gift. After finishing the rest of the chapatti rolls from the "Magical Muncherie", they all clapped their hands and jumped for joy when they saw the unforgettable sight of Nasseruddin the Nutty repeatedly banging his head firmly against a cave wall as sparks from the myriad of wall-embedded stars raced out to splash his face with sparks.

"Where are the others?" Anarkali asked the madman, looking around and seeing no one.

Nasseruddin stopped bashing his head momentarily and then replied. "They are inside this cave, our cave of the Whirling Dervishes."

"Can we please come in to rest our tired legs a while,

Nasseruddin?" Fareek asked, stepping forward and helping to lift Nasseruddin up off the floor.

"Of course you can, my cave is your cave!" whistled Nasseruddin, happily rubbing his pained head and checking his lapis lazuli front teeth.

And with that the tired group entered the cave of the Whirling Dervishes to find Stargasm and Moonmummy in deep discussion with Mevlana, Suleiman and Habiba. The group were obviously arguing about something and had broken off into two camps. It was strictly a boys versus girls situation. The girls, Stargasm, Moonmummy and Habiba, sat to one side and Suleiman and Mevlana sat to the other. As the group discussed the recent past amidst gasps and shrieks at the excitement of the story, Mevlana's long white hair fell out of his fez and exuded his rosy perfume.

"Oh no ... he's smelling again!" Suleiman screamed, holding his fingers to his nose.

"Quick, cover your noses!" Habiba shrieked loudly.

"Oh, it's not that bad, quite pleasant really," Moonmummy finished with a completely different perspective to the others.

The tall Suleiman then bent down to offer Anarkali an apple from the golden orchards of the never-ending summer groves of Kamershand. His eyeballs stayed silent and still as he himself began to spin quite slowly. Very soon the tiny Anarkali joined him and as they started to flow in opposite directions around the cave, things started to lift themselves up from the floor. The others simply watched in amazement as the two most incredible spinners on this side of the universe complemented each other's spin perfectly.

"Aren't they beautiful together?" Stargasm sighed, watching the movement of the two, simply bewitched and entranced.

"Even if one is only four and a half feet tall and the other well over seven feet," Moonmummy answered giggling like a schoolgirl.

Watching them spin, Moonmummy and Stargasm quietly reflected on their position.

Habiba joined in with her exuberant manner. "Well they've come back from Ancient Zeegypt."

"Wonder how they got there?" Moonmummy replied.

"It doesn't matter," Habiba added as Stargasm finished knowingly.

"Yeah, they were on a mission from St Stan."

"And by the sacred beanies of St Stan they've returned with a golden scarab!" Habiba said, full of excitement.

"Wonder what it can be used for?" Stargasm asked, patting her collapsible broomstick which had floated to the level of her eyes.

"Something brilliant no doubt if it's going to go to Fairlight!" Habiba replied, smiling.

"Perhaps it's an extra special magic potion to fight Lucifer with!"

"Wouldn't it be a wonder to end all wonders?"

"Let's ask Fareek, Tarquin and Mellow Tron!" Moonmummy butted in.

"Why?" Habiba asked, her hooked hand toying with her multi-coloured burnoose.

"Can't you see what they're doing now?" Stargasm asked in a knowing manner.

"What are they doing?" Habiba replied, looking madly around.

"Stop asking so many questions and look properly," Stargasm finished with a sweeping sigh, yet not explaining anything.

And there just outside the Cave of the Whirling Dervishes, Nasseruddin, Fareek and Mellow Tron were having an argument over how to put on pantaloons. Nasseruddin's the Nutty's, of course.

Tarquin was the first to explain. "Pantaloons are difficult things to wear!"

"What do you have to do?" Nasseruddin asked childishly, as Tarquin continued.

"Simple, you have to hold the trousers up in mid-air with ropes from either side."

"And then what?"

"And then you take a running jump from a distance of one hundred yards and try to jump into the pantaloons!"

"It's easy, Nasseruddin, have a try," Fareek said, trying to hide his ever-growing smile.

And having tied his orange pantaloons five feet up into the air, Tarquin asked the diminutive Nasseruddin to take a long run up from the corridor and jump into them. The frustrated Nasserudddin tried umpteen times gnashing his teeth but failed each time. It was time to move on. Leaving Habiba, Stargasm, Moonmummy, Suleiman and Mevlana in stitches watching poor Nasseruddin trying to get dressed, the group waved goodbye as there was still Fairlight to find.

Suddenly, they all heard the refrain of a most beautiful ringing in their thunderstruck ears, a tune like no other. There were three parts to it: treble, mid-range and bass, and the harmonies were breathtaking in their sheer simplicity.

"We are now in the Land of the Sleeping Dreamtime," Anarkali said slowly to the others in a cascading, dreamy voice.

"How do you know?" Tarquin asked, not too sure.

Anarkali did a graceful spin and whistled. "I feel sleepy."

"And I feel as if everything's a dream," Fareek added, his gown shimmering in the half light and making him look rather saintly.

Mellow Tron said confidently, "We must be in the Land of the Sleeping Dreamtime all right which means we only have to cross this level and then we will finally be down to the level of the Land of the Awakening Dreamtime where we will surely find Fairlight . . ."

"Yippee!" squealed Anarkali.

"Brill!" Fareek exclaimed, expanding both eyeballs to the size of dustbin lids and dancing on the spot.

"Far out and most wonderful!" Tarquin explained, hitching his falling pantaloons up higher. They all stood and pondered.

But where exactly was the intrepid group? The Land of the Sleeping Dreamtime was a mighty big place they felt as Tarquin led the way and they followed the incredible song that emerged into the corridors with golden flashes of luminescent flame that flared up and down the cave walls endlessly.

"Look, I know where we are now," Tarquin gasped after a while, bouncing down the path at a quicker rate.

Anarkali following quickly behind, asked, "Where are we then, Tarquin?"

"Easy peasy, don't you remember?"

"Yes, it's the Sisters Nazneen singing!"

"We must be near the Cave of Blissful Echoes!" Anarkali finished with a joyful scream and raced onwards to be the first to reach the legendary sisters.

Tarquin ran to catch her up, answering gleefully. "It's the 'Om Song' in its infinite variations and still singing well I hear."

"Come on, let's hurry on down and we can catch them," Fareek hollered taking Mellow Tron by the dreadlocks and running fast to catch up with Anarkali.

Very soon they had located the exact source of the sound and crashing in through the cave doors of the Chamber of Blissful Echoes, they found the incredible Sisters Nazneen valiantly singing the finale of the "Om Song". As everyone watched entranced the sound waves from their respective throats flowed out of their mouths like honey and clearly and visibly raced up the walls to enter the main artery of the Lost Catacombs as beautiful sonic rings. Watching the sonic rings grace the walls and then disappear, the three sisters finally flumped to the ground with a sigh.

"Where have you all been?" Ambrin started, wiping her sweaty face.

"We've all missed you terribly," Ayesha added, peeling apart her Hypno-Tantric Hijab and peering out.

Najma was not one to be left out and finished in a voice so deep that it shook the cave. "Song and dance wasn't the same without all of you funny people."

Tarquin took the time to scratch his head awhile before replying. "We've been away."

"To Zeegypt, as a matter of fact," Anarkali added in a twirl of ankle bells.

Ambrin wasn't so happy. Grimacing like she'd sucked bitter lemon, she said huffily, "If you went on holiday you should have told us!"

"Yeah, we'd have loved to have gone to Zeegypt!" Ayesha said, looking disappointed that they hadn't been invited.

"But we took a little break anyway and went on holiday too!" Najma finished, feeling a bit sorry for the Beat Boys.

"Where did you go?" Mellow Tron asked quietly, starting to eat a samosa that Najma had offered him.

"We went to Waziristan to see our grandmother and, of course, we went to Zindia before that to look for the Magic Mantras!"

"But I though your grandmother lived in deepest Darkistan" Fareek asked with surprise.

"No, the other one, silly, the one who taught us how to sing," Ambrin said, patting little Anarkali on the head.

Anarkali tried ineffectually to get out of the way and so she tried another tack. She asked Ambrin a question. "Have you spent much time in Pearly Green?"

"You mean the overland?" Ambrin asked now starting to preen her own, ample, raven hair.

"Yes."

"No, we've mainly all been here practising the infinite variations on the 'Om Song'."

Mellow Tron had taken a good look at the cave and decided to complement the sisters on their home. "Your Chamber of Blissful Echoes is simply brilliant."

"We know," Najma replied, picking a rose out of her head and watching it change into a narcissus before their unbelieving eyes. Picking a whole bunch and then offering them to Anarkali, she continued in her big brassy manner. "It was a good thing that Ayesha found this amazing cave."

"Yeah, it's unique, out of all the caves in the Lost Catacombs, it's the only place where sonic rings coming from people's mouths can actually be seen as luminous golden waves that cascade up the catacomb walls," Ambrin chuckled, picking a narcissus from Anarkali's bunch and putting it in her hair.

The group sat around on the carpet-strewn floor and exchanged views, news and crunchy bananas for ten minutes until it was time to move on again. No doubt they would soon meet when playing a gig but for now they would have to part. Fareek had explained the mission and the Sisters Nazneen understood that Fairlight couldn't be kept waiting.

After another hour's travelling through the Land of the Sleeping Dreamtime, they suddenly hit the pink diffusing light of the Land of the Awakening Dreamtime populated with shoals of twinklefish swimming around them in the air.

"Hey what's happening to me?" Fareek cried, trying to shake them all off his holographic gown unsuccessfully.

"Fareek, you're disappearing in twinklefish!" Anarkali chuckled, spinning once more up into the air again and throwing down some bits of fluffy pink candyfloss that she had discovered.

"Where am I?" Fareek insisted, pulling Tarquin into view and hammering on his chest.

"You're in the Land of the Awakening Dreamtime," Anarkali screamed, showering him with more bits of wandering candyfloss but he still wasn't satisfied.

"No I mean where's the path? I can't see a thing, these damn fish are blocking my sight."

"Never mind, you should see yourself, you look a very pretty picture," Tarquin teased, unclenching Fareek's fingers from his designer jacket. The trip was getting stranger and stranger which was only natural for all trips and most adventures. The deeper and further they got from their starting point, the weirder the whole trip would become and the Lost Catacombs was a fantastic case in point. Loneliness and desolation could be everywhere if one's heart wasn't at home but if the very universe was home as well, then one need never be alone. Of course, the First Holy Truth stated that "you're never alone being alone" and the intrepid group knew this well. That's why they were travelling together. They were well-educated even if they couldn't read and write. They knew their Four Holy Truths, the Four Humble Truths and the Three Serene Sillinesses but were still looking for the Magic Mantras.

The Land of the Awakening Dreamtime was the culmination of all the magic and trippery of the three levels above as the whole of the Lost Catacombs was in reality, one organic whole. The Land of the Living Dreamtime merged into the Torrible Zone. The Torrible Zone metamorphosed into the Land of the Sleeping Dreamtime whilst most incredible of them all, the Land of the Awakening Dreamtime synthesised the different elements of all of the above levels and made it its own. And why was it called the Land of the Awakening Dreamtime? Simple. For those present there would awake and never fall asleep ever again. This was the land of Enlightenment. This was the Land of Entitlement. This was the dream of liberation as a perfect right for one and all. It was the simple destiny belonging to everyone and everything. But what was Enlightenment anyway? It was illu-mination and as Anarkali flowed deeper and down she saw flashes and pulses of incredible multi-coloured light grace the walls. And what was Entitlement? Entitlement was what was one's own by right. It was the bequeathing of the universe to each and every being as a natural inheritance. It was the fight for the right to be free expressed by every living thing that flew in the oceans, swum in the skies, raced around on broomsticks, cloudboards or magic prayer-mats or fell asleep strumming guitars under sacred apple trees somewhere in the summertime in the golden apple groves of Kammershand. Entitlement was the right to trance with dainty twiglets in sunny Kashtent. Enlightenment and Entitlement were separately profound but together they were simply stunning in their simplicity. However for now, as Fareek stumbled blindly along bathed in a robe of shimmering twinklefish, this was the land of fantasy for sure.

"Oh wow, we're near home," Tarquin trilled, rushing forwards.

"What can you see?" Fareek bleated, more or less asking Tarquin to be his eyes.

"Home, Fareek, simply home!"

"Wow!" gasped Mellow Tron standing still and taking a good look at what lay around them.

"Brilliant!" Anarkali sung, racing up and down the air like a cool cucumber on hot naga chillies.

And then they saw some caves that made them really feel at home. From inside Catweazel Phil's "Emporium of Laser Lights", they could see the manager of the "Bum Note" do his stuff. Through an endless array of the most incredible mirrors, he was refracting the emerging and descending sonic rings coming from the "Chamber of Blissful Echoes". He was refracting them into many levels of colours and shooting them off the Awakening Dreamtime walls whereby they would race up through every level and give every inhabitant of the Lost Catacombs an exquisite thrill. They waved hello to the black hatted wizard and, as usual, Frogamatix the pug-ugly thousand year old tree-toad sat contentedly on Catweazel Phil's shoulders. Only a few caves further along was the Music Studios, the cave of Anarkali and MMA but Mellow Tron stopped them going in and guided them on further.

"Hey, can we go home first?" Anarkali pleaded but to no avail. Mellow Tron was on a mission.

"No, just a little bit more!" Fareek decided to get into the act.

"We've come a long way, we can go a little bit more."

"Where are we going, Fareek?" Anarkali pleaded yet again in a voice full of triste and tiredness.

"I don't know but I think the twinklefish are leading me to the Sonic Temple of King Psychedelix."

"Okay, let's all follow Fareek," Tarquin gasped, swallowing one of his everlasting gobstoppers and feeling rather eternal as a consequence.

"Yea, let's ride the wave, Fairlight can wait ten more minutes!" Mellow Tron chuckled, coming up close.

"Why not, he's been waiting over five thousand years for the sacred scarab!" Fareek added, laughing at his own joke.

Mellow Tron was impressed and asked respectfully, "That's brilliant logic, how do you do it?"

"I don't think it's me, it's being here inside the Land of the Awakening Dreamtime that does it!"

"You too!" Anarkali squealed, laughing her little head off and spinning.

"No, me three!" Fareek finished, peering through the cloud of twinklefish and giggling too.

Twinklefish were still swarming around Fareek when he entered the vast Sonic Temple of King Psychedelix as Mellow Tron, Anarkali and Tarquin followed close behind. Tarquin stopped moving and looked under his feet at the moving waters of the River of Crystal Light that could clearly be seen whirling and swirling.

"Amazing!" Mellow Tron beeped excitedly.

"Great to be back home again!" Fareek wheezed with a happy sigh.

"What do you mean, I thought your home was in the music studios?" Anarkali said, coming in to land gracefully by their feet.

"It is and more."

"This place is big enough to hold the whole universe, we belong here too. Our separate caves are one home but this place belongs to all of us," Tarquin went on to explain, holding Anarkali by the hand and giving her his warmth.

"Well said, you sound pretty enlightened!" Anarkali said, looking Tarquin in the eye.

"Nah ... I'm simply being entitled!"

"Wicked ... you is a real geezer!"

"And you is a real queen!"

"Only of Kathak mind!"

"Was there ever any greater queendom than that?"

And with an abounding atmosphere of love and compassion towards each other and all living beings, they looked around at the vast starry night and the incredible stars that were shining on them. The vast expanse of this temple was completely flat, no rocks or boulders marred its perfect smoothness and there was simply nowhere to hide. Anarkali was the first to see them; out in the distance, right smack bang in the middle of the temple were three figures sitting on the floor having cucumber sandwiches and oblong oysters.

Tarquin suddenly caught Anarkali's gaze and shouted, "Oi ... its Mullah Ullah!"

"And the Genie of the Lamp!" Anarkali screamed.

"And next to them is the grinning Jabberwocky, for sure!"

"Let's go towards them!" Fareek said, instinctively going forward and leading them all on. Anarkali realised they were simply miles away.

"But it's miles, how are we going to get there?"

"Easy, just follow me," Tarquin chuckled, preparing himself for the next move.

And they did. Tarquin suddenly jumped up in the air and landed on the flat ground where the waters of the River Alph could clearly be seen and with that single bounce, the floor gave way and concaved itself and tossed Tarquin right to the middle of the temple where the Genie of the Lamp, Mullah Ullah and the smoking Jabberwocky greeted him with pats on the head.

"Me too!" Fareek cried like a happily demented child, copying Tarquin's moves

"Me three!" Mellow Tron screamed, bouncing only half a step behind Fareek.

And very soon Fareek and Mellow Tron reached the centre of this universe too. Anarkali simply flew gracefully like a true lady and still got there before Fareek and Mellow Tron.

"How does she do it?" Fareek gasped, tears streaming from his eyes.

"Magic . . . Hee . . . Hee . . .!" Anarkali chuckled, landing softly on the ground.

With everyone assembled Mullah Ullah looked at each of them in turn. His lungi flapped up and down in the slight breeze inside the Sonic Temple and he welcomed each of them in courteously.

"Welcome all, what brings you here?"

"We've been away for a long time," Fareek started earnestly as Mellow Tron seconded:

"We just wanted to come home again."

"Yes, the Sonic Temple is the true home for all of us, where we can all put away our differences and be as one," Fareek finished, sniffing the air excitedly and panting like a puppy in the park.

"Well said, young Master Fareek," said the Genie of the Lamp still emanating from his golden lamp like a true magician. He felt hungry looking at the swarm of twinklefish still surrounding Fareek. He was currently only about twenty feet high and definitely not as scary as he might have been, especially not as scary as he had been in the sands of Afrostan. His body shone like a deep-sea pearl and he examined each of the group in turn. Finally, flicking his golden earrings with a huge hand, he picked Anarkali from the air and gently placed her on his shoulders.

However, they weren't the only ones there. Unseen and invisible, the friendly ghosts of Phineas Freakville and Cynthia Cruickshank were circling the group below and chuckling magically in a ghostly language of their own.

"Dear Phineas, they are here at last" Cynthia whistled as Phineas quickly replied while picking his teeth.

"Good thing!"

"Well if they are here then what about those who have gone to Topping, Madame Serendipity included . . .?"

Phineas put a ghostly finger through his green velvet smoking jacket before replying. "I don't know, maybe they can only come back when they have completed their task."

Phineas Freakville tugged at his long moustache and his meerschaum pipe together. Under a tatty top hat, his friendly face and merry smile beamed out while his twinkling eyes focused themselves on the object of his affections, Cynthia Cruickshank. His pince-nez had fallen off his long, thin nose and he buffed his velvet green smoking jacket to make it as shiny as grass.

The beautiful Cynthia Cruickshank meanwhile whirled her diamond tiara around her head and adjusted her pearl necklace. As Madame Serendipity's acolyte, Cynthia spent much of her time weaving too. As she sat in the air Cynthia continued stitching her Tapestry of Never-Ending Time. "What's happening, Phineas?"

"A very good thing, Cynthia, the plot is thickening, Lucifer's forces are getting stronger, we are in for an incredible explosion!"

"What do you mean?"

"I think there's going to be a fight and all these different elements that Sidney Arthur has manipulated to do his bidding will come back to fight Lucifer with a vengeance."

Cynthia twirled around in the air for a while before happily asking, "That's an excellent thing, is it not?"

"Yes but anything could happen, take a look down below," Phineas said, pointing below with his long white finger.

Cynthia cast her ghostly eyes downwards and stopped stitching on the tapestry. Mullah Ullah and the Genie of the Lamp could be seen gesticulating madly

"Its Hare Bonk . . . Hare Stonk . . . Hare Poo!" Fareek screamed at the top of his voice. "Those are the true Magic Mantras".

"No, Scribbidy Git . . . Stronky Dog . . . Wibbit . . .!" Mellow Tron gasped, looking equally as uptight as Fareek and gnashing his teeth.

Tarquin had had enough of the other two and was sure he was

the one that was right. "No, it's neither ... it's Frug ... Frux ... Friggit ...!"

From high in the air Phineas closed his eyes and muttered. "Oh no ... they are arguing about the Magic Mantras again ... who cares what they are anyway ...?"

"You're so right but the whole of the Idiot's Path depends on knowing them. We know the Four Holy Rules, the Four Humble Truths and the Three Serene Sillinesses, with the Magic Mantras we will know everything," Cynthia said breathlessly, watching those below fight with an interested eye.

"I suppose you're righ,t" Phineas replied, passing her the smoking Meerschaum pipe and whizzing on down to be closer to those that were visible.

And so after ten minutes of useless argument, Fareek, Anarkali, Mellow Tron and Tarquin calmed down and finally got up. They had almost forgotten that they were on a mission and had Fairlight to find so they rushed out of the Sonic Temple and ran through the corridors to get to the Fantasy Factory.

"Fairlight!" Fareek started

"We've ..." Tarquin interjected

"Come ... Anarkali butted in

"To give ..." Mellow Tron commenced

"You ... a ..." Fareek tried again

"present ...!" Anarkali finished in a squeal of giggles.

Fairlight stopped leaning over his work-table and prodded Osric who was sitting there slumbering in a comfy armchair in the middle of the laboratory. The magic potion maker greeted them all enthusiastically, his pirate's beard complementing his white dinner jacket and tuxedo. His dark brown hair was expertly pulled up and tied in a top knot above his head. Putting various samples of magic potions into the deep pockets of his lab coat, he demonstrated his calm and collected manner by standing absolutely still as Fareek raced around the Fantasy Factory chased by his host of twinklefish. Meanwhile the others jscreaming their heads off now that they had completed the task from ancient Zeegypt. All except for Anarkali of course, for she was still in the air and floating at the level of everyone's eyes.

Fairlight looked thoughtful before speaking. "So, you're home."

"Yes, we just got back," Tarquin replied, almost starting to giggle like Anarkali and coming up close to the magic potion maker.

"And what have you brought for him?" Osric asked in a sleepy voice, sitting up in his armchair and scratching his aquiline nose. His pale face looked quite bemused and his eyes stared out at Fareek as he put the wooden box right into Fairlight's hands. Osric smiled his lopsided grin and put on his orange-coloured woollen jumper as a cooling breeze had entered the Fantasy Factory along with the visitors.

Everyone waited for Fairlight to open the wooden box and as the golden scarab came out Fareek simply said, "The Old Blind Man of Thebiz and Granny Cass told us to give you this."

"And that you'd know what to do with it," Tarquin added as Mellow Tron butted in enthusiastically.

"Do you know him? Is he a friend of yours?"

"Maybe ... Maybe ... Who knows?" Fairlight said, enigmatically throwing his head back and chuckling.

Meanwhile the scarab had crawled out fully from the box and was climbing up Fairlight's arm.

Fareek was still dissatisfied with Fairlight's explanation. "What are you going to do with it?"

"Hmm ... just wait and see!"

"Yippee! More magic potions for me to try out!" Osric screamed with gay abandon and they suddenly realised what Fairlight was going to do.

Having performed their task, they stumbled and bumbled back home to the Music Studios to crash out on the many bean bags Fareek had ensured they kept there. And there they slept like never before because it must be remembered, they had not slept for over five thousand years.

27

Teatime at the Fantasy Factory

FAIRLIGHT THE EMULATOR had been cooking for hours and it had been over three days since he had received the golden scarab and he hadn't stopped or slept and neither had Osric nor Princess Amrita. They were in the cave with Fairlight, arguing and spluttering while Hussain the Insane and his dear friend, Nasseruddin the Nutty made mischief and mayhem. Everything was as it should be. Osric was tied to the bamboo chair where Amrita was tickling his nose with the peacock feather. Of course, it was Osric's job to test all the magic potions that Fairlight made and Amrita's task to make them all laugh as her childish giggles also went into the mixture. So, as Fairlight hung around looking cool, Amrita took turns in tickling herself and the scruffy Osric.

Fairlight ignored the crazy shenanigans and got back to work. In the screen on the computron, double helixes of DNA rushed around doing their funky stuff and the many shoals of twinklefish that had swum in with Fareek swam around in the air. On the work-table various chemicals, test tubes, different batches of Anatta and piles of coloured powder (some of them mushroom spores) were waiting for Fairlight's attention. As he worked and Osric swallowed whatever the Princess was stuffing into his open mouth, what were Nasseruddin and Hussain doing? Hussain's brown wavy hair had fallen out of his turban and was tickling his waist. He was staring at Nasseruddin the Nutty who was going around the cave taking orders for tea yet something was odd. No, it wasn't the inexplicable behaviour of Osric and Amrita or the quiet intent of Fairlight, there was something odd about Nasseruddin's request for tea.

"More tea anyone?" Nasseruddin asked, going around the room and asking each in turn. His head bobbed up and down as his cloudboard whizzed around the room teasing the twinklefish. It was then that Hussain the Insane understood the plot in a moment of pure quicksilver satori and quickly joined in. Rushing around the room with a silver samovar he followed Nasseruddin's footsteps and mimicked his every movement.

"More tea anyone?" Hussain spoke only milliseconds after Nasseruddin had finished them.

The Whirlistani dwarf raised his head looking behind at the other and chuckled. "Oi, stop copying me!"

"Oi, stop copying me!" Hussain repeated as if they were standing in the Chamber of Blissful Echoes and not Fairlight's Fantasy Factory. The end of his turban was on the floor now.

Nasseruddin was starting to get annoyed with his Banglastani friend and shouted, "Shut up, you fool!"

"Shut up, you fool . . .!"

"Ha . . . Ha . . . Ha . . . Ha . . . Ha . . .!" Hussain the Insane laughed, getting well into play and beginning to enjoy himself thoroughly.

"Hee . . . Hee . . . Hee . . .!" Nasseruddin the Nutty chuckled as a modicum of peace took over.

The brothers in lunacy politely went around the room doffing their turbans at the laughing twinklefish and asking everyone what they wanted to drink. These two weren't just supreme idiots, they were master illusionists too and as Hussain minced around the room with the samovar, Nutty Nasseruddin suddenly produced one of the Artful Dodger's stolen silken handkerchiefs from behind Amrita's imperial ear, making her giggle intensely. Nasseruddin quickly covered the samovar with it and then intoning in a serious voice, he passed Osric and asked, "And what would you, dear Osric, like to drink?

Osric sat up, wriggled at his bindings and said, "I'd like some tea please, what do you have?"

Hussain giggled like crazy as Nasseruddin continued sagely, tugging at his teeth. "This samovar has very special tea inside and only the tea that is appropriate to the specific person will be poured."

"And what sort of tea shall I get?" Osric asked, pushing aside Amrita who was trying to stuff more magic potion into his mouth.

"Let us think!" Nasseruddin said, scratching his nose and ponderously pondering. Having thought a while he continued while conferring. "What do you reckon, Hussain?"

"Mutter . . . mutter . . . mumble . . ." whispered Hussain the Insane, bending down towards Nasseruddin's ear for a full six and a half seconds.

"Mumble ... mutter ... mutter ... " went Nasseruddin, suddenly standing up to his full height of four feet and replied cryptically as Osric waited with bated breath. He then continued. "You, Osric are much too much of a dreamer and so you need Reali ... Tea."

"Reality ... Ha ... ha ... ha ... Absolutely brilliant!" chuckled Hussain the Insane from the back, almost spilling the samovar in his laughter.

"Wicked!" Fairlight beamed finally.

"Far out!" trilled Princess Amrita, totally thrilled at this new game of delusion and illusion conjured up by the insane Nasseruddin and Hussain.

And as Osric smiled Hussain poured a whole stream of orange-coloured liquid into a magically produced cup of the finest china. Everyone started clapping their hands.

"And what about you, Hussain?" Nasseruddin suddenly cried, turning around backwards to face his friend.

"Oh ... um ... I'd like a Zindian tea please."

"Hmmm ... let me think," Nasseruddin muttered, taking the silken cloth off the silver samovar again and pouring tea into another china cup. Hussain the Insane then peered into it awhile and cackled. Nasseruddin couldn't wait any longer and quickly asked, "What is it then, Hussain, What is it?"

"It's Sobrie-tea!"

"Yes, you of course, drink too much elderberry wine and need this drink more than anyone else ...!"

"Tee ... Hee ... Hee ... Yummy yummy ... Thanks, it's nice!"

And with that Hussain slurped it all down, dancing a jig and simply loving the joke. He laughed and laughed before suddenly straightening up as sobriety is always a very sober brew. However, by now others were getting impatient.

"Hey, what about me?" Fairlight cried, putting his test tubes and samples of magic potion down as Nasseruddin was rather busy helping himself.

"Just wait a minute, I'm pouring myself a cup."

Hussain poured Nasseruddin an amber-coloured liquid which the dwarf drunk quickly.

Watching the proceedings with incredulity Fairlight buffed his nails and asked, "What type of tea is it?"

"Its Equanimi-tea, designed to give you balance of mind. I have none so I drink lots of this."

"Brilliant, it's what you need, being a bit nutty!" Hussain the Insane chortled, throwing away Nasseruddin's empty china cup in mid-air where it instantly vanished leaving nothing behind, not even a tea leaf. Somehow, from somewhere, Hussain materialised another cup as Nasseruddin giggled like a blushing schoolgirl confronted with her first kiss.

"Very nutty, you mean ... Hee ... Hee ... Heee!"

"Well, whatever!"

However, the master maker of magic potions was getting impatient.

"But what about me?" Fairlight hollered. Hussain and Nasseruddin ambled over and poured Fairlight his tea after swishing away the illusionary golden handkerchief that covered the silver samovar. Fairlight sipped it slowly appreciating every little drop before asking, "Well what is it, Nasseruddin?"

"This is Humani-tea and it's specially brewed for you in thanks for all the work you are doing on behalf of all humanity through the creation of your incredible potions and the superb brilliance of the Anatta you design!"

Fairlight stood there simply gobsmacked before exhaling. "Wow!"

"So, everyone can drink this?" Osric asked, sitting up in his bamboo chair and ineffectually trying to loosen his bonds.

Nasseruddin pulled at his nose and answered. "No, not really, what about the magical creatures inside the Lost Catacombs? They can't drink this as it's only for people." In confirmation the dancing twinklefish swooshed around the cave and Fairlight instantly understood that they agreed.

"Oh, wow!" whistled the master potion maker completely knocked out by Nasseruddin and Hussain's game of tea-making. It was then that Hussain the Insane spoke up loud while stuffing the end of his turban into the seat of his pants.

"Here's a drink stronger than Humani-tea that can be drunk by everyone!"

"And it's the drink that Amrita's going to drink," Nasseruddin said as Hussain poured her out a drink.

"What is it?" Osric asked, bouncing around the cave-floor, still tied to his bamboo chair.

"Ambigui-tea?" Fairlight screamed, starting to lose his cool and loving every moment.

"Necessi-tea?" Osric squealed from his chair, suddenly getting a crazy desire to want to drink all these teas by himself.

"Normali-tea?" Hussain the Insane suggested shyly, still holding the silver samovar that was still not running out of liquid.

"No, good try, Hussain but Princess Amrita gets the ultimate drink – Enigmatic Totali-tea, also known as Sereni-tea."

"Wow, it can be drunk by any living being?" Amrita chuckled, tossing her head back and drinking it in one greedy gulp.

"Most definitely, yes!" Nasseruddin chuckled as everyone (except for Osric of course) danced a merry jig around Hussain and himself. And with their separate, wonderful teas inside them warming them up, they got back to work.

Fairlight beamed inwardly as the respective teas began to take effect and rushing around in a blur of fantastic speed, he got the golden scarab out of its wooden box and very gently attached tiny transmitters onto its wings. A shower of golden pollen fell from its wings into the test tube that Fairlight had nearby. The transmitters were attached to rows of other test tubes and nearby were the different piles of spores, sonic starfish DNA and other such magic. Fairlight deftly mixed all these ingredients together while the twinklefish swam excitedly around the room. Finally, after much mixing of the ingredients in the mortar and pestle, he jumped up to exclaim, "Anatta – Mark 4 is finally ready!"

"Yippee!" screamed Amrita, bouncing crazily across the floor.

"Hoorah!" hollered Osric, now realising he was going to be set free.

"Brilliant!" whistled Hussain the Insane, crazily pulling at Nasseruddin's lapis lazuli teeth.

"Give us a go!" Nasseruddin squealed, punching Hussain squarely on the nose and jumping up.

At this juncture Fairlight was firm in his decision. "No, Osric first, that's the way its always been and that's the way it always will be."

"Okay, we can wait," Hussain the Insane trilled, waiting patiently in the line behind Osric.

"Speak for yourself!" Nasseruddin laughed, pushing Hussain out of the line and taking his place instead.

Slowly unstrapping Osric from his chair, Amrita finally stopped tickling him with the peacock's feather as Fairlight rushed over to stuff three tabsules of the new Anatta into his mouth.

"Should be enough," Fairlight said to no one in particular but Nasseruddin and Hussain overheard.

"Are you sure? We always take a hundred."

"Each!" Hussain the Insane interjected with an obvious lie.

"Hour!" Nasseruddin finished with a lying smirk.

Fairlight was starting to lose his patience. "You two are filthy little fibbers, just be patient while I deal with Osric first."

"Okay!" laughed the dwarf stepping back with a graceful salaam.

"Tee ... Heee ... Hee!" chuckled Hussain the Insane, looking more crazed than ever.

Suddenly and completely out of character, Osric got up and started dancing and Amrita soon joined in as Fairlight questioned him closely.

"Osric, how are you feeling?"

"Brilliant, but I've got this sudden desire to want to dance. I need to find Anarkali and get her to teach me a few tricks."

"I see."

And with that Osric ran out of the cave but not before jumping up and down a few times. The stompings were so heavy a whole row of test tubes clattered and smashed to the ground. Of course, Amrita joined him in the stompings and almost made the same amount of mess herself but Fairlight pulled at his beard and pondered. Something wasn't right. Osric had never shown any interest or inclination in wanting to dance before and Fairlight found his desire to find Anarkali very odd indeed and got even odder when Fairlight saw the greedy hands of Nasseruddin the Nutty and Hussain the Insane both gobble a handful of new Anatta. Very soon, they too were twitching and stomping the ground in rhythm. Fairlight naturally wondered what was so special about this new batch of Anatta.

"Wonder what the fuss was about the scarab?" he muttered, untying the beetle from the tiny transmitters and letting it go free. Flying instantly up into the air, the golden scarab joined the shoal of swarming twinklefish and raced around the cave happily. As for Nasseruddin and Hussain, they rushed out of the cave too but not after stomping up and down on the ground a few times, knocking more things off the shelves. Fairlight let them go. If they didn't, there would be simply too much mess in the Fantasy Factory. Very soon Fairlight was left alone in the cave to tidy up the mess but he seemed perturbed and looked distinctly quizzical as he was yet to understand what exactly he had unleashed upon the world.

28

The Band of Doom Tunes Down (or up)

THE VALLEY OF Dry Bones, somewhere east of the Black Hoggar Mountains in Afrostan, was rocking. The air was blisteringly hot and scorched the skin off the backs of the grasshoppers that jumped up and down in the air pointlessly trying to get cool. Tiny frogs and lizards many feet below in the golden sands hopped around on alternate legs trying to keep cool but most were gobbled up by cruising pelicans that raced out of the sun at about three o'clock. Life was a real bummer in the Valley of Dry Bones but all the same Hoggaristan was rocking its roots off. But why?

Beyond the incredible sandstorms that were brewing in the scalding desert air, the crumbling ruins of the amphitheatre lay like a set of broken teeth across the horizon and was now filled to the brim with much screeching and stamping. Ghouls, gremlins, afreets, bhoots, demons, diabolics, geeks, gooks, goblins and major and minor devils, clapped their heads and stamped their feet, sitting or standing or generally flying around. But why were they doing this? The Afreet Orchestra were now practising their scales and after that the most incredible Black Magic Mysterons would join them and more colours would disappear from the skies. On the mammoth stage made of dinosaur droppings, the poison ivy was still connected to the six hundred and sixty six banks of samplers, grumplers and angst arpeggiaters. It screamed in satanic sympathy with the scrapings and bangings of the Afreet Orchestra as the level of the sounds got even scarier.

The Afreet Orchestra were ripping through their hypnotic scales, its undead members playing well. The afreets, banshees, bhoots, ghouls, vampires and other monsters that made up the Afreet Orchestra were playing the unfinished Satanic Symphony again but this time the skeletal trumpeters were blowing their rancid horns with much more precision. Essentially they were playing the

Grumble Glitch once more and as we know the effects of playing the Grumble Glitch on the inhabitants of Pearly Green and beyond were profound.

"Aaark . . .!" went the vampire violinists as they scraped the hot air from the bent bows of their stolen violins and the emaciated kettle-drummers bashed on mammoth skulls. Then the banshees and preets played their horns like dogs baying for blood. Last but not least, the bhoots, blowing on bones, shivered and shook like falling autumn leaves as they pursed their lips and lungs and blew like crazy. Suddenly a blackness began to spiral into the demented grey-black skies and colours from the Chuckle Stream began to fade out.

Azrial flapped his wings to the beats and stood to attention on the battered Roman column that acted as his plinth. As he waved his baton to the stage many feet below the phantom dancers, shiggling in their hula hoops, changed back to wearing ballerina gowns while the Afreet Shape-Shifters changed from Draconian Draculas to quivering hamsters faster than the eye could blink.

Suddenly Azrial looked angrily down from his stupendous plinth and screamed. "Right, Vampire violinists . . . Play more crescendo and drummers, you're banging out of time . . . if you do that one more time . . . I'll bite your heads off!"

"But our heads are already off!" screamed the emaciated kettle-drummers but their squeals were conveniently ignored.

Azrial chewed on his conductor's baton for a while before saying, "Oh, I see, it was just a figure of speech . . . Get back to the beat . . .!"

"Yes sir . . .!"

"And you bhoots blowing bones, you're blowing out of time."

"Okay, sir . . . won't do it again."

Azrial threw an angry look to his left and shouted "And you skeletal trumpeters, don't dilly-dally with the sound, I want it short and sweet, this isn't jazz, you know, it's the Satanic Symphony!"

As the Afreet Orchestra bashed and blew their horns and bones, the appreciative crowd cheered as bats flew deliriously overhead and crapped black bat-droppings. In the distance the Black Magic Mysterons were getting ready to come on stage. The musicians in the orchestra pit quivered with excitement while the Black Magic Mysterons clambered on stage as the warlock wave-engineers and spectral sound-programmers finally gave a bony thumbs-up.

"Wicked Hoggaristan, welcome to Hell!" shouted Fruggy, the first to come on stage. The three bony skeletal forms of Fruggy, Fruzzy and Total-Frux ambled on. They had just had their usual snakebites before they had come on stage and the Frux brothers' eye sockets were like burning white coals. Each dressed differently from the next. Wearing schoolboy shorts and an old school tie, Fruggy rushed behind the set of Bad Beat Drums and began whacking them. Fruzzy then jumped onto banks of mixers, samplers and grumplers and played them with his right hand while he smashed a power chord with his left onto the battered blood-red electric guitar slung around his neck. And then it was up to Total-Frux to tickle the rotating poison ivy which was connected to Fruzzy's kit. The combination was toxic and as the sound of the music increased, Total-Frux increased the slider up on the scrankler and the effects were immediate. And the band began to play the electronic version of the Satanic Symphony with breathless abandon. Devils, monsters and baddies they may have been, yet they were superb at what they played. Yes, perhaps their music was of the dark kind that robbed the Chuckle Stream and dripped the colours from the skies so that the whole world became a gloomy place but they were still brilliant at what they did. The crowd loved them and kicked each other's heads onto the stage for the Frux brothers to boot them back into the crowds with obvious derision.

The noxious aura of this music of the spheres played by the nasty Afreet Orchestra rose up into the skies to start draining the colours off the Chuckle Stream. Azrial flapped his angry wings and conducted and the demonic dancers shiggled and wiggled also like never before. They moved to this side of the beat, that side of the beat and the very best of them, right in the middle of the beat as they rattled each other's bones until it started to happen. Colours were leaving the Chuckle Stream and the world was becoming a far darker place than before; the rate of colours was bleeding from the rainbow's end at a much faster rate than ever because the Band of Doom had perfected their dark assignment.

Under Azrial's guidance the amphitheatre of Hoggaristan started to spin in an anti-clockwise manner, slowly at first and then picking up speed to 666 rpm, it gave the cheering audience a superb thrill that tickled the socks off their ears and the underpants off their toes. It was wondrous, wicked and wild but as the skies got darker and darker, there was not much left to see as even the night stars had scurried off. The Man on the Moon sitting on the crescent of the moon strummed the sympathetic strings on his cosmic hurdy-gurdy and doffed his harlequin's hat. The golden bits of yesterday suns and the silver bits of old full moons fell down from his hat onto the sands but nobody saw as they were far too busy going round and round and head-banging to the Satanic Symphony. The Grumble Glitch was back with a vengeance.

29

A Pirate in Pearly Green

"AAAH . . .!" SCREAMED Captain Kidd as the drop fell away from his frightened feet. Suddenly he was being extended in two ways, his body and feet were falling through a hole while his head remained fixed, or that's what he believed happened at hangings. But then, he'd never been hanged before. Captain Kidd looked out at the cruel world before him and thought fast. It was all too much as he looked out at the cruel world for the last time as he fell through the air to his certain death.

"Aaah I'm falling ... where am I going . . .?" he screamed as he tumbled and fell and fell.

"Why is my neck still all right?" he thought as he found himself tumbling through the trapdoor and to the bottom of the gallows.

"Ah, the noose has torn," he spoke calmly, seeing the noose still around his neck. Malik Slik Sylvester's Magic Muslin had worked and all the hard work of the holy ghosts had finally paid off. Although the knot was still clearly there, the actual noose itself had just dissolved and saved his neck.

"Quick Charlie, get ready to row," BB screamed, two foot away from the fallen Captain.

"Hurry up, don't waste any time, just boot his backside into the boat!" Charlie replied, urging his brother-in-arms to more speed.

"All right, but hold on and be patient for just a little while more, remember, he's nearly been hanged!" BB said, pulling the confused Captain Kidd up by his arms.

"Well, if we wait any longer, he'll be hanged again," the Artful Dodger shouted from the boat, his cheeky face looking unusually serious.

"All right!" BB spat out, rushing back to work.

As the stumbling pirate staggered to his feet, his hands still bound around his back, he took one look at the astonishing beatnik and choked on his condemned man's last breakfast.

"By the balls of St Stan, who are you?" he said in a voice of pure wonder.

"My name's Bilal but you can call me BB and my friends in the boat are Charlie and the Artful Dodger, we are all here to set you free!"

Captain Kidd was still confused and poking BB in the belly to see if he was real asked hurriedly, "Where are you from? I have never seen spectacles like yours before?"

BB rubbed his stomach before replying. "I'm a Banglastani Beatnik wearing kaleidoscopic spectacles and we all come from Pearly Green!"

"That's here."

"Of course, but we have come from three hundred years in the future to save your neck, now hurry up!"

Captain Kidd scratched his head and pondered a while. "Why have you done this?"

BB hadn't the time for all these explanations here and now and so he tugged at the captain's tassels and replied quickly. "Simple, because you're the best thief this side of the universe and we need you to help us in our fight against Lucifer."

"Lucifer – bit of a tall order?"

"Hurry up now, the executioner's coming to check what happened to you," Dobbins urged, clearly seeing both the gallows level and the underground from his perspective on the boat only feet away.

BB wasted no time and threw Kidd head-first into the tiny wooden boat that Dodger had stolen earlier. The boatman on the Greenwitch side of the river whose boat it was, could clearly be seen jumping up and down and waving his hat in futile frustration for its return. The Captain's three pointed red and blue hat went whizzing through the scorched air while his beautiful green and black parrot flew back to land on the Captain's braided left shoulder. It had been less than half a minute since the bungled hanging and the executioner had pulled his own hood off and was coming down fast to inspect what had happened and he wasn't pleased.

"Oi matey, hurry up!" Charlie shouted in irate Kockneestani, his slanting eyes looking grim.

"Yeah, no time to look at anything else now, we have to split or we'll all get our heads chopped off!" Dobbins squealed, pulling madly at his oar.

"Yippee, we made it!" BB screamed as he jumped into the aptly named 'The Mite Leek'. After having stolen it two hours earlier, the Artful Dodger thought it said "The Mighty Leek" and had visions of a giant green vegetable but as they were to soon find out 'The Mite Leek' was a well-named boat.

So the plan had worked and up above their heads, the ghosts circled joyously in the air because the plan which the sly foxy Sidney Arthur had stuffed into Bilal's head had done its thing. BB now laughed and laughed while clapping Charlie and the Artful Dodger on their backs and egging them on as they rowed the boat from different sides. Charlie had a long oar and a long arm while the Artful Dodger had a shorter oar and a wicked look. His hair flew underneath his hat and he yelled obscenities in the direction of the passing gallows as they all jeered and cheered as BB asked Charlie, "Quick, give me your love grenades!"

"All right, they're in me pockets."

"Got 'em!"

And with that BB started lobbing the last of their love grenades in the direction of the gallows pole and within seconds thousands of blooms of marigolds, daisies, jangoberries, junipers, orange petal, hibiscus flowers, oleander blossoms, cherry blossoms and wild apple flowers burst into full bloom and there was havoc everywhere. The gallows pole was covered three foot in petals and all of them smelled divine and the very last love grenade landed squarely on top of the executioner's head and as he found himself bursting into a thousand blossoms, the fat man hollered in the direction of the departing company. "Oi ... Come back ... We ain't finished with him yet!"

"You're not having him back," the Artful Dodger yelled, chucking a manky looking tench he had grabbed from the waters.

"But we've got to start on the beheading and then the quartering!" bemoaned the fat executioner, waving his fists.

"Find someone else, you fat oaf or better still hang yourself, we're not coming back!" Charlie added, sticking up two fingers and picking his nose for fun.

Some of the crowd awaiting the hanging, beheading and quartering were cheering the happy fact that Captain Kidd had got away and an effervescent ripple could be heard throughout the crowd of the wickedly naughty refrain of the "Stinky Billy Song" getting louder and louder. Others in the crowd jeered the executioner and pelted him with rotten tomatoes when he came back up to the gallows, his axe lonely and unused and firmly wedged in the giant wooden block. So half the crowd were pleased and half the crowd were not but they were all gobsmacked to see Captain Kidd disappear – a magic trick to end all magic tricks!

Nevertheless the escape of Captain Kidd had not gone entirely unnoticed by the powers-that-be and whole battalions of sailors and soldiers had been released to look for him. The most dangerous man in the empire had to be caught and hanged, however many times it took.

Sidney Arthur saw their intention and shouted, "Billy, we've got to stop the soldiers and give Captain Kidd a chance!"

"What do we do, Sidney?" Billy asked, cruising up at great speed.

"Yeah, what do we do?" Danny asked, streaming in from the opposite direction and coming to a mid air stop.

"Easy peasy, we just trip them up on crunchy banana skins," Sidney Arthur replied with a laugh

"From where?" Billy enquired, looking confused.

"Look up!" Sidney Arthur finished, grabbing their chins with either hand and pushing them up.

And they did. Suddenly above their heads they could see a whole grove of ghostly crunchy banana trees waving in the wind on a magically floating island. How they had materialised there no one knew and more importantly, no one cared. They quickly picked up hundreds of crunchy bananas and peeled them before giving them all to Billy Blake to eat. Madame Serendipity chucked the empty skins to the ground like manna from the crazy skies. Suddenly, there were hundreds of slippery crunchy banana skins on the ground and the soldiers and sailors stumbled, slipped and fell all over the place to the entertainment of the crowd. The chubby Madame Serendipity smiled, shook her frilly ballroom dress and checked the forever-shifting scenes on her Tapestry of Alternative Endings and became very excited by what she saw.

"What can you see, Madame Serendipity?"

"Brilliant, Sidney Arthur, I can see Captain Kidd and the others escaping through the boat on the river into the underworld at Brickie Lane three hundred years later!"

"Yippee!" yelled Danny De Foe, stabbing the air with his wooden leg with obvious pleasure.

"Hurrah!" screamed Sidney Arthur in sympathy.

"Bluuurgh … Puke!" went poor Billy Blake as he vomited from the skies and watched his ghostly puke plummet into the waters below. He'd overdone the crunchy bananas a bit.

On the tatty boat, introductions were soon being made.

"Hello, who are you again?" Captain Kidd asked the Banglastani Beatnik as the always useful Artful Dodger deftly untied the knots on his hands behind his back.

Once they were free Captain Kidd quickly shook the pins and needles out of them as BB rubbed his spectacles and replied."I'm BB, he's the Artful Dodger and he's Charlie!"

"And I'm Captain Kidd!" Captain Kidd exclaimed, straightening out his hat and sitting upright in the tatty boat.

"We know!" whispered the Artful Dodger, beaming.

"How do you know?" asked Captain Kidd, confused and rather bewildered.

"Oh, we've been following you for some time, an hour and a half at least!" BB retorted, tucking in his shredded purple kurta into his jeans and waiting patiently for a reply.

"Brilliant, and thanks for saving my neck!"

"Pray don't mention it, it was an honour," BB finished as the Artful Dodger got out a few dusty bottles of "Rudolph's Reminiscing Rum" which he had stolen from somewhere or other. Suddenly, there was a distinct flash of light.

"By the sacred beanies of St Stan, what are those?" Charlie hollered, suddenly poking BB with his long oar.

"What?"

"Sitting at the end of the boat," Charlie insisted, now flapping like an upside down turtle.

"Aaah … leprechauns but how did they get there?" said BB before screaming again and stumbling.

They almost jumped out of their skins as a whole bunch of foreign-looking leprechauns suddenly appeared to sit on the starboard side accompanied by Percy the parrot. There were Banglastani leprechauns wearing lungis, Bongostani ones wearing maroon robes, Zeegyptian ones wearing silken one-piece gowns, Bagpipistani ones with knobbly knees wearing short kilts and even the odd Mayrish one dressed all in green. Along with the international leprechauns there was also Abdul, the meditating chappie from Danny De Foe's desert island. (Danny floated down to say hello but the other simply couldn't see him because he was now a ghost.) The lama had a handful of seashells in his grasp and while Charlie and the Artful Dodger rowed, he skimmed them across the flat waters of the River Thames where they suddenly rose up into the air and struck the many soldiers clambering into wooden boats to chase after them. The rest of these seashells were caught by Seashell Sally somewhere in the future, a different time but not a different place. Seashell Sally would then naturally give a single seashell in turn to each of her forty lovers before singing a song of pure loveliness.

So much for the leprechauns, the lama and Seashell Sally's astonishing presence, there was something more immediate to worry about. Suddenly, sitting up, Charlie decided to make a point. "Oi Dobbins . . .!"

"What?"

"What sort of boat have you nicked?"

"Yeah, have you noticed, it's starting to leak," BB added, feeling decidedly wet and uncomfortable. Water was coming in through the wooden floorboards under BB's leaky, torn, pink plimsolls.

"Why did you nick this one?" Charlie asked, having stopped rowing and looking grim. Dobbins decided to dodge a smile and weasel his way out of this predicament so, rubbing his long nose and chewing his fingernails, he answered, "Cos the name's excellent."

"But you can't read."

"No, not very well, I got the owner to read it out to me anyway."

"But it's letting in water now!"

"It sure is!" BB said, adding his two pennies' worth of opinion.

The Artful Dodger squirmed in his seat and thought all this criticism rather unfair. "Don't blame me, I chose it cos of its title – 'The Mighty Leek', it made me think of Jack and the Beanstalk, a mighty vegetable or something."

Charlie was definitely not amused. "But it's not 'The Mighty Leek', you idiot, it's 'The Mite Leek'!"

"And it sure is leaking now," BB finished with a sigh, feeling his feet getting wetter and wetter.

Many boatloads of armed soldiers had clambered into sturdy-looking boats to give chase and what with the leak and the additional weight of the many leprechauns things were not looking good. And then the firing started. A fusillade of bullets fired from some of the approaching boats had an immediate effect as *The Mite Leek* started sinking at a faster rate, it now being even leakier with bulletholes. However the leprechauns were very fast and dodged out of the way of the flying bullets; they were impossible to hit and only smirked and stuck out their tongues. The Holy Ghosts were not slow on the uptake as they looked up to see the miracle. There, thirty feet above their ghostly heads was the floating island where Princess Amrita, Little Lucy and Astral Alice once played on the crumbling sandcastles of King Osric's palace and it was whizzing towards them at speed. This occurrence was more flotsam from the mystic mayhem of *that* night at Metta-Morph-Aziz so long ago in the future. Billy took out his mystical hourglass with the single grain of diamond-white light stuck in the middle and correctly guessed the time to be somewhere near to eternity.

Madame Serendipity was meanwhile checking to see what the shifting figures on her Tapestry of Alternative Endings were saying. The Holy Ghosts were tremendously excited and raced through the air to land on the floating island and began frantically picking the funky coconuts to drop on all the king's men below.

"Yippee . . . they've stopped firing!" BB shouted as *The Mite Leek* slowly paddled to freedom with Charlie and the Artful Dodger on the oars and a few friendly leprechauns stoppering up the many leaks with their thumbs and fingers. It was then suddenly that recognition took place.

"Aaah, I know you!" Captain Kidd screamed, prodding the nearest leprechaun with his finger.

"Of course you do!" muttered the leprechaun from Treasure Island, stepping forward to shake Captain Kidd by his hand and playfully pull at his long black wig.

"You're from Treasure Island, aren't you . . .?"

"Yes, my name is Abdul and I lived there for a while. So are many of the others here and we are here for a reason."

"And what's that?"

It was then that Abdul lifted up his maroon robes which were now getting rather wet, cleared his throat and spoke simply but clearly. "We've just come to give you a letter, don't forget to read it."

"Is that it?" Captain Kidd asked, bemused as Abdul gave him a letter in a sealed envelope.

"You don't have to read it now but don't forget to read it later," said Abdul enigmatically.

Captain Kidd pondered on this for a while as the boat began to sink further. Desperately trying to keep everything afloat, the leprechauns, Charlie and the Artful Dodger simply did their best. BB could think of nothing better to do so he swigged down two bottles of "Rudolph's Reminiscing Rum" with no help from anyone.

A particularly big boat full of Stinky Billy's soldiers was now racing towards the slowly disintegrating *Mite Leek* and it started firing but luckily, missed. However, in no uncertain terms, the leader of the boat made it quite clear that Captain Kidd should stop and everyone give themselves up. Standing up to his full height, Captain Kidd quickly scribbled a note which said "I love you", rolled it down into an empty bottle of rum, stoppered it up with a cork and chucked it as far as he could into the muddy waters. (Many years later when retired, rich, fat, happy and living again on Treasure Island, Captain Kidd went fishing one day for transcendental trout in the exquisite turquoise waters of the Pazific when what should turn up and tickle his toes but the self-same bottle with the message for him because now he truly loved himself.) Captain Kidd pulled his black wig straight and turned to port-side to face the oncoming attackers and simply shouted.

"There ain't no seaside rock.
There's only fluffy candyfloss.
There ain't no gain.
There ain't no loss.
Its only thieves and Buddhas
who don't give a toss!"

The soldiers on the boat jeered and fired this time knocking off the hat of a very surprised Mayrish leprechaun and spooking the parrot. By now *The Mite Leek* was living up to its name and sinking fast and as for the ghosts, none of them were calm; none sanguine, none choleric and Sidney Arthur particularly, was full of bile.

"All our hard work is going to go to waste," he cried, looking decidedly depressed.

"Why, Sidney Arthur?"

"Simple, Billy. It's because Captain Kidd and the others aren't going to get to Pearly Green!"

Danny flew up close to be of some comfort and added, "Yeah, Billy can't you see? Sidney Arthur's right, they are all going to get shot or drown."

"Oh!" Billy gasped, catching the point.

"Get it now?" Danny said sadly, making sure that Billy had finally got it.

As they panicked, they flew in fast circles and increasing speeds around Madame S. checking and rechecking her Tapestry of Alternative Endings, desperately searching for a happy one. Sidney hovering sixty foot above the sinking boat thought that the scam was off. They had tried but they had failed and for the want of a good boat, the kingdom was lost. Sitting cross-legged up the air, Sidney Arthur sighed and cried. It didn't look like they would ever get free he thought, looking tearfully down below and waiting for the inevitable to happen.

It was at this crucial moment when all hope was lost that the Artful Dodger decided to save the day and reaching into his overflowing top hat he grabbed a handful of Anatta left over from *that* night and handed them around.

"Here boys, let's finish off the last of this before they finish us off!" he shouted over the sounds of cascading water.

"Where did you get them?" BB snorted disbelievingly but alert to all possibilities.

"Been saving them for a rainy day, stole them from Fairlight didn't I?"

"Brilliant idea. Let's have it washed down with the last bottle of rum."

"Okay!" Charlie said confidently, still slapping the murky waters with his long oar as they swallowed together.

Capitan Kidd then looked briefly at the greenish tab of Anatta that Dobbins was pressing into his hand and swallowed it. The trip was suddenly on and taking no longer than two and a half seconds to activate in their bloodstreams, BB could just burble with wonder as the Anatta came on faster than he'd ever known it before.

"Aaah, the boat's finally sinking!" the Artful Dodger hollered as the water level got higher and higher.

"Naah! We're going to be shot!" Charlie screamed as the longboat with the many flintlocks raised got closer and closer.

BB seemed to disagree with the gloomy situation. Gurgling and sinking he blurted, "No, I'm going to drown, you're going to be shot!"

It was then that the pirate captain put in his penny-worth. "No, I'm going to be hanged, beheaded and quartered into a thousand pieces!"

"Oh, shut up you three and enjoy the ride!" the Artful Dodger shouted and this was something they needed to know.

The Anatta was slowly dissolving their world when Charlie shouted in surprise. "Where have all the leprechauns gone? "

"Glug ... glug ... rats leaving a sinking ship eh?" BB said half a second later, thrashing about in the water.

"Who cares?" finished the Artful Dodger, checking to see if their end had really come by grabbing onto a silken pocket watch streaming out of his Victorian top hat and checking the time. The time said one minute to twelve, a high noon for sure, thought Dobbins as he tried to keep his head above water.

"Forget about them now and try not to get shot!" BB shrieked as the longboats of King Stinky Billy's sailors got closer and closer. They were now no more then ten yards away and flintlocks were being fired furiously as the Anatta took them over completely. In milliseconds flat the magical potion of Fairlight's incredible potion had begun to do its trick and as the hole-ridden boat finally sank into watery oblivion, the trip turned itself full-on.

"Far out, the Anatta's saved us," the Artful Dodger squealed as everything went magic!

"Don't be too quick to judge!" Charlie spat back, ever the cautious one.

"Hold on to your handkerchiefs for the ride!" BB giggled before yelling at the top of his Banglastani beatnik voice. All was well except that Captain Kidd seemed rather confused.

"Excuse me, but what's Anatta?" he asked but no one apart from his parrot answered him.

"Squawk, but what about me?"

Captain Kidd managed to look bemused and sorrowful at the same time but had no words. He just waved and smiled weakly.

"Aaaaahhhh!" they all screamed as the white flash of lightning flashed all around and they were spinning through spirals of white light, tumbling and twisting and falling in patterns known only to their karma. They were moving at the speed of light and hurtling through time as if they were skydiving from the moon until the fields and parks and cobbled streets of Pearly Green appeared.

"Yippee, we're coming back home!" BB yelled joyfully as they fell.

"We're in our astral bodies and so we won't have to jump through the tandoori ovens!" Charlie squeaked wisely as he took the lead.

"Yeah, but who knows where we are going?" said the Artful Dodger artfully dodging a whole flock of fantasy flamingos two hundred feet from the ground.

"Yeah, but who cares? We've come home and that's enough!" BB insisted sailing through the air to be close to Charlie and the incredulous pirate who was having the time of his life.

"Most incredible, the world looks so different from this perspective. Much better than dangling from a scaffold!"

BB tended to agree with him and said so. "You're right there, Captain, hold on, we are coming in to land."

They were all holding hands in their astral forms as they plunged into the Lost Catacombs. Whizzing through the Land of the Living Dreamtime, they tumbled through a flock of penguins, startled a group of flying psychedelic pigs and flashed right through a herd of sacred cows out nibbling moss in the corridors. Ripping past Kid Kurry's Magical Muncherie, they fell through the Torrible Zone where they went right through a surprised group of Master Fagin's Funkadelic tribe, Habiba and some Hashemites and then through the cave of the three Whirling Dervishes too. Nasseruddin the Nutty giggled like a child as Captain Kidd's astral body whizzed through his physical form leaving no visible trace of any damage except a supreme desire to itch. Suleiman the Spinner and Mevlana were scratching like mad as Sid and Charlie raced through them. And then they were all falling through the Land of the Sleeping Dreamtime and deftly missing Twynklyn, Blynkyn and Nod. The tiny Dreamweavers were out giving free wishes to anyone who wanted them. And then finally they were whizzing past a grinning Jabberwocky and BB realised that they must be somewhere near the Sonic Temple. They all tumbled horizontally through cave and corridor walls as if they were made of paper to squarely land inside the mysterious cave of Malik Slik Sylvester.

"Ohh . . .!" moaned Charlie as his lanky form found itself on the floor once again.

"Groan . . .!" groaned Captain Kidd, his black wig almost falling off his confused head.

"Never again . . .!" BB said, rubbing his pained head and sitting up.

"That's what you say all the time" Charlie retorted, doing much of the same.

"Well never again till next time then!" BB said cockily, slowly getting up and taking his bearings.

"By the balls of St Stan where are we?" Captain Kidd crooned, dusting himself off and straightening up his wig.

"Oh wonderful! Guests!" Malik Slik Sylvester cried happily as the others slowly re-materialised into their physical forms. Malik's impish face didn't look perturbed as he rubbed a thin hand through his usual unshaved three-day-old stubble. His long tapering fingers scratched his cheeks and the head of Future Fashions Inc and the incredible inventor of magic muslin laughed at the incredulous sights of these bumbling fools. Dressed in a one-piece gown of spider-woven silk, Malik went quickly over to check his looms and spiders before releasing a large canister of hallucinogenic agaric-flies for them to eat. Folding a few Hypno-Tantric Hijabs to the side, he also put away a battered book he'd been reading about the Magic Muslin Weavers of Gobbinfields of yore and took note of what he had learned. He soon recognised the lads but pinched his nose on seeing the queerly dressed Captain Kidd. As he pondered, Malik suddenly saw the noose made of magic muslin still tied around Captain Kidd's fortunate neck.

"Aha, the magic muslin that was missing, so that's where it went. I did wonder!"

"This, young man, saved my life and so I should thank you," said Captain Kidd fingering the noose and going to shake Malik by the hand.

By this time Charlie, BB and Dobbins had got up slowly and uncertainly onto their wobbly recently re-materialised feet. Dusting each other off they proceeded to stretch their arms and legs and become re-accustomed to being back in their physical bodies again.

Captain Kidd, however, was in the midst of demonstrating his gratitude. "Yes, thank you for your fine weave, it saved my neck for sure." Malik shrugged his shoulders and smiled before replying. "Glad to be of use but I didn't save you, I wonder who did? BB, wont you introduce us?"

BB hobbled on over to do as bid. "Malik, this is Captain Kidd and Captain Kidd this is our Malik Slik – the most amazing inventor of magic muslin . . .!"

Both shook hands and Captain Kidd's golden earring glistened like the sun as it took in the glowing stars in the Sleeping Dreamtime walls. It was time for Malik to become a polite host and he decided to make some tea for everyone.

"Right, who wants tea?" he asked, clapping his hands and stroking his stubbly chin.

"What have you got?" BB asked examining the holes in his pink plimsolls curiously.

"I've got everything, Sereni-tea, Equanimi-tea, Humili-tea, Humani-tea, Futili-tea and, of course, Normali-tea."

"I'll have Normali-tea," BB replied quickly, not liking the sound of the other fancy brews.

Captain Kidd took his three-pointed hat off, exhaled deeply and said, "And I'll have Humili-tea, certainly not Futili-tea, after my experiences I don't like the sound of that one."

"Make mine a Humani-tea," Charlie said, squeezing the last of the water out of his damp socks.

The Artful Dodger was the last to reply. "And mine a Sereni-tea, please, Malik!"

And with that they all cheered spontaneously and started dancing a jig around the cave, alive and back home. (Well, Captain Kidd's real home was of course Treasure Island but he was glad to be alive if not at home yet.) As Captain Kidd danced around, his three-pointed hat askew, his twinkling blue eyes took in the wondrous sights of the Land of the Sleeping Dreamtime and he gasped at the translucent colours that were dripping off the cave walls and into his heart.

As Malik returned with the teas for everyone they all sat around in a circle on some small work stools and drank in silence until BB exclaimed, "Hey Captain Kidd, we've been reliably informed that you are the best thief this side of the universe!"

Captain Kidd didn't bother to even look up but simply asked nonchalantly, "Am I?"

"Yes, now can you tell us how you do it?" BB insisted, wanting to know everything.

Charlie added his support by saying, "Yeah, do you have a philosophy or something?"

"That would be telling," Captain Kidd exhaled but BB would have none of this and continued in this vein.

"Well then, tell us, after all we've done for you and all!"

Captain Kidd slowly slurped up the rest of his tea and then said resignedly, "Well all right, I might as well teach you about Thieves' Philosophy, it's got four parts."

"Go on!" the others all said in unison, sitting up and looking excited.

"One – Nothing ventured, nothing gained, this means living in the moment of the here and now when committing the theft, not to think about the past or the future but just to live in the moment and allow yourself to be present in the present."

"Wicked! What's the second?" Charlie asked, totally entranced by what his Kockneestani ears were hearing. Captain Kidd went on.

"Two – There is never a loss, only gain. You can never lose even if you lose. Look at me I had lost but was still pretty cheerful considering they were going to hang, behead and quarter me."

"And the third?" asked the Artful Dodger, firmly giving the Captain his full attention.

"Never keep anything you have stolen but give it away to others who need it more."

"This is a bit like Robin Hood, robbing the rich to feed the poor!" BB said enthusiastically, remembering some of the stuff he'd heard so long ago.

"That's right, we work along similar lines."

"And the last?" Charlie interjected quickly before the Captain's flow could be spoilt.

"That's simple, remember there is no higher honour or loyalty than the honour amongst Buddhas and thieves!"

"Wow!" went Dobbins and Charlie together, clapping their hands in time as BB spoke up defiantly.

"Oh sorry, I was falling asleep. Sorry. Please. Thank you. Could you say all that again please?"

"Oh mate!" gasped the Artful Dodger pulling BB's ears and chuckling.

Charlie then had a bright idea. "Look, let's just eat our cakes and drink our tea and think about how we are going to use this philosophy to rob Lucifer of his dearest possessions."

"Yes we have to use it to steal the mountain of gold from Fort Cox and maybe the horns from Lucifer's head too!" whistled the Artful Dodger merrily, though it was a bit of a tall order.

And so they drank and ate and pondered. Malik smiled glad of their boisterous presence as they talked well into the night of their mission from St Stan and how they still had to take great care.

30

The Sonic Temple of King Psychedelix Comes to Life

Big changes were happening to the residents of the Lost Catacombs or to be more accurate, big changes were happening to the Lost Catacombs and this was having an incredible effect on the inhabitants. All the three different lands of the Living Dreamtime, Torrible Zone and Land of the Sleeping Dreamtime had coalesced into the Land of the Awakening Dreamtime. In fact, there was nothing left of the Lost Catacombs except for an incredible expansion of the Sonic Temple of King Psychedelix. Early one morning, after a mad night before, all the inhabitants of the Lost Catacombs had found themselves suddenly falling through the central artery where the River of Crystal Light flowed on both sides. Rather like Astral Alice falling through the rabbit hole so long ago, everyone descended to the deepest level and the Sonic Temple. But why was this happening one may ask? The answer was really simple. It was all to do with the rebirth of music inside the Lost Catacombs and could be totally blamed on Mellow Tron, Tarquin and Fareek. Ever since they had been experimenting with an ancient Zeegyptian juniper-spludberry accidentally found in Mellow Tron's locks, they had been synapsing this plant with all their beat-boxes, samplers and synthesisers and life had become very different. King Funky had given the future his golden scarab through the Old Blind Man of Thebiz to make a new Anatta but this accidental juniper-spludberry plant was making them all dance and trance splendidly. All the inhabitants looked totally gobsmacked and the whole of the caves in the Lost Catacombs arranged themselves in the best manner possible in the giant flat expanse of the Sonic Temple.

"Flumph . . .!" went the sound as cave after cave sailed through the air to settle themselves nicely into their new positions in the temple and the caves that had previously been next to each other were together and next to each other still. "Kid Kurry's Magical Muncherie" was right in the middle feeding all the hungry people, elves and leprechauns as usual. Kassim, Karim and Dilly the Silly could be seen bossing the waiters around when the crowd shouted for more. And next to that there was Malik Slik Sylvester standing outside the cave of Future Fashions Inc enticing whole crowds of gobsmacked people to come inside and look at his wondrous raiments. Next to his cave the Wicked White Witches of the West could be seen cruising through the air above the Sonic Temple on their collapsible broomsticks. Moonmummy and Stargasm waved a hello to the Jabberwocky, Mullah Ullah and the Genie of the Lamp who had come out to see what was going on.

"Wow, do you realise what this means?" Mullah Ullah asked, rubbing his psychedelic gatta.

"What?" enquired the Genie of the Lamp, cruising out to get a better look.

"Grunt. Poot ... I know!" stammered the waddling Jabberwocky, stumbling forward on its short green legs and flashing its colour-changing scales to everyone and anyone who could be watching.

The Genie of the Lamp replied first. "I don't know, Mullah Ullah, I wasn't here during the last great adventure!"

Mullah Ullah was sympathetic. "That's right Genie of the Lamp. OK then, Jabberwocky, tell him."

"All right, grunt, grunt ... now all the caves have come and the new music is activating the Sonic Temple of old King Psychedelix, what it, grunt, grunt, means is that we shall soon be going on an adventure! What do you reckon Mullah Ullah?"

"Very soon the whole of the Sonic Temple will start spinning off into St Stan knows where and we shall all be with it!"

"Oh, what fun!" whistled the Genie of the Lamp, coming fully out of its lamp and into the air. The Jabberwocky was just as amazed.

"Grunt ... Grunt ... incredible!"

"And is everyone going to go?" the Genie asked, flying down for a bit.

"Everyone who's in the Sonic Temple when it takes off will go!"

"How will it take off, Mullah Ullah?" the genie asked inquisitively, flicking his golden earrings to make them glisten.

The Mullah explained. "It all depends on Anarkali, when MMA are making their wonderful Hypno-Tantric Trance and the Sonic Temple is grooving when Anarkali trances, the whole of the whole of the Sonic Temple and, may I say, the whole of our world will take off."

Meanwhile, as everyone looked, the Giant Hypno-Tantric Love Monster that had not been seen for a while, came tumbling down the central shaft of the River of Crystal Light. Over three hundred feet tal, it was made up of the astral bodies of thousands. Landing onto the ground with a soft thud it brushed itself off, laughed at the world and what it saw through its thousands of eyes, bounced up and down like a three year old before doing cartwheels and back-flips across the vast expanse with a big smile on its face and pulling its vast form up onto Osric's floating island. Where it had been and what it had done, no one knew. All the inhabitants waved deliriously to the Love Monster and saw the countless faces of their friends and families whom they had not seen since *that* night. The Love Monster was back and that was a good sign, another friend to have in the fight against Lucifer.

As Osric's island floated over, the coconut trees blew in the breeze and the growing melody of gladness blew its ascendant notes into the cascading winds. But there was something special about the island now. Although the sandcastle palace had long dissolved and the very grains of sand been reclaimed by the sea, some very special beings were now living here. It was the ten thousand Buddhas that had rushed out of Osric's heart so long ago. However, leaving Osric's heart these Buddhas had to find a new home and this they did by landing on the floating island. The place was perfect and they didn't need a palace to live in either.

Deep down below, the original owner of these ten thousand Buddhas (but not of the one green garden gnome) put a hand through his spiky, collar-length hair. His kajol-stained eyes were staining the rest of his face as usual and a lop-sided smile was slowly spreading over his sleepy face. Osric, once king of the funky coconut swaying island where his ten thousand Buddhas frolicked with the one green garden gnome and once in the past the most incredible King Psychedelix, monarch of the whole of the Lost Catacombs, pulled up his scruffy jeans. Standing next to him was the seven-year-old terror and next to her was the grinning Jabberwocky, smoke snorting out of its nostrils. Amrita laughed before dexterously jumping up onto the Jabberwocky's back and asking it for a ride.

The Jabberwocky got up slowly and plodded around the floor

just to please the very last in line of the Gigglistani princesses, and said to Osric in a smoky syntax, "Osric, you know that you are the king of all you survey?"

"What does that mean, Jabberwocky?" Osric asked, confusedly.

"It means exactly as I said . . . grunt . . . king of all you survey."

"But all I can survey with these tired eyes is the love, light and laughter of my many friends and family."

"That's right! That's your kingdom!"

Osric looked yet more confused and asked again. "Does that mean I'm not king of a real place?"

"What you mean like a country or something . . .? But Amrita is just like you . . . She's last in the line of the legendary Gigglistani princesses . . .!"

"What exactly does that mean, Jabberwocky?"

"That means she's the princess of chuckling, giggling and laughter . . .!"

"Hee . . . Hee . . . Hee . . . that's right!" Amrita grinned, slapping her pigtails under Osric's nose and running away.

The Jabberwocky clapped its front legs together, stood on its haunches and replied. "To be the Princess of Laughter is so much better than being the Baroness of Pearly Green or the King of Butlinistan or the Queen of Snootyland, you are special, you are the future form of King Psychedelix!"

"Yeah, I know, he gave me such a fright when he whizzed out of my heart he did!"

"You are a king because your kingdom is that of perception. You have the most amazing way of looking at things. The most original and dare I say it, the most far out, and that floating isle going above our heads where all your ten thousand Buddhas are looking out at the ocean, is yours. There Amrita, Astral Alice and Little Lucy built a sandcastle palace for you because to them regardless of who you really are, you will always be king!"

Osric pulled his own ears and whistled. "Sheesh!"

The smoking Jabberwocky allowed him no respite and carried on. "But we are not here to go on about the past, we have to live in the present, in fact it's the only place you can live but me and Amrita are here now to check that you know your stuff."

"What stuff?"

The Jabberwocky came up close, stood up on two short legs and smokily whispered in Osric's ears. "The stuff you need to know if you really are the future rebirth of King Psychedelix, the most far-out monarch of all time and space!"

"Oh come on, Osric!" Amrita grumbled, jumping on his toes.

"If you were who everybody thinks you were then you shouldn't have much difficulty remembering anything, it's not much, is it?"

The chuckling Jabberwocky changed the colours on its fins in delight, adding. "Well said, Amrita, of course, it's not much, we are now going to check to see if Osric knows the Idiot's Path or not!"

"If you are going to rule as King Osric, you have to know, there's no getting away!" Amrita chirped, wiser beyond her years.

"All right!" Osric gasped, changing his vacant look for something more awake.

The Jabberwocky grinned a bit more and smoked testily out of his glowing nostrils.

"What's the first Holy Rule?"

"Er Um ... 'you're never alone in being alone'!"

"Excellent and do you know what that means?"

Osric looked rather sheepish.

The Jabberwocky looked serious and explained. "Well I'll tell you then, loneliness is a terrible thing but aloneness is OK. We are all alone even when we are together and being alone is the very nature of the universe. However, when lots of beings who are alone get together nobody is lonely anymore and that's a great thing, so what's the Second Holy Rule?"

"I know this!" Amrita interjected, pulling the Jabberwocky's fins trying to get his attention.

The Jabberwocky nudged her gently and said, "Not yet, Amrita, only help him out if he struggles!"

Looking more sheepish than before, Osric bit his lips before replying, "Laughter is the first language, isn't it?"

"Simply brilliant, Osric and look here. Amrita demonstrates this better than anyone else I know. Laughter comes before language and brings the world together. Without it, serious philosophy would swamp the world and drown it of chuckles."

"Ha ... Ha ... Ha ...!" Amrita laughed, perfectly demonstrating her personal philosophy.

After a while the Jabberwocky butted in. "You can stop laughing now, Amrita and help Osric with the Third Holy Rule!"

"Er ... em ... er ... um ... I don't know!" Osric bleated like a lost sheep in Queen Angie Park.

"Grunt . . . tell him Amrita."

"Okay. 'All roads lead to home'."

The Jabberwocky snorted from its smoky nostrils and muttered. "That means that the world and the universe is a single unified place and it doesn't matter where you are it will still be home!"

Osric gasped at the sheer simplicity of the Jabberwocky's argument. "Far out, oops! What I meant to say was that I knew that."

"So what's the last?" the Jabberwocky asked with a wry expression on its face.

"Easy I can't forget this one, its 'What you see is what you get, what you get depends on you'."

"Excellent, now you know your Holy Rules, let's check to see you know your Humble Truths."

Osric paused for a while and then started with gusto.

"All right then, the first is 'Freedom is a basic necessity'."

"Bravo! Freedom for all sentient beings that move, crawl, swim or fly."

Osric didn't stop as he was on a roll. "And the second is 'Freedom will not come by waiting'."

"Superb!"

Amrita meanwhile was jumping up and down with her hand in the air. "And I know the third!"

"What is it, Amrita?" The Jabberwocky inquired, gently singeing her buttocks with its smoke.

Amrita felt the tickling warmth and chuckled her answer. "Because freedom will not come by waiting it has to be sought for, fought for and won!"

"Excellent, and the last?"

Osric stood there visibly amazed at how much Amrita knew and exhaled deeply as he replied. "Freedom doesn't come for free, there's always a price to pay!"

So far they had been correct and the Jabberwocky wasted no time and asked him now for the Three Serene Sillinesses.

Princess Amrita had had enough of the Jabberwocky's bossiness.

"Oh give him a break. I'll tell you what they are," Amrita said intent on protecting her friend.

The Jabberwocky smiled at this change of tack and replied. "Okay then. Shoot away!"

Amrita pulled at her dress and started. "Time flies like an arrow is the first one."

"Correct and the second?"

"Fruits flies like a banana."

"Crunchy of course, but correct!"

"And the last is dragon flies straight for the heart."

"Absolutely perfect ... grunt ... in all of them ... grunt ... well done!"

And then the three danced once again as the Jabberwocky finally said, "All we need to know now are the Magic Mantras which we don't know yet and that, my friends, is the whole of the Idiot's Path wrapped up like a betel nut inside a betel leaf and chewed."

The Hypno-Tantric Trance was booming across 387 giant wall-embedded speakers with a loudness that was so loud, smaller caves were exploding like popcorn in the process. On the centre of a hastily constructed stage, Fareek's flashing holographic zoofi gown was dancing in time to the music as he whacked up the controls on the umpteen phazers and flangers connecting the Juniper spludberry to the whole array of beat-boxes, samplers and synthesisers. Next to him Mellow Tron's face looked wiser beyond his years as his tiny body jumped up and down perfectly to the beat. Tarquin, meanwhile, was sitting behind a set of synsantooric tablas and banging away for dear life. His handsome Bollywood bloomers had been hitched up and an overwhelming smile began to spread over his face as his happy fingers slapped the skins like no one else.

"Thud ... thud ... thrippity ... Thud ...!"

"Hey, Mellow Tron, what do you think of the juniper spludberry you brought back from Zeegypt in your hair?" Tarquin screamed over the deafening loudness and, letting his dreadlocks fly free for a change, Mellow Tron answered as quick as a flash.

"It sounds great, mate. Wonderful what the dreadlocks can hide when they are in a secretive mood ...!" Tarquin then quickly turned his attention to Fareek who was playing around with the plant and adjusting the filters.

"Oi Fareek, more Astral Ale to the roots of the plant I think!"

"It's crying out for a drink," Mellow Tron added turning the faders up so high, the glorious twinklefish raced towards the ever-expanding ceiling of the Sonic Temple.

Fareek pondered a while, chewed his lips and then said, "All right, but just a drop ... This Astral Ale is really strong stuff."

"Not as strong as 'Rudolph's Reminiscing Rum!' Tarquin chuckled, opening a bottle himself with one hand and swigging the lot in one go.

And so Fareek dropped some drops of Astral Ale into the pot-holder and lo and behold in five seconds flat the pot-holder containing the juniper spludberry began to spin around in an anti-clockwise direction, faster and faster. It spun to the beats as the music went up in clarity and volume. The elves and the fairies danced in the glow and above all the crazy hullabaloo, the ghosts of Cynthia Cruickshank and Phineas Freakville danced invisibly, arm in arm and she hid her beautiful face in Phineas's shoulder as they did the foxtrot together. Phineas's merry smile shone past his glassless pince-nez while Cynthia's unfinished Tapestry of Never-Ending Time traced her every footstep and her voluminous gown followed her closely. Things were getting crazier by the second.

"Oi Fareek, do you remember, we have to remember something!" Tarquin screamed above the sounds, edging closer to his pal.

"What?" Fareek asked, not having remembered anything.

"I said, do you remember?" Tarquin began again.

But Fareek had heard him properly. "And I said 'What'. What am I meant to remember?"

"Oh I see, what I wanted to say was do you remember the promise we made to King Funky!"

"What promise?" Fareek asked while delicately connecting the feed wires from the liquid food and the spinning juniper spludberry.

Tarquin looked aghast and shouted over the howling sounds. "We said we'd be back one day and that he could be the funky drummer in our band."

"Oh right!"

"It would be brilliant, it would complement what I play on the synsantooric tablas!"

"Well, what about it?" Fareek asked, never taking his eyes off the spinning plant.

Tarquin looked at Mellow Tron for support and simply said, "I reckon we should start making a drum kit up for him now."

"Good idea, but with what?" Fareek asked, starting to feel flabbergasted.

Tarquin smiled as he had everything worked out. "Easy, look above your heads, Osric's floating island is passing again and things are dropping off from it and onto the floor!"

"What sort of things?" Mellow Tron asked in a haze.

Smilingly Tarquin continued happily. "Oh, I think they look like giant coconuts shells, pumpkin gourds and thousands of pretty sea shells."

"What can we do with those?" Mellow Tron asked and Tarquin took no time in explaining.

"We can make King Funky a drum kit, the giant pumpkin gourds can be bass drums, the giant coconuts the tom toms, the pretty seashells can be the cymbals and bells."

Fareek was impressed but he still wasn't fully satisfied. "That's all very good but what are we going to use for the snare and hi-hat?"

It was time for Mellow Tron to step in. "For the snare, Tarquin can give him his own from his synsantooric tabla set-up. He never uses it anyway."

"But what about the hi-hat?" Fareek insisted, scratching his head in wonder.

"Don't be silly, King Funky doesn't need one, he's already got a high hat on his head ... the twin crowns of upper and lower Zeegypt," Mellow Tron replied rapidly.

"You've gone completely bonkers now!"

"No, you are the one who's lost the plot!"

"Stop arguing you two, and dig the beat!" Tarquin screamed, suddenly slapping a different set of rhythms on his ever-present synsantooric tablas. They did.

And as they played Fareek checked to see if the juniper spludberry was all right. It was and so he took the time to quickly jump off the stage and rush underneath the floating island. The construction of King Funky's drum kit had finally begun.

"Brilliant, got three giant pumpkins for the bass drums, now just need coconut shells for the tom toms," Fareek whistled rushing to show Mellow Tron his stash of bass drums and then running back to stand underneath the moving island again.

The Buddhas had gone back to their music and while five thousand were playing biscuit tin guitars, the other five thousand were playing their coconut drums but they only needed one half of the coconuts to use as drums and as they played, the gnome went around picking up hundreds of empty coconut halves that were being chucked off the island to be gathered by Fareek. This was, of course, King Psychedelix's Sonic Temple they were all in, where time and space could behave in very disturbing ways.

"Oh wicked! Giant clam shells! They can be cymbals and pretty pink seashells, they can be bells. The drum kit, I think we've got it!"

And while Buddhas and little girls frolicked as a laughing gnome looked on, people, elves, fairies and funny creatures of all sorts jumped around to the incredible music made by the juniper spludberry with a little help from the MMA. As Mellow Tron and Tarquin watched dumbfounded, Fareek rushed around backstage to set up King Funky's fantastic 108 piece drum kit in record time. It had 3 bass drums, 65 tom-toms, 30 cymbals, 9 bells and one snare and was the greatest drum kit ever seen either in Brickie Lane or underneath it.

Mellow Tron watched his beat brother run around with total astonishment but then he couldn't help himself and asked, "How do you know we'll ever see King Funky again? We last left him inside the largest of the pyramids!"

Fareek turned around as quick as a flash to say, "Karma will join us up all again, I know it!"

"You wish Fareek. Do you mind if I give the drum-kit a go?" Tarquin asked, itching to have a go behind the largest drum kit he had ever seen.

Without batting an eyelid Fareek replied phlegmatically, "Be my guest."

Jumping off from his synsantooric tablas Tarquin jumped behind the monstrous 108 piece kit and starting whacking all the drums together at the same time ...

"Boom ... Booom ... Boom ... Boooooom ...!"

Everything inside the Sonic Temple thundered and the sound was bone-shatteringly loud. Fairies, gubblies, elves and funny creatures went flying through the air from its heavy reverberations while people just stood around and laughed. Tarquin and the drum kit were brilliant together but as the bedrock of King Osric's floating island started to crumble earth onto their heads, Fareek called it a day. "Wicked, Tarquin, but enough, we know the drum-kit works, let's leave it for Funky when we meet him again."

"You sure of that?"

"Absolutely positive!"

And with that Tarquin sat behind his synsantooric tablas again and normality prevailed once more. And then as the music rose to a crescendo, the three Sisters Nazneen shimmered to the centre of stage and started to sing. They had brought their Chamber of Blissful Echoes with them and their high notes, mid range and bass reverberated like crazy and echoed forever through the cavernous space of the Sonic Temple.

"Wow, they're groovy!" shouted an elf to a gubblie as the Dreamweavers watched with growing interest.

"They're great!" shouted Nasseruddin trying to pull his lapis lazuli front teeth out for no reason.

"They're better than ever!" Hussain the Insane said sensibly, secretly pouring Nasseruddin another cup of their favourite, Dirty. And they *were* better than ever.

As the Sisters Nazneen burst into song, Anarkali shot off into the air and was dancing in the very space where the bright blue skies of the Sonic Temple met the crystal clear waters of King Osric's isle and in this space she turned round and round, faster than the eye could see and then the whole temple started spinning. The Chuckle Stream was increasing and as it increased the whole of the Sonic Temple spun faster and faster. With a cheer hip hip hoorah, all the participants started getting into the swing of it, singing, dancing, trancing and generally having the wildest of times. So all was well in this the best of all possible worlds except for one little thing. And what was that? As the whole universe started spinning in an anti-clockwise direction with Anarkali as the spinning centre, a bewildered Captain Kidd sat and finally opened the golden envelope. It was the secret and yet so important letter that Abdul had sent him through the vistas of time via Zeegypt. He looked thoughtful as he took out the letter and there in childish handwriting the lama had written nine simple if confusing words in the centre of the page:

"Tickle his toes and his horns will fall off"

31

Stealing the Horns of Lucifer

THE CONSPIRATORS WERE busy planning. They had all been waiting for Captain Kidd to return from the past and now that he was here their plans could proceed and in one of the most secret recesses of the Sonic Temple, BB, Charlie, the Artful Dodger, Mullah Ullah, Stargasm and Moonmummy were busy muttering and throwing beetles on the ground in an attempt to divine the future. As Moonmummy threw the many black little things not a single one landed upside down, they simply hid under her gown.

"Drat and double drat!" Stargasm spat as she peered intently at the escaping insects. Moonmummy looked really annoyed as no amount of coaxing would make the beetles fall on their back.

"Maybe Mellow Tron was wrong about this beetle thing, Stargasm!"

"Or perhaps he threw golden scarab beetles in Zeegypt, here we have to unfortunately put up with simple black ones."

"Never mind, you two. Get close together, there's much to discuss!" Captain Kidd started, more daring than ever. The Captain's humorous mouth flashed up and down getting everyone and everything in order. He had decided that as he had been brought back from the past at great risk, he should take the lead in this particular adventure.

"Oi Captain Kidd, enough of your bossiness. What do we need to do and where do we need to go?" BB shouted and Charlie wasn't long in joining him either.

"Yeah, tell us and make it clear."

Above their heads the ghosts of Sidney Arthur, Danny De Foe and Billy Blake listened with great care.

"This bit's really important, we'll be able to work out whether or not they have caught on to our plan!"

Now it was the turn of the witches to get interested.

"All right then, Captain Kidd. What's the plan?" started Moonmummy.

"Yeah, and have you worked out the meaning of the letter yet?" Stargasm asked insistently, her curly blonde hair flashing like the sun.

Moonmummy muttered a few spells and then continued. "What exactly does 'Tickle his toes and his horns will fall off' mean?"

"One question at a time, good people ... first I'll take BB's question. The plan is to go to the deepest darkest recesses of Hell and find Lucifer!"

"Wow that sounds dangerous, then what?"

"And then Charlie, I've worked out the meaning of the letter in my dreams last night. It's very simple, it means that if you tickle Lucifer's toes his horns will fall off!"

Charlie wasn't satisfied. "And what does that mean?"

"Well, Lucifer's power is all in his horns, if they come off he's lost it and will be easy to defeat!"

"Brilliant, Captain Kidd, it's a good thing that you are here and weren't hanged, drawn and badly quartered," Moonmummy said with a smile.

"I'll say but that's not the end of it, we are going to steal his gold and share it with the whole world, we are going to practise Thieves Philosophy and make everyone really happy."

"Wicked!" went BB, smiling.

"Far out!" giggled Charlie.

"Excellent!" Moonmummy mumbled.

Stargasm still had some questions. "But how are we going to carry all the gold?"

Captain Kidd stroked his beard and replied. "I've thought of that, I've had a chat with Mellow Tron about how Cassandra raised the gold in the air and made it move. She taught him how to do it and in turn, he taught me."

"So, it shouldn't be a problem then," Stargasm asked more in exclamation than question.

"No, not at all!" Moonmummy answered swiftly.

It was then that Captain Kidd clapped his hands for everyone's attention again. Pointing his hat at a rakish angle, he cleared his throat and continued. "Hmm ... Hmm ... you do all realise the plan is extremely dangerous and we may not escape ... But we are going for two reasons."

"And what are they?" BB asked with a serious look.

"Firstly, we are going to steal all the gold and give it to the leprechauns. I've been dealing with them my whole life and the plan requires us to give all the gold we steal from Lucifer to the leprechauns!"

"Why?" the others all asked at the same time. Captain Kidd remained enigmatic. "I can't tell you, it's still a secret."

"Do you know why then?" Stargasm asked quickly, the first to take the lead.

"Of course, I've been stealing gold off the English and Spanglish off the coast of Treasure Island many centuries before you were born and believe me I can't tell you why yet!"

BB, scratching his head and looking rather puzzled, suddenly asked, "Will we get to find out later on?"

"Of course!"

Charlie was still rather sceptical and wanted to carry on in the previous vein. "And how will the leprechauns appear?"

Captain Kidd stood up to his full height before answering. "They will appear suddenly once we have stolen the gold and defeated Lucifer. This part of the plan is number three in Thieves Philosophy: 'Never keep anything you have stolen but give it away to the poor and undeserving!'"

And that was that, having said his piece, Captain Kidd sat down and played with his earrings as the conspiratorial group conferred once more. They were having endless meetings and whilst they argued over how many crunchy bananas they were going to take and how ripe they should be, the pirate whistled between his impatient teeth and started peeling a transcendental plum. He wondered whether or not it would be better to go on his own when he realised he didn't know the way to Hell or have the means of transport. Captain Kidd laughed as he realised that his chosen form of transportation, his wonderful ship *The Leprechaun's Deligh*t had been lost in the mists of time. He exhaled deeply and felt wistful and wondered what ever had happened to his old shipmates likes Seaman Stains, Master Bates and the others. He then turned around to look at the others who were still arguing.

"I want to go by broomstick!" Stargasm shrieked, excitedly jumping up and down like a child without a lollipop.

"Me too!" shouted Moonmummy like a child without two.

Charlie stuck up his hand and rapidly put his point of view

across. "But they're far too slow and the heat in Hell might burn them up!"

BB then bit his fingernails and said, "What about psychedelic flying pigs? Me and Charlie want to go on those."

"No, they'll just get roasted up by the fires of Hell and the demons will eat them up!" Stargasm said abruptly but most eloquently.

Meanwhile, two Holy Ghosts hovering above their heads conferred with Sidney Arthur very quickly.

It was Danny who started first. "What's the most important thing, Sidney?"

"That we travel there together and in comfort," Sidney Arthur replied, buffing his fingernails with a quiet confidence.

"Well said!" Billy agreed emphatically, sidling up to be next to Sidney Arthur.

Prodding Sidney Arthur with a grubby hand Billy proceeded patiently. "Yeah, go on Sidney, open your carpet bag of trickster ideas and get an idea, stuff it into Mullah Ullah's head and make sure the Genie of the Lamp isn't watching. I'm not too sure but I think that he can see us."

"All right, here goes!" and with that Sidney Arthur opened the carpet bag of wickedly trickster ideas and getting out an incredible idea, planted it into Mullah Ullah's wonderful brain. His psychedelic gatta started to shine like a beacon as a warning but Mullah Ullah luckily ignored it and the hovering mischievous presence of Sidney Arthur and the other two was quickly forgotten.

Suddenly without realising it, Mullah Ullah opened his mouth to ask if anyone would like a samosa when all he came out with was, "Why don't you all go on the Genie of the Lamp's Giant Magic Carpet? It will fit you all in no problem."

"Wow, a giant magic carpet that will fit us all," BB gasped, sucking his thumb and more excited than ever.

"Brilliant! Never been on a magic carpet before," Moonmummy squealed like a psychedelic flying pig cart-wheeling over the air of Brickie Lane.

Mullah Ullah tugged at his nose and said while remembering his magic prayer-mat, "They are very roomy, smooth and most comfortable!"

"Excellent idea, Mullah Ullah go on ... call the Genie of the Lamp," Captain Kidd replied impatiently.

"And anyway, how do you know so much about Hell?" Captain Kidd asked Mullah Ullah.

"Yeah, have you been there before?" BB asked breathlessly.

Mysteriously and enigmatically Mullah Ullah did not explain or expand upon the subject but simply gave the golden lamp in his hand a firm rub. Quicker than a ferret could fart, a smoky-blue seriousness whizzed out of the end of the golden lamp and the genie appeared.

The Mullah looked it straight in the eye and said, "Genie, I've come to ask you to get the magic carpet out of your living room floor and bring it here immediately please."

The Genie of the Lamp groaned and mumbled and after diving back into the lamp, soon returned with a giant carpet rolled up and carried over his right shoulder. Dropping it and unrolling it out the Genie of the Lamp turned to Mullah Ullah and asked, "Is this your second wish, Mullah Ullah?"

The Mullah wasn't to be so easily caught out.

"No it isn't, it's your first act of altruistic generosity, you big Blue Meanie!" Mullah Ullah replied laughing, secretly glad that the Genie of the Lamp had accepted his lame excuse. He still had two wishes left and he crossed his fingers hoping the genie wouldn't mind. As Stargasm and Moonmummy watched enchanted, the Mullah made the Genie of the Lamp explain how special the carpet was. It was of Merzian origin and made by the hand of blind one-handed Kohistani princesses. With one stitch stitched every decade, the giant carpet had taken many thousands of years to make.

And then the Genie tried again. "And so I give you the incredible Magic Carpet!"

"Yippee!" went BB and Charlie together.

The Genie of the Lamp looked down and asked again. "It's your second wish isn't it, Mullah Ullah?"

The Mullah was still on his toes. "Good try, Genie of the Lamp. It's not my second wish but it's your first gift!"

"Oh ... okay ... mutter ... mutter ...!"

And without further ado, the Genie of the Lamp told them the simple instructions to the Giant Magic Carpet and how it worked. It didn't take more than three minutes for everyone to learn but then Captain Kidd, who had been used to mastering a whole ship of his own, took over the controls as the carpet was rising fast. The colours on the magic carpet were simply incredible with each stitch being woven of a different colour that had faded at a different rate because many years separated one stitch from another. The

Banglastani Beatnik made sure he'd polished his kaleidoscopic spectacles well before he clambred on board. Charlie squashed his bony form up next to BB's who was finally sitting still while Moonmummy and Stargasm leapfrogged like monsoon frogs getting out of the rain. The Genie of the Lamp sighed deeply, worrying that the group were going to make a mess out of one of his grandmother's heirlooms. It rushed around tying up the frayed corners of the incredible carpet to make sure that it didn't split on the journey to Hell. Like a panicking housewife it thrashed the hovering carpet from underneath with a fly-swatter stolen from Malik Slik Sylvester. Meanwhile, Sidney Arthur smiled a sly aristocratic smile as pulling Danny by his peg-leg and beckoning Billy by pulling his silly nose, he jumped them all onto one corner of the huge carpet.

"Come on stop mucking around Danny, and Billy behave yourself, we're going to be off soon . . .!"

"How do you know?" Danny asked, screwing his peg-leg in and looking up but Sidney Arthur was giving nothing away.

"Look, stop asking silly questions but I'll tell you this, a long time before you were born and even longer before you were dead I took the journey into Hell sitting on this carpet."

Danny was not impressed. "What a load of dobb! Is that another one of your tall stories?"

"No, honestly, it's the truth but it doesn't matter if you don't believe me even though I am the oldest ghost in Ghost Town, just hold on tight and we'll all fly to Hell faster than the wind beating inside my excited heart!"

But Billy was suddenly holding up some carpet wool in his ghostly hand. "Aaah some stitching's come off."

"Oh Billy, that's about three hundred years of work!"

"Sorry, Sidney, I'll take more care," Billy said with a sigh, now realising the sheer pricelessness of this special carpet. And then with everyone on the carpet, Captain Kidd stood in the centre at the rear and gave the signal and, waving goodbye to Mullah Ullah and the Genie of the Lamp who were not coming, they were off.

Captain Kidd steered and the others sat around drinking bottles of Astral Ale as they raced towards the seas. It took a few short minutes to get out of Slumdon and reach the coast and they were now going to go west to Fort Cox, the deepest darkest recess of Hell itself. Captain Kidd seemed to know where to go but in truth he had quietly mumbled the destination of where they were to go to the Giant Magic Carpet which took over its own navigation across the Spatlantic, flying at about three hundred feet above the choppy waves, and was enjoying every moment.

"Carpet, veer three degrees to the left!" Captain Kidd hollered in the rages of the ravishing wind and the great undulating body of the Kohistani carpet moved to the side.

"Why are you telling the carpet to move to the left? I thought it knew where to go," Stargasm asked, slowly coming over to where Captain Kidd stood defiantly.

Captain Kidd smiled sheepishly and said, "It does but I like telling it where to go. It makes me feel like a sea captain at the helm of my own ship again!"

"Then you'd better tell the carpet to get back on course."

Captain Kidd doffed his three-cornered, red and blue hat and agreed. "Three degrees to the right carpet, to Hell!"

"By the way where is Hell and where exactly does Lucifer live?"

"Easy, Lucifer lives in the deepest darkest Hell at Fort Cox!!"

"And where's that?"

Captain Kidd let out some very spectral laughter as he replied. "Somewhere inside the secret bit of your heart!"

Stargasm was not amused and flounced away saying, "Very funny . . . Ha . . . Ha . . . Ha!"

And then with Stargasm and Moonmummy holding onto the edge of the carpet and looking down at the dancing phantoms of the surf below, the Artful Dodger bounced up to be near Captain Kidd and Charlie. Captain Kidd steered them brilliantly as they whizzed past the playgrounds of his youth, the incredible Karibbean and the Spanglish Main. Captain Kidd doffed his hat as they passed Treasure Island many feet below and soon they were passing parallel to the mountains of Central Spamerica. It was then that the carpet turned left and plummeted through the air towards a giant volcano that lay in the middle of the narrow strait surrounded by the busy oceans of the Pazific and Spatlantic on either side. And then the carpet wobbled and everybody screamed as they fell down the huge opening of the huge volcano all desperately hoping that it was extinct.

"Wow, it's a bit like Dante's *Inferno*!" Billy Blake screamed as they fell into the yawning abyss faster than the speed of descending fear.

"It is exactly like Dante's *Inferno*!" Sidney Arthur screamed back as the wind ripped through his ghostly body.

"What do you mean?" Billy asked, holding on tightly to the carpet.

Sidney Arthur smiled, clearly enjoying the ride and answered. "What I mean is to say that Dante the medieval Italian poet came to this place with me on this very selfsame Kohistani carpet many moons ago!" Billy looked at him aghast as Sidney continued. "And then he wrote the *Inferno* describing the different rings of Hell and the unfortunate creatures that live there!"

"Of course he did, he was an excellent poet you must consider," Billy added with a greater respect for Sidney Arthur than ever before.

However, hanging on to one corner of the giant carpet with a set of ghostly teeth, Danny had had enough. "Oi, shut up about this Dante geezer, I'm not a poet like you Billy, I'm just a shipwrecked sailor. What interests me more is that Sidney's been here before! ... He must know what to do."

Billy tugged at his lank ghostly hair and then asked, "Is there any place you haven't been to then, Sidney?"

"Yeah!" Sidney Arthur replied, examining the holes in his crumbling waistcoat.

Billy was most interested and asked persistently. "Where's that?"

"Simple. Heaven!"

Danny had had enough again and asked angrily, "But you always told us that Heaven ... "

"And Hell ... " added Billy.

"Are only states of mind," finished Danny, intently watching the expression of fear on everyone's faces as they fell faster and faster.

Sidney Arthur buffed his smile this time as he said, "And it's all a case of mind over matter. I don't mind and you don't matter."

Billy could see the joke and laughed. "Hee ... Hee ... nah be serious!"

And then Sidney Arthur began to sing: "Heaven is where the heart is but my heart is not at home."

Danny who wasn't feeling so optimistic had had enough of this and made his voice heard. "Oh, stop singing Sidney and help us work it out, it's bad enough being ghosts and watching all your friends and family go to heaven when you're condemned to eternity as a ghost!"

Sidney stopped smiling, turned to Danny grabbed his arm and said, "Yes, I already know that cos if you've forgotten, I am the oldest ghost in Ghost Town! Look down below, can you see the different rings of hell?"

Danny took a good look and replied, "Yes ... Sidney Arthur ... I can see them!"

Grabbing Billy's attention, Sidney Arthur elucidated. "Wrongdoers of different kinds are left to suffer in the different burning pits and Lucifer is lord of all he sees."

As they descended the visions of heckles, speckles, bhoots, demons, diabolics, vampires and all the other nasties appeared all around them but the other denizens of Hell were far too busy in their task of dragging huge, iron balls attached to their legs to see the Great Magic Carpet or the frightened inhabitants on it. It was Hell all right and as the crew watched, scared witless, from the curling edges of the giant carpet, the brave Captain Kidd grabbed Bilal by his tatty Zindian kurta and described all the different levels of Hell and the various creatures that resided there. Captain Kidd was a great fan of Dante and had read *Inferno* many times. As BB watched, flabbergasted, Kidd recounted the activities of each level and the punishment involved.

Very soon they landed in the deepest realm of the lowest ring of Hell and knew exactly what to do as they had practised back at the Sonic Temple. Immediately upon landing, the two Wicked White Witches of the West started dishing out a varied assortment of Magic Muslin Hypno-Tantric Hijabs that made the wearers invisible. Charlie rolled up the carpet and carried it on his shoulder and BB and Dobbins ran around slipping a few Hypno-Tantric Hijabs onto the carpet to make it invisible too. However, this meant that in carrying the carpet, Charlie was fully occupied and would be of no use in the likely event of battle. Many of the demons and devils guarding the huge stashes of gold sensed their presence but weren't sure as they couldn't see them. Eventually, they came to the first major stash of gold that they had been looking for. Stargasm and Moonmummy stopped, sensing that this would be the right place to begin the robbery.

"What do we do now, Moonmummy?" BB asked, straightening up his spectacles.

"I'm not quite sure, BB."

Captain Kidd approached as stealthily as a cat and said, "We have to steal the gold!"

"We know that, silly, but how exactly are we going to do it?" Stargasm said, not too impressed by Captain Kidd's brains.

"What do we have to do?" BB asked, looking as innocent as a child.

It was then that the Artful Dodger spoke up. "Tarquin told me something Stargasm about what happened to them in ancient Zeegypt!"

"What happened, Dobbins?"

"Well, apparently when they were trying to steal all the gold inside the pyramid, the blind seer called Cassandra had a special incantation for making the gold rise and hover in the air."

"Excellent!"

"And not only that, she could make the hovering piles of gold follow her like faithful sheepdogs."

"Well, what use is that to us?" Stargasm asked.

The Artful Dodger decided to get to the point quick. "It's of perfect use because Tarquin told me and Captain Kidd what the incantation was."

"Oh wonderful, what is it then?" Stargasm asked as the Artful Dodger gargled his throat and then sang in his husky voice:

"Gold. Gold. Here to stay.
Rise up into the air, day by day
Gold. Gold. That we steal
Make Lucifer's wrath
Something we don't feel."

"Oh brilliant!" squealed Moonmummy and Captain Kidd together as suddenly the Artful Dodger's words had a real effect on the nearest mound of gold bars. Slowly but surely, it rose to about twelve feet into the air, luckily unobserved by the demonic guards, and stayed there.

"Quick, what do we do now?" Stargasm asked quickly.

"We have to do something quick as the guard is asleep and hasn't noticed yet," Moonmummy said immediately.

"We have to make the gold invisible!" BB said, rather worried.

"We can't use any more of the hijabs!" Charlie added, looking just as worried as his mate.

"Why not?" Stargasm interjected quickly before she got dejected.

"Because we used the last to hide the Giant Magic Carpet that Charlie is carrying," BB said sadly, feeling the heat of Hell rise up.

Stargasm however wasn't that bothered. "Not to worry, us Wicked Witches of the West have a few tricks up our sleeves too."

"Go for it, Stargasm! What are you going to do?" Charlie asked, starting to feel the weight of the heavy carpet.

"Me and Moonmummy are going to spell the risen gold and make it invisible."

"All right then, get ready, let's go!" Moonmummy said, getting out her wishing wand and very soon the two sisters were singing.

"Gold. Gold, lovely stuff
Don't you think Lucifer's got enough?
Gold. Gold disappear

But whatever you do, don't wander far from here."

And then suddenly, the hovering piles of gold that Artful Dodger had made rise, disappeared under cloaks of invisibility that the invocation invited. Sidney Arthur, Billy Blake and Danny De Foe observed what was happening and chuckled.

"Look Sidney, they are stealing the gold right from under Lucifer's chin!" Billy cheered like a demented schoolboy at half-term.

"No, his nose you mean!" Danny said, feeling rather cheerful now but it was Sidney Arthur that always had the last word.

"Look what they are doing now, simply brilliant!"

And it was true. As the invisible group went around with the Artful Dodger in the lead making the stashes of gold in each vault rise, Stargasm and Moonmummy's invocation would make them invisible. So, while Charlie had the responsibility of carrying the huge carpet, BB went around checking his trigger happy finger and ensuring that his love grenades were perfectly pinned. They would, no doubt, soon be needing them.

"Cor, have you seen the amount of gold in these caves?" Charlie said to BB as they tiptoed on their feet past each and every vault.

"Yeah, the result of millennia of pilfering."

"Do you reckon Anarkali, Tarquin, Fareek and Mellow Tron saw this much gold in Zeegypt?" asked the Artful Dodger, totally amazed at the sight.

BB coughed and spoke up in reply. "I doubt it. What we have here is the biggest stash ever. Well, in this world anyway."

Charlie decided to make his point felt. "Look at the invisible mound rising into the air."

"It must be hundreds of feet wide," BB added with an increasing grin on his beatnik face.

"And thousands of feet high," finished the Artful Dodger with a smile even wider than BB's and far funnier too. The three decided to get a second opinion.

"Well Captain Kidd, what do you reckon so far?"

Captain Kidd came up and said gladly, "Everything is Ticketyboo and going to plan!"

BB needed further clarification though. "Where are we on Thieves Philosophy though?"

"We are on Rule One – nothing ventured, nothing gained and allowing yourself to live in the present."

"Great!" BB said, quickly stifling his chuckles in case the demons awoke.

Moonmummy, however, brought them all down on a sensible note. "Take care though, our invisible stolen gold is bound to attract some attention."

And as they went from vault to vault stealing Lucifer's gold from under the sleeping noses of the demons and diabolics sent to guard them, they cringed and shivered as they heard the hollering of the many tormented souls in all the different rings. The moaning and the groaning were all too much and the Artful Dodger almost fainted as the sounds of sentient suffering continued. However, although the guards from eighteen vaults hadn't noticed any different, there were still seven more to go.

BB suddenly had a thought and asked, "Hey, why are all the demon guards sleeping in every vault we pass?"

Moonmummy gave him a secret smile and answered. "It's because me and Moonmummy muttered some sleeping spells."

BB was astounded and looked so. "Oh, and I thought it was an amazing coincidence that the guards were going to sleep every time we passed!"

"We are Wicked White Witches of the West, we know stuff that would make your hair curl!" Stargasm added, trying to look serious but BB was totally confused.

"But my hair curls anyway, Stargasm." Then it was his turn to get serious. "I must tell you that it's getting rather unwieldy under the Hypno-Tantric Hijabs."

"Why, what's happened?"

"Well, for a start Charlie is almost toppling under the weight of our transport. Captain Kidd is going crazy fighting invisible enemies. The Artful Dodger's getting gobsmacked at the sight of Hell and I'm starting to finger my love grenades."

Moonmummy and Stargasm stopped walking and listened very carefully as he continued.

"And something else too!"

"What?" Moonmummy aske, very much interested.

"I think the gold we've stolen and made invisible is going to tumble!"

"How do you mean?"

"Well look behind you, see how the very air totters. It means we've stolen about as much gold as we can carry."

Stargasm and Moonmummy however, were made of much sterner stuff. "No, don't be such a scaredy cat, we need to steal all of Lucifer's gold and leave him penniless. Come on this way, only seven more vaults to go!" Moonmummy said emphatically, prodding Stargasm to take the lead.

And so everyone followed Stargasm and the Artful Dodger and the plan to deprive Lucifer of his ill-gotten gains proceeded as planned. However, just when they thought they were going to succeed BB suddenly decided to flip put. Having fingered his love grenades for over three hours, his finger suddenly slipped and he blew up under the cover of his Hypno-Tantric Hijab. Luckily the hijab didn't tear as it was made of Malik's best cloth but BB tumbled out of the invisible protection of the hijab and crawled over on the floor concussed.

"Quick, something's happened to Bilal!" Charlie shrieked, running forward to take a peek under his robe.

"What?" asked the Artful Dodger, almost tripping over his own feet.

Charlie grabbed his lapels with one hand and shook him, saying "He looks like he's concussed, damn fool, always fingering the love grenades when he should have had them safely in his bag!"

"What shall we do?" Dobbins bleated sorrowfully.

"We have to revive him somehow."

"Any idea?"

"Yeah, I know," Charlie said with a sigh, continuing."What you have to do is shoot some flowers through my fantasy flintlock right through his head."

"Are you sure?"

"Yeah we have done this to each other many times when we have been blown away by the force of the love grenades!"

The Artful Dodger went to pick up Charlie's fantasy flintlock when suddenly he cried out. "Good idea, but I'll have to do it fast, I think the devils and demons have discovered us!"

"Oh no!" Charlie screamed while desperately trying to hold on to the heavy carpet which was promising to knock him over.

But it was true. While Dobbins raced to shoot some rare blooms right through BB's head in order to revive him, the loudness of the explosion had wakened the sleeping demons. Taking a quick look around them they saw that their golden stashes were no more and roared with rage. Flapping their black and red wings, they raced towards the ceiling and looked down. They couldn't see anything but the sleeping form of a young Banglastani Beatnik on the ground, dozing gently with flowers coming out of his head.

Quicker than a hummingbird could hum a siren sounded out in the cavernous halls of Hell. Now, a whole legion of heckles, speckles, demons, devils, diabolics, bhoots, preets and afreets raced out from every corner to attack the supine one. At this point, the Artful Dodger rushed out of the protection of his Hypno-Tantric Hijab, pushed his grubby hand out and dragged BB's sleeping body back under its protection. The demons got there too late and when they did arrive on the ground, all they saw were the blooms of ten types of fantasy blossom that the Artful Dodger had shot through BB's head.

"Gaaarrrk . . .!" screamed the monsters, realising that the Banglastani Beatnik had got away but there was something fishy going on too.

A heckle suddenly began to take notice. Baring its angry fangs it breathed fire and asked angrily, "Where's all the gold gone?"

"It's simply disappeared!" a speckle relied quickly.

"It can't just disappear. What will we do? Lucifer will have our heads for this!"

And then suddenly the conspiring heckle and speckle felt the invisible mountain of gold move somewhere to the right.

"Quick Grrr . . . that way . . . something's hiding from us!" a major demonic rasped to its cohorts in the hot sizzling air.

"Which way Srr do we go boss . . . which way?" a minor bhoot quickly replied, standing still to attention.

The major demonic rasped its furry lips and grunted. "Just follow me, I'm going down to ground level to penetrate that magic force I can feel there!"

"And all us others?" asked the heckle and speckle together flying sideways to be near and huddling up together with the others.

The major demonic grunted even louder this time before replying. "All of you can follow me, I think we'll soon find the perpetrators."

Stargasm and Moonmummy then muttered spells that could knock the socks off anything and patiently waited for the ghouls to enter their sacred space.

"Gnnr . . .!" roared a preet flapping its big ugly wings in the air and coming closer.

"Snark . . .!" sneered an accompanying warlock as it joined the preet.

"Aaark . . .!" groaned a devil, in fury.

"Vaark . . .!" went a vampish vampire, fast approaching the two who were not slow on the uptake.

"Oh wow, Stargasm, what's happening?" Moonmummy asked a gawping Stargasm who remained too astonished for words.

"Oh brilliant BB, you're waking up!" Moonmummy then said, poking him in the ribs.

BB was not amused but he was confused. "What's happening?" he mumbled, trying hard to sit up.

Moonmummy decided to enlighten him. "Your love grenade got us the attention of the monsters."

It was time for Stargasm to step in. "Now they know we are hiding under here and that we have stolen the gold."

"Moonmummy, is the spell working?" BB asked propping his invisible body into its cross-legged position by the judicious use of his arms.

"It sure is, they can't enter inside this force field!"

"Oh, brilliant and most excellent!"

"It's more amazing than that because although they can't enter inside we can still throw things out at them."

"Like what?"

"Like love grenades to blow them up, fantasy flintlocks to shoot them through with the arrows of love and a wide variety of magic spells of course."

The fight had come to a standstill. Although they were

surrounded by thousands of major and minor devils, the Pearly Green crew were protected by the magic of Moonmummy and Stargasm but they couldn't make their escape with the umpteen tons of stolen gold. BB, Charlie and the Artful Dodger threw love grenades out from under their Hypno-Tantric Hijabs while the witches held the fort by flashing an endless range of magic spells from their wishing wands.

The good guys like the gold were invisible and it was at this point that Lucifer himself decided to come down and have a look, flying down from the fifth ring of Hell where he had been torturing errant philosophers, and screaming, "Where's all my gold gone?"

"It's been stolen!" whimpered a cowering minor devil, hiding underneath its own wings.

"By whom, you useless demons?"

The minor devil came out from hiding underneath his wings and said fearfully. "By those hiding under the magic spell of invisibility down there!"

"How do you know it's them?"

"Because of the love grenades they keep chucking out from under there, your lordship."

Lucifer then slapped the demon a good few times before replying. "Right, I've had enough of this, do you know how many thousands of years it took to steal that gold?"

"No sir, but we can imagine, a very long time," moaned the cowering demon, but Lucifer was in full swing and continued.

"That's right and I'm not going to let a few mere humans stop me now!"

"What are you going to do, sir?"

"Watch!"

Lucifer grew about one thousand times in size and roared and every level of Hell felt his vibrations and shivered but the intrepid crew refused to be scared and while the two Wicked White Witches continued streaming out spells from the end of their wands, the others decided to work on Thieves' Philosophy to see where they had got to.

"Where are we now, Captain Kidd?" screamed Charlie, shooting out a stream of fantasy blooms from under his hijab.

"We are all living in the moment!"

"That's rule number one of Thieves' Philosophy isn't it?" Charlie whistled, immediately reloading his fantasy flintlock with more blooms.

The unstoppable Captain Kidd wasted no time in answering. "That's right, enjoy the present!"

This last comment confused Charlie somewhat. "What do you mean, enjoy the fear of getting killed by Lucifer?"

"Why not? Enjoy each moment, it might be your last. And remember we have stolen all the gold, not for ourselves."

"But for what?"

"The thrill of course!"

"Wow, now you're really talking!"

"Have you realised something, BB?" Captain Kidd turned to the beatnik and asked, seeing him clamber to his knees and then feet.

"What?

"Rule number two of the Thieves' Philosophy."

"What you mean – there's never a loss but only gain?" BB replied fingering the love grenades twitchily.

"Correct!"

"What that means is that you now know how unified we have become since the start of this story so long ago and how this unity is helping us in our fight against Lucifer," Charlie said helping the lad to his shaky feet and smiling. "We are learning how to be happy and live in the moment, understanding whether we live or die, there is never a loss, only gain."

It was then that Bilal decided to ask a pertinent question. "What is happiness, Captain?"

"Nothing special!"

"What do you mean?"

"Big happiness is made up of lots of little happinesses that lay out sequentially one after each other!"

"Wow, so there's no big happiness?"

"No, it's all made of little bits."

"Oh, wonder of wonders!"

Seeing that he couldn't intimidate them with his huge size, Lucifer decided to become no larger than the Genie of the Lamp. Approaching the brave group fighting under the Hypno-Tantric Hijabs, he roared and Captain Kidd rolled onto the ground close to Lucifer's feet.

"Brilliant!" screamed Charlie as he instinctively knew where things were heading.

"Go for it!" BB screamed catching up pretty quick and Stargasm also roared in sympathy.

"You know what to do!"

And while the others kept Lucifer distracted Captain Kidd who would have been clearly seen by Lucifer if he'd looked down, crawled slowly towards Lucifer's foot. Achilles had an Achilles' heel and no doubt Lucifer would have a Lucifer's toe so, getting his frisky fingers ready, Captain Kidd remembered the words from the letter given to him three hundred years earlier on a leaking boat on the River Thames:

"Tickle his toes and his horns will fall off."

"Aaah ...!" screamed Lucifer, seeing the tiny form of the frisky pirate at his feet and he was just about to squash him into oblivion when, without warning, his two red horns quivered on top of his skull before tumbling into the air where they were deftly caught by the grinning Captain Kidd, who quickly stashed them into his pockets.

Lucifer screamed and screamed while the pirate disappeared under the Hypn Tantric Hijab again and taunted, "You forgot about Thieves' Philosophy, mate! You thought you were the biggest thief and all. Rule number two states there's never a loss only a gain ... Ha ... Haa ... Haa ... in this case it's your loss and our gain!"

"Roar ...!" went Lucifer trying to throw down a basketful of black magic spells but they just trickled down like dirty water and did no harm.

"Look Stargasm, he's lost his power!" Moonmummy yelled in her sister's face, gobbing excited flecks of spittle.

"Amazing, isn't it?" Stargasm replied, quickly wiping her face with her wattle and daub gown and chuckling.

"Captain Kidd was right all along!" BB added, rubbing his spectacles clear of any illusion.

"And that's why we had to save him, so he could do this now." Charlie laughed.

"Yippee, Lucifer's power's gone!" sung the weird sisters together, giggling like crazy and dancing a delirious jig.

"AAAAAAAHHHHHH ...!" Lucifer screamed, clamping his hands to his head where his red horns had once been as he flew away to another ring of Hell where he could not be followed. He knew he stood no chance against these adversaries and their magically enhanced powers. In a quicksilver moment his many minions suddenly lost their power too and howled disconsolately.

As soon as Lucifer departed with his minions hollering for a haven, an incredible flash took place in front of their bedazzled eyes. They quickly took the Hypno-Tantric Hijabs off now that the danger was over.

"What's happening?" Stargasm screamed as the blinding light scuppered all their thoughts and plans.

"Can't see a thing, the light's too bright!" Moonmummy hollered, pulling back and holding her fists up just in case.

Rubbing his spectacles for the umpteenth time BB shouted out above the din. "Hold on, wait a minute, what is that?"

The most incredible international gathering of leprechauns materialised in front of all their disbelieving eyes.

"They've come back to take the gold!" Captain Kidd cried as the others watched, astounded. In a magical wave of their hands, the leprechauns made the entire stolen gold move like it was no heavier than a feather and as they worked their tiny arms in conjunction with each other, the gold suddenly became visible again and moved through the air like a leaf flowing in a mountain stream. It was at this point that Captain Kidd picked up the nearest leprechaun, Abdul, the Bongostani one, and kissed him smack on the face, shouting, "Never keep anything you've stolen but give it away to others who need it more!"

"Wow! That's rule number three of Thieves' Philosophy," BB said, totally entranced by the pirate's actions and prodding Charlie who was equally bemused and peering intently down.

Abdul turned his happy face towards Captain Kidd and asked, "You read my note then."

"What's going to happen now?" piped up Charlie.

"Just you wait and see," said Kidd and Abdul in perfect synch.

All the little folk clapped their hands and countless jute sacks appeared, were immediately filled to the brim and in another flash they all disappeared again! Stargasm and Moonmummy tried to find out where they'd disappeared to with the aid of their wands but couldn't. The leprechauns had simply disappeared but hovering invisibly the Holy Ghosts laughed and laughed.

"Oh brilliant! Things are going to plan!" chuckled Sidney from one side of the giant vault that they were in.

"What do you mean?" Billy Blake asked to which Sidney Arthur replied excitedly.

"There's a chance that we will all get out of this!"

"What do you mean?" Billy repeated, catching his inflection of enthusiasm.

Sidney Arthur smiled now that he had their full attention. He chuckled, continuing, "Simply that we may all become free now that the leprechauns have got all the gold!"

This was too much for Danny who thrashed around in the air before putting his mouth to Sidney Arthur's ear and shouting, "Tell us, tell us clearly!"

Sidney Arthur giggled like a lunatic, shrugged his shoulders and then replied. "No, can't tell you any more, wait till the end!"

As Danny and Billy screamed in frustration, suddenly there was yet another flash of brilliance in the skies above Hell as the crazy sight of a ghostly galleon came into view. This shimmered in the coverings of pure cobweb where a ghostly skeletal crew waved a hurrah below and ripped into song – the infamous "Stinky Billy Song":

"Stinky Billy, fat pudding and pie,
Kissed the girls and wondered why."

"Wow, it's the *Leprechaun's Delight*!" Captain Kidd shrieked as the ghostly galleon settled in to land.

"Are you sure?" BB asked running up to be next to the ecstatic pirate.

"Surer than anything I have been in my life!"

"But how do you know for sure?"

"Look it says the *Leprechaun's Delight* on the side, doesn't it?"

"Yes it does (BB bluffed) but the only thing is that I think the whole crew's made up of ghosts!"

"Ghosts, just like us!" Billy screamed, his eyes greedily examining the ghostly crew many feet below.

"Real ghosts! More like us!" Danny squealed, hitting himself on the head with his wooden leg in overblown excitement. The last of the Holy Ghosts then paddled his oar into the muddy waters of their enchantment.

"About time too and can I remind you that they are skeletons, they can be seen. We, on the other hand are invisible," Sidney Arthur shouted above the growing catcalls from Billy and Danny but down below others were equally mystified and bewildered.

"Oh wow, your crew-men are ghosts," BB said, entranced and a little scared.

Captain Kidd deftly replied, "I don't care if they are ghosts or not, I haven't seen any of them for over three hundred years!" He took a swig of rum and beamed a huge smile. He himself was rather astonished to see his crew turn into skeletons but tried to pay it no mind.

The ghostly galleon hovered a hundred feet in the air and a rope was now chucked down as two of the craziest-looking seamen ever seen slipped down it. One was a chubby skeleton wearing a red bandanna around his head and the other was a skinny skeleton, tall and very bony.

"Ah Seaman Stains and Master Bates, long time no see! Give me a hug!"

"Love to, Captain but we're such brittle old bone, if you hugged us we'd crumble to pieces!" said Seaman Stains coming up to shake the Captain's hands gingerly. Captain Kidd didn't stand on ceremonies and neither did he sit on his bottom in fragile moments such as these and pursing his lips he blew them both a kiss.

"Never mind, here's a flying kiss!" he whispered, delicately blowing into their skeletal faces.

"Thanks, Captain!" muttered Master Bates, a ghostly tear falling down his skeletal face. Captain Kidd tried not to look embarrassed as the two sailors burst into tears and then hugged each other in true comradeship.

Clearing his throat, Captain Kidd asked, "What brings you to this neck of the woods?"

Seaman Stains tugged at his bandanna and replied. "We've come to take you home."

"Back to Treasure Island you mean?"

"Yes, of course, we have much piracy to perform!"

Captain Kidd hummed and hawed, bit his fingernails and looked shy. Then looking up again he whispered, "I can't go just yet as I have to go with the others down to the Sonic Temple inside the Lost Catacombs. This great adventure's not over yet!"

"It just gets better and better," the chubby Master Bates replied jiggling his earrings and looking lairy but Captain Kidd hadn't finished.

"That's right and I want all of you to come with me, something tells me something incredible's going to happen."

The two witches, along with Captain Kidd, were returning to

Pearly Green on the pirate ship with some ghostly stowaways and the lads were going to fly back on the carpet beside them. As they sailed Stargasm decided to ask Captain Kidd a question that had been preying on her mind.

"Captain, why have the leprechauns taken the gold?"

Captain Kidd, who was back at the helm of his ship controlling the giant wheel, turned around to Stargasm to say simply, "Sorry, Stargasm. I know the answer but I can't tell you."

"Well, what else can you tell us about Thieves' Philosophy now?"

"Easy! Look at my shipmates, they've turned to skeletons waiting for me to return but wait they have and now we are reunited again and I am master of my own ship once more!"

"So?"

"This clearly demonstrates part four of Thieves' Philosophy – There is no higher honour than loyalty amongst Buddhas and Thieves!"

Stargasm decided to start taking the piss. "Oh wow ... but I didn't know you were a Buddha!"

These intrepid heroes who had harrowed (and robbed) Hell itself, arrived in glory at the Sonic Temple on the giant magic carpet and the *Leprechaun's Delight* to an enormous party with awesome music and Anatta Mark-4 flying out of Fairlight's fingers into their mouths.

In the third ring of Hell, Lucifer nursed the gaping wounds on his head and instructed his minions in Hoggaristan to take revenge. Azrial was still conducting the Band of Doom and as he waved his baton, the amphitheatre, where the Afreet Orchestra and the Black Magic Mysterons were playing so well, started to move in a clockwise direction and began to rise into the air. Meanwhile, back at the Sonic Temple, the same thing was happening but in an anti-clockwise direction. The Sonic Temple was quickly changing into a spinning Starship and ripping through the cobblestones of Brickie Lane to shoot off hundreds of feet into the skies and taking with it every inhabitant of the Lost Catacombs. And little Anarkali was spinning and spinning through the air in the middle of it all scorching her burning footsteps with mysterious mudras of mind-blowing magnificence. They were all getting seriously high.. In the air that is.

32

The Battle of the Bands

EVERYONE WAS GETTING swept along in the Cosmic Dance: gubblies, Dreamweavers, members of Master Fagin's Funkadelic Tribe, wizards, witches, sorcerers and cats with cosmic cream; Princess Amrita, Fairlight and Osric were chasing their magic potions; Fareek, Tarquin and Mellow Tron playing their wondrous tunes; BB, Charlie and Catweazel Phil firing fantasy flowers and exploding laser lights; Captain Kidd kidding no one and chucking his three-pointed hat into the air; the ghostly sailors merrily drinking without a care; Habiba and the brothers scurrying around the stage arranging all the holodisks to play for Seashell Sally; Kid Kurry, Kassim, Dilly the Silly and the Banglastani waiters still going around the floor offering nibbles from silver salvers. Moonmummy and Stargasm were whizzing around in the air on their broomsticks when Abdul appeared shouting, "Hurrah! Who cares?" Ayesha, Ambrin and Najma were on stage singing, Mullah Ullah was going baboolah with the Genie at his side while the Zoofis pulled each other's ears, Abraxas had his beard tied to Azeem's and his was tied to Hussain's. Nasseruddin just made sure that nobody was bored. Mevlana the Mage and Suleiman the Spinner were flying in circles on the Genie's Magic Carpet while Anarkali was spinning fast. Far far below Malik smiled, looking at the well-dressed dancers, all in his own fine clothes and Dobbins, time streaming out of his hat, was busy drinking elderberry wine. Little Lucy was throwing down funky coconuts from somewhere on King Osric's floating desert isle, Astral Alice blew her bloomers and held Lucy's hand for a while. Twynklyn was blinking and Blynkyn was Nod and what they saw was what they got. The gubblies rode the Love Monster bareback, and what the Funkadelic Tribe could not steal, they stuffed into a jute sack. The Jabberwocky was feeling happy with the Sabre-Toothed Pussy at its side, Frogamatix the Tantric toad was dripping in woad and last but not least the White Rabbit and Dylan were munching toast with marmalade and smiling like it was the party at the end of all time.

So much for all the characters but what was really happening in the middle of the sacred skies hundreds of feet above the Sonic Temple? Spinning around anti-clockwise in the up-draught caused by the feet of Anarkali, Mevlana and Suleiman looked above their heads as the Magic Carpet battled the cosmic storms, and pointing to Anarkali Suleiman screamed:

> "Mevlana, look at the perfect one
> at the circle's centre. She spins and
> whirls like a golden compass
> Beyond all that is rational
> To show this dear world
> That everything, everything in existence
> Does point to God!"

Mevlana was not put out a bit and deftly replied, "Yeah, she's a geezer to beat all geezers!"

Suleiman threw his peanut shells into the swirling maelstrom and let out a high piercing shriek saying, "And she's only a geezerette!"

Mevlana peered out from the edges of the bucking carpet and stared down at the swirling madness below as he shouted into the blistering air. "And such a young one at that!"

But Suleiman wanted some answers and poking the other in the ribs asked affirmatively, "What's happening, Mevlana?"

"We are all going someplace special!"

"Where are we going?" Suleiman asked, thunderstruck.

"We are going to the Battle of the Big K!"

"How do you know?"

"I'm not called Mevlana the Mage for nothing."

"What's the Battle of the Big K?"

Mevlana smiled a perfect grin and said, "The Battle of Kurukshetra."

"And when is that, exactly?"

"Its five thousand years before St Stan."

"Wow, that's early!"

"It sure is, Suleiman."

And they gazed as all their friends and neighbours danced through space and time like never before. They all held each other's breaths and jodhpurs while the very air around them scorched like fire and little Anarkali danced faster and faster but seemed as still as the eye of the hurricane until the light was absolutely blinding and the sensation of time travelling backwards collywobbled the marrow in their knees and made them all shake and shiver like autumn leaves in a storm. Looking earthwards, they saw the confluence of the rivers where the Khumb Mela was held and then a vast plain on which the Sonic Temple now landed, the party persisting with vigour.

Suleiman caught a movement in the corner of his eye and turning to look, shouted, "Look up at the sky!"

"Why, what's happening?" Mevlana whistled.

"We were followed."

"Why? What's up?"

"Look at that dark cloud up there, what is it?" Suleiman sighed, picking Mevlana up and putting him on his shoulders so he could get a better look.

"Oh no, it's the dark spinning cloud of Hoggaristan that's followed us."

"What a bummer!" Suleiman snorted, instinctively curling up his moustache and putting it out of harm's way.

Mevlana understood the situation very quickly. "This must mean that there's going to be a big fight!"

"Between who?"

"Between us and them, silly. Hoggaristan and the Sonic Temple!"

"Oh dear, what shall we do now?" Suleiman sighed again this time much deeper.

Mevlana soon gave him encouragement. "What do we do? What do we do? We hold on to our hearts and hope for the best ..."

And then with a thundering crash the amphitheatre of Hoggaristan shook the very earth as it landed about half a mile away. Karma Korma and the billowing updraught from the Starship had wrenched it from the Afrostani desert and made it follow the Starship to their present position. Both parties took their time to settle in and recover from the effects of time-travel when BB and Charlie finally put their heads out of the side and spoke.

"Charlie, where are we?" BB asked sheepishly, rubbing the dust off his kaleidoscopic spectacles.

Charlie knew his history and said as quick as a flash, "Ancient Zindia on the plains of Kurukshetra, 5000 years before St Stan."

"How do you know?"

"I overheard Mevlana talking to Suleiman."

"Wow!"

And then Charlie pointed out to an incredible sight that surrounded them on both sides. They were sitting in the middle of a vast plain which tapered up to a valley. On each slope of the valley ghostly apparitions of the most amazing beings could be seen.

"Can you see those thousands of spirit-warriors dressed in their golden finery and sitting on spirit horses and chariots on each side of the valley?"

"Are they ghosts?"

"Not exactly, they are spirit-warriors. You have to remember what this place is all about."

"What's it about, Charlie?"

"It's about a big fight. Doesn't matter who, just that it's between opposing sides!"

BB was soon getting the point. "It's like we've interrupted the spirit-warriors in the middle of a battle."

"Yeah, in the middle of a battle that never ends!"

"Or perhaps we are the new battle," BB said, cracking his knuckles.

Charlie was getting into this new game too. "That's right, that's why the soldiers on either side are waiting!"

"We will have to fight Hoggaristan and Hoggaristan will have to fight us!"

"Wow and wonder!" Charlie chuckled, picking up his trusty fantasy flintlock and shooting a few blooms into the air.

BB joined him, chucking love grenades and laughing. "And it's going to be a battle of the bands ... Hypno-Tantric Trance versus The Band of Doom!"

Charlie watched his fantasy flowers pretty the skies before bending down to speak to BB again. "Yeah, nothing so gross as blood and guts, remember we are fighting pure evil which is subtle so we have to fight it in equally subtle ways!"

"Are you sure?"

"I would bet my bottom dollar on it," Charlie replied, hitching up his falling pantaloons.

However, BB had seen a problem with Charlie's theory. "But you never have any money!"

"Ha . . . Ha . . . Ha . . . Be quiet!"

They waited as musicians from either side slowly set up their sound systems knowing full well it was they who would call or rue the day, sound was going to fight sound and there could only be one winner. The sounds started emanating slowly with the sound check from the bejewelled stage where Fareek, Mellow Tron and Tarquin fingered their instruments lovingly and where the Sisters Nazneen stroked each other's vocal chords. On the stage of dinosaur droppings and tyrannosaurus teeth, Azrial was flapping his wings prodding the Afreet Orchestra to play in tune while the three Frux brothers, the inestimable Black Magic Mysterons mooched on stage with live snakes rammed into their open arms, enjoying a quick fix of pure poison. Everyone was readying for the fight and the Battle of the Bands began.

The Chuckle Stream and the Grumble Glitch were to thrash it out in the sands of the plains of Kurukshetra. Trance versus Doom. The Zindian spirit-warriors stood in silence and watched contemplatively as the monsters and the trancers started cheering and jeering. It was going to be a fight like no other. Charlie and BB both loaded their flintlocks with cheerful abandon.

"Gollygosh, Charlie, looks like there's going to be a big scrap."

"This was bound to have happened some time!"

"I can understand the monsters jumping around to the Afreet Orchestra and the sounds of the Black Magic Mysterons driving everyone crazy but what I can't understand is who are those spirit-warriors?"

"Those are the Pandavas and the Kauravas!"

"The who?"

"Forget it, doesn't matter, just look out!"

And they did.

It was then that the Giant Hypno-Tantric Love Monster stared out over the plains as an endless stream of eyes, hands, feet reached out of its body. It looked more like a Zindian god than any Zindian god had ever looked before. Zindian gods usually had four sets of arms and legs whilst Trans-Tibetan gods had perhaps a hundred if they were lucky, but the Love Monster invaded the battlefield with ten thousands arms and legs and a trillion pairs of eyes.

"What's it going to do, Mullah Ullah?" the Genie whispered with apprehension and the Mullah tugged at his droopy nose before replying.

"I think I know."

"Well, what is it then?" the Genie of the Lamp stammered.

The Mullah grabbed his lungi where the melting red sun was trying to race up towards the top and replied seriously. "I think this fight needs a referee and the Giant Hypno-Tantric Love Monster has decided to be one," Mullah Ullah intoned, exhaling deeply.

Nearby, two flower-power warriors were listening intently. "Did you hear what Mullah Ullah just said?"

"Yeah Charlie, sounds wicked, it's going to be a fair fight with a decent referee around," BB exclaimed, rubbing his nose and spectacles.

Charlie prodded him with the end of his fantasy flintlock and continued. "Not only that but I think the Man on the Moon is going to have the final say in these refereeing decisions!"

"Totally wicked, geezer!" BB was obviously impressed but Charlie had his doubts.

"And do you think we have a hope in Hell then?"

BB was full of blustering confidence and let the other one know so. "Of course we have. We are going to win through the force of karma."

"What, you mean the calmer we are the karma we get?"

"Naturally."

But Charlie wasn't totally satisfied. "But the Baddies are nastier than us, they bite and spit!"

BB cracked a grin and suggested with some authority, "So what? We know our Four Holy Rules, our Four Humble Truths not forgetting the Three Serene Sillinesses. All we need to know now are the Magic Mantras!"

Charlie wasn't so sure about this overly simple reasoning and said excitedly, "These Magic Mantras have caused more dissension within our ranks than an army of hedgehogs under a duvet!"

Suddenly next to them, Mullah Ullah had something to say. "It's going to be a very fair fight!"

"How can you tell, Mullah Ullah?"

"Look at the spirit-warriors, the heavily gilded horsemen, the Pandavas and the Kauravas. They have been fighting since the dawn of time and still no side has yet won!" said the Kockneestani.

The Genie of the Lamp exuded a cloud of blue smoke before

replying. "Yeah, both sides look perfect with nary a scratch on them!"

It was then that the Love Monster bounced back from his chat with the Man on the Moon and standing squarely in the centre between the two opposing forces and in a voice so sweet it called for all participants to be silent. As seething black smoke billowed from Fruzzy's electronica, the Love Monster smiled first at one side and then at the other before saying, "We all know why we're here, don't we?"

"Grrr ... Grrr ...!" gnashed the demons, devils, bhoots, preets, afreets and other assorted monsters stomping up and down. It was righteous. It was raucous. It was rage.

"Yeah ... Yip ... Yip ... Yap ...!" screamed the Pearly Green posse, waving at Anarkali who had spun herself into the air again. The sight was stupendous. Over at the amphitheatre, hundreds of thousands of demons and assorted droks jumped up and down hollering as Azrial raised his baton and brought it down with a sharp snap. He flapped his wings and the music began.

"Thunder ... Thunder ... Screech ...!" roared the monsters as the vampire violinists scraped their bows across their demented violins. The trombone players and the skeletal hula-hoop dancers jumped to the beat as the Black Magic Mysterons came into view magically rising onto the stage. Looking timeless and as ethereal as ever, the skeletal form of Fruggy mooched into view, his day-glo silver leotards perfectly complementing his tutu and glitzy gown. Jumping behind his tablatronic set-up and spectral snares he whacked the bad beats into play, sending shivers up Tarquin's spine. Fruggy was good and this was the gig to end all gigs and as he screamed effortless obscenities from his toothless gums, he rammed his scary fingers onto the six hundred and sixty-six banks of mixers, samplers and grumplers. The sounds coming out were simply awesome, enveloping, precise and damn scary. Then slamming some power-chords on the violently red battered electric guitar slung low around his neck, Fruzzy stuck his tongue out which, at almost three quarters of a mile long almost sucked the monocle off the very surprised White Rabbit who scurried off in abject terror. As Fruzzy retracted his tongue he slapped a few demonic kettle drummers who were playing out of time and whacked a couple of banshees playing bones. He was well on form tonight. It was now Total Frux's turn to terrify. Bouncing onto stage in his schoolboy shorts, his skilful fingers coaxed the living strands of poison ivy to do what he wanted. Dressed in mirror-shades and platform boots, his right hand turned on the scrankler and real hell burst out. The Love Monster grinned, chuckling all the time. He finally spoke, trying to look serious.

"Anybody who does not want to be in the Battle of the Bands can leave now!"

"Grr don't bet your life on it . . .! Anyone leaves.. they are finished . . .!" Azrial screeched back, flapping his burnt wings with tension.

Meanwhile, BB and Charlie noticed something. "Look, some minor devils are flying off!"

"Yeah, they look like they are slinking their tails."

Excitedly standing up to his scarecrow height, Charlie asked acutely, "Who is that monster standing and flapping his wings on that stone plinth so high up in the sky?"

BB could see everything clearly in the distance and replied hastily, "He's the most respected conductor of the Afreet Orchestra – Azrial."

"Wow, he looks really pissed off that the minor devils are going off, there must be at least fifty of them."

"Yeah, those devils are in trouble when they get back home," BB chuckled.

"Yippee!" roared the rest of the happy crew seeing that no one from their side had left.

The evil razor-edge to the immutable sounds of Lucifer's Band of Doom spiralled into the azure skies and proceeded to rip the colours from the Chuckle Stream. The sun stood no chance either and the light of the plain began to dim immediately.

"Oh no, the Chuckle Stream's being robbed!" Stargasm screamed, waving her broomstick up and down.

Moonmummy came immediately to her aid. "Don't panic, Stargasm, our musicians haven't started to play yet!"

But Stargasm still wasn't fully convinced. "And what will happen when they do?"

Moonmummy stood there quaking before replying. "The Chuckle Stream will return in all its glory and the colours will come back into the rainbow's end and the sun will get much brighter!"

"Are you absolutely sure?"

"Yes, have faith!"

Stargasm remained unconvinced. "Faith, Don't make me laugh, I'd rather have a tea! An Enigmatic Totality that is!"

And then the witches looked out at the chaos of the Sonic Temple. It was incredible, the eyes of every single creature there lit up in the ensuing darkness.

"Moonmummy, look at us, just look at us, however are we going to win with such crazies on our side?"

Moonmummy was getting tired of trying to convince her. "Speak for yourself, Stargasm, having an army full of crazies is just what the doctor ordered."

And then Stargasm looked around and took in the collective sights. It was a sight to take your breath away. The lovely little girls were still sitting on the floating island gathering seashells for Sally to give, with love, to the Hashemites, still on bended knee and loving every moment. The Pyramid in Prism Buddhas sat meditating around the edge of the island and the ghostly *Leprechaun's Delight* was moored nearby somewhere in the middle of the air ready for a quick escape. Stargasm looked down, ignoring all the mandrills and gibbons that scurried about and watched Fairlight coaxing magic potion into Osric's mouth as Fareek, Mellow Tron and Tarquin got ready to play. Delicately adjusting the juniper spludberry brought back from Ancient Zeegypt, Fareek found everything was as it should be. Mellow Tron's dreadlocks were twitching with anticipation as they badly wanted to get out and play, not just tune up. Mellow Tron adjusted the controls of his Deep Space Muffle Wubbles just as Charlie shot a stream of fantasy blooms into the air to fall on everyone's heads. Next to him Catweazel Phil and Frogamatix fired off lasers into the skies. Sidney Arthur, Billy Blake and Danny De Foe sat drinking carafes of periwinkle wine as they'd done their bit.

Habiba was rubbing her hawk nose while her hooked hand began to play the spinning holo decks expertly. Her Scarabian burnoose was swept to one side as she looked at the three burkha-clad Soul Sisters of Awareness and beckoned them to sing. Looking incredible, dressed in Malik Slik Sylvester's Magic Muslin, they began to get into Tarquin's and Habiba's beat and started the "Om Song" as the Sonic Temple began to circle again.

"Hey, we're moving again!" Stargasm screamed as the howling wind got louder.

Moonmummy grinned as she replied. "And look, the Baddies are starting to spin too."

And it was true, the two separate spinning worlds were going in opposite directions to each other as the creatures of both the spinning worlds began to float up in the air. Dobbins directed his whole tribe of knee-high weenie thieves into the fray. Twynklyn, Blynkyn and Nod whirled and swirled above the maelstrom smiling tiny fairy smiles and filling hearts with gladness while the thirty-foot-long tiger shone its luminous stripes yellow, orange, red on black, changing faster then the speed of thought as its bright eyes looked all around. And as for the grinning Jabberwocky, its colour-tipped scales were matching the changes of the Power Pussy and its funny crocodile teeth snapped at the crazy world while its spark-ladelic tail swung from side to side with the beat. Stargasm twirled as the Sonic Temple began to move faster and faster and there was no one left to look at when the many speakers embedded in the walls boomed out.

"Yeah . . .!" raved Stargasm, jumping effortlessly to the new beat.

"Brilliant!" replied Moonmummy, stuffing her face full of oblong oysters and joining her.

"About time too!" Stargasm shrieked joyously.

"Well Stargasm, what do you reckon?"

"Excellent, now we can hear two sounds."

"And look at our music climbing into the skies and replacing the depleted Chuckle Stream . . .!"

"Wicked Sis! Absolutely wicked!" Stargasm finished, picking up a handful of squidgy oblong oysters and munching on them hungrily.

And it was true, with the scrapings of the Afreet Orchestra and the stompings of the Black Magic Mysterons, the sounds of the happy Hypno-Tantric Trance were increasing bit by bit and threatening to take over the world but the battle had just begun.

Fairlight seemed to know something special but he wasn't telling anyone as he ran around clockwise within the vibrating perimeter of the Sonic Temple, frantically distributing the latest batch of Anatta. Simultaneously, Osric went around in an anti clockwise direction doing the same.

"Let's eat it!" Karim the Kid Kurry hollered rushing up and looking fantastic. Kassim the Sun-Trance Kid nodded and doffed his purple Stetson, looking as tasty as Mr Naga himself. (That's Mr Naga – king of the cosmic chillies, not Mr Naga – king of the cosmic snakes.)

"Yippee for Fairlight for being such a scream!" yelled Karim, his mouth full of Anatta.

Yippee for Osric for being such a dream!" Kassim squealed.

"Three cheers for the good guys!" Dilly the Silly shouted, doing a perfect back-flip into the "Magical Muncherie" closely followed by Karim and Kassim.

Within minutes, all of the newly made Anatta had been munched and the Band of Doom hadn't yet noticed anything. Their psychic monster in the form of a colour-sucking python rushed out from the very centre of the amphitheatre to grapple with the sparkling, psychedelic, many-coloured ten-headed cobra rising above the Sonic Temple. As the Man on the Moon chuckled and passed the enormously huge Giant Hypno-Tantric Love Monster a bottle of ever increasing grins, they watched with eyes aglow as the two swirling, whirling, fighting and writhing snakes fought viciously and valiantly for supremacy. From thousands of feet below, Azrial waved an angry baton egging their serpent on while Mellow Tron turned up the sliders on the Deep Space Muffle Wubbles and Tarquin beat the heavens out of his tablatronics. So the Battle of the Bands was truly raging and everything was still totally unpredictable. The whole of the Sonic Temple began to get into the cosmic dance and from the door of his laboratory, Fairlight looked amazed as he began to feel the beat of the ten thousand trancers stomping up and down on their five- or six-toed feet, flapping their wings, racing through the swirling skies on magic prayer-mats, snowcamels, broomsticks, cloudboards, psychedelic flying pigs or just the power of prayer alone. Their very stompings made the air pulse with a pregnant pause.

"Absolutely brilliant, Fairlight!" Osric muttered with another lop-sided grin, looking even more unkempt than usual.

"Totally wicked but I'm hoping for the best!" Fairlight guffawed excitedly, his nervous energy making him more confident than ever. Having exchanged his lab coat for a tuxedo had definitely made a difference.

"What are you hoping for exactly?" Osric continued, smudging the kajol from the corner of his stained eyes and looking less kingly than ever.

Fairlight prodded his friend in the ribs and continued. "Well, have you noticed one thing, Osric?"

"What is it, Fairlight?"

"It's very simple, look at them all dancing, does something seem usual to you?"

Osric rubbed his unknowing head for a few moments before replying. "Ummm, I think what's weird is that they are all jumping in sequence together. They have never done that before!"

Fairlight brushed a hand down the front of his tuxedo and said, "Exactly! They are all jumping in time to the beat and all together."

Meanwhile, Osric had had enough and he grabbed Fairlight's attention and collar and for once spoke clearly and loudly. "Er umm ... I beg to disagree with you, I don't think anyone, and that includes little Anarkali doing her Kathak stomp up there is jumping to the beat!"

"What do you mean?" Fairlight asked, startled.

"I mean exactly this, the dancers are jumping in the middle of each beat and using each beat like a hurdle that they have to precisely jump over!"

"You're right, they are all trancing in between the beats and doing it rather well!"

"What can it mean?"

"I don't know, we'll just have to wait and see," Osric finished, having the last word for once.

The Anatta was taking its course through the thousands of bloodstreams in the ever spinning temple as Fairlight and Osric took in all the wondrous sights all around them. It was magic, myth and mayhem and it couldn't have been done without any of them. Individually they were wicked. United simply unbeatable. Osric was the first to open his mouth after a few minutes of simple gawping.

"This is wicked, Fairlight!"

"Absolutely wicked, I'd say too, Osric," Fairlight replied, flabbergasted.

However Osric sucked his index finger and asked, "Have you seen Amrita? Haven't seen her for absolutely ages."

Fairlight, knowing how attached Osric was to Amrita, decided to play it gently. "I think she's growing up Osric, and prefers to play with people her own age now."

Osric sighed, looked at the floating island above his head and just caught sight of Princess Amrita strewing dustbin-loads of Anatta onto the disbelieving crowd joined by the ever chuckling Astral Alice and Little Lucy. Osric sighed again and then smiled. "You still wouldn't be able to make the Anatta that you make without any of her chuckles though, Fairlight."

"Absolutely right again but it's nice to see her play with Astral Alice and Little Lucy. She couldn't always be cooped up with us adults you know."

Osric rubbed his bleary eyes and said with a frog in his throat, "Each of them is so special."

"Yeah ... Little Lucy's always in the clouds throwing down diamonds for a grin."

"And Astral Alice has the strangest sense of logic I have known any little girl to have."

"That's odd coming from you, Osric."

At that precise moment the three little girls whizzed over their silly, fiddledum heads and things were really changing fast. The stompings in the Sonic Temple were beginning to knock things over.

"Oh no Osric, you know what's going to happen?"

'What?"

"Do you remember when we invented this batch of Anatta, people started to stomp clumsily and things started to fall over everywhere?"

"Yes, I do!" Osric said with an exclamatory cough, standing up straight and starting to take great notice.

Fairlight grabbed him by the arms, looked him directly in the face and continued. "Then I've just thought of it, this is dangerous and if the stompings continue the way they are then the whole of the temple could crumble!"

"Are you sure?" Osric said, quickly breaking away from Fairlight's manic stare.

"Not totally, but I have a damn good idea."

"What do you reckon?"

"Its called Atomic Trancing!"

"What is?"

"This is, silly!"

"What do you mean?"

"What I mean to say is simple, by dancing between the beats the trancers ripple through the middle of each atom and vibrate it to destroy it!" Fairlight finished with what had been obvious effort but Osric was not slow to catch on.

"But that's terrible. What's going to happen to the Sonic Temple?"

"We'll be destroyed and Lucifer will win," Fairlight explained with as much patience as his growing excitement could muster.

"We can't let that happen, not at all!"

"Calm down, Osric. We'll find a way to deal with this."

"What shall we do?"

"We shall sit down and think and do nothing." Looking up at King Osric's floating island and seeing the Buddhas stock still in meditation Fairlight got an idea which he put into practice immediately. Grabbing Osric by his nose he pulled it out of joint and exclaimed emphatically, "Wonderful idea! Let's take a feather out of Dylan the black bunny's hat!"

Osric wasn't so impressed especially as his nose had been pulled out of joint. However rubbing it he still asked, "Why, what does he do?"

"Nothing usually but he does it really well."

"Okay, let's do nothing."

Fairlight and Osric sat cross-legged on the floor and did absolutely nothing. Both with closed eyes, they swirled the two forms of music through the maelstrom of their brains and contemplated.

Sidney Arthur, sitting above them with Billy Blake and Danny De Foe, had had enough. "Look at Fairlight and Osric down below!" he chuckled as Danny De Foe stomped over.

"What are they doing, Sidney Arthur?" he asked.

"Yes, what exactly are they doing?" asked Billy, and waited for Sidney to answer.

"I think they are waiting for the answer to come into their heads."

This answer wasn't good enough for Danny De Foe who stomped his wooden leg harder in the air and asked irritably, "The answer to what?"

"The answer to their problems," Sidney Arthur said, gingerly fingering his carpetbag of wickedly trickster ideas.

"Which is?" Billy Blake added in a smile to counterpoint Danny's seriousness and flowing through the ghostly bodies of the other two like a divine dolphin.

Danny was having none of it though. "What shall we do if the trancers' stompings crumble the temple?"

"Well, what are you doing Sidney?" Billy added insistently.

Sidney Arthur however remained as enigmatic as ever. "I'm going down to help them with their answer."

"Aren't you going to tell us what it is?" Danny snorted angrily.

"No . . . work it out for yourself."

"He never tells us anything!" Billy said, shrugging his shoulders and nudging Danny in the ribs.

Danny finally stopped being angry as there simply wasn't any point and exhaled, muttering under his breath. "So, you just noticed."

Sidney Arthur flew down to join Fairlight and Osric who were now examining each other's navels for an appropriate answer. Osric's pale face was looking more confused than ever as in examining Fairlight he couldn't find a belly button at all so he made do with examining his tuxedo buttons instead. It was at this point that the hovering Sidney Arthur blew another of his spectral ideas up Fairlight's nostrils and raced back up to join Danny and Billy who were still examining the crazy world below.

"Er, did you pick my nose or something, Osric?" Fairlight muttered, scratching his nostrils like mad and for once not looking so cool.

"Oh me, no, far too busy picking mine," Osric replied sheepishly, slowly opening his eyes and revealing to Fairlight his strange pose. His legs were crossed way up above his heads and his toes were merrily picking his nostrils.

Fairlight was still waiting for an answer. "So, were you picking my nose, Osric?"

"I don't think so, Fairlight, I was only picking my own," Osric replied holding on with grim determination to the pose.

And with that Fairlight let it go because a beautiful germ of an idea was rapidly growing in his head.

"Wow Osric, I've just had an idea!"

Osric, still coming to terms with his contortions, was not particularly impressed.

"So what, you always have ideas."

"No, this is a really good one of how we can save the Sonic Temple from destruction."

"How's that?"

"It's very simple really." Fairlight added, rushing over to help him get up.

Slowly but surely Osric was picking up on his enthusiastic vibes. Picking himself the right side up, he questioned the magic potion maker. "What do we do?"

"We get hold of Anarkali," Fairlight spat back faster than a water drop could fall down a waterfall.

"What will that mean?"

Fairlight continued scattering verbal bullets in Osric's unsuspecting direction rapidly stood up. "Well, seeing as the position is like this, we have to have an effective plan. The Baddies are brilliant musicians too. Theirs are just as good as the tunes the three Beat Boys and Habiba are making up and that's why the two fighting snakes thousands of feet up in the sky can't get the better of each other. No one seems to be winning. But we have a dancer far better than any of their hula-hooped skeletons!" With that Fairlight paused for breath.

"Oh yeah, Anarkali of course," without her none of us would have got here in the first place," Osric admitted with a wry smile. Her dancing brought the Sonic Temple here."

Fairlight clapped his fingers now Osric was starting to see the point. "So the plan is very simple."

"You always say that Fairlight but I still never understand."

"All right, I will put it in simple words. If you add up the energy of all the thousands of trancers here they still don't add up to the amount of dancing energy that our little Anarkali has."

"But I don't understand."

Fairlight laughed and began to sing. "Easy Peasy pudding and pie."

Osric stopped the song immediately before the verses came in. "Not the Stinky Billy song again, I can't stand it. Captain Kidd sings it all the time."

Chuckling like crazy Fairlight went on to explain. "No, not the Stinky Billy song, I promise."

"Well, what then?"

Getting serious for a moment, Fairlight set his speech pattern to machine-gun speed again and fired away.

"Okay, if we get Anarkali to trance the other way to the stompers then the forces of nature will be equal and the Sonic Temple won't crumble into dust."

Osric still wasn't fully satisfied. "And what will happen to the Baddies over there?"

"That remains to be seen."

Osric scratched his head and finally nodded. "It sounds like a wonderful idea!"

With that Fairlight grabbed the tail of Hussain's snowcamel as it came near to him and told the plan to Hussain's disbelieving ears before the Banglastani Zoofi rushed two hundred feet in the air and grabbed the spinning Anarkali by the hem of her Kathak gown to explain the plan to her. Having heard it, her emerald eyes twinkled in the shifting breeze.

"What are you going to do, Anarkali dear?" the hundreds of voices on her embroidered dress began to question but Anarkali just smiled enigmatically. Her silver ankle-bells tinkled to a newer rhythm of her cosmic Kathak show.

"Feet do your stuff, make me dance like magic.
Like cosmic powder puff
I don't need Anatta cuz I'm superbly wonderstuff.
Feet, impress me with your feats
I may be small but I'm big enough!"

It was a strange and amazing thing that Anarkali, the most magical dancer this side of the universe, really knew no magic spells at all. She used to make them up all the while and although it wasn't always poetry they worked perfectly. BB and Charlie were observing everything whilst firing brilliant blooms, love bombs and grin grenades into the throng.

"Can you see her? Something's happening!" Charlie asked as he towered over BB and showered him with fantastic petals.

"Yeah, the air is being scorched."

Looking beyond the immediate pleasure of grin grenades and love bombs, from somewhere in the corner of their spinning circular world, Charlie beckoned BB to stand up and pointed something out while saying, "No not just that, something else too."

"What?" the beatnik asked as an anxious Charlie grabbed him by the arm and pointed out to the skies again.

"Feel it! The air is now beginning to slow down."

"What you mean the whole of our spinning?" BB said rubbing his nose to see if was still there.

"Wow, wicked!" Charlie retorted, jumping up and down as BB had finally got the point.

"Absolutely brilliant! How does she do it?"

"Nobody knows, not even her." Charlie chuckled.

"She must be the eighth wonder of the world!"

"She is!" Charlie screamed as the molecules around them began to vibrate.

As the air burnt like streaky black bacon left cooking in the pan on a lazy Sunday after a heavy Saturday night before, sizzling smoke began to emanate and Anarkali began to slow down and began foot-slapping and spinning the other way. Now she was spinning in a clockwise direction whilst the many thousands of stompers below continued in the anti-clockwise direction, gasping at the incredible wonder above their heads. All this wonder was simply too much for Anarkali and she let out a gasping peal of pure joy as their temple slowly slid to a stop, vibrating dangerously.

"Whay! What's happening?' screamed Stargasm, bouncing up and down on her broomstick, looking menacing.

"We've slid to a stop," Moonmummy added beside her, trying hard to get control of her disobedient broomstick.

"Oh no, maybe we'll fall off the Sonic Temple ... off the edge of the universe and into oblivion!" Mevlana the Mage cried, cruising up on his wobbling cloudboard to be next to Stargasm. It was left for Suleiman the Spinner who came whizzing by in the other direction to explain.

"Don't be silly, the universe is supported by a giant purple turtle!"

"What do we do then?" Stargasm asked in agitation, accidentally kicking off a sandal and hitting Hussain's snowcamel right on the head, many feet below. Giving Stargasm his pair of rubber flip-flops, Suleiman continued to explain.

"Do what we have always done – trance!"

"Is trance the same as dance?" Moonmummy asked, quickly running a hand through her silvery hair.

"Yes, it's dancing with a T," Mevlana added, staring at the scene and seeing the inner visions of the others, particularly liking the stuff going on in Stargasm's powerful head.

"Do you mean like Equanimi-tea and Humili-tea?"

"No, I mean T as in transcendental," Suleiman said scattering his unstoppable laughter like bubbles.

"Ha ha funny ha ha!" Stargasm tittered, revving the broomstick to take them both higher into the clouds.

"No it's ha ha funny ... Hee ... Heee ...!" Suleiman suggested, suddenly goading himself and Mevlana further into the fray. Everyone then shot off in directions known only to their conscience and their karma.

And the beats went on, the Sonic Temple rang out with Love and Joy and the shrieks of the geeks and the gooks, the bhoots and demons and diabolics rose to a terrible crescendo while the Black Magic Mysterons turned the scrankler up. The music was awful, hideous and full of awe.

"Eeek aaark ... what's happening?" Fruggy cried, whacking the Bad Beat drums harder than ever, his ballet tutu way over his skeletal head and flapping in the breeze.

"Snarl ... I've got no idea," Fruzzy added, thrashing power chords to no avail. It was time for Total Frux to get a word in. Ramming a poisonous green mamba directly into the jugular on his scrawny neck, he chucked his mirrored shades into the crowd and howled. "The Goodies have stopped!"

"Nark ... no they haven't ... they're just vibrating," Fruggy shouted back, chucking a broken snare into Fruzzy's direction and throwing off his glitzy gown.

And then the miracle happened. As Mellow Tron turned up the Deep Space Muffle Wubbles on his bass machine, his dreadlocks went racing off his head to fight the evil snake thousands of feet up in the sky. As Mellow Tron continued playing, oblivious to his new hairstyle, Tarquin whacked his tablas harder than ever before while Fareek jumped around looking busy until something odd began to happen in front of their startled eyes.

"Aaah no ... Aark what's happening?" Fruggy cried, starting to feel really panicky and nervous now. In damming frustration Fruzzy chomped a big hole out of his battered electric guitar and shrieked at Total-Frux who was madly connecting the synaptic filters with the poison ivy. Total-Frux began to understand what was happening.

"Snarl ... it seems like our amphitheatre is starting to crumble ..."

"Nark ... Snark ... It can't be!" Fruggy yelled, seeing an instant end to all their hard work.

Fruzzy, out of sheer fright and forgetfulness, forgot to run his bony fingers up and down the keyboards and just left his hands there playing a discordant note of total hellishness. Spitting like a rabid dog in the midday sun, Fruzzy stuck his abnormally long tongue out and asked, "It's true ... Vark ... Snark ... what are we going to do?"

"No idea. Just put the music up!" Fruggy yelled from the back, whacking the Bad Beat drums like his very life depended upon it.

But Total-Frux who was in charge of the mixers screamed, "It's as loud as it will go!"

"Noo!" Fruzzy shrieked, chomping yet more holes out of his guitar.

"Boo!" cried Fruggy from the back, now starting to chuck a whole row of tom-toms at the orchestra now swooning in their pit. Their amphitheatre was crumbling fast, whole blocks were falling out of it while it was still spinning at fantastic speeds and coming apart like rotting teeth. The blocks and smaller stones went hurtling into the air and narrowly missed those ravers in the Sonic Temple as they shot off to fly through the two fighting serpents thousands of feet above.

"Wow!" gasped BB, swallowing his surprise. His spectacles were starting to make a spectacle of themselves as the lenses began to whirl around and round keeping in sympathy with what else was happening.

"Incredible!" Charlie wheezed, putting his flintlock down on the ground and just taking in the sights. He could see better than BB who had to stand on tiptoe. Charlie looked rudely at the Banglastani beatnik with more cheek than ever and he swiftly swished up his friend's tiny frame and plonked it on his shoulders.

"Thanks, Charlie!" BB gasped, pleased with his new perspective of the world.

"Don't mention it," Charlie said politely.

"What do you reckon?" BB asked in a tone of pure awe.

"Simply unbelievable!" Charlie whistled as BB, who could see more than his friend for a change, continued.

"Anarkali's doing it again!"

Charlie needed more clarification. "Do you think she's responsible for it all?"

"Of course, the power of Natraj and all that."

"Who?" Charlie asked, rather surprised.

BB continued talking with his eyes still focused on the horizon where the amphitheatre continued to crumble. "Call him Shiva if you like? With one foot slap he creates and with the other he destroys."

Now starting to feel the delicious effects of "Rudolph's Reminiscing Rum" Charlie smiled from somewhere down in the pit of his stomach and simply said, "Isn't destruction a bit naughty though?"

"It's the natural end of the creative process."

"Wow, oh Boogie!"

"Yeah Boogistan, the place of dance!" BB finished expertly, jumping off Charlie's shoulders.

At that very moment, with a thunderous crash, the amphitheatre came apart completely. With hideous shrieks scary enough to scare granny on shivering winter nights, thousands of geeks, gooks, spooks, afreets, bhoots, ogres, vampires, heckles, speckles and other assorted monsters raced out into the scorched air eager not to get destroyed as crumbling stones fell all around them. Even Azrial's plinth toppled like a piece of overcooked spaghetti as the musicians played on. Luckily, although the amphitheatre was gone for good the stage made of fossilised dinosaur droppings remained intact as did the Afreet Orchestra's pit. Bravely and valiantly the Black Magic Mysterons, vampire violinists, skeleton kettle-drummers and ghostly hula-hoop dancers did not give up. The three Frux brothers smiled through gum-less teeth as they realised that this would be their last gig.

"Krank ... Kronk ... Jhong ...!" Fruzzy smashed sonic superstition after sonic superstition as amplified angst.

"Snark eeek yip ...!" Fruggy added excitedly, still playing gamely on as their world crumbled around them.

"Snork ... Pork ... Yap ... Let's Rock ...!" finished Total Frux, smiling like a gibbering baboon.

However, playing their happy Hypno-Tantric Trance from over half a mile away the three Beat Boys and Habiba perked up and it was only then that Fareek noticed.

"Wow, the Band of Doom didn't get blown away!"

"They might be bad but they are certainly brave, don't you agree?" Tarquin added, rubbing a Bollywood hand through his hair.

"I'm totally impressed. They are true musicians to the very core," Mellow Tron added.

"Yeah, they are brilliant, it's a damn shame we can't be friends," Fareek interjected, his holographic zoofi gown cascading colours like sparklers lit under rainbows.

Tarquin meanwhile had a point. 'Who says? We never tried!"

"Look, don't get so dewy-eyed, look what's happening to the skies," Mellow Tron said tersely, adding more psychedelic filters on the Deep Space Muffle Wubbles.

"What is happening?" Fareek asked, suddenly biting his lip and trembling.

"They have somehow put the volume up and the black snake in the sky is getting bigger and more violent!" Mellow Tron elucidated for them all as Habiba's frantic beats brought them all back into the groove again.

"Oh this is terrible, their music will drown our music out and their snake will destroy ours!" Fareek finished angrily getting back into the mix.

It was all absolutely true. Although the demons had no home to speak of, their music and power was still racing into the skies and sucking the colours off the Chuckle Stream and this dark musical energy was what the evil snake was feeding on. The demons shrieked as the psychedelic snake got repeatedly bitten by the dangerous fangs of the black serpent of unvanquished evil and then with a sudden dive the evil snake blew its poison towards Anarkali.

"Aaah, she's falling!" Moonmummy shrieked, a few hundred feet directly under where Anarkali had been dancing until then. She revved her broomstick towards Stargasm and hollered, "Was she bitten by the snake?"

"I don't think so," Stargasm spat back in agitation.

Moonmummy breathed a sigh of relief. "You're right, it just spat in her face."

"That's lucky."

"Not really, she's still falling fast through the air."

"Quick! Somebody help her!" Stargasm finished, racing around in circles trying to find someone that was close enough to Anarkali to be able to help.

And with that the brave foolish dwarf that was Nasseruddin the Nutty raced up through the glittering air on his cloudboard to catch her before she fell to her certain doom. His lapis lazuli front teeth lit the way and with outstretched arms he caught her just in time and brought her to the ground in a flurry of fantastic flying. As the black serpent grew and grew as a direct result of the expansive power of the Band of Doom, the good guys were left dumbfounded. They had destroyed the amphitheatre but that wasn't enough. The darkness of the evil music was still sucking out the colours out of the rainbow's end. What were they to do next? Mullah Ullah was riding on the Giant Magic Carpet with the Genie of the Lamp beside him and the psychedelic gatta pulsed and itched his face in warning.

"Hey Genie, there must be something we could do."

"There is," the Genie replied, looking dazzling as he had just taken a bubble-bath in his lamp.

"You have an idea?" the Mullah enquired with grave concern.

"Of course I do but there's a problem."

"What problem?"

"Quite simply, your meanness!"

Mullah Ullah was shocked and the carpet rocked.

"What do you mean?" the Mullah asked, looking bewildered.

"Exactly what I said . . . you're a Meanie Mullah."

The Genie of the Lamp had really got up Mullah Ullah's goatee and it was starting to show.

Mullah Ullah tugged desperately at it before answering. "Why do you say that, am I not a kind master?"

"Exactly that, you see me as a serf and you are no different from the one thousand and one masters I have had before," the Genie said emphatically, rubbing his giant hands with obvious glee.

Mullah Ullah was left almost speechless but he managed to stammer out some words anyway. "Erm . . . sorry . . . anything else?"

"Yes, here you all are looking at your own liberation and you don't care two figs about mine."

"What do you mean?"

"Well, I could solve this problem by using a magic spell but as you only have two of those left after they are done I shall be gone, free for ever!" The Genie shrieked as the sonic winds buckled the carpet even more.

Mullah Ullah picked at his gatta and pondered. "Now you put it that way I suppose you're right," he whispered in painful admission, adjusting his lungi nervously.

"You know I am," the Genie persisted, glaring into the Mullah's perturbed face.

The Mullah decided to make a brave face and continued. "Erm . . . Okay, sorry for having been so mean and wanting you by my side for ever. Is there anything you can do to help the situation now?"

For the first time in ages the Genie of the Lamp smiled before replying. "Yes of course, but it's you that has to make the wish."

After he'd flown around surveying the terrific scene of the battling serpents and hearing the horrendous music of evil trying to outdo the Hypno-Tantric Trance, Mullah Ullah rubbed the lamp and the Genie appeared dutifully.

"What is your wish, oh master?"

Mullah Ullah hummed and hawed before stammering. "I'd ... I'd ... like to destroy Lucifer's Band of Doom."

"That is your second wish, oh master."

"I suppose it is!"

"Then I must obey."

With a sudden flash the Genie of the Lamp turned his body in the direction of the Band of Doom and pointed his finger straight at them releasing golden sparks to shower the unfortunate group.

"KERFLASSSSSSSSH ...!"

"Aaark ...!" went the afreets tumbling.

"Screek ...!" screamed the bhoots toppling.

"Scrok ...!" shrieked the demons bumbling

"Nark ...!" hollered the nasties falling.

"Noh ...!" yelled the yellow skins turning .

"Oook ...!" went the gooks, geeks, scronks and spooks howling.

"Eeek ...!" went the rest as the monsters were finally put to rest, scowling.

"CRASH ... CRUMBLE ... TOPPLE ... SMASH ...!"

Suddenly the music stopped. Their sound system had been blown up, thousands of speakers, all the instruments, drum kits, keyboards, synthesisers, grumplers, samplers and scranklers and the poison ivy all smashed to smithereens. The Black Magic Mysterons and the Afreet Orchestra were aghast at the mess before them.

"Aaark, what do we do, Fruggy?" Fruzzy screamed, his silver leotard looking quite tattered while his platform boots had lost their soles.

"Grr ... got no idea, ask Total-Frux," Fruggy retorted, examining with abject horror his set of smashed drums that lay around his feet like broken seashells on the seashore.

"Snurk ... I don't know either," Total-Frux finished, his skeletal face burning with incandescent rage.

"Wow, look up at the skies!" Stargasm shouted above the raucous din, revving her broomstick round and round.

"What's happening?" Moonmummy retorted, flowing close on her beautiful heels.

"Look what's happening to the black serpent!" BB yelled to Charlie, rubbing the mist off his spectacles to make sure. Although the flower-power warriors were on the ground they could clearly see what was taking place thousands of feet in the air.

"Yippee ... it's diminishing in size and falling to earth!" Charlie screeched back, stretching even taller and chucking another love bomb into the skies for good measure.

"With no dark music to feed off it's got no power!" BB exclaimed joyfully to Stargasm giving her a big hug as Charlie did the same with Moonmummy.

"Look, its even stopped fighting!" Charlie yelled, forgetting to let go of Moonmummy and feeling her crush the heebie-jeebies out of him.

"Yippee ... that's brilliant," Stargasm commented, making her hovering broomstick collapse into a tiny telescopic form once more and pocketing it gladly.

"Wow ... it's dissolving into the very air!" Moonmummy added, finally letting go of Charlie.

BB decided in his blissful happiness to jump and jive like never before. "Now, there's nothing to worry about any more!" he continued, taking Stargasm by the hand and leading her in a merry jig.

However, Charlie meanwhile had seen something else. "Look, the Pandavas and the Kauravas are now bowing in our direction!" It was true and from either side of the valley they had their hands clasped and were bowing down in their direction.

"Wonder what that means," Moonmummy wondered aloud, shaking the brick dust off her boots and checking to see if her eyebrows were still where they were meant to be.

"And something else too," Stargasm added quickly looking back into the skies again.

"What?" BB asked, still dancing a merry jig, all alone this time.

"All the colours are coming back into the rainbow's end!" Stargasm yelled joyfully, pointing her wand at the sky.

"And the Chuckle Stream is getting funnier too," Moonmummy added, taking BB's defunct arm and going round and round in circles with him to his delight.

" I think we've won!" he hollered madly like a monk on skunk.

"Yippee ... I've never won anything before!" Charlie squeaked.

"Look the world is getting so beautiful again!" Stargasm bleated beatifically, now pointing her wand all around them.

"And all the colours of the rainbow are falling onto our fiddledum heads!" BB insisted, observing the magic around them with glee.

"The game is over!" Charlie added, getting into the swing of things.

Moonmummy wasn't so sure and quickly interjected. "No, it's only just begun!"

"All the same, whatever? The fighting's stopped and we can relax!" Stargasm finished, conjuring up a load of crunchy bananas and handing them around.

At that moment, towering over the crowds one thousand feet in the air, the Giant Hypno-Tantric Love Monster smiled the all-knowing smile of St Stan and looked down at the battlefield below with its stream of endless eyes and chuckled. With its countless hands it waved to the many coloured Buddhas still fishing for minnows on King Osric's floating island and with its many mouths it quickly conversed with the Man on the Moon. The Man on the Moon of course was dangling at the end of the crescent moon playing his cosmic hurdy gurdy in perfect tune to the happy Hypno-Tantric Trance emanating from way below.

"Shall we tell them, Man on the Moon?"

"Yes, it's better that we do."

With that the Love Monster coughed through its many mouths, stamped its huge feet, grabbed everyone's attention and shouted. "Now look here, me and the Man of the Moon have conferred and come to a decision."

The assembled stopped what they were doing and looked up.

"What is it?' a demon ranted, waving a pitchfork perilously close to a vampire's head.

"Yeah, don't keep us in suspense any more," Charlie shouted, lobbing a whole stream of love bombs into the direction of the friendly giant.

Gently tossing the love bombs aside and smiling through a haze of bursting fantasy blooms, the Love Monster smiled again and said, "Okay then, for a start it's clear that happy Hypno-Tantric Trance has won the day!"

"Hoooray!" went the trancing crowds, breaking into a cosmic jig and jumping up and down on the ground.

"Yippee!" went BB, accidentally firing his fantasy flintlock straight through Charlie's head. Charlie smiled serenely and watched fascinated as fantasy petals emerged out of his ears. However, not everyone was so pleased.

"Snark . . . Unfair . . .!" moaned the monsters, gesticulating rudely to the giant referee, screaming and bawling and pulling their horns out.

It was time for the Giant Hypno-Tantric Love Monster to be placatory and it spoke out clearly and loudly, anxious to avoid further trouble. "Yes, but we have also agreed that the diabolics played really well and deserve extra credit for playing while their whole world was crumbling around them."

"Grr yeah . . .!" roared the monsters, feeling a bit better with this extra snippet of information and a hovering group of heckles decided to collectively cheer.

"Hrrr . . . yippee . . . Long live the Black Magic Mysterons . . .!"

The Giant Hypno-Tantric Love Monster continued. "And furthermore, neither of us have seen such a fantastic battle or heard such incredible music in all the time we have been alive . . . and that of course has been a very long time for both of us."

"Hurrah!" went everyone, now really getting into the swing of it.

Then, with a fantastic smile that spread from one side of the universe to the other, the Giant Hypno-Tantric Love Monster said its last words. "And so we declare the battle over and the party on!"

Perfectly on cue, the Love Monster pointed a fractal finger at the Sonic Temple until it stopped vibrating and everyone looked out at the infinite plain of Kurukshetra, at the smiling spirit-warriors of the Pandavas and the Kauravas still sitting on their golden horses. When they all looked up the psychedelic cobra suddenly evaporated when the Man on the Moon sharply clicked his silver fingers at it. Right on cue and waving goodbye to the world below, the Giant Hypno-Tantric Love Monster jumped on the dangling crescent moon, paddled like crazy with its ten trillion arms and simply floated away with the Man on the Moon beside him laughing their heads off. In fact, both of them faded out of view as night ended and another day awoke. The Chuckle Stream had been saved for sure and colours had stopped bleeding from the rainbow's end. The leprechauns would, no doubt, be totally delighted. However, just as Fareek was about to turn the faders up on the volume control so the party could begin again in earnest, an enormous sight filled the skies that made everyone and everything tremble like autumn leaves in the middle of a cosmic gale. Something very big their way came.

33

The Big, Blue Cheese

"IS IT A BIRD?" screamed Moonmummy, flapping crazily up and down in the air like a twiglet in a storm. Her silvery hair was blowing all over the place and she looked like a maelstrom in the middle of a cosmic blizzard.

"Is it a plane?" Stargasm hollered madly.

"Is it a monster?" Charlie shouted, jumping up and down like there were mice in his pants.

"Eeek, it's so big!" BB spat back, staring up at the incredible apparition in the sky which obscured the sun. The apparition grew and grew until it almost filled the skies.

"And it's coloured so black!" Moonmummy sang out but Stargasm had other ideas.

"No, blue, silly!" Stargasm rejoined instantly, barely managing to keep her broomstick under control.

However BB had other ideas and simply shouted, "You're both wrong, it's Blackness with Blue!"

"What's that?" Charlie asked querulously.

BB kicked him in the shins and asked irritably, "Don't you know anything?"

"Of course not you idiot and nor do you!"

Scratching his head BB pondered a while before replying. "Oh yes, I remember now!"

But now it was Stargasm's turn to get excited. "Aaah, what immense size! What unique colour!"

"Its colour is the very colour of space itself …" Charlie added quickly.

Looking slightly perturbed Stargasm replied testily, "Oh no, we must be dealing with the original spaceman himself!"

Waving her wand pointlessly in the air, Moonmummy added, "You don't mean the Man on the Moon do you, cos he's just floated away?"

It was at this point that BB suddenly realised what was up. Pointing crazily at the demented skies he grabbed the others' attention and screamed. "No it's the Sweet Lord himself!"

"Lord what?" Charlie asked a bit miffed. There was a time and place for religious sentiment and this wasn't one of them as a giant foot had appeared from nowhere and was coming down fast.

"Lord a mercy, the giant foot is going to squash us completely into mango pulp!"

And it was true. The giant blue black foot half a mile across was preparing to place itself smack-bang right in the middle of the plain. Quickly picking up on the vibes of fear Stargasm screamed in sympathy. "Please no, Bigfoot. Spare us from a squashy doom!"

Clearly able to see another giant foot descending, Charlie spoke out for them all. "Na ... we don't want to die ... not after all we've been through anyway!"

"Nooooooooooo ...!" joined BB in sympathy, covering his face with his trembling hands and fearing the very worst.

And then the movement stopped. The descending foot suddenly stopped descending and hovered three miles up in the sky, as a stentorian voice said, "Oh, hello earthlings!"

"It's Lord Krishna!" Sidney Arthur squealed deliriously.

"What did you say, Sidney Arthur?" Danny asked, thirty feet up.

Sidney Arthur looked bewildered. "I said, it's Lord Krishna!"

The two other holy ghosts looked at each other dumbfounded.

"Is he like Father Christmas then?" Billy Blake asked, circling Sidney Arthur from the left.

Now starting to tremble uncontrollably and sobbing, Sidney Arthur stammered. "Er ... Er ... Sometimes ... but he's usually a lot older ... oh no, he's come back to finally get me after all these thousands of years!"

"What are you talking about?" Danny asked, forcefully tapping Sidney Arthur on the head with his wooden leg to try and get some sense out of him. Both Billy and Danny were amazed. They had never seen Sidney Arthur look like this before and he had definitely lost his cocksure confidence and was looking frightened.

"What I'm trying to say is that I've been waiting for this moment for thousands of years."

"But you don't look very happy to see him," Danny added,

whacking him on the head a few more times for good measure.

"Happy? ... I'm delirious ... Boo ... Hoo ... Hoo!"

"Then why are you crying?" Billy added from the other side, now completely interested in the sudden change that had come over their usually supercilious friend.

Danny then stopped hitting Sidney Arthur on the head and asked more gently this time. "And you do you look so scared."

Sidney Arthur stopped snivelling and looked up. "Me ... I'm not shivering, am I?"

So much for them but what about Krishna? What was he hollering about? He was so high that the earthlings could only see up to his knees about a thousand feet up in the air.

In a vibrating voice that shook the very marrow of their bones he spoke again. "Hey, can you hear me down there?"

The volume of his voice was simply incredible and the thousands of earthlings below just couldn't take it. They all shouted back in unison. "Yes, Lord Krishna but please don't shout as we don't think our eardrums can take it!"

Lord Krishna giggled for a while and then spoke up again. "Ha Ha Hee and can you see me?"

The people, spooks and gooks all spoke out in one voice again. "We can only see up to your knee-caps!"

"We bow down to your greatness!" Charlie shouted up into the air, as Krishna continued.

"Perhaps my incredible size and dimension is intimidating you?"

"Yes sir, quite a bit!" Charlie replied as the others decided to get their words in too.

"No sir ... a lot ... it's absolutely freaking us out!" Moonmummy shouted.

Meanwhile the God of all he surveyed got out his bamboo flute and tapped himself on the head with it. As he did so he laughed his incredible laugh yet again. "Oh, how I do love grand entrances ... Ha ... Ha ... Ha ...!"

Stargasm, who was never scared of anyone even if they were gods five miles high, put on a steely expression and screamed way up into the clouds. "Please stop laughing like that, Lord. Your breath is blowing all the spooks and gooks away and they have already had a hard day!"

Lord Krishna laughed once more and fingered his bamboo flute with anticipation as he cleared his godly throat and said to the crowds below, "All right, good folks, I've had my fun. It's nice being five miles high and twenty-five years old but I think my grandness is simply intimidating you."

"Now that you come to mention it, Lord – yes!" Charlie yelled loudly.

Surprisingly, Krishna decided to respond in the positive. Stroking his chin he looked down again and whispered, "All right then, in that case, I'll come down to earth. Can you see me clearly now?"

"No we can't!" yelled a cast of fifty thousand as Krishna's image began to blur uncontrollably so he decided to try again.

"Well I'm in fifty-seven dimensions at the same time. Can you see me now?"

Everyone just nodded and so Krishna descended yet again and asked gently, "I'm now half my size and only in thirty-two dimensions simultaneously. Is this still too much for you?"

"Yes!" shrieked Stargasm speaking up for everyone, waving her broomstick up and down like a loon.

"Scrook!" went the spooks, for once agreeing.

"Most definitely!" BB shouted firing a whole volley of fantasy blooms into the direction of Krishna's head but only reaching his ankles.

Krishna meanwhile was soberly listening to everyone's advice. "All right then. I'll go down again, I'm now only half a mile tall and connected into twelve dimensions!"

"Still too much, our sweet lord!" screamed the multiple voices as he began to land.

In a voice as clear as a waterfall he called out, "OK then, here goes, I'm coming in to land ... watch out!"

And then with an almighty flash, Krishna burst out of the skies and onto the ground. He shook with laughter as he danced in the centre of the former battlefield. He then began to chuckle again saying, "Tee hee ... Watch out world, here I am!"

However as both sides began to cheer, realising that they were not going to be squashed into pulp, one invisible voice in the whole crowd expressed his fear clearly. It was Sidney Arthur of course, who muttered, "Oh no, he's chosen the form of the seven-year-old boy again!"

By this time Danny De Foe had had enough and slapping Sidney he asked pointedly, "What are you so worried about?"

Fingering his hourglass in ghostly agitation, Billy Blake pulled his rotund shape forward and added, "Yeah, how can a seven-year-old kid be scary? Not as frightening as the five-miles-high monster he just was!"

Sidney Arthur let out a plaintive wail and a sob and explained, both hands flapping uselessly in the air. "You don't understand. Lord Krishna can choose any form he wants, sometimes he's a young man dancing with gopis, sometimes a baby stealing ghee and sometimes a seven-year-old boy!"

Billy looking rather confused, blurted out, "What are you looking so troubled for then, Sidney?"

Sobbing dementedly, Sidney Arthur wrung his hands in desperation and elucidated further. "Well, to put it mildly when Lord Krishna's in his seven-year-old form he's much more powerful than when he's a giant."

"Oh wow!" went Billy and Danny together, profoundly shocked at the importance of Sidney's words.

It was Danny who then spoke. "How strange but true, but why are you looking so worried? It's not as if you know him!"

"I wish that were true but I do know him and I've been dreading this moment for thousands of years!"

"Oh Sidney, what have you done?" Billy finished, watching Sidney Arthur dissolve into a pool of tears again.

As the two holy ghosts began to comfort their pal, Krishna who was now a mere four feet tall began to play his flute. Everyone and everything else was completely entranced in seconds and his blue-black form shone like space itself. Mischievousness and spiritual glory were the hallmarks of Lord Krishna for sure and as he played with great delicacy, the world seemed to stop spinning in his beautiful presence. However, as most gasped with wonder, somewhere thirty feet in the air, Sidney Arthur clapped his hands over his ears and tried to block out the glorious refrains.

"What are you worried about?" Danny asked, holding Sidney Arthur by his lapels and turning him around.

"Never seen you in this state before," Billy added shaking him up and down to no avail.

Releasing a torrent of tears Sidney Arthur cried like crazy and in between sobbing gulps went on to explain. "He's come to catch me for wrongdoings!"

Billy needed clarification and, in fact, demanded it. "What wrongs, Sidney? What are you going on about? We've never known you to be doing wrongs, ever!"

It was then Danny added his bit. "You're a bit naughty at times but that's just high spiritedness but you've never done anything downright malicious. Tell us what's up."

Sidney Arthur sailed around the air followed by the faithful Billy and Danny who still didn't understand. The assembled crowds below were standing, flying or gawping, totally entranced at the sound of the beautiful bamboo flute And then suddenly out of the cosmic skies the solitary grey crapping pigeon which had been chased through time and space by the ever ravenous flock of fantasy falcons burst into the scene. The poor pigeon seemed like it was on its last legs or in this case, wings. Seeing Krishna it raced towards him and landed safely on his left shoulder. Instantly, the fantasy falcons raced off the other way not willing to risk the wrath of the great god. The freewheeling pigeon panted and puffed deliriously on Krishna's shoulder with relief. It was home. It had travelled thousands of years and even more miles to find solace and as it panted and crooned to the great god's bamboo flute, Lord Krishna looked at it and smiled, having missed his special friend.

"You mean that humble pigeon is Lord Krishna's friend?" BB asked, flabbergasted.

"Looks like it," Charlie added, slanting his eyes back as far as possible to get a better look.

"What, it's not even a very special bird ... not like a dodo or flamingo," Moonmummy suggested.

"Or even a pelican or a penguin pulling a palanquin!" Stargasm said at the sight of this insignificant bird sitting prettily on holy shoulders.

It was at this point that BB began to remember. Tugging furiously at his hair he mumbled mysteriously. "This little bird's been chased through time and space everywhere by those hungry fantasy falcons and it still got the better of them all."

"Yeah, I remember seeing it in Pearly Green," Nasseruddin the Nutty shouted, whizzing down on his cloudboard.

"And we a saw it in ancient Zeegypt," Mellow Tron rang out sidling up to be close to the group. He was still a baldhead as his dreadlocks had not returned but he didn't care.

"And we saw it at the Khumb Mela ages ago!" Stargasm suddenly remembered as the mystery began to clear itself.

Now, standing confidently tall as a beanstalk, Charlie added, "And we saw it in eighteenth-century Pearly Green!"

"That little bird's been everywhere," Nasseruddin chuckled, shooting back off into the skies again, taking his teeth with him naturally.

"And for that matter, so have we!" Moonmummy added in a peal of laughter.

While they were laughing a very worried ghost darted invisibly in the crowds but he was no match for Lord Krishna who fixed his third eye firmly on him and there was no way that Sidney Arthur could get away from its vision. He then told his ghostly mates the secret he had been keeping.

"Many thousands of years ago, long before either of you had been turned into ghosts I used to live quite happily under the canopy of giant mystic mushrooms at Queen Angie Park. As you both know I am the very oldest ghost in Ghost Town and so I have seen and done things that neither of you can imagine."

Danny wasn't too impressed. "Stop showing off, so what?"

Sidney stopped to brush away a ghostly tear and continued. "It was at this time I was given the job by Krishna of cavorting with his sacred cows as he is the ultimate shepherd of all beings and I was given the task of looking after this herd of especially sacred cows."

"Wow, you a shepherd. I can't believe it!" Billy whistled excitedly, while Danny became impatient.

"Get on with it."

"Well I preferred gambolling with the lambs rather than looking after the calves."

"What did you used to do with the lambs?" Danny asked, fascinated.

Looking him squarely in the eyes Sidney resumed his story. "We used to sit cross-legged on the grass drinking rye and playing gin-rummy."

"And then what?" It was Billy's turn to ask as he too became transfixed by the tale.

Sidney sighed deeply and went on to explain. "One day I was fleecing the sheep as usual when we were all playing cards while smoking cigars . . . when the smallest calf in the herd of sacred cows that used to wander Queen Angie Park fell into the lake and nearly drowned."

"Wow, go on!" Billy blurted excitedly as his fingers twirled his mystical hourglass round and round distractedly.

Ignoring the sight of its spinning Sidney continued. "And if it hadn't been for the friendly blue octopus that lived at the bottom of the lake, it would have been a different story for sure but it lifted the drenched calf out and saved it from drowning."

"I see ... so that's why Lord Krishna's angry with you!" Danny whispered with disbelief through his ghostly teeth.

"... and that's why you have created this incredible plot!"

"Yeah, why have you done all this, Sidney?" Danny then asked, looking more serious than seriousness itself.

Shaking himself free of the clutches of the other two, Sidney Arthur almost shouted in deliriuous response. "For a start, so that you two and other ghosts can become liberated and finally stop being ghosts!"

"We'll believe it when we see it, mate!" Danny whispered disbelievingly as Billy simply asked, "What else?"

Sidney Arthur looked up and offered a weak smile. "So that everyone in Pearly Green can have the greatest adventure ever known, become free and have fun while doing so!"

The cynical Danny remained unsatisfied. "But tell us the real reason, I think you're hiding something."

His facea ablaze with fury this time, Billy asked Sidney Arthur, "Oh yeah, tell us the complete truth now or we'll feed you to little Lord Krishna ourselves!"

Sidney Arthur decided to come completely clean.

"By the balls of St Stan, all right I'll tell you. I created this whole story and involved the thousands of characters in all the adventures so that when this moment comes and when Lord Krishna finally gets me I simply wouldn't be on my own!"

"So admit it, you were scared to face the Lord's wrath on your own," Billy said, just as furious as ever and angrily putting back his hourglass away.

"I most certainly was, I've never been so scared of anything in my life!"

Danny needed to get a very clear understanding. Looking wizened and wise he asked Sidney Arthur a very pertinent question. "So Sidney, you simply wanted your mates around you to give you protection when he finally got to you ...?"

"Yeah, that's right! You don't know how frightening it's been all these millennia waiting for the blue god to jump on my back!"

Finally, having caught on to the plot and the incredible extent of Sidney Arthur's manipulations, Billy asked in a voice like a storm, "And so you thought by helping to devise and manipulate a plan that would lead to the liberation of thousands of people and other furry beings, Lord Krishna would go easier on you and be less harsh as to his punishment!"

"That's right boys, you got it in one!" Sidney Arthur replied with a sheepish grin.

Danny decided to get to the end as fast as he could. "And you mean to say that this entire tale and the most fantastic adventures that we all have had were simply due to the fact that a single sacred calf which you were meant to be shepherding fell into the lake in the middle of Queen Angie Park some time many thousands of years ago?"

"That's true."

"That's the most fantastic story I've ever heard Sidney tell us Billy . . . what do you think?" Danny said, turning around to look at Billy who was starting to smile.

Billy's reply was phlegmatic in the extreme. "This is amazing, it's the first time that he has told us anything about anything without having his teeth pulled out first!"

It was at that particular moment when Billy and Danny were considering whether to give Sidney a cuddle or beat him up when Lord Krishna patted the grey pigeon, crooning happily on his shoulder, and pointed his right index finger at the familiar ghost, the visibly quivering Sidney Arthur who he now drew towards him with the other two ghosts in his slipstream.

"What's happening?" BB screamed as what was invisible became suddenly visible.

"Can you see them?" Charlie yelled crazily, whilst prodding Moonmummy in the back with a bony finger.

"What can you see?" Stargasm shrieked, surveying the strange new sights and not knowing whether she liked them or not. Then hastily getting her act together, she flashed her wishing wand in a northerly direction and hollered like a banshee. "There are three ghosts moving towards Lord Krishna, Moonmummy!"

"Are you sure, Stargasm?" Moonmummy yelled back.

It was then BB's turn to put things straight. "Stargasm's right, Moonmummy, look, you can make out three distinct figures."

Turning quickly to Charlie, Moonmummy shouted at the top of her voice. "It looks like they're being dragged along."

"It's like some kind of magic force is drawing them along!" Charlie replied, quickly bending down to get a closer look.

However, this all may have been OK for those still living but what about the dead? How were they faring in this whole unpredictable process?

"Scream!!! ... What's happening Sidney Arthur?" Billy Blake shrieked, his face looking distinctly scared and his lank hair flying in all directions.

Sidney Arthur, being the first ghost to be drawn by Lord Krishna, tried unsuccessfully to hide his quaking fear and replied, "I don't know, Billy, but we can now be seen!" Dragged through the air only inches behind Sidney Arthur, Billy Blake was none too impressed.

Neither was Danny De Foe flying madly through the air at the back. His wooden leg clanked through the breeze as he shouted,. "Oh no, what a drag after all these years of being able to see and not be seen we are now just the same as everybody else!"

"Dead right, Danny!" Billy fumed, suddenly wanting to hit Sidney Arthur over the head with Danny's leg again but unable to as he was travelling towards the finger of the beckoning god.

However, it was the right time for Danny to pontificate to Billy. "Dead is the specific word, it's like we've all come alive again."

"And we are all moving towards Lord Krishna's little finger like something on fire!" Sidney Arthur yelled towards the back, his frown still visible on his tired, ghostly face.

Billy pointed out to Sidney Arthur the crowd of thousands staring at them and the obvious discomfort he was starting to feel. "And look at the people staring at us, I don't like it one bit!"

Those that were living found the scene completely enthralling.

"Look at the old thin ghost at the front, the one with an aristocratic nose, that must be their leader!" BB screamed to Charlie, impervious to the gentle rain that was starting to fall and permeate the holes in his plimsolls.

Charlie was quick on the uptake too. "And followed closely by the fat one with the white hair!"

The witches suddenly burst into chuckles seeing this strange sight and Stargasm was the first to laugh.

"Hee hee and look at that stretched one at the back clanking through the air with his wooden leg. They're ghosts!"

"Are you sure, Stargasm?"

"Absolutely!"

Now it was time for BB and Charlie to wonder aloud.

"Wow, Stargasm reckons they're ghosts!" BB said to get Charlie's attention.

Charlie soon got the point. "Wow, now we really have seen everything!" he replied, randomly chucking a few love grenades around for fun. Flowers of romance bloomed everywhere but the ghosts had something else on their frazzled minds. Sidney Arthur was the first to scream as they crash-landed right at the exquisite feet of the child-god.

'So, you are finally here, Sidney Arthur?" Krishna said with an expansive chuckle.

"Boo hoo hoo . . . don't punish me too much, my Lord!" Sidney Arthur cried, grovelling on his knees and looking rather silly.

Looking at Billy, Danny asked quickly, "Wow, he really is going to punish him, Billy!"

"Don't doubt it, he is the Lord, after all."

Lord Krishna then tittered like the child that he was as he watched their discomfiture for a while before stating, "Dearest

Sidney Arthur, you thought you had deceived me all these thousands of years. But no, I have been watching you very closely." Sidney Arthur could only sit up on his knees and cry. "Boo hoo hoo!"

Krishna continued, "You thought with your actions you could stay invisible for so long but you were wrong because your actions were visible all the time just as you are now."

"Wow, Charlie, now I know they are ghosts."

"And did you hear what Lord Krishna just said?"

"Yeah, something strange is cooking!"

And then, looking very serious, young Krishna beckoned Sidney Arthur closer.

"You have devised this incredible set of adventures, helped in the invention of Anatta and also helped in the creation of this amazing music. What do you call it?"

Wiping his snotty nose on the hem of his tatty overcoat Sidney Arthur stood up and bawled at the top of his voice. "Hypno-Tantric Trance, Lordy. Boo hoo hoo!"

Lord Krishna was not impressed. "Oh, stop blubbing!"

"I can't help it!"

"I know and have always known about your scam!"

"What scam?" Sidney Arthur cried.

Not batting an eyelid Lord Krishna said hurriedly, "Simply this, that you have helped liberate thousands of beings through your manipulative machinations and got nowhere yourself!"

This was an interesting change to the plot and the two other holy ghosts perked up their ears. Billy was the first to comment. "What did he just say about our Sidney?"

"He said he'd got nowhere himself," Danny replied, totally astounded at the words he had just heard from the little god's lips.

"What?" Billy blurted, unable to keep his amazement and wonder to himself any more.

Lord Krishna went on to question the flabbergasted ghost. "Go on, admit it, Sidney, what have you done wrong?"

But Sidney Arthur was in no fit state to be able to talk, so it was up to Krishna to explain everything to the thousands of beings gathered there on the plain of Kurukshetra.

"Sidney Arthur, you were my very best shepherd and I gave you the whole of the incredibly beautiful Queen Angie Park to shepherd my flock of sacred cows and what did you do?" Krishna said in a voice so authoritative that the very air shuddered with his sovereignty. Sidney Arthur didn't say a thing and so Krishna carried on.

"I'll tell you what you did, you preferred gambolling with the soft cuddly lambs and playing gin-rummy whilst fleecing them of their fleece and all the while you were having fun!"

Sidney Arthur could do nothing but nod his head to the rhythm of his sobs.

Lord Krishna then said curtly, "And what you don't realise is that you Sidney Arthur could have been liberated long ago!" the voice of the lord reverberated in the sonic wind.

"What?" Sidney Arthur suddenly looked up as Krishna's voice strode on mercilessly through the caverns of his consciousness.

"While you were busy planning and scamming and liberating countless beings through your magic, you yourself could have been liberated and stopped being a Holy ghost."

This was incredible news for the two other hungry ghosts who jumped up immediately.

Billy was the first to respond with rapid fire enthusiasm. "Did you hear that, Danny?

"I sure did, Billy!"

"What does it mean?" Billy asked again, scratching his nose in confusion.

Sidney Arthur had meanwhile stood right up and with falling tears and fears he hollered dementedly at the little god's face. "I could have been free thousands of years ago?"

Danny and Billy were not slow on the uptake either.

"Wow! Sidney could have been free simply ages ago!" Danny whistled getting Billy up off the floor by the scruff of his neck and standing themselves up.

"Then why was he hanging around with us?" Billy asked, looking more confused than Sidney.

Danny quickly decided to put him out of his misery. "I think he didn't know that he could have been free ages ago."

It was now time for Lord Krishna to interject. "That's right, Sidney didn't know, he thought he was the cleverest ghost in Ghost Town when really he was the most foolish."

Meanwhile these very words were enticing some real human living ears too.

BB was the first to react. "Wow, did you hear that?"

"Yeah, Sidney Arthur's an unwilling Bodhisattva!"

"You what?" BB replied, not sure he'd heard Charlie right.

Stargasm decided to put the metaphysical boot in quick. "Well a Bodhisattva is a being that doesn't choose to go to heaven until every other being has got there first."

Hearing these incredible words Sidney Arthur burst into more tears and Krishna gently asked him why he was crying now.

"It's because I could have been free a long time ago and I spent all these thousands of extra years in Ghost Town without a cause."

"That's right and that has been your real punishment, I didn't really need to add to it!" Krishna replied, with a strangely compassionate look in his godly eyes. "Yes, you thought you were scamming me when in reality you were only scamming yourself."

"And me, the oldest ghost in Ghost Town!" Sidney Arthur screamed stomping up and down on the scorched ground.

Lord Krishna decided to tease him further. "That's right, there's no fool like an old fool."

It was time for Sidney Arthur to get heavy and he did. "But you could have told me Lord Krishna then I would have admitted to everything!"

"What would you really have admitted to? Almost losing that single calf that fell in the lake?"

"Erm well . . . no."

"And would you have admitted that to me and gone on to explain that if it hadn't been for the octopus, the calf would have drowned?"

"To be honest, no."

"Well then, what do you expect Sidney Arthur? You were once the best of my shepherds and then you turned into the most mischievous monster of them all. All in all you have been a very naughty boy!"

There was a moment's hesitation after which Sidney Arthur stopped sobbing, smirked a bit and deftly replied, "Sorry, Boss, I was on a lucky streak gambolling with the lambs and I just couldn't stop."

Lord Krishna paused a while to scratch his head and then smilingly asked, "The question is, you mischievous ghost, shall I let you off or not?"

Sidney Arthur scratched at his kneecaps where his carpet bag of wickedly trickster ideas hung and simply replied in one magic word. "Please."

Krishna smiled a subtle smile of such beauty that the skies above lit up. He continued, looking much like a seven-year-old god but even more radiant, "Dear Sidney Arthur, I have decided to forgive you for your past misdemeanours simply because yesterday is history and tomorrow is just a mystery and so today is a gift!"

With a face full of delight, Sidney asked Krishna, "You mean the gift is today, the here and now?"

Lord Krishna hummed and hawed for a while before replying. "The present is the present of course so live in the moment, it's the only place that counts!"

Sidney Arthur bowed low, knowing the true import of those words and simply uttered, "Thank you!"

Lord Krishna comically cupped his hands to his ears and asked again, "What did you say?"

"Sorry, Please and Thank you!"

Lord Krishna then raised his voice so the whole crowd could hear. "You've just said the three most important mantras in the world after the word 'love', they are, of course, 'Sorry', 'Please' and "Thank you'."

"The Magic Mantras!" Moonmummy shouted, throwing her broomstick into the air where it flew away on its own whim.

"Yippee, we've found them!" Stargasm joined in the other's expansive excitement.

"After all our searching!" Moonmummy gasped with the hint of a growing sob.

"Yeah, they were always here, deep in our hearts!" Stargasm

screamed with total happiness exuding from her very pores. Then it was left to the master of all ceremonies to explain everything in a clear manner so the truth was plain for everyone to see. Lord Krishna, the tiny seven-year-old god who was really timeless, elucidated the issue for all to hear.

"The very best mantras are always the simplest and after 'love' these three are some of the most useful. Reciting these three you can always be happy and make others happy too!"

"Oooh!" went the Whirlistanis in unison, jumping up and down on their cloudboards

"I didn't realise the Magic Mantras were so simple!" Stargasm shouted clobbering Nasseruddin the Nutty accidentally with her returning broomstick. Her witchy sister had discovered something also.

"That's why it was so hard to find them!" Moonmummy shrieked like the real banshee that she was when excited. Her black robes were trembling as she bounced up and down like one possessed. Sidney Arthur's trial was now over and it was obvious from the expanding grins on both Sidney Arthur's and Lord Krishna's faces that the oldest ghost in Ghost Town had been forgiven for his past misdemeanours. And then Lord Krishna waved a tiny arm once and everywhere simply lit up and no one knew what to do as tens of thousands of ghosts became visible as if they were appearing magically from a hole in the ground somewhere. There were fat ones, thin ones, spooky ones and demented ones, creepy ones, crawly ones, funny ones, serious ones, sane ones, bad ones, crazy ones, happy ones, horrendous ones all being liberated at the same time. And before they were all disappearing into the Land of Gold someway over the rainbow, they became visible to the whole of the astonished crowd. Ghost Town had finally lit up for good as they doffed their ghostly hats at the stunned and bemused crowds and dissolved somewhere inside the sunrise.

"Wow, this must be Nirvana!" BB shrieked, poking Charlie in the back of his knees.

Charlie looked bemused and asked Stargasm, "I thought they were all going off to heaven!"

Stargasm turned round to look up at Charlie, sharply waved her wishing wand, and cracked up laughing in the most stunningly amazing of replies.

"Oh, this is much better than that, much better than any heaven!"

Charlie had a sudden urge to shoot a whole volley of fantasy flowers through Stargasm's head but his fingers could only tremble on the trigger as he peered down asking, "What do you mean?"

Stargasm suddenly looked wiser than her years. For a while she looked very serious as she replied. "Heaven is a place you can get to but when your good karma runs out it's back to the lower planes for you."

"So it must be Hell that all the hungry ghosts are going to."

Stargasm had other ideas and speaking to Charlie in the same manner one would speak to a little child, she enunciated her words very clearly and said, "No, in Hell when your bad karma runs out you go back to Heaven, Earth or whatever plane you came from that is."

By this time Charlie had had enough of these enigmatic puzzlements. "Then just where are they going, know-it-all?

"Nirvana!"

"Is that a bit like Never-Never Land!"

"Precisely!"

Stargasm's self confidence was getting a bit too much for Charlie who quickly dropped his sarcasm and asked in wonder, "And how?"

Stargasm smirked and explained. "They have all won the game."

"The game of what?"

"The eternal game of births and deaths and those that were once the hungry ghosts are now truly deathless and birthless!"

Charlie, BB and Moonmummy stopped to consider this for a moment and after a while's hesitation, BB stepped forward to shyly ask, "Does that mean they'll never be born again?"

Stargasm, looking every inch the cosmic queen, cackled like a hyena before replying, "That's right, because they can't be born they simply won't die either!"

"Wow!" BB gasped, gobsmacked at Stargasm's answer.

"Incredible!" Moonmummy shrieked, clasping her arms around Stargasm's shoulders and smothering her in a gigantic hug.

Charlie, however, still wasn't satisfied and had a question that needed answering. Peering down to look intently at Stargasm's shining eyes he persisted. "But tell me, is this Nirvana better than heaven?"

Stargasm was dancing and would only answer whilst in full movement. "Oh much better, there's no comparison really!" she shrieked. However, BB had other things on his mind. Turning away from Stargasm he suddenly saw what was happening on the plain and shouted. "Incredible, just watch those millions of ghosts!"

"We are . . . we are . . . we are . . .!" Moonmummy and Charlie sang in unison as Stargasm continued her merry jig around the others. Watching this cavalcade of ghosts appear to disappear into Nirvana, the ghosts of Danny De Foe and Billy Blake sat to one side not moving as Sidney Arthur sat to their left, still sobbing, but this time with relief.

Danny and Billy were not happy though as Sidney's incredible scam had blown their minds completely. They were both starting to see the incredible complexities in Sidney Arthur's scam and Billy, particularly, was not in a forgiving mood. Snarling and snorting like a pain-maddened bull, he scratched his head, suddenly realising the enormity of the plot.

"No Danny, the plan is much worse than we realise!" Billy whispered with an element of real vengeance in his voice. Something was eating him up from inside.

"Why, what's up?" Danny replied hastily, noticing a very real change come over his friend.

Billy's whispers became louder. "I don't think Lord Krishna has told us everything."

"Whay! What do you mean?"

"Just this, what's to stop us having been liberated simply aeons ago?" Billy wheezed, becoming angrier and angrier.

"What?"

"Listen carefully to this."

"All right, Billy . . . fire ahead!" Danny answered, puckering his face up in total concentration so as not to miss a word.

Billy grabbed his friend by his lapels and spoke so loudly that a bunch of hovering demons could hear him very clearly and took fright.

"Krishna said to Sidney Arthur that he could have been free ages ago if he wasn't so intent on facilitating the liberation of others as a coy way of avoiding Lord Krishna for his deplorable escapades."

"Yeah, I just about got that," Danny answered breathlessly trying hard to keep up with the incredible speed of Billy's thought processes.

"Well what I'm trying to say is that if Sidney could have been liberated then, in all probability, we could have we been as well."

"I'm beginning to see."

Billy suddenly hesitated for a split-second and exhaled with a great tiredness. "Sidney Arthur got everyone into his brilliant scam and who were the first ones that he trapped in his net?"

"You and me Billy ... you and me," Danny replied slowly but surely, catching the drift of Billy's argument.

Quickly getting his breath before it scampered away into oblivion, Billy finally let go of Danny's lapels and explained. "Correct, we've known him longer than anyone else and he's always bossed us around. And that's exactly like he's always bossed other ghosts around too."

Danny considered this for a moment and scratching his chin, simply nodded.

"Totally correct Danny, Sidney's adventure has been our adventure and Sidney's downfall has been our downfall too!"

"What do you mean?"

"Well if Sidney wasn't so scared about facing Lord Krishna on his own then he wouldn't have got us embroiled into his plan either and we would have been free to fly off to Nirvana all the quicker."

"The dirty, low-down scheming rotter!" Danny replied with a sudden burst of vengeance which even took Billy by surprise.

Giving his fuming friend a slap on the back, Billy wheezed impatiently. "He's a rotter to end all rotters!"

"What shall we do, Billy?" Danny glared back as angry as Billy who gnashed his teeth before replying with a strange smile on his lips.

"I don't know Danny but we should just cheer up."

Danny, however, felt completely different. "Why, I don't feel like forgiving him at all, the obnoxious scoundrel. Palookah to end all palookahs!"

"We have to remember that we are holy ghosts and today is the liberation day for all ghosts."

"Does that mean we'll go to Nirvana as well?"

"Probably, just as soon as it's our turn!" Billy emphasised by getting out a ghostly bottle of "Rudolph's Reminiscing Rum". He forced Danny to swallow a big swig, making him cough in reply.

"Yeah ... cough ... cough ... maybe we should just forgive Sidney. No point carrying all these bad vibes on our way to Nirvana!"

"Yeah, you're right, no point at all."

"However, there is one thing I'd like to ask about our Sidney. One question that's still unresolved and keeps going round and round in my head."

"What's that?"

"Well, after Sidney Arthur himself, you and me are the oldest ghosts in Ghost Town and he's made us part of his adventures ever since I can remember." Danny smiled as he spoke, feeling the currents of rum course warmly through him.

"You're right!" Billy bleated, taking a huge swig himself.

Danny tapped his wooden leg in the air and continued. "He's been scamming us since we were baby ghosts!"

Billy paused in swallowing the rum to consider what Danny had suddenly said.

Then he replied in a cool, clear voice. "That's right and he's done it to thousands of others as well, not just ghosts but people too."

"That's how we have had this most incredible adventure, isn't it?" Danny asked, a growing smile upon his thin face. He continued in a similar vein. "Yeah, we should forgive Sidney too but there's still that single unresolved question."

"What's that?"

At this point Danny's face took on the most cryptic expression it had ever taken. Having mystified Billy with this look, Danny tapped his wooden leg in time to his enigmatic words and answered. "To what extent is Sidney Arthur's, or in that case, anyone's, love and compassion just bleedin' self interest?"

Billy was gobsmacked for a while and just didn't know what to say. Then picking up Dutch courage he cleared his ghostly throat and chuckled. "Wicked Danny, what a simple question!"

"Well what do you reckon, Billy?" Danny asked, impatient for an answer to the predicament that he had posed. Billy fingered his hourglass and stammered, "Oh, the answer's easy!"

Danny wasn't so sure and continued with his persistent questioning. "What is it then clever clogs?"

Billy clapped his hands and finally spoke up loud and clear for all to hear. "The answer is all of it! All compassion and love is only total self-interest in the long run."

In response, Danny spun around the air faster than a snowflake in the nether regions of Hell. It was obvious that Danny was pleased with Billy's answer.

"Absolutely brilliant, Billy! That's what I thought too. Sidney

Arthur has shown us one last trick up his sleeve, his love and compassion towards every being, living or otherwise, has only been total self-interest."

Billy, now whizzing around the burning air too, chuckled like a madman and roared. "He's tried to set everybody and everything free so he can be free himself!"

"And the funny thing is that he didn't have to try, hee hee!" Danny replied quickly, joining in for all he was worth.

"Yeah, he was already liberated but he didn't realise it!"

Billy now held onto his stomach as he span through the air. "Krishna certainly had the last laugh!"

"Tee hee!" Danny agreed, with his chuckles saying more than words ever could. Both ghosts laughed, trembling in their ghostly forms watching the trillion ghosts around them arise from nowhere, clasp their hands as if in prayer in the direction of the smiling Krishna before disappearing into the centre of themselves – Nirvana.

"I've worked it out," cried Billy.

"What have you worked out?" Danny screamed back, twirling and doing a perfect pirouette, three hundred foot in the air and looking like he was having the time of his life or in his case, death.

"The incredible meaning of my most mystical hourglass!" Billy answered, racing up from ground level to catch up with Danny in less than three seconds flat.

"What do you mean?"

"The single grain of diamond-white sand that doesn't fall this way or that within the mystical hourglass has just shown me the meaning of everything."

"Famous last words but what exactly do you mean?" Danny finished with a quizzical look at his friend whose face was taking on an indescribable look. And then as Billy looked at Danny, his face too was taking on the exact same look and they felt themselves transforming moment by moment from their ghostly bodies into bodies of light. Billy still had some explaining to do and he did it as the blue of his eyes turned green with wonder and his body slowly disappeared into light, feet first. He clenched his hourglass, turned to Danny who was swiftly disappearing into Nirvana and whispered his final worlds on this plane or any other.

"To see a world in a grain of sand
And heaven in a wild flower
Hold infinity in the palm of your hand
And eternity in an hour."

And the two holy ghosts instantly dissolved.

"Whay!" cried Sidney Arthur, sobbing at seeing his two oldest friends disappear for ever. Still crying and not knowing why, he sat up and surveyed the wondrous scene with a painful heart. Trillions of once-hungry ghosts were getting liberated but not him. Madame Serendipity was waltzing into Nirvana with Rob Indranath while Phineas and Cynthia were striding in a spiral of ever-decreasing circles as her Tapestry of Never-Ending Time flew off in the sonic wind, its thousands of stitches unravelling. Behind her, a long unsatisfied stream of befuddled suitors bawled their eyes out knowing that they had lost her for ever.

"What's happening?" Phineas Freakville asked, looking Cynthia straight in the eye.

"I've just realised that I've been in love with you all along!"

"Fine time to tell me, Cynthia!"

"Better late than never!" Cynthia replied coyly as they too dissolved.

The whole of the plain went completely silent then as everyone realised that not a single being had been killed in that mother of all battles; a few broken bones and a lot of broken egos, for sure, but no actual deaths. Former enemies now embraced and Krishna repeated the Magic Mantras with exuberance.

"Thank you!" tittered a Bongostani leprechaun as it lent a little green hand to help up a befuddled demon.

"Please!" pleaded a vampire violinist, offered a glass of rum by Dobbins but much preferring to take a swig of bat's blood that it kept in a little flask. Meanwhile, some spooks, bhoots and afreets were stating their perspective with the Dreamweavers.

"It's sorry!" screamed a spook, trying ineffectually to tweak Twynklyn's fairy nose.

"No, it's please before thank you!" Blynkyn responded, quickly pulling Twynklyn out of reach.

"No, it's sorry before please!" an Afreet insisted, holding on to Nod's tiny wings before Amrita swooped down to flick its ears and making it let them go as Nod had the last word.

"No it's always thank you at the start and thank you at the end."

The plain was changing fast, all enmity had gone and demon drummers and hula-hooped dancers were making friends with the Wicked White Witches of the West. Captain Kidd and his merry pirates were befriending the terror trombonists from the orchestra whilst BB and Charlie were sharing their rum with a bunch of thirsty-looking Afreets. The Whirlistanis tried to dazzle a group of bhoots with their flying skills but the bhoots ran rings around them and the Zoofis from Banglastan were sharing snowcamel husbandry with a group of pitchfork-raising demon who were hungrily eyeing the sacred sheep that Sidney Arthur was gathering together into a fold.

Malik Slik Sylvester's spiders were making clothes for a whole row of hideous hag horn-players who stood there meekly as they were garbed in dresses so fine that they were the hautest form of haute couture. Malik was sitting nearby smoking a pipe with Azrial, each trying to outdo the other in the outrageousness of their respective smoke rings and in the centre of this unbelievable scenario Mullah Ullah, Anarkali and the Genie of the Lamp rode contentedly on the precious rug, giving rides to whoever wanted one. Seashell Sally and the Trans-Tibetan lama were squatting on their haunches sharing a bowl of oblong oysters with a whole host of devils, donks and scronks while the Hashemites crooned love songs to Seashell Sally with the Sisters Nazneen providing a perfect three-part harmony.

However, it was somewhere near the temple stage that things were getting really interesting as the Black Magic Mysterons, looking ashen-white and blown away by the complete destruction of their stage and kit, tottered up onto the stage where the Beat Boys were getting ready to play again.

"I still don't think they're as good as us, Fruggy," Fruzzy said with a twinkle in his eyes.

"Yeah, I agree," Fruggy replied, the smoke still coming out of his ears.

"We got more banks of samplers and synthesisers!" Fruzzy insisted.

Total-Frux wasn't so sure and with an irritable snort replied, "The word is 'had' . . . now we don't have any!"

"You're right Total-Frux, so right!" Fruggy finished, chomping his teeth and trying to look as respectable as a battered muso could do after being dragged through the maelstrom of the second wish. They approached the members of Metta-Morph-Aziz.

"Who is this menacing trio, then?"

"You don't know anything, Mellow Tron, but I know who they are," Tarquin hollered from the back, slapping the synsantooric tablas like no one else but eyeing the newcomers suspiciously.

"Well, who are they then?" Mellow Tron asked again with an edge of annoyance.

"Easy, that's the Black Magic Mysterons – Fruggy, Fruzzy and Total-Frux!" Tarquin screamed from the back, quickly changing tempo.

"You don't say, let's get their autographs. They're famous!"

"Be cool, we're just as famous as them," Fareek insisted, throwing his head back like an arrogant stallion and conveniently forgetting to mention that he had secretly bought all 17 of their albums and played them to death.

Tarquin meanwhile had stood up from his tablatronic set up and was clearly stating loudly, "But we beat them fair and square."

"No we didn't, we had help from a genie!" Mellow Tron replied, ever the fair one.

Fareek meanwhile had had enough of this dissent and pleaded, "Look, why are we arguing again? We're both as good as each other."

"Let's say hello," Mellow Tron added as Fareek's words revealed his adoration of the Mysterons.

"But I'm shaking, I'm so nervous!"

"Grow up!" Mellow Tron chuckled.

The Mysterons came ambling over to look at the Hypno-Tantric Trance set-up and Fareek, Mellow Tron and Tarquin jumped quickly off stage to shake their hands. This was rather difficult as each of them was over seven foot tall but the lads managed it nonetheless.

"Greetings, Fruzzy," Fareek whispered looking bravely up into his burning eyes and trying to hide his secret adoration of their consummate and inimitable style.

"No, I'm Fruggy," Fruggy replied, removing his mirror-shades.

"Sorry," Fareek answered sheepishly as one last Mysteron introduced himself.

"And I'm Total-Frux," Total-Frux boomed, looking hard at Fareek who simply said, "I could tell that just from your looks, mate!"

"What do you mean by that?" Total-Frux enquired, suddenly looking menacing.

It was left to Mellow Tron to save Fareek's hide from a good hiding. "He doesn't know what he's talking about. Fareek's better left spinning the holodecks or playing around with the hydro navigation unit than talking to professionals like yourselves."

This seemed to placate Total-Frux who turned his back on Fareek with a huff and lazily examined the kit.

"Who plays drums in your set up?" asked Tarquin.

"Played drums, don't you mean?" Fruggy said with a sigh, wistfully remembering his set of Bad Beat drums and spectral snares which were wonders of the worlds, the dark ones anyway.

"Yes, er . . . sorry," Tarquin replied.

Fruggy looked at him and sighed again. "I used to play the drums."

Now it was Tarquin's turn to be enthusiastic. "You played brilliantly too. I just play this Tablatronic kit, my name's Tarquin."

After comparing notes for ten minutes and guzzling almost three bottles of rum, they all buckled up with contagious laughter. It was only after they had finished the final bottle which Tarquin had hid behind his tablatronics that Total-Frux took his mirrored shades off, tugged at his glitzy gown and said, "So who's the little blue-black fellow playing the flute?"

"Oh, that's Lord Krishna, he's a god!" Fareek replied, casually peeling a purple plum he had found in the folds of his zoofi gown.

Fruggy replied in a voice almost approaching enthusiasm, "Oh, isn't that an interesting fact, I know for a fact that we're devils," Fruggy said with a grin, stumbling over the words like a drunkard over gravestones.

Fruzzy came immediately to his help. "What Fruggy is trying to say is, what's all the stuff with the Magic Mantras?"

Fareek continued. "Oh, easy! Lord Krishna said that the three words . . . 'Sorry', 'Please' and 'Thank you' were some of the most powerful mantras in the universe."

Everyone stood still while absorbing the importance of these words.

After a moment's break Fruzzy carried on where he left off. 'Is that right, little friend? Then I suppose it's only right that we should practise them, don't you think?"

Fareek quickly looked at Tarquin and Mellow Tron who gave him no support whatsoever so he carried on bravely himself. "Oh I agree, absolutely."

"Thank you Fareek, I think I'm getting to like the sound of these Magic Mantras!" Fruggy finished. It was only left to Total-Frux to say, "Sorry my head went through your bass-bins!"

Tarquin, ever the polite one, could only say with another reciprocal bow, "Don't worry but you could always thank me for smashing you in the face with your guitar!"

"Why yes, thank you!" Tota-Frux wheezed, his eyes illuminated with this newer understanding of the Magic Mantras.

And so, on the battlefield they continued learning the real value of the Magic Mantras. Those that were enemies were now friends. Fruzzy was offered a battered red electric guitar exactly like his old one and Fruggy was shown to a set of bongos which he caressed lovingly while Total-Frux made himself at home behind a set of more modest samplers and synthesisers than the Black Magic Mysterons had been used to. The musicians like the elves, leprechauns, ghouls, spooks and gooks were getting their act together. Together.

As Lord Krishna looked out at his domain he smiled boyishly and played along to the happy Hypno-Tantric Trance that all of the musicians were now jamming to. Squatting at his feet, Sidney Arthur looked disconsolately at the thousands of ghosts disappearing into Nirvana but he was going nowhere fast.

The Genie of the Lamp decided to cheer him up and now spoke. "So Sidney Arthur, the whole of this story hinges on a cuddly lamb that almost drowned and your fear of what Krishna would do to you?"

Sidney Arthur turned around to look at the Genie and replied in the most mysterious manner that he could muster. "The karma you are, the calmer you get and the calmer you are the karma you get!"

The Genie of the Lamp had little time for these mystical whimsies but asked, "Is not the desire for personal liberation just another craving? I should know, I was stuck inside that damn lamp for countless centuries!"

Sidney suddenly perked up transfixed by the Genie's comment and replied quickly, "Of course it bleedin' well is!"

The Genie threw his half-munched cockroach away and simply asked the most intelligent question that Sidney had ever heard anyone ask. "Is not the greed for the desire of personal enlightenment just another greed?"

"Heh heh heh! Of course it is!"

The Genie looked quizzical for a while, whooshed off into the air, flew around in crazy circles and then swooped back to where he had came from to ask yet another simple question. "What makes us free then, Sidney, seeing as it looks like you and me are never going to achieve Nirvana?"

Sidney Arthur scratched his head, chuckled and replied faster than a passing twinklefish. "Liberation, my good friend, depends on our own actions and nothing else ... No gods can condemn us down to hell or raise us up to the heavens ... I feel free of the past now that Krishna has forgiven me for the regrettable incident in the park. But now, I feel free and won't have to worry about his wrath anymore, chasing me through time and thrashing me at any unexpected moment. Sorry. Please. Thank you, Lord Krishna ... "

It was then that the blue-god suddenly perked up and asked Sidney, "Have you anything else to say?"

And then in a moment of satori, Sidney Arthur jumped to his feet and mischievously chanted:

"There ain't no Goddess. There ain't no God.
There ain't no gain. There ain't no loss.
It's only Thieves and Buddhas who don't give a toss!"

Krishna dissolved into a pool of giggles and Sidney looked his employer straight in the eyes once more and shouted, "Who the hell do you think you are? Who are you to tell me when I can be free?"

"Amazing answer, Sidney, my, you have come a long way."

And with a beatific grin he disappeared in a puff of fragrant blue.

"Yippee, the Boss has gone!"

"Thank god for that!"

"I thought he was never going to leave."

"Now we can party for ever, Genie!"

"And we shall, Sidney, we shall."

The party had kicked off again and everyone was delirious and happy when Mullah Ullah felt his psychedelic gatta itch like never before and so he grabbed the microphone off Fruzzy who was preparing to wail himself into oblivion, and called out, "Is everybody happy? The never-ending party to the end of all time has just begun but there remains a single question to ask. Is everything resolved?"

"Yes! All's well!" roared the crowd, except Fareek who begged to differ and shouted. "No, there is still something yet to be resolved!"

"What's that, Fareek?"

And Fareek hollered, "We told King Funky we'd be back in Zeegypt one day with some more Anatta and music and that he could play in our band – the most brilliant funky drummer in history!"

"Okay then – Genie of the Lamp – come over here."

In a split second the Genie arrived beside him and the Mullah.

"What is your desire, Mullah Ullah?" he asked in a smoky voice, admiring the countless thousands of wild party people before him.

Mullah Ullah hitched up his lungi with one hand and grabbed the mic with the other and announced: "Time for you to be free, Genie! Time for the third magic wish."

"Your wish is my command?"

"Take us all to the Temple of Zarnak at Thebiz!"

And in an atom-splitting second, the Sonic Temple and its inhabitants moved through time again, all except for Sidney Arthur and the Genie of the Lamp who, having been granted freedom with the final wish, simply stayed on the ground with his new pal.

"Where are we going?" Stargasm shouted as the swirling winds took them higher and higher aloft.

"Ancient Zeegypt!" BB screamed as a crescendo of blinding white light flashed before them.

"What do you mean, 'ancient'? We have just left 5000 BS!" Charlie screamed, holding onto his head in the teeth of the cosmic wind.

"What's BS?" Moonmummy asked, trembling with both agitation and anticipation.

"Before St Stan, silly!" Stargasm deftly replied, shaking on her broomstick as BB put them all right.

"Okay then, we are actually going 1000 years into the future!" he said, bravely holding onto the spectacles that were threatening to fly off his face.

And they most surely did. They flew westwards and further forward in time towards the ancient-future city of Thebiz where the ever-patient King Funky awaited their arrival with bated breath and funky drumming!

34

King Funky's Joy

THE STARSHIP HAD landed again and BB rubbed his smeary glasses, and nudged Charlie who was next to him.

"Where are we?"

Bending down to be nearer to his friend, Charlie turned to the shivering beatnik and simply said, "You heard Mullah Ullah speak to the Genie of the Lamp didn't you?"

"Yes, he said something about Thebiz!" BB gasped pulling out a handful of sooth-saying sea slugs that had got into his earholes.

Charlie pulled him up to the level of his eyes by grasping his shoulders and said, "This is where Anarkali and MMA got to when we ended up in eighteenth-century Topping."

"Oh, is that so?"

"That most certainly is, matey," Charlie replied emphatically, coughing for good measure. He watched BB's confused eyes for a moment and then shook him hard to get the rest of the sooth-saying sea slugs out.

Shaking himself free BB asked with a grin, "Is everything resolved now?"

"It seems to be and look at who is running up wearing an unusual headdress juggling tangerines!"

BB took a good look at the two tiny figures running up towards the Sonic Temple, one thin and one fat but both panting. Releasing himself from Charlie's grip he tumbled to the ground saying, "That's King Funky!"

Patting him condescendingly on the back Charlie asked, "Then who's that fat slaphead running beside him?"

BB screwed up his eyes to get a better look, thought for a while and then replied. "Must be his faithful sidekick, Plebmoses!"

"Hold on! How do you know what they look like if you've never seen them before?" Charlie asked suddenly.

"Easy! Tarquin told me what the king looked like and the double royal crown of upper and lower Zeegypt is a dead giveaway," BB replied earnestly.

Meanwhile Charlie was examining the scene and scratching his unshaved chin. Kicking both his black boots into the earth to make sure he was on solid ground, he blew his nose into one of the Artful Dodger's stolen silk handkerchiefs and exclaimed, "Oh wow, we are most certainly in Ancient Zeegypt."

"But don't forget it's the future to where we've just come from . . .!"

"But 4000 BS still sounds pretty ancient to me . . .!"

As all the inhabitants of the Sonic Temple, good or bad, came to their senses and finally stopped throwing up all over the sides, they looked astounded as Tarquin, Mellow Tron and Fareek rushed to greet the fantastic pharaoh. Anarkali was the first to fall into his arms, however.

"Anarkali, you're here!" screamed King Funky as he stared at her. His delicate nose sniffed her equally delicate aura while his perfectly etched black eyebrows shot off on either side of his face in a manner only Moonmummy knew how.

Anarkali replied with a smile, "Yes King Funky, how could we not?"

At this point Mellow Tron, Fareek and Tarquin came racing up. As the two groups raced towards each other like lovers who hadn't met for thousands of years, everything and everyone inside the Sonic Temple either cheered or jeered magnanimously. Racing towards King Funky faster than the speed of wonder, Fareek crash-banged right into the delirious pharaoh and little Anarkali was sent spinning into the air once more.

"Yippee, you too!" King Funky squealed happily and grabbed Fareek by his holographic gown.

"We told you we'd be back!" Fareek panted, kissing the king firmly on both cheeks. Slowly but surely extricating himself from the reciprocal shower of kisses Fareek tidied up his messy hair and said, "I know we said we'd be back but I didn't believe it."

It was time for Mellow Tron to paddle his oar. Coming up to the bewildered king, the diminutive Skankmaster of Jah quickly asked, "How long have you been waiting for us, King Funky?"

King Funky, finally letting Fareek go, embraced Mellow Tron and said, "Oh I've lost count. It's been endless days and nights and there's been no one with me but the faithful Plebmoses . . .!"

At this juncture the bald, fat, sweaty Plebmoses stepped forward to say with exquisite courtesy, "Your wish is my desire, your highness!"

King Funky decided not to stand on ceremony and replied as quick as a flash. "Oh, I know that silly but you've been faithful all the same!"

Plebmoses bowed as King Funky adjusted his moving head-dress of the two joined crowns of upper and lower Zeegypt and asked.

"What's happening now, Fareek?"

"We have got the music for the great party together and us lot and Habiba are making it with the additional help of Lucifer's Band of Doom."

"Sounds absolutely brilliant!"

It was now Tarquin's turn. "You can put away your solar-powered CDs now King Funky and join the band!" he said.

"What me?"

"Yes, you of course, silly!" Tarquin said irreverently while Fareek picked at his nose before speaking.

"Why, we've made a special 108-piece drum kit for you so that you can join us."

"Being the best funky drummer in history, ancient or future!" Mellow Tron added, ignoring Tarquin's kick as the synsantooric tabla player obviously wanted the last word.

King Funky looked at the four each in turn as Anarkali had come back by now and with a teardrop in his eyes he finally said, "Oh, I don't know what to say."

"Then simply don't say anything at all and join our band," Tarquin said forcefully, happy to finally have had the last word.

By now the Starship had settled for good and on the bejewelled raised stage Habiba could be seen spinning the disks with members of the Black Magic Mysterons beating out the bongos, immersed in banks of synthesisers and wailing out on a battered old electric guitar. It was just like before. Fruggy, Fruzzy and Total-Frux were having the time of their lives. The party had not stopped. It had simply moved on. They were all living in the moment and the even once distraught members of Lucifer's Band of Doom were loving every moment; the Anatta helped! On centre-stage as the three Sisters Nazneen wailed their "Om Song" looking beguilingly resplendent in their shimmering Magic Muslin Hypno-Tantric Hijabs, the hawk-nosed Habiba spun the holo disks with absolute precision as the three beat-boys and King Funky caught up with themselves. However, she was not spinning them with her sabre-toothed hand any more. She had given the sabre tooth back to the long suffering Power Pussy and was playing the disks with her hawk nose instead. She looked rather silly but the music blared out beautifully, just the same. The Great Gig in the Sky, the best party this side of the universe was finally getting grooving. They had all set their controls for the in-estimable heart of the sun and were rocking like nothing else seen or ever heard before. Just below Habiba the skeleton hula-hoop dancers were serenading their funky stuff. The Black Magic Mysterons were still playing their dark music but now it somehow blended well with the happy Hypno-Tantric Trance and no one minded as it gave the music that the boys and Habiba were making a dangerous new edge and the crowd were loving it.

King Funky was being encouraged most persistently to sit behind the incredible 108-piece drum kit and Fareek exclaimed, "Don't be scared, King Funky, we built this especially for you."

"Yeah, it will make a change from playing bongos!" Mellow Tron added as King Funky slipped his slim body behind the incredible drum kit and patted his pet cheetahs who had ambled up to join him behind the drum kit.

"Wow! it looks wonderful. What's it made of?" he finally gasped

Fareek, Tarquin and Mellow Tron had rehearsed this part well. In perfect three-part harmony they answered the king in exquisite cadence. Fareek was the first to start.

"Well, the bass drums are made of giant pumpkin gourds."

And then it was Tarquin's turn. Fingering his bloomers in anticipatory agitation, Tarquin blew the king a raspberry and said, "The tom-toms are made of coconuts that have fallen from King Osric's floating island."

King Funky looked at his drum kit rather like BB in a sweet shop, not knowing which to go for first. Controlling his merriment and trying hard not to pee his pants King Funky simply asked, "What about the snares?"

"They are giant clam-shells that Seashell Sally found," Mellow Tron replied faster than the other two. The tiny bass master of Deep Space Muffle Wubbles went on to elucidate further. "And the cymbals are made of assorted seashells that a Bongostani leprechaun has been skimming to Seashell Sally for years!"

King Funky looked at him with the strangest look that had ever clouded his eyes and screamed, "Wonderful, now I finally get to have a drum kit of my own!"

"That's right! About time too."

And then it really was time. Gingerly, King Funky adjusted the royal crown of lower and upper Zeegypt properly upon his head, made himself comfortable on the giant mushroom that served as his stool and looked around. Jubjub birds flying out from tumtum trees chased the pretty pink flamingos that chased the penguins and pelicans pulling palanquins through the cosmic skies. Buddhas and mandrills, still sitting atop King Osric's magic island, threw crunchy bananas down to the delirious crowds who ate them like popcorn. The Whirlistanis and the witches swapped cloudboards for broomsticks and raced each other through the air like children playing catch. Fairlight was finally smiling now the story was coming to fruition and grabbing Osric by the scruff of his neck, pointed his head down at the ground. BB and Charlie were indiscriminately throwing love grenades and firing fantasy petals so the earth was covered in petals. Rose and tulips and mangoberries divine were getting mixed up with lilies and lotus and other things sublime. Kassim was berating the Banglastani waiters as he pondered awhile. Billy Blake, now in Nirvana, had left his timepiece behind and both witches started to observe the magic within a poem unfurled and scribed upon the silk scarves coming out of Dobbins' top-hat:

> The Sisters Nazneen sang directly to Mullah Ullah
> who picked his at his gatta like the madman he was,
> slapped his head and wondered why
> they all thought he was boss.
> Abraxas the Long Beard and Azeem the Dream
> were thrashing Hussain the Insane.
> He'd forgotten to feed his snowcamel again
> and was feeling much pain.
> Captain Kidd was doffing his hat and explaining the seas
> to the floor,
> they loved this sweet pirate and soon asked for more.
> Stains and Bates were climbing the rigging,
> sails flapped in the breeze and sailors were jigging.
> Nasseruddin the Nutty was playing with putty
> while Mevlana the Mage was eating plain yam.

Suleiman the Spinner had the final last word
as he shouted, "Never eat spam!"
St Stan, high up in the sky, looking down on all this,
exhaled a sweet sigh
and porridge is good for us, just never ask why.
Anarkali was still queen of all she surveyed;
danced her trance and, in cosmic winds, swayed.
Malik Slik Sylvester jigged with his spiders
amongst bales of magic silk
taking Anatta with ale and some milk.
And me, I'm dodging from nobody now
as this adventure has been so sound,
We freed Captain Kidd without whom
no peace could ever be found.
Archangel Azrial, once a bad boy,
was now having fun,
he'd put on some pork
and now weighed a ton.
The orchestra's new instruments had been given for free,
Biscuit-tin guitars and pipes made of reed
it was a good thing that Buddhas still had their creed.
The Black Magic Mysterons were really on form,
Fruggy whacking bongos and Fruzzy on synths
sharing ale with drongoes, looking like a prince!
Total-Frux, with snakebites up on the stage,
cobra and mamba, looking like a sage!
Jabberwocky was cocky, Power Pussy at its side,
Tears in his eyes because no one had died.

And in this tall tale no one had!

(It was thought that the ditty had somehow impressed itself directly from the Artful Dodger's brain onto the silken scarf in his topper!)

As for leprechauns, they were there in their many thousands. From Bongostan, from Trans-Tibet, from Banglastan, from the kingdom of Chin, Zeetpong, Mayland, Zeru, Treasure Island, Bagpipistan, Zongolia, Kathakstan, Merzia, Queen Angie Park and of course from Dooblistan to Mehra Dhun and Tunkirk to New Zork, leprechauns were there from everywhere and none of them were eating pork.

And then King Funky stared to play.

Fareek gasped with delight, quickly adjusting the synapses on the juniper-spludberry Mellow Tron had inadvertently brought back from Zeegypt so long ago and now, here it was back there once again, playing its delicious little soul out.

Mellow Tron pondered a while before continuing. "Great idea to get him a drum kit."

"I know. He complements Tarquin brilliantly!"

"You know what we have to do?"

"What?"

"We'll have to ask him to stay in our band." Mellow Tron added with a smile. Fareek answered quicker than a fish could blink. "Even if it means leaving Zeegypt where he's a pharaoh?"

"Oh I'm sure he'll have no doubt about it. He always wanted to play in a band!"

And then as the MMA, Habiba, King Funky, Sisters Nazneen and the Black Magic Mysterons played their groovy music, it rose to an incredible crescendo as the thousands of people, fairy folk and magical creatures danced and tranced. Life had never been like this before. From the centre of the stage a smoky-blue aura arose like iridescent lilies and the most magical happened.

"What's that?" Nasseruddin the Nutty screamed while cruising in spirals fifty foot up in the foggy air.

"What is that?" Stargasm hollered this time like a banshee gone bananas as the crazy Whirlistani pulled at his lapis lazuli teeth and exclaimed, "Just incredible!"

"Do you know what that is?" Stargasm shrieked, totally aghast at the oncoming vision.

Nasseruddin blinked rapidly a hundred times before answering. "No ... but it looks like three pyramids flying in our direction."

And it was true. Above all their fiddledum heads three pyramids could clearly be seen cruising the astral skies at three hundred feet, slowly but inexorably coming closer. All three were of different sizes with the smallest at the front followed by the middle sized one with the largest at the rear.

"They're the Pyramids of Geezer!" Tarquin shouted not missing a single beat on his burning synsantooric tablas.

Turning around Mellow Tron looked at him and exclaimed, "But they are usually at Kayro ... how come they got here? Do you know the date today, Tarq?"

Scratching his handsome head with one hand and slapping the tablas with the other Tarquin replied fast. "It's midsummer's night!"

And then Fareek suddenly remembered. "Can you remember something special about midsummer's night that the Old Blind Man of Thebiz told us?"

"Oh yes!" screamed Mellow Tron and Tarquin in perfect unison.

"What is it then?" Fareek asked as the three hovering pyramids came even closer.

"He said something about a Spirit Light alignment!" Mellow Tron said excitedly as his snake-headed dreadlocks hungrily snapped at the air at passing twinklefish.

"What do you mean?" Fareek gasped as the shoals of pretty twinklefish swam right through his holographic gown.

It was Mellow Tron's turn to scratch his head and think. "I can't remember . . . I forgot!"

The musicians contemplated in the only manner they knew how. Getting down on bended knee they gazed at each other's navels but still they couldn't work it out.

And then it happened and in the manner of the best Zen Satori. As they stared up at the incredible apparition of the three floating pyramids above their eyes, Mellow Tron suddenly cried out, "It's Granny Cass and her hubby!"

"Are you sure?"

"Absolutely!" whistled Mellow Tron between his cracked and cheroot-stained teeth.

"Great!" said Tarquin and Fareek in perfect synch as their intellect gave way to intuition. They looked high above their heads and gasped.

Mellow Tron was right. At the top of the largest pyramid, Cassandra's Afro could clearly be seen undulating from side to side while next to her, the Old Blind Man of Thebiz was eerily looking out at the world beneath with the cold, blank eyes of the truly blind. Cassandra, of course, had plenty of inner vision and had no problems seeing this world and a few others too. They seemed to be navigating the three pyramids in an incredible line to a few hundred feet away from the stage and about two hundred and fifty feet up above them. The Old Blind Man of Thebiz was running around whilst Cassandra sat serenely scattering scarab beetles which fell upside down on their backs in order to divine the future. Members of Master Fagin's Funkadelic Tribe rushed around followed by an equally large number of sooth-saying sea slugs who scattered happy endings everywhere.

With Cassandra's inner vision lighting the way very clearly, she looked at the patterns the beetles had made and shrieked, "The beetles have got it just about right. There will be no more adventures for now and we have come to the end of this one."

Hearing her delicate voice pierce the wind like a damascene dagger going straight through silk, everyone hooted. As for King Funky, he got up off his mushroom stool and stopped playing as something truly amazing was happening right now in front of everyone's Anatta-dazzled eyes

The whole of the main Pyramid of Geezer was turning to glass and multicoloured diamonds were shooting off from the sides. Seeing the enormous prism change into some of her most precious gems, Little Lucy screamed her head off and it was left to Astral Alice and Princess Amrita to keep throwing her bag of emeralds and pearls into the crowd. Lucy was so far gone with the visions of what she had seen, she could only hang on to the Giant Magic Carpet and weep.

Osric lazily propped himself up, pulled at his nose to see if it was still there and gasped. "That pyramid has turned into glass and is showering diamonds at a rate that not even Little Lucy could manage."

Fairlight tugged at his tuxedo and finally let his topknot go free. His brown hair tumbled like waterfalls down to his chest. Adjusting his cascading hair with a deft hand, Fairlight whistled in the wind and wondered. "I know and that's not all, just look at the other two pyramids."

"What's happening to them, do you think?"

Fairlight, now wobbling to his feet to get a better look, simply answered in the shaky breeze, "They are changing to mother-of-pearl!"

"Just incredible, man ... it's so far out!"

It was time for Fairlight to pick up on Charlie's tip and he decided to get philosophical too. "Or far in, it doesn't really matter as we can all clearly see that change is all that we have!"

"Oh wow, Fairlight. You're absolutely right," Osric burped.

As this incredible transformation to the three pyramids was wowing the assembled crowds, the Old Blind Man of Thebiz began to work with the Spirit Light.

"What's he doing, Moonmummy?" Stargasm gasped to her sister-in-arms as they flew side by side.

"I don't fully know Stargasm but I think the old man's aligning the lasers so that it goes through the top of each pyramid . . . "

"That's just incredible!"

"Can you see what's happening now Stargasm?" Moonmummy asked, grinning from ear to ear.

"Yes, the three separate lasers that the old man was shining on top of the three pyramids have turned into one."

"And the power of the laser seems to have increased also," Moonmummy chuckled

The Old Blind Man of Thebiz was doing something wonderful with the Spirit Light and the resulting laser-beam had intensified. Instead of being six inches in diameter and with the three separate beams shining onto each separate pyramid, the light was now six feet across and piercing finely through the pinnacle of each pyramid.

King Funky threw his crown into the tremulous crowd and swiftly ran the five hundred yards to the bottom of the largest pyramid. Still clutching his golden drumsticks in his hands he hollered at the top of his delicate throat. "Hello Cassandra . . . Hello, Old Blind Bloke!"

"Your majesty, how are you doing?" King Funky's two pet cheetahs had caught up with him now and, purring like illuminated sages who had found the answer to the riddle of life, they jumped up and down and chased a flock of passing sooth-saying sea slugs as if they had been some of Sidney Arthur's long forgotten sheep. Cassandra was still waiting for King Funky to reply.

"How am I doing? Perfectly, as you well know but things are getting better all the time!"

Cassandra peered at the tiny figure below and shouted. "We haven't come too late for the greatest party in the universe have we?"

"No, you've come just in time. Won't you join us down below and boogie like the rest of them?" King Funky hollered with a growing smirk and beckoning them down with arms moving like semaphore signals.

Cassandra had other ideas. "Afraid not, we have work to do," she stated.

Her husband managed to get a word in edgeways at last and continued. "And we're doing it now."

King Funky scratched his head, now mercifully free of his heavy crown and asked, "What are you doing exactly? Is it something to do with the Spirit Light?"

"You have got it in one and very soon you'll find out the full extent of the story!"

"What story, Cassandra?"

"Your story, silly!" added the Old Blind Man, now laughing at the confused king. It was time for Cassandra to put him out of his misery.

"I'll give you a clue – the Spirit Light is getting stronger and stronger and very soon you'll have to eat your words."

This was all getting too much for King Funky who scratched his head more earnestly than ever and asked plaintively, "Why, what have I done?"

"Don't tell him any more, Cassandra!" interjected the Old Blind Man before his wife could give the game away.

Biting her lips whilst blowing her nose, Cassandra simply said, "OK, I can't tell you anymore, dearie, except to say that it will blow your mind!"

King Funky, snappier than a snapdragon, had the answer on his merry lips. "That's not a problem, not with all the Anatta I have just taken, my mind seems to be totally blown anyway!"

King Funky doubled up in laughter and rode the waves of inner bliss as Mullah Ullah's vacant prayer-mat was hi jacked by Catweazel Phil and Frogamatix and through the scorching air they flew higher and higher until they reached Cassandra and The Old Blind Man of Thebiz who were awaiting them.

Looking at Catweazel Phil with her inner eye Cassandra was the first to ask. "Oh goodie, why are you?"

Momentarily taken aback by the abruptness of the question, Catweazel Phil scratched his chin for a moment before answering. "My name's Catweazel Phil and this is my froggy friend, Frogamatix."

"I know that because I can see everything with my inner eye," was Cassandra's prompt reply and it was up to the Old Blind Man of Thebiz to ask the next question.

"What she asked was why are you?"

Looking the Old Blind Man of Thebiz straight into his dead, blank eyes Catweazel Phil simply said, "What a strange question, old man. I thought the answer was very obvious."

"Croak . . .!" went Frogamatix in empathy as Catweazel Phil went on to explain.

"Well, we are here with you now because we also control lasers except we do it at the Bum Note and the Lost Catacombs while you pick a pyramid."

"Oh, is this what you call the Spirit Light?" the Old Blind Man of Thebiz asked, much softer this time.

"That's right. We call them lasers."

"Then perhaps you two would like to help me in the final stages of this wondrous act?"

"Of course we would. That's why we flew up here," Catweazel Phil said with a sigh.

"We know that as we are seers!" Cassandra suddenly intoned, patting Frogamatix on his huge head.

Now it was Catweazel Phil's turn to feel miffed. "Then why are you asking again?"

"Oh, just making polite conversation," the Old Blind Man said with a chuckle, giving Cassandra another quick hug.

The controls of the Spirit Light were very simple. In fact they were child's play. They were just short bamboo sticks stuck inside the rocks. The whole console looked exactly like a Stone Age version of the very complicated electronics that Catweazel Phil was used to back at the Bum Note. In less than half a minute he had understood how they worked and Frogamatix, being rather more intelligent, took even less time. As Cassandra waved her body mysteriously in the wind, perched perfectly at the pinnacle, the other three, just inches below her, controlled the Spirit Light in a manner only known to experts. The Old Blind Man of Thebiz was in the middle and the other two on either side. Together they bent and shaped the light in exquisite patterns and hit them through the tops of the three pyramids with a grace that had not been seen for a few thousand years.

"What are we doing now?" Catweazel Phil asked demurely as the stormy wind promised to blow both his hat and his head away.

The Old Blind Man rubbed his blind eyes and retorted quickly, "We are doing something rather special."

"Croak!" went Frogamatix, bending his great, ugly head forward and agreeing with everything the old man said.

Phil was not satisfied. Bending his skinny body towards the old man he asked petulantly, "What do you mean?"

Looking straight through Catweazel Phil as if he wasn't even there the Old Blind Man of Thebiz replied without a care in the world. "Well now we have the Spirit Light aligned perfectly we are now going to make it hit the thousands of statues in the Temple of Zarnak itself."

Catweazel Phil scratched his nose and pondered for a while before he spoke. "That sounds wonderful but won't it destroy them?"

"Don't be silly young man ... why, look at my wife, she is standing in full force of the beams themselves and it's not doing her any harm."

The infamous manager of the once even more infamous Bum Note looked at Cassandra the seer and considered. "You're right, the lasers seem to be going right through her."

They both looked up. It was an incredible sight. The laser above their heads was going right through Cassandra, a beam six foot wide. And Cassandra was just standing there and letting the full force of it go straight through her.

Catweazel Phil chucked his bobbing wizard's hat right into the air and chuckled like a hibernating hyena. With a sonic scream he grabbed the old man in a mighty bear hug and growled, "Just amazing!"

Surprisingly, the Old Blind Man of Thebiz had more decorum and insisted with a cough, "Be quiet, young man and aim a little to your left!"

"OK, you're the boss!" Catweazel Phil wheezed finally letting the old man go and gripping the bamboo sticks of the control console with two excited and sweaty palms.

"Hmm ... I know," tittered the Old Blind Man of Thebiz getting them all back to the wonderful show.

For about six minutes they continued increasing the power and the velocity of the giant laser beam and then suddenly without much ado, the Old Blind Man of Thebiz shifted his control stick to the right and rammed the beam right into the top of the head of one of the thousand statues that there were there at the Temple of Zarnak. Here it must be explained that this temple was a giant rectangular plain with one thousand eighty-foot stone statues surrounding it on all sides. Here and there in the middle too there were statues as well and some were so beautiful they were simply indescribable. These were the faces of the pharaohs, kings and the occasional queen that had ruled Zeegypt for three thousand years. Their faces had been delicately carved by master stonemasons and sculptors and all beamed their enigmatic smiles. There were statues of Queen Neftari, King Akhenaten, King Amenhotep (one to six), Ammit, King Apophis and Princess Esemkhet. In addition to these, there were also sacred statues and carvings of the many gods that permeated the beliefs and lives of the worshippers. As if the statues of the monarchs weren't amazing enough, the statues of the gods were simply profound. There was Amen, Aten, Hathor, Horus, Imset, Khnum, Nephthys, Osiris, Selkis, Thoth, Anubis and even the sacred bull, Apis, to name but a few.

"Why are we shining the light on top of their heads now?" Catweazel Phil asked as the very lights seemed to explode all around them.

The old man was not slow to reply. "Just follow my lead!"

However the ecstatic Catweazel Phil was not to be deterred. "Look at the way their faces light up when the lasers shine on them!"

"You just wait, there's a lot more to this than meets the eye now. Just be a little bit more patient," the older man said with a smile.

Pointing to a statue below Catweazel Phil rapidly asked, "I like the smiling face of that statue down there, who is it?"

"Oh, that's Hapy!"

"Well he's certainly living up to his name, he looks damn happy now," Catweazel Phil said, starting to notice what a wonderful improvement a growing smile made to the old man's usually fierce visage. He continued pointing out statutes one by one and demanded an explanation. "And look at that carved, black basalt statue down there, who's that then?"

Without batting an eyelid the Old Blind Man of Thebiz replied quicker than a passing thought. "That's Tutmoses the third, he was seriously heavy!"

"Baddies and Goodies together, simply amazing!"

"Croak!" added Frogamatix blowing raspberries at them both in equal measure and seeming to enjoy it very much.

However Catweazel Phil still wasn't satisfied and with his fingers still pointing continued to ask, "And whose are those statues over there?"

"Those are of Kings Menkeperre and Merenptah and next to them is that of Queen Meresankh," said the old man taking a break and passing his control stick to Frogamatix who greedily took over.

Giving his faithful frog his control too, Phil pointed excitedly to one particular statue and said, "All these statues are amazing but I think the one with the most beautiful face is that statute in the front to the left."

The Old Blind Man of Thebiz cleared his throat and continued. "Naturally. That was our most esteemed queen, Hatshepsut. In my personal opinion she was better than all the male monarchs put together."

"You mean even better than Good King Funky!" Catweazel Phil asked with a start, unable to believe that any monarch could be better than the mischievous pharaoh jumping up and down many feet below.

The old blind chappie decided to be non-committal, momentarily looking up to see if Cassandra was all right. She most certainly was. With her tattered rags billowing in the breeze her whole aura was lit up in a special green as the huge laser beam ripped though her body. She was loving every minute of it and wanting more. However, the Old Blind Man of Thebiz had still to reply to Catweazel Phil. Taking his set of controls back off of Frogamatix he flashed his beam to the heart of the sunrise and chuckled.

"Oh, Funky! He's absolutely in a world of his own. Look behind Hatshepsut now, there are the statues of Imset, Ineni, Isis, Princess Mattkhare, Queen Nefertiti, Ramses (one to nine), Sekhmet, Seth, Sothis, and Tutankhamen."

The old man was on a roll and nothing could stop him now. However Catweazel Phil had had enough. "Stop mate! I can't take it any more!"

The old man looked offended for a while and then said, "But we have only listed a hundred. There's 900 yet to go."

"Please don't bother, I get the point. There are loads of these dudes and now all have our Spirit Light shining above all their heads. What's this meant to achieve?"

And then as the flabbergasted Catweazel Phil stared Frogamatix blew him another existential raspberry and everything became clear. As Catweazel Phil turned to look at the rows and rows of statues of gods and monarchs again, he bit his lip in wonder as he saw a most amazing sight.

"The statues are coming alive, they are most definitely coming alive!"

"Dead right, young man. The dead are coming alive!"

As the green spectral light of the lasers enveloped each and every statue, a definite and imperceptible change was coming over them. They were starting to shiver, tremble and move. From way down below others were starting to notice it too.

"Oi BB, can you see what's happening?" Charlie asked, throwing a love grenade in BB's direction just to get his attention.

BB waited for the waves of love to overwhelm him completely before he replied. "I think my kaleidoscopic spectacles are playing up again."

Charlie wasn't taking no for an answer so he grabbed BB by his kurta and said loudly, "No they're not . . . look closer."

"The statues are moving. I'm sure of it!" BB gasped, rapidly taking off his spectacles to get a clearer look.

Charlie patted him on the head like a schoolteacher congratulating a specially intelligent child and simply said, "You're right, they are!"

And still cruising at about a hundred feet, the two Wicked White Witches of the West were seeing it too.

"Look Moonmummy, the party's getting to the very rocks and stones," Stargasm gasped as her broomstick swayed dangerously in the sonic breeze. She was flying at the height of the middle pyramid but flew down lower to get a better look.

Moonmummy was finding the sights incredible too. "This is simply unbelievable, the damn rocks are moving!"

"They aren't damn rocks, they are the statues of esteemed gods and monarchs!" Stargasm shouted.

"Whatever, they're moving now!" Moonmummy insisted, holding on tightly to her broomstick before she fell off onto the dancing plains many feet below.

Stargasm flew to be close to her and gasped. "They seem to be trembling on their bases but it won't be long before they get off and move with us."

"I think they are trying to dance."

"I hadn't thought of that but dancing they surely are!" Stargasm finished rubbing a hand around her face and still looking beautiful.

In quick, intuitive communication both Moonmummy and Stargasm raced to the ground to check out this amazing phenomenon for themselves. They weren't disappointed. Mammoth blocks of stone, hundreds of tons in weight, were coming alive and rising into the air.

Moonmummy gasped seeing this simple wonder and bleated, "Wow, now they are rising into the air, Stargasm!"

"Yes, Moonmummy, nothing to worry about, they are just partying like the rest of us."

"Yippee! More party people, does this party never end?"

"Not if we can help it!" Stargasm whistled deliriously like a lunatic set free from an asylum.

But what was happening to Funky as this was taking place? By now he had given up trying to speak to Cassandra up on high and was simply consoling the blubbering Plebmoses for whom the sight of the moving statues was all too much.

"Why are you crying, faithful friend?" King Funky asked, lovingly putting his arm around his shoulders.

Plebmoses bawled for a while longer, his tears the size of watermelons, before he answered, blowing his nose on his one-piece cotton gown. "Oh nothing, sire, it's just the sight of so many of your ancestors on the move again makes me want to weep."

"Oh that's nothing, bloody ancestors. I've been living with them all my life, can't get away from the past even if you tried. What worries me is if the statues which are now floating all around the plains just above the people's heads topple and spoil the party."

"I'm sure the Old Blind Man of Thebiz has it all under control." Plebmoses finished straightening up and starting to feel rather better.

From the side about fifteen yards away BB and Charlie had heard everything the two had said and ran on over to join them. "And don't forget about Catweazel Phil, he's the best laser tekky in the whole of Slumdon!" BB said in fraternal support, wondering exactly what Catweazel Phil was doing with Frogamatix on top of the highest pyramid.

With a respectful bow Charlie bent down and added, "Don't worry, your majesty, we have great faith in the skill of our wizard friend."

Jumping up and down like a schoolboy wanting to answer a question, BB squealed, "And as for Frogamatix, he's even better."

Plebmoses now fully happy again beamed himself into an everlasting smile and said, "I'm not worried. What could happen ... the sky fall on our heads?"

King Funky stroked his chin thoughtfully and answered. "Not the sky but bloody great big carved rocks which would kill the joy of any party person."

Seeing the good king's confusion, Captain Kidd, who was nearby, hollered over for the king to hear, "Ah don't worry about the statues, I'm sure everyone will be all right. Come over here King Funky . . . I've got a little secret to tell you . . ."

King Funky stopped what he was doing immediately and ambled over towards the swashbuckling pirate, who was sitting down and gamely ignoring all the thousands of trancers bewildered with the sights of the giant floating statues and dumbfounded with the quality and quantity of magic potions coursing through their veins. His loyal crewman joined him in an instant and very soon they were all sitting in a sacred circle and drinking rum (preferring piracy to Nirvana). The circle opened to let in a bewildered King Funky.

"So you're Captain Kidd?" King Funky asked hesitantly.

Captain Kidd decided to put him at his ease. "I most surely am your majesty, do you know why I called you over?"

"A secret?" King Funky replied with perfect aplomb, surveying the strange seamen around him.

Captain Kidd sat up and replied. "That's absolutely true, your majesty. Master Bates, give your seat up for his majesty please"

"Yes sure, Captain," Master Bates replied, jumping up like a firework and giving way. With that the crew moved aside and let King Funky sit squarely in the middle of the sacred circle that they had created. The sailors sniggered and giggled because they knew what was coming, a home truth that was a long time in the making. For three minutes the Captain just sat and stared at King Funky, making the latter feel more uncomfortable by the minute. Pulling at his beard, the sparkle from Captain Kidd's twinkling blue eyes mirrored into a smile. Toying with his gold earrings he chuckled a bit more and watched King Funky look more confused than ever. Finally with a valiant swig of rum, Captain Kidd spoke.

"We have a lot in common, you and us."

"Oh, why is that?"

"Because we are both thieves. I know that you are a tomb robber."

"What are you trying to say, Captain Kidd?"

"Just this, we are blood-brothers, you and me. You may be a monarch of all you survey and me just a freewheeling gallows cheater but essentially, we are the same."

"Do you mean to say you play bongos as well?"

"Not exactly ... never been musical in my life, but something else!"

There was an uncomfortable silence and then Captain Kidd continued as he meant to go on.

"You rob the past while we have always robbed the present and it's robbery I want to talk to you about."

"Oh, right!" said King Funky gamely shrugging his shoulders and taking a swig of rum.

Captain Kidd held his sides in laughter as he truly was having the time of his life. Doubling his body up into the craziest folds he waited a good minute for the laughter to subside before he carried on. Clearing his throat and winking his eyes at his crew he crept up close to King Funky's ear and said conspiratorially, "We know all about the leprechauns."

King Funky jumped up as if he had been touched by a live wire.

"Don't try and bullshit us, your majesty, we are all from Treasure Island and the whole place is full of leprechauns!" Captain Kidd said, looking the other directly in the eyes. This seemed to do the trick.

"Oh! all right then, I give up!" gasped King Funky sitting down once more.

As the general laughter around him subsided, Captain Kidd smirked and went on to explain. "I only ever stole gold from the English and the Spanglish so I could give it to the leprechauns at the rainbow's end!"

King Funky gave a deep prolonged sigh and continued. "I've been giving gold that I've stolen from my ancestors to the leprechauns as well but I've never known why."

It was time to put King Funky out of his misery and Captain Kidd surely did. "The answer is very simple, I gave it to the leprechauns so they could melt it at the rainbow's end."

"But why did you do that?"

"So that they could turn up the sun for everyone!"

"What do you mean?"

At this point Captain Kidd laughed and elucidated further. "To put it simply and to save you from any further confusion I have to explain one thing – the sun is made of gold!"

"What?" cried King Funky bouncing up and down like a beach ball.

Ignoring his plaintive squeal Captain Kidd thundered on. "You heard me right. The sun is made of gold and it's the job of the leprechauns to keep the world bright and warm by melting gold into it. They melt it at the rainbow's end and the sun becomes brighter for everyone and as you've been doing the same with the leprechauns, you can see the bright sun of Zeegypt is pure gold!"

"Oh, is that why?"

"Correct!"

"And I never knew."

"Well you know now!" Captain Kidd finished with a breezy smile.

And with that King Funky jumped up and danced with each member of the crew and with a yip and a shout raced to jump back onto the stage. He was starting to miss the music and the golden drumsticks were burning a hole in his hands. He needed to get back on stage with Habiba, the Sisters Nazneen and MMA, not forgetting the three grinning members of the Black Magic Mysterons. Before Captain Kidd could finish his rum King Funky was back on his giant mushroom stool whacking out the beats on the 108-piece drum kit so carefully made just for him. As he turned to what he knew best, whacking out the beats in perfect sync to Tarquin and Fruzzy on the tablas and bongos respectively, his smile grew by leaps and bounds till it spread off his face and into infinity beyond.

"I know the answer!" King Funky shouted excitedly above the raucous din of the ever-growing music.

"To what, funky one?" Fareek screamed back jumping up and down to the beat as if his soles were on fire.

King Funky carried on explaining. "To why I've been giving the gold away to the leprechauns," he squealed as the music drove them all higher and higher.

"That's nice, now don't waste any more time, riddim come forward, my funky selecta!" Fareek said, loving every moment.

"Yes sir!" replied King Funky, thundering a new set of tom-tom rolls.

And the everlasting boom-boom beats went on, now accompanied by the leprechauns all singing.

"The sun is happy. The sun is bright.
We did everything right and it's outta sight.
The sun is more than golden, it's actually made of gold.
We have won the battle and no one needs to be cold."

"Yippee!" went the crowds stomping up and down as the music reached a fiercer crescendo. Things just couldn't get more amazing than this, could they?

And as the leprechauns trilled in their countless tiny throats, something special seemed to be happening to the most beautiful statue of all. This was of course the stunning statue of Queen Hatshepsut. Sixty foot up in the air and still rising, as countless lasers bounced off her stony form like transcendental bullets in a game of love and not war, she came truly alive and as all the statues of all the pharaohs, kings, queens, gods and goddesses doffed their headgear, the statue of Queen Hatshepsut beamed her incredible face down towards the stage and spoke in a voice so deep, the very pebbles under the earth shook like never before.

"Funkanathen, this is your great great great grandmother, Queen Hatshepsut. Thank you for inviting us to the party."

"Hello Gran! Thanks for coming!" King Funky screamed from behind his drum kit, taking a break yet again and exasperating Tarquin with his stop-start attitude.

The giant statue then leaned forwards in an almost horizontal position and intoned again mysteriously. "Don't interrupt me when I am speaking. As I was saying, me and the rest of your countless relatives have known about your grave-robbing for a long time and what's more, we thoroughly approve of it . . .!"

"You mean you don't mind?" King Funky said, rather like a schoolboy let off from breaking a window.

The statue of Queen Hatshepsut went on to explain. "Us, mind? Not in the least, what use is gold unless you can do some good with it? And you have made a lot of people and, dare I add, leprechauns, very happy!"

"So you're not going to punish me are you?"

"For what? You never did any wrong!"

"Brilliant, Granny!"

As the fragrant smoke-bombs thrown by the mind-blown crowds cleared the air of all despair the statue went on to elucidate further.

"And what's more, me and the rest of your family have all come to the agreement that you are the most loved pharaoh that's ever been, even more loved than me and that's saying something but more importantly than that – you're the best funky drummer this side of the known universe!"

King Funky pondered a while and scratched his head before adding. "But only the second best thief because Captain Kidd beats me on that score!"

The smile of Queen Hatshepsut's face grew bigger and she looked ebullient even if she was upside down.

"You can't have everything, Funkanathen. Oh, there's one more thing to tell you!"

"What's that?"

Righting herself, the statue of Queen Hatshepsut descended another thirty feet and explained. "We played a little trick on you. We paid the temple priests to foresee the future wrongly and tell you that your life will be short because, knowing your nature, we knew that as soon as you had heard this you would start to party. And not only that but you would end all war, feed the poor and make our nation the happiest place on earth!"

"Far out!" King Funky screamed as a whole swarm of passing twinklefish covered him momentarily from view. But Queen Hatshepsut had not as yet finished.

"No, far out to you, Funkanathen, or should I call you Funky?"

Suddenly, as the swarm of twinklefish passed straight through him King Funky responded with obvious glee. "Wicked, Granny, and I thought I was doing it all wrong."

"In that you have been wrong as you have been doing everything right."

As the 999 other statues bowed down to the gobsmacked King Funky, Queen Hatshepsut had the last word. "And the last thing I have to say before I let you resume your funky drumming is this, you have behaved exactly like we knew you would. You wanted to have a clear conscience as you had a good time. From an early stage you realised something incredible and profound, you knew that you can only have a good time if everyone else is having a great time too."

"Thanks, Gran!"

And as King Funky got back to beating out the happy Hypno-Tantric rhythms on his 108-piece drum kit he smiled his brilliant smile again. The past, present and future had locked themselves into an embrace too tender to ever be ripped apart again. As King Funky played like he had never played before and evaporated his beats into the Sonic Temple rainbows, Hell disappeared into the heart of Heaven and King Funky cracked a slow gentle smile. It spread the stars right off his funny face. This grinned over the trillion glowing forms, the gentle, calm, delicate, impenetrable, gracious, wise, perhaps mocking, thousand-fold smile of King Funky. Self was dissolving into others and as he grinned, randomly shooting enlightened ions of light everywhere, his smiley stars raced to the opposite ends of the universe. As Fareek watched him with total astonishment on his happy hippy face, the smiley stars returned as quick as a flash and extremely fast. They'd picked up random interplanetary grins from the far sides and crashed into his face in a complete tie-break as he dissolved into his true essence.

"Far out!" Fairlight quipped, dancing the transcendental tango hand-in-hand with Osric and Princess Amrita as a whole new universe of possibilities opened up. As the musicians played, the happy Hypno-Tantric Trance wound its path through the universe. Deserts blazed with fantasy flowers in fields of gold. From the abandoned cities of Timbuktwo and Timbukthree, long-lost laughter rang once more. Time had been stretched completely. What was once was here again, while what was to be, actually became so, as everybody laughed. Together. Remembrance of Future Times Past was a very simple thing. The present was the present which was ever continuous. Then the light was very white and suddenly very clear.

35

Paradise Found

PARADISE WAS LOOKING beautiful again. Was this some off planetary space or was this Heaven? Certainly not, this was Queen Angie Park and two happy beings were sitting cross-legged under a canopy of giant mystic mushrooms and drinking Astral Ale from large pewter mugs. It was still dawn, just as the sun was rising, and the two characters were, of course, Sidney Arthur and the Genie of the Lamp who had returned here directly after their meeting with Lord Krishna at the Battle of Kurukshetra. They were laughing merrily and chuckling at each other's jokes and having fun in their usual irreverent manner. Sidney Arthur was the only ghost not to have been liberated. However karma is as karma does and he was too happy to care. The Genie of the Lamp however was now well and truly liberated both from the imprisonment of the golden lamp and the eternal avaricious greed of those he awarded three magic wishes to. His last master Mullah Ullah had used the three magic wishes well and was partying in Zarnak with the other thousands of characters so amply described before. As a consequence, Pearly Green was peaceful and quiet. It was just the way that Sidney Arthur liked it and bending his nose towards the Genie of the Lamp, he pulled at the Genie's cauliflower ears, his twinkling blue eyes laughing. Flicking the Genie of the Lamp's golden earrings with a thin spectral finger he pulled at the ghostly daffodils coming out of his crumbling jacket holes and looked around. Queen Angie Park really was paradise. All around them there were hundreds of sacred cows and fluffy white sheep munching up the juicy green grass and the early morning marigolds. Some of the lambs were already gambolling and playing gin rummy whilst pretty pink flamingos raced across the glowing sunrise. Happy twinklefish were swimming in the lake and merrily frolicking with the giant blue octopus that lived at the bottom of it and only ever came up for air at sunrise and sunset. Very special times as we shall see. To the left, crunchy banana trees swayed in the blissful breeze while the mango and mandarin groves looked delicious too. As for a palanquin pulled by penguins and pelicans, the secret occupant inside brought out a white gloved hand as she whizzed around rapidly around the park and threw pearls before the swine. These were the psychedelic flying pigs of course which were ravenously chasing the trippadelic truffles that were scurrying out of their way.

As Sidney Arthur twirled his ghostly form seventeen foot off the ground and pulled down a couple of mangoes, he munched one greedily whilst chucking another down to the Genie of the Lamp saying, "It's wicked here in Queen Angie Park."

"It's a good thing Lord Krishna gave you your old job back," the Genie of the Lamp said hungrily swallowing the mango, stone and all, and noticing the wondrous transformation of his ghostly friend now he was back at the park, the place he loved more than any other in this, the best of all possible worlds. Cavorting round and round in the air like children playing at being whirligigs, Sidney Arthur finally raced back to earth clutching a bunch of bright golden daffodils which he gamely presented to the Genie of the Lamp with a bow. Only a second behind Sidney Arthur, the Genie of the Lamp landed on the ground with a resounding bump and pulled at his friend's lock of white hair.

Gently extricating his hair from the other's huge meaty blue hand Sidney Arthur said, "Yeah, my old job. You know that's all I really wanted, I've always been happy living in the park even when I was alive!"

'Yeah, but I notice that you don't play gin rummy with the lambs any more!"

"Ah, give it time, I'm sure that I will get up to my old tricks soon."

They looked around them again. There were countless fluffy white lambs and sacred sheep going about their usual business and being a sly old fox, Sidney Arthur had already come to an agreement that if any of his flock should fall into the lake, the Giant Blue Octopus would only drag it out again. It was just like old times and Sidney Arthur's smile spelt everything out. He was back on his old hunting ground doing very little and loving every moment. It had been a good idea to leave the raving masses after the Battle of

Kurukshetra and come back home. Exotic places were fine thought Sidney Arthur, taking another sip of Astral Ale, but home was where the heart was and his heart most certainly was at home.

Joyously examining the peaceful vista around them Sidney Arthur finally said, "It's great being homeless!"

"If you mean living under a canopy of giant mystic mushrooms then you are right," the Genie tittered, carving himself a huge slice of the mushroom growing above his head.

Seeing the Genie's quick actions, Sidney Arthur sighed happily and added, "Yeah, it's fine, especially since it's endless summer weather after we beat the baddies at Kurukshetra!"

"Don't you ever miss your old home though?"

"You mean the ancestral crash-pad down in Scoreditch?"

"That's the one!" the Genie of the Lamp said, offering his pal a piece of his mystic mushroom as Sidney lazily replied.

"I never liked it anyway and the place is so crowded now with Bongostani leprechauns I couldn't even fit in even if I am a ghost and the nominal owner to boot."

Both seemed to like the open-air life and both looked out at the spreading dawn whose tentacles were reaching everywhere and turning the early morning frost into syrupy dew. Watching the miracle of nature repeat itself as he had seen it do for thousands of years and never yet getting bored of it, Sidney Arthur suddenly said with a start, "Anyway who needs a house when you have materialised the most incredible palace here in Queen Angie Park?"

The Genie buffed his fingernails and tried to look humble. "Yes, I couldn't resist it!"

Gently toying with Billy Blake's ghostly timepiece Sidney Arthur simply said, "Yes, it's those damn leprechauns again, they have started overflowing out of my old house and have now come to live in your magic palace!"

"Yes, I suppose you are right but where were they supposed to go?"

The Genie of the Lamp let the question remain unanswered in the early morning fog as Sidney Arthur opened another bottle of Astral Ale. They looked in front of them and a hundred yards away was the most incredible eastern palace one could imagine. Its seventy spires curled skywards and ended in infinite domes. The huge central dome was wider than the River Padma of Banglastan at its greatest stretch and it was covered in a glorious damascene inlay of blue and gold. There must have been at least six hundred rooms inside and the whole place was inlaid with precious gems and covered in a sheen of fine gold. The floors were made of the rarest marble and on every wall was carved in silver Scarabian calligraphy the story of the friends of the Lost Catacombs of Brickie Lane and their journey so far. And the fixtures and fittings inside were something else too. There were couches made of the deepest velvet, transcendental tapestries, cushions made of fluffy white clouds, thrones made of bamboo and gilded red and black lacquered doors everywhere. This palace was so beautiful that no eastern king had anything so beautiful. And now it was a home for the countless overflow of Bongostani leprechauns from Sidney Arthur's ancestral home. However there was a catch. Every evening at sunset the Genie conjured up the most amazing palace and this would last until dawn when it would dissolve back into the elemental ether it came from. As it was used by homeless leprechauns and their friends, the elves and fairies, Sidney Arthur and the Genie of the Lamp would get up in the dead of the night and wait to dissolve it. The catch was that dawn happened to be whenever Sidney Arthur and the Genie of the Lamp judged it to be. As a consequence the inhabitants of the magical eastern palace never knew when exactly it would dissolve and invariably got a rude awakening each day. In fact, watching the pale pink sun break out over the horizon, this is what Sidney Arthur and the Genie of the Lamp were now doing, checking to see if it was dawn.

"It's dawn now, we have to turf the squatters out. Hee … Heee … Hee!"

"Dawn's come at the right time today. It's usually in the middle of the night with you."

"No, it was good to give the little blighters some time to rest for a change!" Sidney Arthur said sanctimoniously, trying to hide his sniggers. The Genie of the Lamp couldn't help latching onto the waves of giggles and tittered.

The whole edifice of the eastern palace dissolved in an instant and out tumbled hundreds of distraught and bleary-eyed leprechauns, fairies and elves stumbling into the cold dewy grass. This was an awakening like no other and as the myriad of magical creatures cried and howled, some still clutching their eiderdowns to their still warm and sleepy bodies, they ran holding onto their meagre possessions towards the shelter of the crunchy banana groves just to get away from the mischievous two.

"This has been your early morning wake-up call," Sidney Arthur yelled at the top of his voice, standing at full stretch and laughing like mad. The Genie was not far behind him.

As the grinning monkeys, one ghost and one spirit cascaded into endless peals of laughter they clasped each other's hands and flew in rapid circles up into the air. From their height they could see the magical creatures scurrying for solace wherever they could. Some went up mango trees, some went down badger holes and some stayed exactly where they were. Wherever they went it was not going to be as comfortable as the palace and they would surely be back the next night for a kip. And the next. And the next. Oh what fun there would be in waking them up for ever and ever!

As Sidney Arthur and the Genie of the Lamp flew off to their favourite mystic mushroom patch their laughter subsided and they were left feeling serious once more.

Sidney's voice momentarily took on a sombre tone as he asked "By the way, Genie, why did you choose to come back with me? You could have gone with the others!"

Mirroring Sidney with a look of equal intensity and seriousness, the Genie of the Lamp gazed at him straight in his twinkling blue eyes and replied strongly, "No one tells me when I can be free or not!"

"My sentiments exactly!" Sidney Arthur wheezed getting back to his accustomed laughter.

But the Genie of the Lamp hadn't finished yet. "And anyway, I like your company."

"And I love yours too, mate!" Sidney answered, giving his friend a ghostly hug just as the Genie of the Lamp emphasised his final words with a growl.

"And as someone once told me, to be alone in company is better then being forever lonely on your own."

Racing around the Genie's body to face him upfront again, it was Sidney Arthur that had the last word and laughter. "Funny, that's just what Danny used to say having been a shipwrecked sailor living on his own for centuries. That was, of course, until he found Billy."

And the sun went around the moon and the moon went around the sun and this story ends as it began. In total happiness . . .

Lightning Source UK Ltd.
Milton Keynes UK

174724UK00001B/1/P

9 780956 561206